PRAISE FOR

THE SEVENTH CHAMPION

"I've always admired Sylvia Mercedes for the seemingly effortless skill she brings to her storytelling, and it's on display again in *The Seventh Champion*. With a sunshine-y heroine who's a pure delight, a grumpy hero to swoon over, and a thoroughly entertaining, romance-infused, action-packed plot, this book is the absolute in reading pleasure."

—India Holton, *USA Today* bestselling author of *The Geographer's Map to Romance*

"I was enchanted from the moment I read the opening line, and once I started reading, I could not stop. Full of charming wit, deadly trials, and the most delicious slow-burn yearning. I am utterly obsessed with this grumpy-sunshine pair!"

—Tessonja Odette, author of *A Rivalry of Hearts*

"*The Seventh Champion* was such a fun romantasy read! Featuring a dragon princess and the deadly trials that pit her suitors against one another, this book kept me guessing until the last page. Rosie was a funny and endearing sunshine heroine, and Valtar the perfect broody—and loomy!—counterpart. I can't wait for the sequel to find out what Sylvia has in store for these two!"

—Demi Winters, author of *The Road of Bones*

"With delicious banter and a tightly woven plot, Mercedes once again entices readers into a romantasy world they'll be loath to leave. . . . Sharp dialogue, plentiful action, and well-developed characters build a fascinating foundation for Mercedes's promising new series."

—*Publishers Weekly*

"A thrilling and romantic fantasy adventure. . . . *The Seventh Champion* is a fast-paced and exciting beginning to the Dragon Queen Duology."

—*BookPage*

"Mercedes's [Dragon Queen] Duology opens with a low-steam, action-packed book. Recommended for Sarah J. Maas and Elise Kova fans looking for a story about a young heroine who is waiting to reach her full power."

—*Library Journal*

PRAISE FOR

BRIDE OF THE SHADOW KING

"Sylvia Mercedes hits every note that romantasy readers want in a novel!"

—*New York Times* bestselling author Danielle L. Jensen

"Utterly swoonworthy!"

—*USA Today* bestselling author Elise Kova

"Give me all the 'marriage of convenience to a morally gray hero' stories! This one has vibes of Hades/Persephone and you'll absolutely want to root for the heroine. I'm craving the next installment!"

—*New York Times* bestselling author Ruby Dixon

"*Bride of the Shadow King* is one of my favorite romantasy reads. This wonderfully immersive and emotionally mesmerizing book is a real treasure. It had me completely bespelled by its gorgeous, rich world-building and by the slow, heart-stirring relationship that develops between Faraine and Vor. Sylvia Mercedes writes both cleverly and beautifully, and I hope everyone who loves fantasy romance will discover the magic of her worlds."

—*USA Today* bestselling author India Holton

"The thrilling first in a romantasy [duology] from Mercedes layers plentiful intrigue and action with delicate world-building and vibrant characters. . . . By turns tender and tense, this addictive beginning will leave readers excited to find out what happens next."

—*Publishers Weekly* (starred review)

Ace titles by Sylvia Mercedes

The Bride of the Shadow King Series

Bride of the Shadow King
Vow of the Shadow King
Heart of the Shadow King

The Dragon Queen Duology

The Seventh Champion
The Last Dragon Queen

THE LAST DRAGON QUEEN

THE DRAGON QUEEN DUOLOGY: BOOK 2

SYLVIA MERCEDES

ACE
NEW YORK

ACE
Published by Berkley
An imprint of Penguin Random House LLC
1745 Broadway, New York, NY 10019
penguinrandomhouse.com

Library of Congress Cataloging-in-Publication Data

Names: Mercedes, Sylvia author
Title: The last Dragon Queen / Sylvia Mercedes.
Description: First edition. | New York: Ace, 2026. |
Series: The Dragon Queen duology; book 2
Identifiers: LCCN 2026007895 (print) | LCCN 2026007896 (ebook) |
ISBN 9780593952252 trade paperback | ISBN 9780593952269 ebook
Subjects: LCGFT: Fantasy fiction | Romance fiction | Novels
Classification: LCC PS3613.E678 L37 2026 (print) | LCC PS3613.E678 (ebook)
LC record available at https://lccn.loc.gov/2026007895
LC ebook record available at https://lccn.loc.gov/2026007896

First Edition: November 2026

Printed in the United States of America
1st Printing

The authorized representative in the EU for product safety and compliance is Penguin Random House Ireland, Morrison Chambers, 32 Nassau Street, Dublin D02 YH68, Ireland, https://eu-contact.penguin.ie.

To you, my sister, as we face these trials by fire.
May we learn to roar.

THE LAST DRAGON QUEEN

Prologue

The doll wasn't much to look at: a few scraps taken from outgrown garments, a stocking head stuffed with feathers pilfered from her mattress, overlarge button eyes, and a scraggly nest of hair plucked from both her own head and that of Aeshlin, the slave woman who swept her chamber and served her meals. But it was the only doll the child had ever owned, and she loved it with a tender ferocity no living thing could have long endured.

So when the cruel, ash-flaked wind plucked the little scrap of rags from her fingers and sent it hurtling out the window, the screech which ripped from the child's lips sent the vultures roosting on the gable roof into a flurry of panicked flight. The child ignored their rasping cries but leaned far over the sill, peering down the smoke-stained tower wall, teeth clenched, and eyes peeled. There—she could just see her beloved doll, lying in a little heap on a balcony several floors below.

"Bats' bottoms!" she snarled. At only seven years of age, her vocabulary was still somewhat limited, unfit to express the true depths of her rage. Sometimes she heard the dracori guards who patrolled outside her door use such colorful words, most of which she did not understand but which had a delicious *badness* to them that she would like to emulate. Aeshlin did not approve of such talk, however, and though she was only a slave and more than a little afraid of her young charge, she put her foot down when it came to strong language.

You are a princess, she would say, her sad eyes hard as flints, *whatever else you may be. I'll not have you shame the once-grace of this house with such vile talk.*

The child grimaced and swallowed back all the more delicious phrases for future use. Eventually Mother would grow angry with Aeshlin and feed her to the dragon spawn, and then there'd be a new slave assigned to her rooms. Perhaps the next one would be more lenient. In the meanwhile, she made do.

"Bats' bottoms!" she growled again, and pounded the stone sill with one tiny fist. She'd have to fetch the doll herself. Aeshlin couldn't go down there; that was the prisoner's balcony, and no one was allowed anywhere near the prisoner except the dracori. And if she asked the dracori to retrieve it, they'd either curse in her face or make a point of torching her dolly in front of her just to laugh at her impotent screams of rage. No, there was no one to help her but herself.

And yet . . . she hesitated. It wasn't the height that scared her. Though she had not yet manifested, she was a creature born for flight and held even the most death-defying plummet in contempt. But she had never dared venture anywhere near the prisoner before.

She liked to watch him. Many's the time she'd stood at this very window, half hidden by curtains, and watched him on his balcony below, gazing out across the desolate landscape to where Mount Dracor dominates the far horizon, belching green flame and black smoke. He was several years older than her, but much closer to her age than anyone else she'd ever seen, and thus an object of keenest interest to her young eyes. Sometimes she liked to imagine that he was aware of her gaze; it felt more companionable that way. But he never looked up and certainly never spoke, and she'd never found the courage to call out to him.

There was no sign of him now. Just her dolly, lying there so forlornly, the wind plucking at her ragged hair and threatening to pick her up and send her flying once more, never to be recovered.

"Come on, you little half-formed thing," she muttered to herself in a voice shockingly like her mother's, though she did not know it. "Are you good for nothing?"

Setting her teeth, the child climbed up onto the windowsill. She was created to blaze and conquer, to strike fear in the hearts of all who set eyes upon her. She wasn't about to let a little timidity get the best of her.

The climb down the stone face of the tower was trickier than anticipated. Though her long, talon-like nails dug into the cracks and crevices well enough, her thin little body was so light, and the wind so harsh, she was nearly plucked up in a gust like a rag doll herself and sent flying across the rooftops of the palace. Grimly determined, she plastered herself flat to the stones and continued her descent, feeling her way with her bare feet. The distance to the balcony was farther than it had looked from the safety of her chambers, but she crept down, inch by inch, until she was almost certain if she dropped, she would land on the balcony itself and not sail past the balustrade to shatter her bones in the courtyard many stories below. She was just working up the pluck to make the attempt when the door below creaked suddenly, sending a jolt of fear straight through her heart.

The prisoner. He stepped out onto the balcony just below her feet, his head bent, his gaze fixed upon the doll. Ash dusted his raven-black hair and swiftly turned his blue coat gray. He shielded his face with one hand, while the other was bound to his side, while his arm recovered from the two-part break the dracori had given him a month ago. They seemed to like breaking him an awful lot. He still limped from that time they'd shattered his ankle and it never properly healed. But somehow he always held his shoulders straight and moved with labored dignity.

He stood for a moment over the doll, contemplating it with his head tilted slightly to one side, as though trying to puzzle out some mystery. Then he crouched, pinched the edge of the rag skirt between thumb and forefinger, and lifted the doll to eye level.

"Get your filthy hands off my sister!"

The sound of the sharp little voice directly overhead startled the prisoner. He dropped the doll at once, leapt to his feet, and craned his neck. The child found herself staring down into a pair of black eyes so wide, she could see the whites ringing all the way around them. He blinked twice, then uttered a little huff like a laugh.

"Well, hello," he said, his voice thick with an accent similar to Aeshlin's but more refined. "Is that my fellow prisoner? We meet at last."

The child jutted out her chin, even as another gust of wind nearly yanked her from the wall and sent her flying. Strands of dark hair blew into her eyes, but she shook it away and scowled fiercely. "I'm not a prisoner," she snarled. "I'm a princess."

"Indeed?" He tilted his head again, and his mouth crooked in a half smile. "And yet you live here in the prison tower along with me. How do you explain that?"

She couldn't. And didn't particularly care to. She had far more important matters with which to concern herself. "Give me back my sister."

"Your sister?" He looked down at the doll then back up at her. "This, I take it, is the sister in question?"

"Give her to me."

"Did I not hear you correctly when you said, 'Get your filthy hands off' her?" He folded his arms. "Which is it to be then? I can't very well toss her to you without touching her, you know."

"Give her to me, or I'll blast you with hellfire."

A hint of merriment sparkled in the prisoner's eyes. He seemed to be biting the inside of his cheek. "Well, we can't have that. This is my favorite jacket—wouldn't want the trimming singed."

Bending once more, he plucked the doll, hefting it lightly in his palm. The child let go of the wall with one hand, extending her clawed fingers. But she was much too far away to snatch it from his grasp. "Throw it," she demanded, even as part of her wondered if this was a bad idea. One more ill-timed gust of wind could spell disaster for both dolly and herself.

The prisoner continued to chew the inside of his cheek, his expression no longer amused but thoughtful. "You know," he said after a moment, his gaze still on dolly's ugly stocking face, "I have a brother. But he's not here. Not anymore. He's far away. Across the sea, or so they tell me."

The child frowned. She had little experience with empathetic emotions. After all, the only people she ever saw were slaves or dracori, and what did she care about their feelings? Slaves were little better than rodents, scampering about the place. And dracori, well . . . the less she could have to do with them the better. The only person whose feelings mattered to her above her own was Mother. As was right.

But in that moment, she found herself feeling oddly sorry for the prisoner. He sounded so sad. Lost, somehow, even though he was right there, where he'd always been.

"My sister is far away too," the child offered abruptly.

The prisoner looked at her, eyebrow lifted, and held up the doll.

"Not her," the child admitted. "My real sister. She was stolen a long time ago. Before we had even hatched."

"Hatched?" the prisoner echoed. His brow puckered faintly before realization dawned in his expression. "Oh. I see. So you're . . . you're one of the dragon princesses."

"I already told you that."

"Forgive me. I assumed you were a political prisoner like myself. From Alinar perhaps. Or from the kingdom across the Sarzana Desert."

"You thought I was *human*?" She spat the word with disgust. Then, without preamble, she dropped from the wall to the balcony in front of him, jarring her anklebones in the process. She hastily pulled herself together, however, and drew herself up to her full height, which was not even up to his heart. Somehow she'd always believed they were close to the same size—the result of always viewing him from above. Now, finding herself at a disadvantage, she bristled like a cat, flashing her teeth and curling her talon claws. "I am no human! I am dragon through and through! Daughter of Mhoryga, Queen of All, born of the Dracor Flame. Tremble before me, spawn of dust!"

The prisoner looked down his nose at her, his brow once more slightly puckered. "No, of course. I see it now. You look . . . you look a lot like her up close." A shadow passed over his features. "You have her eyes."

This was not quite the degree of groveling terror the child hoped to inspire. Perhaps she simply needed practice. "I'll be a proper dragon one day," she said proudly, tossing a snarl of hair off her forehead. "When I manifest. Then I will be a dragon queen."

"Yes. I know." The prisoner turned the doll around in his hands then flicked a glance her way. He had a kind face. The child didn't know quite what to make of it; she'd never encountered anything like kindness before in her harsh, narrow existence. "You do know what . . . what Mhoryga does to her daughters, don't you?"

The child gave him a look. "Do you think I'm stupid? Of course I know! When I have manifested, I will offer my heart to feed my mother's fire. It's what I was born for, to sustain the eternal flame of Mhoryga. Only . . ."

She held up one hand, cupping her palm and curling her taloned fingers slightly as she reached down inside herself, down to that place where sometimes she could almost, *almost* feel the fire of her heritage burning. But no matter how she reached, she could never summon the hellflame that was her birthright.

"They say I'm half formed," she admitted softly, as though confessing a terrible sin. She glanced up at the prisoner, searching for condemnation or disgust in his gaze. Met only with more of that earnest sweetness, she continued. "When the thief who stole my sister's egg raided the nest, he sundered our bond, and now neither of us may be able to . . . to . . ." A heavy sigh gusted through her lips. "We might never manifest flame."

"Would that be so bad?" the prisoner asked softly.

"Of course it would!" Her eyes flashed to meet his. "We were supposed to be together—two hearts, one flame. When Mother devoured us, we should have made her great beyond anything this world has ever seen! But now? What use am I if I am half formed? Any fire there is in my heart will not be enough to sustain her."

The prisoner nodded slowly. A series of expressions passed over his face, one after another, as though considering suddenly the vulnerability of this child before him, the great empty plunge below the balcony, the lack of any guards or protections. But the child did not notice, caught up as she was in her own woes. And by the time he spoke again, that moment of temptation had already passed, and the prisoner's voice was as gentle as ever.

"You know," he said, kneeling before the girl and pressing the ugly doll into her hands, "maybe the tragedy of your parting from your sister is a gift? Maybe it's the gods' way of changing the course of your destiny. They may have a greater purpose in store for you and your sister than merely to feed the Dragon Queen."

"What?" The child frowned, puzzled. "That doesn't make sense. The only reason I'm alive is because Mother gave me life. How can I not give my life back to her when she asks it?"

The prisoner shook his head. "I was brought up to see things rather differently. My father . . ." His voice cracked, but he recovered and continued in an even tone. "My father believed it was his duty to give his life for his children."

"Oh! Fathers!" The child scoffed and took a step back, pressing her doll to her bony chest. "What's the use of them? I don't have a father."

"Neither do I," the prisoner replied softly. "Not anymore." His face was once again so sad, the child couldn't help the dart of pain which shot through her own heart at the sight. She wanted suddenly, more than she'd ever wanted anything in her life, to make him feel better. Maybe even to bring back the smile to his face.

"Here," she said, and impulsively grabbed his hand and pressed her doll into it. "You can have her, if you want. So you won't be alone." She shrugged as though it meant nothing, but felt like her heart might crack in two behind her ribs. "I can make another."

The prisoner's lips parted in a little O of surprise. He looked down at the doll, frowned, shook his head. Then his gaze flicked to meet hers again. "Thank you," he said, his voice oddly thick. "I . . . I do get lonely sometimes." He swallowed hard and gently cradled the little bundle of rags and hair against the front of his ashy coat. "Does she have a name?"

"Naevya," the child replied. "That's my sister's name."

"And . . . will you come back to visit Naevya sometimes?"

The child nodded. Then, impulsively: "My name is Nyxia."

The prisoner bowed his head solemnly. "A pleasure to meet you, Nyxia. My name is—"

A loud boom drowned out whatever he might have said as the door to the inner chamber burst wide and struck the wall. The prisoner whirled on his feet, dropping the doll from numb fingers. Nyxia peered around him to see two large dracori step through the doorway and look around the sparse room. One of them turned his head to the balcony, but Nyxia didn't wait to be spotted. With a leap, she sprang for the tower wall and scrambled partway back to her room before daring to look down again.

The prisoner remained where he stood on the balcony, her doll forgotten at his feet. He drew his shoulders back, his good arm straight at his side, hand clenched in a fist. "What is the meaning of this intrusion?" he demanded in a clear, loud voice, even as the first of the dracori lurched out onto the balcony. He was a big man—one of the biggest who patrolled the tower. He was bare breasted, the large, dragon-shaped burn scar on his chest prominently displayed as testimony to the transformation he'd undergone.

Nyxia hated all dracori. They were not Mhoryga's natural children, but humans she'd taken, filled with her fire, remaking them into creatures devoted to her service. They were cruel to everyone—slaves, prisoners, and other dracori alike. But for Nyxia they saved an extra measure of cruelty, for in her, they saw what they themselves could never be: a true dragon. Though she lived under Mhoryga's protection, and they would never dare to hurt her physically for fear of the Dragon Queen's wrath, they found other ways of making her life a living hell.

Her lips rolled back in a silent hiss at the sight of that dracori. Wild temptation came over her to drop on his head and tear at his eyes with her talons, but she couldn't quite bring herself to.

"Mhoryga requires your attendance upon Her Majesty," the dracori growled, his ugly face a stark contrast to the quiet, handsome features of the prisoner. "At once."

"At once, eh?" he answered dryly. "Haven't I time to change my coat? The queen likes her meat fresh, after all."

Before Nyxia could even gasp at his audacity, the dracori lunged and drove a fist into the prisoner's gut, doubling him over. She only just managed to swallow back a squeak of terror, which would surely give away her presence, biting down on her lip until she tasted blood. The second dracori appeared behind the first, and together, they grabbed the prisoner, little caring how they wrenched his not-yet-healed arm. Breath knocked out of him, he managed only a faint whimper of pain, but it was enough to knot Nyxia's heart.

The next moment, they vanished, leaving the child staring

down at the trampled remains of her doll. She could do nothing but cling to the wall, breathing in short, sharp pants for some moments.

Then, with a little snarl, she dropped to the balcony once more and darted into the empty chamber. The dracori had left the prisoner's door wide open in their wake. Bare feet making no sound, Nyxia followed after them into the passage. Her heart surged with a mingling of terror and delight at her own daring, and she raced after them down the winding stairs, clinging to shadows and taking care to remain out of sight. She could not remember the last time she walked the halls of this palace unattended. Perhaps she never had. Of course, that didn't make her a prisoner; princesses must have their attendants, after all. But it was thrilling to feel this degree of freedom. Part of her wondered if she ought not to waste it trailing after the prisoner and his brutal captors . . . and yet, for some inexplicable reason, her footsteps continued their pursuit, almost against her will.

They came to the throne room at last. Nyxia had been here before, on those rare occasions when her mother remembered she had a daughter and sent for her to offer her some amusement. It had been nearly a year since the last time the child had seen her mother, and she found her heart beating with excitement at the prospect of glimpsing her again. There was nothing in this world she loved with such utter adoration as the beautiful Dragon Queen.

Keeping to the shadows, Nyxia slipped into the room and behind a pillar, moving silently as a wraith. No one noticed her—all eyes in that chamber were fixed on the two dracori, who dragged their pale and fainting prisoner between them down the center of the vaulted space toward the great throne at the far end.

The throne was a splendid thing of gold, blackened by years' worth of dragon smoke. It was large enough to dwarf even the tallest human man, to make all eyes in the room remember that it was not the individual who sat upon that high seat who mattered, but the divine office which he had been born to fulfill. So it was with the human kings and queens who had ruled this land in ages past.

Not so with Mhoryga. No throne crafted by human hands could diminish her greatness, her splendor. She was a mighty being, far beyond the lowly inhabitants of this world. Though clad in the shape of a woman, her seven-foot frame could scarcely contain the true power and heat of her dragon nature, which always strained to the brink of breaking free. Her skin was golden, gleaming with jewellike scales, like snakeskin wrapping her chiseled muscles. Her hair was black but glinted with flashes of green fire, and more hellfire gleamed in the depths of her eyes. Long black talons curved from the ends of her tapered fingers and lightly scratched the arm of the throne, tearing deep grooves. She wore very little—a silken gown that only just covered her breasts and loins, leaving much of her magnificent figure on display, for what garment could ever be worthy of such a host? Every movement she made, every tip of the head, every shift of the foot, bespoke a coiled power just waiting to be unleashed.

Nyxia loved her. Just the sight of her was enough to fill the child all over again with such a flood of passionate devotion that she would eagerly lay down her own life for such a woman, such a mother. To have been born for the purpose of serving Mhoryga was a blessing indeed. It was Mhoryga's will which created her, Mhoryga's will which sustained her, and one day, it would be Mhoryga's will that ended the span of her existence.

As the dracori drew nearer to the throne, another figure stepped suddenly forward, pulling Nyxia's gaze unwillingly away from her mother. It was another dracori—younger and smaller than the others, but bare chested like them, displaying the ugly scar that branded him as one of them. Rather to Nyxia's surprise, he reminded her of the prisoner. He had the same fine features, though all the sweetness in that face had been beaten out of this one, leaving behind severe lines which spoke of the ruthlessness within.

But when this dracori saw the prisoner, those severe lines melted away abruptly, and he looked suddenly both younger and more human than he had a moment ago. "Arun!" he cried, his voice echoing in the vaulted space.

"It's been a while, dear brother," the prisoner's voice, slurred with pain, answered. "You're looking well. That's quite the impressive new scar you're boasting. Can't say I like the look of it much, though they seem to be all the rage with the murderous set these days."

Brother? The word pricked in Nyxia's brain. She dared to lean out a little farther from behind her pillar, eager to get a better view. Her hungry eyes devoured the sight of the young dracori turning to the throne and throwing himself on his knees before Mhoryga.

"It's my fault," he cried. "My fault alone. There's no one to blame but me."

"And what exactly is your fault, sweet prince?"

Mhoryga's voice—the voice of fire incarnate. It burned in Nyxia's brain, a delicious pain she craved more than food or drink or breath. Her heart swelled at the sound, and her gaze, fixed upon the face of her mother, was adoring.

"I had her," the young dracori said, trembling where he knelt. "I had her in my hands, pinned down. And . . . and I was going to do it, I was going to kill her, but . . . but . . ."

"Go on." Fire licked from the corners of Mhoryga's smiling mouth.

The young dracori turned, his black eyes desperate as he sought the face of his brother. Judging by his expression, one would think he was the one whose broken arm was even now being twisted. He shook his head and looked up at Mhoryga again. "She was so . . . small. Just a kid. I . . . I didn't know she was just a kid. I couldn't make myself—"

Mhoryga rose from her seat, like a mountain from the sea. Great and goddess-like, worshipful and terrible, she towered over the trembling young dracori, hellfire dancing in her eyes. "Someone must pay, Valtar, my love. Someone must own the price for your weakness."

"I'll pay." The dracori threw wide his arms, baring his breast before her. "I'll pay the price. It was my fault. I'm the one who should suffer. Please . . . please . . ."

"Please what, sweetling?" Mhoryga glided toward him, her scaled skin gleaming in the light of her own flame. Nyxia shivered. She'd seen her mother cast slaves to the dragon spawn before. Once she'd even seen Mhoryga shift suddenly into her true dragon form and devour a trembling prisoner whole. Was she about to witness this dracori meeting a similar gruesome fate? She hoped so. She hated all dracori. Even if this one's face looked so like her new prisoner friend.

But when the young dracori spoke again, the words he spoke sent a blade of ice straight through Nyxia's soul. "Please, don't hurt my brother."

Mhoryga smiled. And for the first time, Nyxia did not think that smile the most beautiful thing in all the world. For the first time, she trembled, not in anticipation, but in sudden, overwhelming dread. Her gaze turned from the dracori to the prisoner. The prisoner who had spoken to her gently. Who had given her back her doll. Who had said such strange, impossible things as though . . . as though she mattered. As though her life was worth something all on its own. Blasphemous things, and yet he'd said them with such kindness in his eyes.

She watched as Mhoryga approached the prisoner, held suspended between those two great dracori brutes. She watched, and her heart screamed, *No, no, no*, though she couldn't begin to understand why.

"Your love for your brother is the source of both your weakness and your strength," Mhoryga said, standing over the prisoner now, but turning to look back over her shoulder at the young dracori. "It is your choice, sweet Valtar, which it will be. Tell me: Are you ready to be strong for me?"

"I am," the dracori said, but his voice cracked, betraying his terror. "I will never be weak again, I swear it."

"Let us hope so," Mhoryga replied. "Because eventually your brother will run out of body parts."

Her talons darted out, viper swift, plunged into the prisoner's eye socket, and ripped out his left eye.

And Nyxia collapsed to her knees, hands over her ears, as Arun's screams racked her soul with horror.

1

Rosie

Sixteen Years Later

We have a saying where I come from: *Never poke a sleeping dragon, for they wake up hungry, and you look like lunch.*

I never thought this little maxim was meant to be taken literally. But it flits across my brain now as I approach the dragon napping in the middle of the empty field, and I cannot help thinking it feels rather too apt for comfort. While the dragon in question currently wears the frame of a pitifully scrawny young boy, little more than a child, I've seen the beast that lurks just beneath the surface of this perceived reality. It's not a pretty sight—all fangs and spines and belching hellfire.

He looks very peaceful now, however, bathed in soft moonlight. He's been asleep for a good twelve hours or more, ever since crashing in that field yesterday morning and burning out in a great, green bonfire that surely alerted any living soul within a ten-mile radius of our presence here. I'd meant to try to wake him long ago and get away from this place before someone came hunting us down . . . but unfortunately, after a meal of lightly scorched rabbit meat, exhaustion got the better of me. I'm not sure how long I was out, but I woke to moonlight, a pile of embers and rabbit bones, and a sleeping dragon boy one field over.

No sign of Valtar anywhere.

I grit my teeth and wrap my arms around myself, shivering against the night breeze. I'd given Valtar's hellfire-proof cloak to the boy after he dropped his dragon form and lay unconscious in the rain yesterday. It had seemed like the right thing to do, but I'm starting to regret it. He, at least, has dragon fire in his veins to keep him warm; all I have is this thin gown and a pair of very damp shoes on my feet. Not the best ensemble for a grand and glorious quest, but I didn't think about that when I plotted my escape from Stromin Palace. I was more concerned with getting out from under that ton of mountain rock and away from King Alderin and the champions and all my kind and solicitous kidnappers. I figured the rest of the plan would come to me as need arose. I am a trained healer, after all. Improvisation is my specialty.

Only now I need a cloak. And water—gods damn, but I'm thirsty! And I'm not entirely certain how I'm going to satisfy either of these necessities. I can't very well leave the dragon boy alone in the field while I go hunting something to drink. If only Valtar hadn't skulked off to who-knows-where on who-knows-what errand.

A little shiver passes down my spine. I can't help craning my neck suddenly to stare over my shoulder. There's nothing but open fields behind me and, a little way off, the lonely copse of trees in which Valtar and I had sheltered from yesterday's downpour. My dragon-born eyes search the shadows, seeing almost as clearly by moonlight as at midday. No sign of my would-be assassin lurking about. Is he even now hidden somewhere, just out of sight? Waiting for his chance to sneak up on me and slip a knife between my ribs?

Nonsense. If he'd wanted to knife me, he could have easily done it while I snored on the ground in front of him.

I wonder, is it true what Iliyani, my old mistress, used to say? Do I really have no more sense than a drunken gadfly? Valtar has admitted, to my face, that he crossed the ocean and ventured deep into enemy territory for the express purpose of ripping my heart out of my chest and delivering it to his queen on a platter. And I just . . . went to sleep?

The truth is, I've never been able to fear Valtar. Not properly. Sure, some prickling of survival instinct now and then tried to pluck at the back of my awareness, but I always squashed it without a thought. Is it just because he happens to possess the face and physique of a marble-sculpted god, offset by a pair of frustratingly kissable lips? I'd like to think there's more to my implicit trust of this man than mere attraction. Maybe some deep part of my spirit recognizes the goodness in him, buried beneath layers of darkness and enigma. Or maybe I'm just that shallow.

With a sigh, I shake off the shivers and focus my attention on the dragon boy once more. Drawing closer, I kneel beside him, my knees squelching softly in the damp soil. He doesn't seem to have moved a muscle since I draped him in that cloak hours ago. I'd worry he was dead, but his whole bony little body heaves with quick, labored breaths. Rhyo—my brother. Of all things, this I find the most difficult to accept, to believe. That I am the sister of dragon spawn, not this boy only, but all of them. All the fire-breathing, hell-born monsters which have tormented this world for generations. That they and I share the same mother: Mhoryga, the Dragon Queen. A demonic entity, escaped from the hellish Dracora Realm to plague the mortal world with hellfire and terror. She has already conquered the entire continent of Khylmira, burning all the noble kings and queens who stood against her. Now her sights are set on the Unified Kingdoms of Belanor, including my own homeland of Anfalen. Everyone I know, everyone I care about, lies under threat of her looming shadow.

And somehow, through a twist of circumstances I still struggle to comprehend, it has become my destiny to stop her. To save the world.

I squeeze my eyes shut for a moment, as though I can squeeze that thought out of my brain. Then, looking down at Rhyo once more, I put out a trembling hand and carefully brush a lock of lank hair back from his forehead. Moonlight gleams on scales, which cover large portions of his skin, like a rash. I bite my lip. He'd been so afraid to take his dragon form. *The more you do it, the less likely you are to turn back again*, he'd said. *Some of them never manage it at all.*

I hate that he was ultimately forced to transform. I can't imagine being forced to become something other than myself, some monstrous creature straight out of my worst nightmares. In the end, we'd had no other choice—either he must transform, or we would never get off that mountaintop. So Valtar had taken matters into his own hands and blasted the boy with hellfire, forcing the issue. Thus we escaped Stromin Palace with our lives.

A shadow passes over my soul as I study that sad, scaled little face. Will he and I share a similar fate in the end? Will I too be forced to choose transformation for the sake of the greater good? Is there truly a dragon inside me, just waiting for the right opportunity to emerge?

Sitting back on my heels, I withdraw my hand from Rhyo's

face. Where is Valtar, anyway? I twist in place, searching the empty landscape for some sign of him again. Gods, I'm pathetic! Have I truly grown so dependent on the man? If I were a heroine out of ballads, I would march off to meet my destiny on my own two feet, purpose fixed firmly in my heart, face set toward adventure. But real life doesn't tend to work itself out in a convenient iambic tetrameter with a neat little two-line rhyme at the end.

I smack my tongue against the roof of my mouth, painfully parched. Surely somewhere in all this rain-soaked countryside there's got to be a convenient stream or rivulet. I'd settle for a puddle at this rate, and deal with whatever parasites I happen to ingest. I get to my feet, turning slowly in place. A gleam of moonlight catches my eye some little ways off, shining on the surface of a little pond.

"Stay here now," I say, looking down at Rhyo. "No running off on me, got it?"

He doesn't stir, not so much as a twitching fingernail. It should be safe enough to leave him for a bit. It's not as though there's much in this world more terrifying than a living, breathing dragon. He may look vulnerable as a kicked puppy, but I know perfectly well what he's capable of if need arises.

Gripping my skirts with both hands, I pick my way over one soggy field, across a little drainage ditch, and into the next field over. Sure enough, there's a small pond here, gleaming like a mirror under moonlight. Ordinarily I wouldn't drink from a scummy little hole like this, but since it's been recently filled with fresh rainwater, I figure it's worth the risk. I kneel, cup some water in my palm, and take a tentative sip.

It's sweet. So sweet, almost too sweet. Sweet enough that, if I weren't so terribly thirsty, I would probably pause and question the sweetness. But I don't. I'm tired, frightened, and so painfully thirsty, that I simply put my head down and gulp straight from the surface. I'll make a point to hunt up some ascal moss later on; it tastes like feet, but it's good for cleaning out the innards. This promise in mind, I close my eyes and drink until I'm fully quenched.

Then, with a little bubbling sigh, I draw back and look down at the pool. My own face stares back at me, reflected with startling clarity and framed by the large, open face of the gibbous moon. If I didn't know any better, I'd think I were gazing into the mirror back in my chambers in Stromin Palace, so perfect is the image before me. I blink, tilting my head so that a golden curl falls across my cheek. Is there a dragon to be found in that face? It's hard to believe. The features before me seem so ordinary, almost painfully human. Yet I find myself strangely frightened. Frightened of the power I now know lurks deep within, the fire waiting for its chance to ignite. Do I really possess inside me a potential rival to the might of Mhoryga? Could I become something so monstrous, so terrible? So magnificent?

And if I do, what will become of me? Of Rosie Harpwood, the apothecary's apprentice? Something tells me she cannot survive such a transformation.

My own two eyes stare back at me. Golden eyes. Dragon eyes. My mother's eyes, or so I've been told. I don't like meeting their solemn contemplation, so I let my gaze drift to my neck where the burn scarring is most obvious. A frown knots my brow. There are no scars reflected back at me in that pool. Is that . . . ? I lean a little closer, uncertain and curious. Are those scales? I put a hand to my throat, but I don't feel any scales. Just the familiar scarring ridges of the old burns. How odd! My eyes shoot back to meet my own puzzled gaze.

Only . . . only those aren't my eyes looking back at me from the water anymore. Instead, two pale, luminous orbs stare out from a slit-nosed face. A wide mouth grins, revealing far too many needle-sharp teeth.

"Oh hells!" I gasp.

Before I can fling myself back from the edge of the pool, a webbed hand shoots out from the water, and a demon grabs me by the front of my gown and drags me into the water.

At first I'm too shocked to be afraid. Shocked by the smack of water, shocked by the rush in my ears and the bubbles bursting in my face. My limbs are stunned by the sudden overwhelming cold—a cold that shoots straight through the bones down to the spirit. Some distant part of me is able to realize that this pond shouldn't be this deep. At most, the water might reach my waist, but I seem to be getting dragged deeper, deeper, deeper, down into a black abyss not of this world. Only those awful moon-lantern eyes glowing in front of me illuminate the watery realm around me, glinting off those hideous, jagged teeth. A *ravara*—a Sixth Realm demon. Gods spare me, it shouldn't even be able to exist in this part of the world! It shouldn't—

Fire roars awake inside me.

I feel it rising, roiling, bellowing up from the depths of my soul. Green and raging and eager to consume. It burns in my gut, spreads through my veins, an agony of flame I've felt before—once when Joro of Rassumen tried to strangle me the night of my Presentation, again when King Alderin called it to life with hellfire.

I can't survive it. It's too great, too hot, and my body is too weak. If I were a true dragon, perhaps it would be different, but I am only myself, clad in this fragile human frame. Such heat, such rage will burn me alive from the inside.

The demon still grips me tight, and my lungs are near to

bursting with the need for air. My choices are reduced to either burning or drowning—there doesn't seem to be much in between.

Rutt that!

With a wrench of one arm, I lash out and jam two fingers directly into those lantern eyes. My nails have done what they always do when I don't make a point to file them down each day—grown into talon-like claws. I feel the moment of puncture, and something in me revolts. The glowing eyes disappear in a sudden gush of black liquid, and the hands gripping my bodice let go.

I kick as hard as I can, cursing my water-laden skirts, cursing the fire burning in my veins, cursing my pathetic lungs that feel as though they will burst in another second if I don't reach air. Disoriented, I don't even know if I'm swimming in the right direction, but I'm not about to give up. Expecting any moment for clammy fingers to close around my ankle and yank me back down, I stretch my hand up as far as I can.

Something latches hold of the hair atop my head. My heart surges with terror, convinced the demon has caught me, when I'm yanked up hard, and my head breaks the surface of the pool. I gasp in a great lungful of air, simultaneously agonizing and blissful, and splash and surge, twisting against that painful grip on my scalp.

"Stop thrashing," a dark voice growls above me. The grip on my head disappears, replaced by an equally strong grip on the back of my gown. "I'm trying to save you."

I open my lips to spit back an answer only to get a mouthful of water. My addled gaze is vaguely aware of the large, broad-shouldered form crouched on the edge of the pool. I reach for him.

The demon bursts out of the water behind me, all many-jointed arms and flaring fins and too-large mouth full of far too many teeth. Its eyes are narrow slits, no longer white but red with rage and streaming black blood. It lunges at me, and I utter a little yelp of terror.

A blast of green fire erupts across my vision, searing my eyes. For an instant, the demon's face is illuminated in the glow. Then my nostrils are filled with an overpowering stench of fried fish. There's a big surge and a splash, which knocks me off my balance so that I once more plunge underwater. But the hand gripping the back of my gown wrenches me out again before panic has a chance to set in.

The next moment I find myself hauled out onto dry ground like a landed trout, coughing and choking and trembling with the awful heat of hellfire still trying to rise inside me. "Rosie?" Valtar's voice is close to my ear, and the warmth of his breath against my skin is a welcome distraction from that other, more dangerous heat. "Rosie, I'm here. You're not in danger."

He's wrong. He's terribly wrong. The fire inside me roars, threatening to burn me alive from the inside. My skin steams as water evaporates into the cold air, and I shudder violently with pain. When I try to speak, nothing moves through my lips but a thin moan.

Realizing what's happening, Valtar wraps his arms around me, pulls my back against his chest. It feels familiar—he's done this before. The last time the fire raged inside me, the last time I thought I would self-combust, he held me just so, urging me to breathe in time with him. Memory of that moment brings with it a rush of hope. I close my eyes, lean my head against his shoulder, shuddering and shaking at the violence coursing through my veins.

"It's all right, Rosie," Valtar murmurs. He rocks me gently, like a child, and I am grateful for his strength. "Listen to the sound of my voice. Listen to me, Rosie, listen."

There's a soothing quality to his tone, a hypnotic sort of rhythm. I try to concentrate on it, to let my awareness focus away from the heat, from the pain. It's almost like song . . . which hardly seems possible. Valtar is the last person in the worlds I would expect to sing. Am I imagining that low, melodic hum, deep as a growl? Wordless but full of faraway and long ago. Full of yearning.

The fire fades. The green glow on the edges of my vision retreats, and I find myself once more safe in the darkness behind my own eyelids. A dark, cool space, where I know myself and don't need to be afraid. The cold sweat on my skin chills under the night breeze, but I press into Valtar for warmth and am comforted.

"Rosie?" he asks, his voice a rough whisper.

"D-d-did anyone ever tell you," I stutter through chattering teeth, "that you have a lovely singing voice?"

He is silent. His arms, wrapped around me, seem to go very still and hard.

"I m-m-mean, I'm not saying you should throw away the deadly assassin gig and run off to join a band of troubadours. Patchwork balladeer's garb wouldn't s-s-suit your menacing aura anyway. But as a hobby, maybe."

Valtar clears his throat. "I'll . . . keep it in mind."

I pull away from him. For just a breath, his arms tighten, and I feel suddenly how easily he could crush the life out of me if he so desired. But he lets go the next instant, and I scoot away from him into the damp grass. Turning, I peer up at his face in the moonlight. All those hard, inscrutable edges, those shadowed black eyes. He's not quite meeting my gaze. But a sudden gust of wind blows a lock of dark hair across his forehead, and the effect is momentarily transformative, softening the sharpest lines, revealing the face of the boy he once was. The boy who survived a kingdom overcome by dragon flame. The boy who watched his father burn at the stake, who fought with everything he had to prevent his brother from sharing that grim fate.

What was he like before darkness overshadowed his soul? Did he like to sing? Did he ever smile?

"If you're going to survive out here in the wilds," he says abruptly, shaking that hair out of his eyes and fixing me with a stern gaze, "you'll have to stop taking unnecessary risks."

"Unnecessary risks like getting a drink of water?" I wrap my arms around my shivering body. "This is going to be one short and miserable quest."

"That was a *ravara*. A demon of the Sixth Realm."

"Yes, I know. I'm not a complete ignoramus. I've seen a demon or two in my time." A shudder ripples down my neck, and I glance at the pool. It looks so still and shallow and unthreatening now. "*Ravara* shouldn't be this far out in mortal lands."

Valtar grunts. "It's the smoke."

"The what?"

"The dragon smoke. From Mhoryga's invasion forces."

I look around at the empty landscape surrounding us. Mile upon mile of fallow fields, forests, and more fallow fields. "It doesn't look to me as though Mhoryga has invaded this far inland."

"No, but the city of Cyran was taken by dracori and dragon spawn last year. The concentration of smoke is intense over that city, and it gets down into the ground and spreads like poison. I saw it happen to my own homeland."

I frown. "They told me that *ilemaara*—Third Realm demons—inhabit the Rothomir Wastes." Another shiver ripples down my spine and knots in my gut. "They didn't tell me there were other demons as well. Certainly not here in Belanor."

"They didn't tell you a lot of things," Valtar says, but adds in what I suspect is meant to be a reassuring tone, "You probably could have escaped without my assistance. *Ravara* are relatively weak, and the air of this world does not agree with them."

"Not much comfort when it's got its hands latched onto your bodice, dragging you down into an interdimensional abyss," I mutter.

"No," he acknowledges. "Not much comfort."

Another gust of wind whips through the grass and bites at my sweat-chilled skin. I wish I could ask Valtar to put his arms around me again, maybe sing more of that haunting song. Something tells me that wouldn't be the wisest choice in this particular moment. I lift my chin, straighten my shoulders, and try to assume a haughty demeanor. "So where were you?" I ask.

Before the words have fully left my lips, a burst of green hellfire explodes on my right. I yelp, scramble to my feet, and whirl to stare at it, open-mouthed. "Rhyo!" I scream, and surge forward three steps. Valtar grabs me by the arm before I can take a fourth, however, and yanks me back. Though I twist and struggle, I cannot break his grip.

Instead I am forced to stand where I am and watch as a writhing, lashing form appears in the midst of that bonfire flame. Two great wings spread, like enormous sails. "Rhyo, wait!" I cry.

It's no use. The dragon boy doesn't seem to hear me. But this isn't the right way to reach him, is it? Recalling the mental connection we'd shared, I try to stretch out with my mind across the space between us to enter his head. I don't know exactly what I'm doing—it's all just instinct and guesswork. And when I reach his mind, there's so much fire, so much heat. It frightens me, and I wrench back again, my physical body staggering in Valtar's grasp.

Helpless, I watch as Rhyo takes to the air. His long, sinuous body undulates as he propels himself skyward. His great wings pulse, and he circles above us once, twice, before choosing a direction and shooting off like an arrow in the night. Soon even my dragon-born eyes cannot see him anymore. Only a host of stars and the lonely eye of the moon fill the sky overhead.

"He's going to Nyxia," Valtar says darkly. "Which means she's closer than I thought."

2

Valtar

Though I hate to waste even a few seconds, I take the time to retrieve my cloak from where it lies in the fire-blasted field. We have few enough resources between us as it is and can't afford to leave anything behind.

Then, without a word, I return to Rosie, take her hand, turn, and drag her into motion behind me. Her footsteps stumble, and she nearly falls but manages to catch herself and lengthen her stride, struggling to keep up with mine. "Wait!" she gasps. "Slow down!"

But there's no time to slow down. No time to be gentle. The dragon boy's abrupt awakening and surge of flame can only mean Nyxia got into his head. Which means she could get into mine as well if she realizes how close I am. Even now, she may be casting out her awareness, searching this very vicinity. Any moment I may feel the stab of pain straight through my skull that foreshadows the arrival of her insidious voice.

We have to move. We have to put distance between us and

this field scorched with hellfire, which will attract the dragon spawn like bees to honey. So I drag Rosie roughly after me, plunging into the dark of the forest. My dracori eyes can see well enough to navigate the dense growth, and urgency drives me forward.

"Valtar!" Rosie gasps behind me, then spits a curse as she trips, staggers, and nearly lands on her face. Only my grip on her hand keeps her upright. "Where are we going?"

"Away."

"That's not—*damn!*—much help."

My teeth set on edge. "If we stay put, we'll be dragon meat by daybreak."

I don't know whether it's my words that shut her lips for the next several moments, or simply the roughness of my grip and the speed with which I yank her along. It doesn't matter—I'm only grateful she doesn't fight me.

We come to a place where the ground abruptly slopes downward. My feet find firm footing easily enough, but Rosie, with a little yelp, slips, lands on her backside, and slides in a small avalanche of broken ferns and last year's leaves. I maintain my hold on her hand, and she ends up in an awkward angle, her feet outstretched, her skirts hiked up to her knees, her arm back over her head. She tilts her chin and glares back at me, upside down.

"All right, Sir Dark and Lurking Enigma Man," she snarls, "I've had enough of this. What is going on? And I mean *exactly.* Don't give me any of your vaguely mysterious nonanswers." Twisting around onto her stomach, she manages to get her knees under her and, with a little assistance from me, scrambles to her feet. When she yanks her hand free, I let it go, and she hastens to arrange her skirts into ladylike folds. Her chin juts at a haughty angle, and those gold eyes of hers flash. "I woke up, and you were gone. Just *gone.* Not a word, not a hint as to your whereabouts."

Her chin puckers slightly, but she grinds her teeth hard. "I thought you'd changed your mind about coming with me."

"I've not changed my mind."

"Oh." The darkness of my voice nonplusses her, and she takes a little half step back, nearly losing her balance on the incline once again. "Well then," she says, gripping handfuls of skirt, "where did you wander off to?"

I don't want to answer. It's not a simple answer to give. But she's looking at me with that narrowed gaze, her knuckles white, her expression as fierce as she can manage . . . which, granted, isn't particularly fierce. Gods above and below, she's so entirely unsuited to this role fate has handed her! She's all soft edges and sweetness. Even when she's angry, it's the anger of a spitting kitten, ferocious but entirely ineffectual.

An image of Mhoryga appears in my head. Mhoryga—the Dragon Queen. My goddess, my mistress. I see her as I first beheld her: a massive darkness wreathed in green flame, wings outspread to overshadow all of Inithana. More enormous than can possibly be described, a world-ending abomination never meant to inhabit a realm such as this.

Memory presents another image: Mhoryga as I last saw her. A giantess, seven feet tall, and more beautiful than tongue can express, her body sumptuous and powerful, covered in scales. Black hair fell in bounteous glory across her bared shoulders, and her heavy-lidded eyes, full of deadly intent, gazed down into mine.

Bring back her heart, sweet prince, she'd whispered in a voice of searing heat. *Bring it to me, or I will have your brother's heart instead.*

Her taloned fingertips stroked my cheek and traced under my jaw, simultaneously sensual and threatening.

Do not fail me, beloved. Bring back this sacrifice for your goddess.

I turn my head sharply, wrenching my mind back into the

present. My breath is tight, and the stink of sulfur lingers in my nostrils. Even with an ocean between us, she is never far from my thoughts. Loathing and longing mingle in my veins, burning with the hellfire she placed there when she transformed me into one of her own damned creatures. I am dracori—demon wrought and demon owned. A monster born from the will of the darkest fiend ever to penetrate the veils of this reality.

Slowly I turn my gaze back to Rosie. She watches me intently, her brow knotted, her lips parted. Some of the fury has faded from her expression, replaced by . . . oh gods! Is that concern? Is she worried about me? It's impossible for her to stay in a place of anger for more than two minutes together. Then she's back to being this empathetic and gentle little person. A person so wildly different from her mother, it staggers the mind even to consider a connection between them. If it weren't for those telltale eyes of hers, I wouldn't believe it.

But those eyes don't lie. Nor does the hellfire I've felt inside her, struggling to rise, eager to manifest in unholy blaze. That fire, which is the antithesis of her very nature and which, should it ever break free, will surely consume her.

In the back of my mind, I hear the echo of my father's screams as he stood at the stake and Mhoryga's flame overwhelmed him. Something deep inside me, something I'd thought I'd long ago killed, begins to tremble.

"Valtar?"

Rosie's voice breaks through the din in my head, like a sudden ray of sunlight cutting through storm clouds. I drag a painful breath into my lungs. Then: "I went to speak to Nyxia."

She blinks. "Nyxia," she echoes slowly. "As in . . . as in my dragon sister, Nyxia? The one who controls you with her . . ." She twirls a finger at her temple, a speaking gesture.

"Yes."

Her jaw rolls, as though chewing on her words before deciding whether or not to speak them. "So what happens now?" she asks in a tight voice, her gaze never leaving mine. "Did she send you back to finish me off? Or are we on our way to her, so you can hand me over personally?"

"Neither."

"And I'm supposed to believe you?"

I press my lips into a hard line. Then, with a single step, I close the little distance between us, looming over her as I stare down into her uptilted face. I stand a good head taller than her and am more than twice her weight and breadth. If I wanted, I could overpower her without a thought. Innumerable methods of murder lurk at my fingertips. I could snap her neck, crush her skull, break her spine. The knife hidden up my sleeve could pierce her flesh in a dozen places, bringing either instantaneous death or lingering agonies over days, even weeks. I've done it before. Men, women, and children too. Whatever sacrifice my goddess required, I fulfilled for her. I've looked into the eyes of countless victims in the last breath before the blow falls, seen their terror, felt their spirits recoil with dread.

But Rosie does not recoil. She never does.

"If I were controlled by Nyxia," I say, my voice a fire-laced shadow, "I would have driven my blade between your ribs, punctured your lungs, and watched you drown in your own blood. Then I would have carved open your breast, pulled out your still-warm heart, and carried it to the appointed meeting place, a gift for Mhoryga." The words fall like molten stone from my lips. "If ever I fall under Nyxia's control again, you will not know it until it is too late."

Her eyes blink once. The line of her cheek tenses slightly.

Otherwise she does not move. My hand lifts, almost against my will, and my fingers slowly reach toward her face, not quite daring to stroke her soft cheek, not quite daring to rest on her throat in that place where I may feel her pulse beating with life. I find it difficult to breathe. I want her to be afraid. I want to see terror limning those eyes of hers, to know that she has at least that much self-preservation. I am the most lethal thing in her life. Sooner or later, I will likely be the cause of her death. If she had any sense at all, she would turn and flee from me even now, never once looking back.

But she doesn't. In her eyes I see worry, confusion, irritation, concern, and . . . and something else. Something I don't dare name. Something she ought not to feel. Not for a creature like me.

But no fear. Never fear.

With an effort, I curl my fingers into a fist and drop my hand to my side. "Fortunately for you, I am not under Nyxia's control now. And I would like to keep it that way." Lifting my chin, I draw a step back, inhaling a long breath of cold night air.

She tilts her head, locks of tangled, golden hair falling across one shoulder. "So," she says, her voice icy, "if you're not under Nyxia's thrall, why did you go to her?"

I hesitate. But at this stage, ignorance will do her no good and may in fact cause harm. "I told her that you have not yet acquired your flame. I told her that, flameless as you are, your heart is no use to Mhoryga."

One incredulous eyebrow lifts. "And? What exactly did you hope to accomplish by this?"

"I told her I am working on a solution to help you manifest your fire and promised to bring you in when it is done. I hoped it would convince her to leave us alone, at least for a little while."

"And did this brilliant strategy of yours work?"

"Judging by the dragon boy's abrupt departure, no."

She opens her mouth to speak, but we've already stood in this place too long. Resisting the urge to take her hand once more, I set off through the forest again, navigating down the incline and pushing through a snarl of young pine saplings. Cursing colorfully, Rosie follows behind, slipping and sliding, but ultimately managing to stay on her feet. "We need to cover our tracks," I throw back over my shoulder. "We'll make for the River Cy. It's not far from here. Can you swim? Dragon spawn find water repellent, running water especially. It may throw them off for a time."

"So is this your plan then?" Rosie huffs, pushing through the pine saplings in my wake. "We're going to run about like lunatics through the forest in the dead of night. No destination, no plan. Just senseless flight?"

I consider Nyxia and those she has with her. Thirteen dragon spawn and twelve dracori. Enough to decimate an entire armed host of fighting men without pausing for a second breath. If Rosie once caught sight of them, she wouldn't be questioning the validity of senseless flight.

Rosie reaches out, hooks my elbow with her fingers, and tugs. I don't stop. I keep plunging forward, pulling free of her grasp easily. She harrumphs and plants her feet. "Valtar Skylock," she calls after my retreating back, "if you don't stand still for two minutes and listen to me, then . . . then I'm going to scream. That's right! I'm going to scream and scream and scream, until Nyxia or Alderin or all the creeping demons of the lower realms come racing to this very spot."

I whirl on her. The temptation is strong to simply knock her across the head, rendering her unconscious so that I can carry her over my shoulders. But . . . gods damn it, if we're going to somehow survive together for more than a handful of hours, we've got to learn how to communicate effectively. I ease a frustrated sigh through clenched teeth. Working with other people is not my strong suit.

"All right," I say. "If you have another plan, go ahead. Tell me."

Her eyes narrow again. "You've got that look about you."

"What look?"

"That look like you're indulging me but you have absolutely no intention of doing anything I suggest. I've seen it enough times on enough faces to recognize it." She crosses her arms. "I don't care to be indulged."

I drop my head back, staring up through the interlaced tree branches overhead to the stars far above. If only I dared pray for strength—but I'm fairly certain whatever gods are out there gave up any interest in me long ago. So I simply breathe out slowly, easing the air from my lungs. Then, looking down at her once more, I say, "Fine. Tell me your plan. And we'll do it. Whatever it is, we'll do it."

She lifts a brow. "You've still got that for-better-or-for-worse tone about you."

"Do you expect your plan to be for better?"

"Well, it sure as hells can't be for worse!"

I clench my teeth and tip my chin, looking at her from under my lowered brow.

"I think we both know," she says at last, "that I've got to manifest. Not just the hellflame, but the whole gods-damned transformation." Leaf-filtered moonlight shines in her eyes, revealing, for the first time, the faintest trace of unease. She shakes it away, however, and firms her jaw. "Much as I hate to agree with Alderin on any given topic, I'm afraid he might be right. If I am, in fact, Mhoryga's daughter, I might be the only one who can . . . you know . . ." She doesn't want to say it. It physically hurts her to utter the words. "Stop her," she finishes at last, lamely. Then, in a lower voice, almost a whisper: "Kill her."

I don't want it to be true. I don't want Rosie to be the one forced to face such an impossible task. If I could take this burden from her shoulders, I would. I hate Mhoryga with a personal virulence unmatched anywhere in this world. Were it possible for me to make myself into a monster great enough to stand against her, I would do it. Whatever the cost.

But not Rosie. She's not meant for this sort of thing. An image appears in my mind, unbidden: the sight of her cradling a gremler kit in her hands, crooning over the little pest. Somehow, she sees value in even the most worthless life. She saw value in mine after all.

"You cannot become a dragon," I say, the words rough in my throat. Do I mean that I cannot bear to see it happen? Or simply that I do not believe it can be done? I'm not sure. Both, perhaps.

Rosie purses her lips, momentarily dropping her gaze. "I've been thinking about that," she says. She hesitates a moment, then continues. "I don't think I'll be able to manifest in the Dracor Flame like Alderin intended. Hellfire burns me—I won't survive it. If I somehow manage to make my way across Khylmira to the Shrine of Drathoridan and dive headfirst into the flame, what good will it do anyone? I'll burn to a cinder, and that will be that."

She's betting on us getting anywhere near Drathoridan in the first place. Which would never happen, not with all the luck of the gods on our side. Alderin was a fool to think it could be done.

Yes, he may have successfully pilfered a dragon egg from Mhoryga's nest, but since then she has increased her defenses beyond anything he can imagine. Ten thousand dragon spawn stand between us and the great fire of Dracor. It cannot be done.

"But there may be another way."

I frown. "There is only one way for a dragon queen to manifest."

"Yes, well,"—a small half smile flashes in the moonlight—"they also said there was only one way for a dragon queen to be born. In hellfire. But I wasn't."

"What?"

She looks excited, the idea which has captured her drowning out all thought of our imminent peril. "Alderin told me the circumstances of my birth. How he stole the egg from Mhoryga and carried it back across the sea to Belanor. They needed a fire of comparable heat to the Dracor Flame to hatch me. So they took the egg to the pyre of Lorayarus, the great phoenix of Inamaer Forest, just as he was preparing to self-immolate." She takes a step toward me, eyes shining. "Don't you see? If I was born in phoenix flame, does it not follow that I will also manifest in phoenix flame?"

I stare at her. Not once did it occur to me to question how the egg was hatched. Now that she shares the story, everything makes so much more sense than it did. This is why she is the way she is. This is why, when the hellfire of her dragon nature tries to rise, as it did tonight, it nearly kills her. Her very essence rejects that flame! She is a being of healing and restoration, not destruction. Hers is a soul of fire, but a very different fire than that of Mhoryga.

As I listen to her detailing her theory, something begins to stir deep inside me. Something I don't like to acknowledge. As though from far away, I seem to hear my brother's voice, whispering softly in my ear: *It's a fool's hope at best, and yet . . .*

"And yet," I whisper.

"What?" Rosie says, her own flow of talk interrupted. "What did you say?"

I shake my head. "Do you know the way to Lorayarus's shrine?"

"I don't," she admits. "But I think Iliyani might. My former mistress. She has connections with the elfkind of Inamaer. I thought perhaps we could ask her. She might be able to find us a guide through the forest to the Shrine of Lorayarus."

I consider this a moment, then shake my head.

"Now see here." Rosie pouts. "You promised we would do my plan, whatever it may be! Are you going back on your word?"

"Alderin will expect you to return home," I say. "He will intercept you long before you reach Anfalen, much less the home of your mistress."

"I'd thought of that." She shrugs. "Is that honestly the worst thing? I'm not saying I'm keen to spend any more time with Alderin, but he is the one who wanted me to manifest in the first place. If I told him my theory, perhaps he would listen. He might even help."

"Does Alderin strike you as the sort of man who listens to anyone else's ideas?"

She purses her lips. Then: "Not really."

"He has fought his own battles for many years now to carry out his plans for you. The championship itself was intended to find a man worthy of taking you to Drathoridan." I almost tell her what Alderin shared with me: that the champion chosen to accompany Rosie on her quest would also be charged with the task of slaying her once her quest was accomplished. She only just learned the truth about the High King, about her parentage, and she's had no time to think it over. I'll find a better opportunity to drop the fact that her own father has been working to arrange her murder.

Instead I finish with: "Something tells me he won't give up on his mission without a fight."

"All right." She sighs and pushes hair back from her forehead in a quick, irritated gesture. "Fine, it's not a great plan, I'll grant you. But isn't it better than simply wandering around aimlessly until Nyxia catches us? I'm ready to try to become this . . . this dragon queen everyone wants me to be. I'm ready to fulfill my destiny. But if I'm going to do so, I need help. In case you hadn't noticed, I'm not best equipped to handle a quest like this on my own."

She's not.

But then . . .

The truth is, Rosie possesses abilities she's not yet begun to explore. There's more to her dragon nature than hellfire, if she can only be convinced to accept it. To hone it.

"I will help you reach Lorayarus's shrine," I say at last. "You have my word. But you must let me decide how and when we go."

She looks at me closely. "You have an idea, don't you."

"Yes. But you're not going to like it."

"Is it better than running around like headless chickens through wild forests in the dead of night?"

"Marginally."

"I like it already. Tell me."

"We must journey to the city of Cyran and build you an army of dragon spawn."

She blinks. "You want to *what* now?"

"You have already discovered for yourself your ability to enter the minds of dragon spawn, an ability you share with both Nyxia and Mhoryga. You can invade dracori minds as well—you've already been on the edge of mine."

She remembers. I can see it in her face. "But . . ." She shakes her head. "I don't know how to control it."

"You can be taught. It is nearly five hundred miles to Cyran from here. We'll have plenty of time to practice. And by the time we reach the city, you'll be prepared to take dominion over the dragon spawn. Perhaps not all of them, but enough to put up a fight against Nyxia. Maybe enough to drive them out of Albhia altogether."

She looks ill. The idea of controlling another being's will is as abhorrent to her as killing. But we have so few options before us, even this wild chance is better than nothing.

"If you cannot control the dragon spawn on any significant level," I continue, "Cyran would still be a good place to lose Nyxia. Out here, where neither dracori nor dragons abound, we are vulnerable. Nyxia doesn't need to get close before she'll be able to sense our presence. But if we can make it to Cyran, it will confuse her senses, and we might be able to shake her from our tail. If, in the process, we manage to turn a dragon or two to our side, so much the better."

Rosie whispers a curse. Then she catches my eye. "Five hundred miles, did you say?"

"Give or take."

"And we're on foot. Gods spare us."

"Until we can steal a horse or two, yes."

"Do you think we can get there before Nyxia finds us?"

I don't. I honestly don't expect us to last more than a few

hours, days if we're lucky. The journey to Cyran will take the better part of a month. How can I hope to keep Rosie alive in the meanwhile? We have nothing but the clothes on our backs and my knives. Hardly well provisioned for all that lies ahead.

"It is our best chance," I say. "Possibly our only chance."

She makes a face. "I . . . I don't know if I could bear to do it. To control them."

"You'll have to practice. On me."

Her eyes flash.

"I am dracori," I remind her. "Hellfire runs through my veins. I am compelled to serve my dragon queen. Which is what you are. Manifested or otherwise, you bear Mhoryga's blood."

She looks sick. "I don't want to control you."

And that right there is what sets her apart from both her sister and her mother most profoundly. That right there is why I would willingly march into the very maw of hell for her . . . and why I believe the other dracori will as well. Once they get a taste of the freedom she offers, they won't want to go back.

But I say only, "You won't have a chance to try if Nyxia gets any closer. So what's it to be, Dragon Queen? Aimless flight through the forest? Or Cyran?"

"We could do what I said before: make for Mistress Iliyani's."

She wants to go home. She wants to throw herself into the care of someone she views as stronger than herself, someone who once gave her world structure. It's a foolish desire, almost childish, but I can't very well blame her. And I did promise I would do as she chose. Come what may, I will honor my word.

Finally, Rosie sighs and throws up her hands. "Fine! We'll go to Cyran." Then she points a finger at my nose. "But you better not be luring me into a trap."

I raise my eyebrows, eyes slightly crossed to look at that

fingertip before lifting once more to meet her gaze. "And what will you do to me if I am?"

She smiles. A smile so brilliant, so devastating, and so unexpected here in this dark world, my heart turns over painfully in my breast.

"I'll kiss you again, Valtar Skylock," she says. "That's what I'll do. Just to teach you a lesson."

3

Rosie

The broad, fleshy leaf is half hidden beneath a layer of red pine straw, and no one who wasn't actively searching for it would have paid it any heed. I, however, have been on the lookout for just this plant for the better part of the last three days and nearly squeal with joy at the sight of it.

"Where are you going?" Valtar demands, mingled confusion and irritation in his voice as he turns to watch me dart away into the trees.

"Won't be a minute!" I toss over my shoulder, ducking under low-hanging boughs and dropping to my knees near the roots of a tall fir tree. I carefully scrape back the pine straw to reveal the dark green plant beneath—an open-faced, ugly thing with scratchy leaves that gives off a pungent and distinctly *green* aroma. I send up a prayer of thanks to the gods and hastily go about stripping the outermost leaves from the array. They're fat, and I can feel the juiciness trapped inside them.

"Is it edible?"

I startle at the sound of Valtar's voice, speaking directly behind me. How he manages to move with such silent stealth across dead leaves and fallen twigs I'll never fathom. Three days of trailing after him over the seemingly endless miles of countryside, I should be used to it, but I'm still not.

"No," I answer, and removing the little pouch from my belt, carefully spread it open in my lap, adding the fat leaves to my collection. The pouch is nothing more than a large strip of cloth torn from my outer skirt and fashioned into a little bag, but it serves the purpose. Over my years of training as Mistress Iliyani's apprentice, I've learned to spot a useful herb, moss, morel, or weed. In the last few days, I've foraged Mercy's Swinies, a pale purple bud that alleviates headaches, spiny yarrow leaves for aiding blood clot, ascal moss for killing internal parasites, and more. But this find is a real treasure.

"Not edible," I say, holding up one leaf and twirling it between thumb and finger. "It's soapweed."

"What?"

"Soapweed," I repeat, and grin. "Trust me, you'll be glad to have it at the next lake or stream we find."

Valtar gives me a look. He's been giving me a lot of those over the last few days. It's subtle, only *just* a fraction of a brow lift, hardly discernible on his stone-stoic face. But I've learned to recognize it. It communicates more eloquently than words a clear sentiment of: *This woman is a lunatic, and she's going to drag me down into madness after her.*

"Look," I say, carefully tying up the ends of my rag pouch, "not all of us are cut out for the trekking-across-endless-miles-of-hostile-terrain lifestyle. *You* may not mind smelling like the hind end of a donkey for days on end, but I find a little cleanliness goes a long way toward keeping up the spirits."

Valtar subtly turns his head, sniffing slightly. "I didn't realize I . . . smelled offensive."

He doesn't actually. Damn the man, even three days of hard travel with scarcely a pause to splash his face in a convenient stream, and he's barely worked up more than a faint masculine musk. Whereas I'm fairly certain an unlucky breeze will alert all enemies to my whereabouts with a single pungent gust.

Rather than answer, I rise, shake pine straw out of my skirts, and give Valtar a curt nod. He ducks his way back out from under the pine boughs, still managing not to rustle so much as a twig in his wake. Far less stealthy, I stomp and crackle my way back out to clearer ground. Valtar waits until I'm by his side, then, without a word, turns and plunges on through the forest. He always manages to find a path. I have only to walk in his footsteps, which can be a challenge, considering how long a stride the man has. Without him, I should have been hopelessly lost in this wild country. Even now, I can't begin to guess where we are, nor have I more than the vaguest sense of where we are going. But Valtar moves with confidence, never varying, following some internal compass.

The man insists on traveling through the thickest parts of whatever forest growth he can find. Groundcover, as he calls it—protection from eyes in the sky. I can't help thinking we could be halfway to Cyran by now if he would just let us cut across open country once in a while. Instead, day after achingly long day, we lumber our way through bracken and briar, twenty miles or more at a stretch, from sunup till sundown. Valtar only pauses long enough to forage for food or water, and even that he seems to do with extreme reluctance. He'll leave me resting under a tree, dart off into the thicket, and come back with a dead rabbit or bird. We then proceed to argue over the merits of stopping to build a fire or simply eating wild meat raw. It's become something of a routine by now, and I know all the parts by heart:

We shouldn't stop. Best to eat as we go.

I'm not eating raw wood pigeon on the march.

A fire will alert pursuers to our whereabouts.

That's a risk I'm willing to take.

Say that again when hellfire rains down on you from the sky.

I will. And I'll be so happy dealing with the hellfire downpour while not *doubled over with cramps from ingesting raw wood pigeon, thank you very much.*

And so on and so forth. Each time I win the day by simply planting my bum on the ground and refusing to budge until a fire is made and my belly is full, or, at the very least, somewhat less cavernous. In those times, Valtar looks rather like he's debating the merits of assassinating me after all. Thus far he's not given in to the impulse, bless his hell-warped heart.

If anyone had told me less than a month ago that I would find myself traveling cross-country in the company of a dracori of all things, I . . . well, I wouldn't have laughed, that's for certain. The very idea would have horrified me. I still have nightmares of that night sixteen years ago when the dracori came to my home village, set fire to my cottage, and burned alive the woman I called mother. Her screams and the screams of the village folk behind me when I fled alone into Inamaer Forest will haunt me to my dying day.

I've believed implicitly, along with every other living soul in Belanor, that the dracori are mindless, soulless, monstrous animals, devoid of all virtue or humanity. Worse than dragon spawn. The dragons, at least, were born the way they are; they weren't given any choice. But the dracori are *made.* Not all survive the transformation, but those who do . . . surely they must have twisted souls to begin with. How else could they support hellfire in their veins?

And yet I've never been able to make myself see Valtar that way.

I shake away that thought, concentrating on the rough ground before me. The soles of my delicate shoes, not intended for forest tromping, are worn nearly through, and I don't want to step on a stray stick or stone and puncture my foot. Every now and then, I peer up between tree branches at the blue sky overhead. So far, despite Valtar's dire predictions, I've glimpsed no sign of any pursuers. Neither dragon nor dracori, nor even the High King and his people. While I know Valtar is primarily concerned about Nyxia and the dragon spawn, they still seem like an unreal threat. Alderin, however, I can easily picture setting out from Stromin Palace with a full company of armed men on the hunt. It won't be easy for him to catch us. Rhyo carried us many miles over several hours, and Alderin does not possess the power of flight.

But the High King of Belanor is the most determined man I have ever met. Did he not unify the six kingdoms of Belanor under his rule? And he organized that ridiculous championship, luring princes from across the continent to compete for the hand of an apothecary's apprentice in marriage! That takes some force of will.

And there's that other small detail which I keep trying to forget: He is my father.

Deep in my mind, that voice of fire whispers again: *You are mine, Roselle. Bred of my blood and bone.*

I still don't believe it. Not entirely. Maybe it's just another of his manipulations, a ploy to get me on his side, to convince me to see and do things his way.

But that doesn't explain away the compelling draw I've always felt for him. A desire, almost a compulsion, to win his approval, even when what he wanted from me went against everything I believed about myself. I'd just assumed it was the natural awe a man like that is sure to inspire in those around him. Now I can't help wondering if it was something more. That some part of me knew him, somehow.

I'd not given much thought to my father over the years. Durona, the woman I believed to be my mother, never spoke of him, and I'd assumed both that he had been Durona's husband and that he had died. Now, putting together the bits and pieces of the story as he's told it to me, along with things he told Valtar, I know that Alderin and Durona were indeed very close. But not lovers. More than lovers—knights-in-arms, sworn to defend each other. Without Durona, he would never have succeeded in his quest to retrieve the egg from Mhoryga. He would have remained Mhoryga's plaything to the end of his days.

For five long years, she possessed my mind, he'd said. *I belonged to her, and in that time, I all but forgot what it was to be a man.*

A shudder twists my gut. That part of the story is almost too horrible to contemplate—that he would give up his freedom, his honor, his very dignity as an autonomous entity, just so that I could be brought into existence. That he should so debase himself simply for the hope that I might come into the world and save it. Do I not owe him for this sacrifice?

No. I set my jaw firmly, fingers curling into fists. Perhaps I've come around to believing the truth of my identity . . . perhaps I've even come to accept that it is my duty to face Mhoryga and either kill her or die in the attempt. But I will not do it as Alderin's puppet. I don't owe him that. I never asked to exist, never agreed to be born. Now that I'm here, I will assume responsibility for my own life and actions. But I will not be responsible for his.

I breathe out slowly and look ahead to where Valtar silently navigates through the foliage ahead of me. Rather to my surprise, he comes to an abrupt stop at the top of a small rise, parts the branches of two saplings, and seems to look out at something beyond this tangle of wildwood.

"What is it?" I call out to him.

Silently he points. Which isn't helpful, as I can't see anything from down here. Muttering curses, I hike up my skirts and trudge up the incline until I stand beside him, looking out from the forest for the first time today. My heart hitches. For days now we've traveled through this wild country with no sign of civilization anywhere. Alderin certainly picked a desolate part of the world in which to host his secret trials. I'd begun to despair of ever seeing any sign of humanity again, but there! Just below us—the rooftops and gables of quite a prosperous-looking little village. There's a mill down by the river, a large building that might be an inn, and a holy house with the distinctive, triangular-shaped front, indicative of the Goddess Eidolo. It's all quite charming, a feast for the eyes after days of wilderness.

"We have reached the border of Albhia," Valtar says.

A little flutter of hope stirs in my chest. Cyran is an Albhian city. While I know we're still many hundreds of miles from our destination, this is the first proper landmark we've come to. Progress at last!

"We must wait here until nightfall," Valtar continues, still in that same solemn intonation of his. "Then I'll sneak into the village under cover of darkness and steal a horse. Two if we're lucky."

I turn my head sharply, shooting him a look. "You're just going to . . . what? Casually stroll down there and steal someone's horse? A horse they bought, paid for, and cared for with their own hard-earned money? Just like that?"

He catches my eye in a quick sideways glance. "What else do you suggest? Have you a secret purse hidden on your person?"

"No."

"Well then. We need horses if we're going to make good time to Cyran."

I scoff, giving my head a swift shake. "Not everything is about us, you know."

"No," he agrees, and looks my way again, more intently this time, holding my gaze. "Everything is about you. In another year, these people will be dead—either burned or suffocated under an atmosphere of dragon smoke. Those who aren't will be enslaved by the dracori or transformed into dracori themselves. That is, unless you manifest and kill Mhoryga." Grim lines frame his mouth. "A stolen horse is the least of their worries."

My stomach knots. There's a cold logic to what he says, but . . .

"Why don't we barter for it?"

He spreads his empty hands. "With what?"

"We have skills between us."

Valtar turns his gaze back down to the village, his brow knotting with thought. "Yes," he says slowly. "Yes, of course. And who do you think down there requires the skills of a dracori assassin? Some disgruntled yeoman's wife, perhaps? Maybe the cobbler has an irreconcilable grievance with the wheelwright next door."

I don't bother to disguise an eye roll. "You can do things besides . . . you know . . . abruptly ending the lives of various individuals." I give him a quick once-over, allowing my gaze to linger on the breadth of his chest beneath the various buckles of his black leather jerkin. "You're a muscular fellow. Offer that muscle in assistance to a blacksmith. Or a stonemason."

"And ask them to pay in horseflesh?"

"Don't be silly."

"I am never"—his lip curls—"silly."

"Agree to disagree."

"Do you have any idea," he persists, "how much a good horse costs? Not just any nag, but a horse fit to carry us to Cyran at pace? I could spend a month or more breaking rocks, and we'd not have saved half of what we need."

"Yes. But you won't be doing it alone."

His eyebrow lifts slightly. "Do you intend to break rocks alongside me?"

"You forget." I sniff, lifting my chin haughtily. "I am an apothecary's apprentice. If there's an apothecary in residence, I can offer myself as assistant. If there isn't, even better for us. There's always work to be had for a trained healer." I pat the little pouch at my belt, bulging with foraged treasures.

Valtar looks slowly down at the pouch then back up at me.

"What's that look for?"

"I'm wondering," he says, "how likely it is that you will give your services away for free. Are you going to demand coin from the first needy widow who asks for a healing poultice for her child's fever? Or the lame old veteran who begs an ointment for his aged joints?"

"That's unfair." I draw my shoulders back, offended. "I know how to charge a price. Mistress Iliyani used to say, 'Fair wages for fair treatments.'"

"And did she live by this mantra?"

"Mostly."

"And you? Will you turn away those who cannot pay?"

I try to hold his gaze, try not to blink or let any telltale expression pass over my features. In the end, I curse softly and turn away, pursing my lips.

Valtar chuckles, a dark and mirthless sound. “I thought not.”

“Well, I’m still not signing off on you stealing a horse!” Whatever else I’m about to become—fire-breathing monstrosity or demon spawn—I have no intention of turning thief. “We’ll venture into town,” I say, “and see what we can get in trade for a day’s services. Perhaps we can stock up on some food supplies. No offense, but I’m positively sick of wild onions and half-scorched rabbit meat.”

Valtar’s face is a cold mask. “A delay could prove disastrous.”

“You keep saying that, but we’ve yet to catch so much as a glimpse of a dragon!”

“If we ever do glimpse a dragon, it will mean disaster has already struck, and whatever chance we had is over.”

I don’t have a response to this. The man is dead set on his perspective, but I’m not about to give up mine either. I’ve said from the beginning of this quest of ours that I would do things my own way, and I mean to stand by it. No casting myself headfirst into the Dracor Flame. And no horse thievery.

Pushing through the last of the forest foliage, I take three strides toward the little village. I stop before taking a fourth and look down at my ragged self. Gods spare me, I look like a madwoman, with my torn skirts and worn-out shoes, and my hair all in snarls and—I’m almost certain—crawling with unwelcome visitors. I cannot possibly offer my services as a healer to anyone looking like this. Not to mention the smell.

Biting my lip, I cast about, wondering if I dare plunge into that winding river. There are too many dwellings along its shore, however. The last thing I need is an audience for my ablutions. Instead, I turn on my heel and march back into the trees.

“Where are you going?” Valtar demands sharply.

“I spied a lake back this way, a half mile or so,” I call over my shoulder. "I mean to have a bath. Or at least a splash-about. And try to scrape off some of this grime, maybe pick the bugs out of my hair."

He growls audibly.

"You're welcome to saunter on into town on your own," I continue blithely. "I won't be long, and I'm perfectly capable of taking care of myself."

"The last time you went for a swim, you were nearly drowned by a demon."

I don't bother to answer that I'd rather be drowned by a demon than spend one more minute with my own smelly self. Something tells me Valtar wouldn't approve. He follows me, despite my bold declarations of independence, a silent shadow trailing after my crackling progress. I refuse to look back at him, but make my way through bramble and snarl until I come at last to the very lake I'd espied earlier.

Only when I reach the water's edge do I hesitate. Though the late-afternoon sunlight glitters pleasingly off the surface, I'm conscious of the dark depths lurking below. Having learned my lesson, I kneel and scoop a handful of water to my lips, testing for sweetness. I should have been aware three nights ago, when the pond water tasted sweet, that it was most likely a demon trap. This water just tastes like lake, however. It's shockingly cold, the melted ice of winter not yet warmed through by the late-spring air. Despite my bold intentions, I'm suddenly hesitating to take the plunge. Perhaps just a little splash-off will do? But no . . . a quick sniff under my arm is enough to dispel that notion.

Valtar strolls to the edge of the lake a few yards away from me. He looks around, scowling, even as I untie the pouch from my belt and dig out a soapweed leaf or two. "Do you plan to watch?" I ask briskly.

His sharp gaze catches mine for an instant before flashing away again. The muscles in his throat tighten as he swallows. Then, without a word, he turns and marches back into the trees. Only after he's disappeared does his voice call back to me: "Don't be long."

I snort softly, but my hands hesitate as I reach for the front laces of my bodice. It's not as though I think he'll peek. In fact, I'm quite certain he will be the perfect gentleman and keep his back turned for the entire time I'm disrobed. Am I . . . disappointed?

Hastily, I shake off that idea. Gods spare me, we have a long journey ahead of us, and the last thing either of us needs is to be complicating matters with . . . with . . . well, with anything! So Valtar will keep his back turned, and I will keep my mind from wandering down paths it has no business pursuing, and we'll both comport ourselves respectably. That's simply how it has to be.

This thought firmly in mind, I hasten to strip off my bodice and ripped outer skirt and petticoat. I swiftly add the boned corset to the pile, along with my shoes, stockings, and chemise. Soon I stand shivering on the edge of the lake, clad in nothing but my lace-fronted breastband and small linen pantalets. I cast a last glance over my shoulder, then shake my head and face forward again. Briefly, I consider discarding my small clothes as well, but there's only so much exposure I'm willing to risk under the circumstances.

"Hells," I mutter. Then, with a little squeak, I splash into the shallow water and dive in before I have a chance to think better of it. The shock of cold is enough to make me gasp out a stream of bubbles. I surface again with a splutter and another "Rutting hells!" uttered through chattering teeth. I wrap my arms around my body, convinced my bones will simply shiver apart. Lakeweed wraps around my ankles, and the sensation makes me yelp with the memory of clammy demon fingers.

But nothing grabs me and pulls me down, and, despite the cold, the lake is very still and peaceful. Sharp-beaked cormorants swim lazily about not far from me, casting disdainful looks my way. The season is still too early for water bugs, and a delightful freshness fills me.

I swim about a few minutes, floating on my back and letting the cold water wash my hair. My body adjusts to the initial cold, and I begin to enjoy myself. After a quick return to the shore to fetch the soapweed leaves, I break them open and squeeze out the milky substance inside. I run it through my hair and over my body, and while it doesn't exactly work up a lather, the effect is almost as good as a strong lye soap. Layers of grime peel away, and my skin glows once more a golden brown, save for the tinge of blue chilling my fingertips and toes.

Discarding the broken leaves, I paddle back out into the deeper lake and dive under once more to rinse off. This is a far cry from the luxurious baths Philippa drew for me back in Stromin Palace, but it's nonetheless wonderful to feel clean again. I surface, whipping hair out of my face, and begin to make my way for the shore and my discarded garments. I'll have to use the outer skirt to towel myself off before I dress, then wring it out as best I can before I—

Commotion disturbs the underbrush along the near shore. I blink, startled. A frisson of fear shoots up my spine. "Valtar?" I quaver, jaw chattering slightly.

A moment of stillness. I hold my breath.

Then, with an explosion of crashing noise quite unlike his usual subtlety, Valtar bursts through the trees and races down to the edge of the lake. Still fully clad in his black ensemble, complete with boots, buckles, and belts, he plunges into the water, splashing toward me in a rush of foam. "What in the—" I begin.

His arms are around me, cutting off my voice as the breath is knocked from my lungs. Before I can even close my eyes, we both plunge underwater.

This is it, I think as cold closes over my head and bubbles burst in my face. *This is how I die.*

Did he suddenly decide I'm just one bother too many and it's time to put an end to me? Or did Nyxia arrive out of nowhere, and this is the abrupt and unexpected murder he warned me about? I wouldn't have thought assassination by drowning was Valtar's preferred method, but then who am I to speculate? I can't help noticing that, though his arms around me are firm, they aren't crushing. He's got my back pressed against his chest, my wrists captured in his hands, his body bowed around mine. This doesn't feel like an assassination attempt, despite the pressure in my lungs.

And for some reason, the fire inside me doesn't awaken. Not like it did when that demon dragged me into the pond. Shouldn't it be doing something to try to protect me? Or is even my latent dragon nature simply unable to be afraid of this man, even when he's in the act of ending my life?

Just when I think my lungs cannot hold out a moment longer, Valtar's muscles surge, and we burst through the surface of the water. I emerge with a loud gasp, my long hair plastered over my face, blinding me. I try to shake it away, but it's too heavy, and I can't break Valtar's grip on my wrists. "Valtar!" I splutter, choking on a mouthful of lake water. "What in all the gods' names are you—"

"Hush," his voice growls in my ear. "Dragon."

"What?"

"Only one, I think. A scout. But if it senses us . . ." He breaks off with a sudden "Take a breath."

"Now wait just one—!"

Then we're under again. Back down in the icy blackness. At least my hair floats off my face, but I definitely did not get the large breath I need. I struggle helplessly in Valtar's arms, but he only tightens his hold, pinning me against him. I'm painfully aware of all the hard buckles of his garments digging into my naked flesh. I try to work an elbow free to dig into his ribs but can't quite manage it. My lungs positively scream for air.

Just as darkness starts to creep in on the edges of my vision, Valtar pushes up from the lake bed once more, and we surface. This time, to my relief, the hair is swept out of my eyes. I choke and gurgle, trying to make sense of the world around me. My heart throbs and . . . well, if I'm honest, I can't say it's with fear. Fury, maybe. And something else. Something brought roaring to life at the reality of being nearly naked in Valtar's arms. While I never imagined this moment under quite these circumstances, still . . .

I crane my neck, trying to get a look at him. His head is tilted back, his black hair plastered around his sharp cheekbones, somehow managing to emphasize the chiseled lines of his face. He stares up at the sky, even as he slowly turns us in circles in the water.

"I-i-if you needed a bath so badly, I would have loaned you some s-s-soapweed," I snarl.

"Quiet," he says sharply. "It could circle back."

I blink water out of my eyes and lift my gaze to the sky. I see nothing but drifting clouds. Remembering that I've always been able to sense the proximity of dragon spawn, I try to reach out with my mind, only to find it oddly garbled and wishy-washy. "I d-d-don't sense anything," I say.

"Of course not." Valtar glances briefly down at me. "Water deflects dragon senses. I've told you this."

Has he? I'm about to protest that he's never mentioned this helpful tidbit, when his gaze drops a little lower. For the first time, he seems to realize my state of undress. His mouth closes with an audible clunk, and a faint red flush stains his cheeks. Hastily he turns his gaze skyward once more. But there's something about the way he stares so hard that tells me he's not actually seeing anything anymore.

Shivering hard, not entirely with cold, I wriggle. "Are you going to let me go?"

"We must wait," he answers shortly. "Make certain the dragon doesn't return. If it senses us, if it even suspects our presence, it will bring Nyxia down upon us. Even if we manage to escape, Nyxia will burn the village just for the sport of it."

I gulp. My shivering is getting more uncontrollable by the moment, and even the distraction of Valtar's large, muscular presence isn't helping much. After what feels like an eternity, I say, "If you don't let me out of this w-w-water right now, I'm going to f-f-freeze to death."

He glances down at me, then away again almost immediately. With a grunt, he begins to take me toward the shore. "No!" I protest, struggling against his hold. "You go first. And stand where I can see you with your back to me, th-th-thank you very much!"

He hesitates. Then, without a word, his grip on my wrists unlocks, his arms unfold, and I immediately regret it. Without his support, I begin to sink, my limbs too numb to work. Valtar, realizing the truth, scoops me up, one arm under my knees, the other around my back. My teeth are chattering too hard by now to protest, and anyway, Valtar makes a point to keep his eyes pointed skyward as we emerge from the water.

He carries me to shore, staggering only once as he catches his balance. Spying my pile of garments close by, he makes for them and sets me down, still with his gaze averted—though I think perhaps he shot one short glance down at my lace-fronted breastband before turning his face fully to the side. Cheeks burning scarlet, he catches up my dirty petticoat and wraps it around my shoulders like a blanket. "I'll . . . make a fire," he mutters, more to himself than to me, I think. Rising hastily, he darts for the trees.

"Don't trouble yourself!" I growl after him. But when I try to clutch the petticoat and wipe off my dripping skin, I find I simply can't. I can feel my body shutting down. Where is that godsdamned dragon fire when I need it? Just now, I'd be happy to risk accidental self-immolation rather than freeze to death over a simple bath.

Valtar returns momentarily with an armful of gathered wood. It does not look dry enough, but he hurriedly stacks it into a pile. To my surprise, he stretches out one hand and simply blasts it with hellfire. A yelp catches in my throat, and I flinch away. "When you said you were going to make a fire, that's n-n-not what I envisioned."

He doesn't answer, but his face speaks volumes. He looks almost angry, his brow so stern, his mouth so grim. Turning from the green blaze, he drops to his knees in front of me and begins to rub my arms roughly through the draped petticoat fabric. I try to protest but can't. My body seems to be folding in on itself. With a little sigh, I lean forward, half collapsing against his chest as he continues to rub my back.

"We've got to get you warm," he mutters against the top of

my head. His hands pause for a few breaths. Then, gripping my shoulders, he pushes me away from him. I mewl a little protest, then bite my lip when I see him beginning to unbuckle his jerkin, rip it from his torso, and set to work unlacing his black linen shirt.

My eyes lift to catch his. "D-d-don't get any ideas, sir."

"I haven't any idea," he growls, "other than getting you warmed through again." So saying, he tears open his shirt, and I am offered, not for the first time, an up close view of the hideous dracori scar burned across his torso. The sight of it makes my stomach knot. The pain he must have experienced receiving that brand is more than I like to imagine, but everything it represents is so much worse. Once again, I'm faced with indisputable evidence that this man is not the hero, the champion, or the prince I want to think he is. If the hellfire blaze warming my skin weren't testimony enough of his damned soul, this scar is all the confirmation anyone could need.

But even in my half-frozen state, I can't help noticing other things as well. Like the splendor of his chest muscles, and how they move as he pulls his shirt off and wraps it around me. Or his abdomen, all chiseled and defined. These things certainly have a heating effect down low in my gut.

He pulls me to him, turning my body so that he can place my mostly bare back against his torso, then wraps his arms around me underneath the folds of petticoat. I find myself enveloped in the warmth of his skin. My body aches, my frozen veins struggling to pump blood through my limbs, but I can feel it all slowly warming. I close my eyes, lean my head back against his shoulder, shivering. How hot his skin is to the touch! It doesn't take much to imagine the hellfire blazing inside him, seeping through his flesh.

How long I remain like so, sitting before that green blaze, wrapped in Valtar's arms, I'm not certain. I'm too numb to think. It's easier just to be. To rest against him, to study the play of dancing flames as they devour the stacked branches. To listen to the swift pulse of his heart against my back. Valtar's breath is very tight, as though he's trying not to breathe.

"Was there really a dragon?" I ask after a time, my teeth no longer chattering.

He is silent for several moments. Then: "Yes." After another pause, he adds, "Did you think there wasn't?"

"Men have come up with crazier ruses to get women naked in their arms."

He stiffens. His heart rate, already quick, doubles, thudding wildly behind me.

Slowly I turn my head, looking up at him. The day has lengthened, the sun already beginning to drop behind the trees. His pale features are illuminated by the glow of the green hellfire, and it makes him seem very strange, not quite of this world. He's carefully not looking at me, his gaze turned toward the lake. "Valtar?" I ask softly.

His throat constricts. He lets out a short breath. "I am responsible for your well-being," he says very quietly, the words rumbling in his chest. "I would never . . . I could never . . ."

"Never what?" I whisper. After all, I still have quite a vivid memory of a moment shared between us. A moment of hot breaths and grasping hands lifting me up, pressing me against a stone wall. A moment of lips devouring mine with the urgency of a man grasping at his last hope of heaven. Was it all part of his ongoing deception? Part of his plot to lower my defenses so he could end my life? Or was it something . . . real?

His black eyes flicker, looking down at me at last. The heat in his gaze is extreme, and for possibly the first time since meeting him, a little thrill of fear trembles in my gut. It's a delicious feeling. Cradled in his arms as I am, nestled between his legs, I can't help but notice a stirring in his lower regions. His cheeks, ordinarily so drained of color, are flushed a scarlet which even the green hellfire light cannot disguise.

I turn in his arms, trying to get a better look at him, my petticoat still draped around my shoulders. His eyes lower, focusing on my lips, and I have the wild thought that . . . well, I'm clean for the first time in days. And he certainly smells fresh and delightful following his dip in the lake. If we're being tracked by dragons and as likely as not to be burned to a crisp at any given moment, shouldn't we take advantage of whatever little time remains to us?

"Valtar," I say softly, "do you want to kiss me again?"

His lips move, wordless. It's like he's forgotten how to speak. His eyes slowly lift, meeting my gaze once more, hard and searching.

I tilt my head to one side, my frizzy hair falling over one shoulder. I'm much warmer now, almost too warm, and my belly flutters with a delicious heat entirely unlike hellfire. Not in a million years could I have dreamed up a moment like this—sitting beside this green blaze, in the arms of a dracori assassin. Everything about it is so wrong.

But he isn't just some dracori assassin. He's Valtar. The only person in sixteen years who has made me feel safe. And while I may not feel exactly safe in this moment, neither do I want to let this knife's edge of danger pass. Not before exploring it further.

Biting my lower lip, I let the damp petticoat drop a little, exposing one bare shoulder. He stares, his mouth parted in a little huff of breath. Slowly, he lifts a hand, tracing a finger along the ridges of my burn scar. He follows the scar all the way to my neck, up to my jaw, then back down again, a lazy trail that ignites bursts of sensation across my flesh. My breath catches.

He looks into my eyes again. "Rosie," he says, his voice thick, "those scars . . ."

I frown. This is not what I want from him. The last thing I want in this moment is to discuss my scars, to allow any thought of them to lead me back into memories of the darkest night of my life. I want to stay right here, right now. With him.

But his eyes, like black pools of abyss, hold mine hard. "You need to know—"

Before he can say another word, I lunge, catch his lips with mine. It's an awkward collision, too hurried, too impatient. I'm almost certain my teeth are involved in ways they shouldn't be. I start to pull back again, embarrassed.

Then his fingers, still on my shoulder, grip suddenly hard, dragging me into him, and I have to catch myself, hand splayed across his bare chest, to keep from losing my balance entirely. His mouth moves, overwhelming mine with a force that silences any thought of retreat. He changes angle, demanding and rough and so desperately hungry. I slide my hand up from his chest, slipping it around into the still-damp hair on his neck. Parting my lips in invitation, I flick my tongue against his.

He groans, an agonized sound. That grip on my shoulder tightens painfully even as he pushes me back, wrenching his lips away from mine. "Rosie, wait. Before . . . before we . . . Rosie, I've got to tell you something."

"I don't want to talk," I say. This distance between us feels so great, though it's really only a few inches. I need to close the gap, need to fit my mouth and body to his. Applying pressure to the back of his head, I just manage to draw his lips down to mine in the briefest of touches.

"Rosie," he growls, turning his head to one side. "No."

"Why not?" I whisper, kissing the corner of his mouth, trying to catch his lips once more. I turn more fully toward him. With a little shrug, the petticoat falls away, and I kneel between his legs, bare save for my wet and clinging pantalets and breast wrap.

My chest rises and falls quickly, short little gasps for air. I've never been so exposed to a man before. What if he . . . what if he doesn't like what he sees? My scars are unsightly, I know, and though I am young and strong, I'm also underfed. Life is hard on the borders of Inamaer, and while I never starved in Mistress Iliyani's service, there was certainly never a surplus of provisions. I am more angles than curves, and even the weeks of luxury I enjoyed in Stromin Palace have all been undone by the last three days of hard travel on a mostly empty stomach.

But whatever insecurities I may have harbored vanish in an instant. Valtar's gaze slowly dips to contemplate my body. My scars, my imperfections, he takes them all in. Firelight dances in his eyes, revealing the wideness of his black pupils. "Gods," he breathes, his voice raw with distress. His eyes linger on the laces of my breast wrap. "Gods," he says again, a painful, rasping sound.

I wait, my body tingling with suspense, with anticipation. With hope. Somehow I know I cannot make the next move. He has to choose this; he has to choose me. He has to be the one to turn that agonized *no* into a *yes*. I cannot do it for him. So I wait, heart tight in my chest, hands resting on his shoulders.

His gaze lifts back to mine, dragged there unwillingly. Hot, quick breaths heat my skin, and I know suddenly what is about to come. For a moment, I wonder, *Will it be all right?* I don't know how to do this, but . . . but instinct will probably help. And I want to. While we're still alive, while we still have a chance. And yet he hesitates, giving me an opportunity to retreat, to change my mind.

I lick my lips. Then, gently, I run a hand through his hair, pushing a dark lock back from his forehead.

He lunges forward, kissing me again. His arms pull me to him, as though he will crush me with his need. One hand presses into my back, fingers digging into my skin. The other runs up my neck, tangles in my hair, gripping the back of my head firmly as he angles it into his rough embrace. Desire explodes inside my chest, like feral magic unleashed from realms beyond. I wrap my arms around his neck, opening my mouth to receive his sweeping tongue. My knees are between us, preventing the connection I want, the contact of my skin against his. I spread them, shift my angle to straddle his lap.

Now I fit. Now he can press my body flush against his, and I can experience fully the hardness of his abdomen, the solidity of his chest. What's more, I feel his urgency pressed against me, right through my small clothes. His hand runs up my spine, pulling at the back of my breast wrap. Then he brings that same hand around front, pressing it against my rib cage, his large thumb trailing under the curve of my breast.

"We can't, Rosie," he gasps suddenly, pulling his lips from mine. I welcome the opportunity to drag in a lungful of air but refuse to release my hold on his shoulders. He leans forward until our foreheads touch, staring down at the swell of my breasts above the delicate fabric of my wrap. His thumb moves, touching my perked nipple through the fabric. An embarrassing whimper vibrates in my throat. "We must . . ." he murmurs, "we have to . . ."

He stops speaking. One finger hooks the front laces of the wrap. A single pull, and they begin to untie.

He breathes out a long exhale. "Rutt."

"Well, if you insist." I grin, then let out a little "Ah!" as the hand gripping the hair at the back of my head yanks hard. His mouth finds my throat, kissing, nibbling, lingering over the scars even as he did all those nights ago in that dark cavern space, illuminated by a fallen *scintil.* I wriggle in his lap as he works his way lower, sitting upright to offer him access to whatever part of me he wants. His finger slips under the fabric of my breast wrap, touching me in ways I've never before experienced, provoking a series of mortifyingly unladylike sounds from my lips.

Then his mouth is on mine again, hard and hungry and delicious. I squirm against him, shocked at what that little bit of friction does to me, at the inexplicable pressure and pleasure building up inside. I run my hands over the muscular hardness of his back, digging in my fingers, pulling him closer. I want him to consume me. I want to be completely lost in this inferno of his, to burn with him right here, right now. I want to—

He pushes me back. His lips swollen, his pupils dilated, he turns his face away, staring into the forest. I'm both too startled and too breath-taken to speak. I lean forward, try to kiss him again, but he pulls away, sliding me off his lap. He rises, and, bereft of his support, I tumble into the discarded petticoat, my breasts heaving under my half-unfastened wrap. "Valtar!" I protest.

"Hush." He makes a sharp gesture. All passion banished from his face, he looks once more like the lethal assassin he is, dark and hard as stone. He stares into the trees with all the intensity of a wolf on the hunt.

Then, without a word, he stalks away, leaving me by the fire.

I want to call after him, but press a hand to my mouth, stifling the impulse. My heart is racing, my body prickling and throbbing in all sorts of strange places, and I want more than anything to summon him back to do more of whatever he wanted to do to me.

Instead I reach for the petticoat, draw it around my body once more, covering myself. Something is out there. Not a dragon, for I would have sensed that. A vivid memory of the *ravara* demon flashes through my brain, and I hold my breath.

A shout shatters the still air.

I press folds of petticoat into my lips to stifle my own startled scream. Sounds of a scuffle, cracked branches and shushing leaves. The next moment, two figures appear, one striding, one stumbling. Hellfire light reveals Valtar's deadly features. He's got one hand gripping the collar of a small, bent figure with long, green-snarled hair. He pulls the stranger's head up, revealing a face as gray and weathered as tree bark, framed by long, tapered elfin ears.

"It appears we have a visitor," Valtar snarls.

4

Valtar

In the short time I've known her, Rosie has always been very much herself. Obstinately, defiantly, against all pressures and pains. Even with the will of nations and kings fighting to make her into something she is not, she continuously manages to stay true to that center of selfhood which so few of us ever come to grips with. I've learned to expect nothing less of her and would be shocked indeed to see her act out of character.

But there are times when she somehow manages to be even *more* herself than usual. This is one of those times.

"Valtar Skylock!" she exclaims, scrambling to her feet and clutching that petticoat around her body as a cover-up. "Let that poor woman go at once!"

"She could be dangerous," I answer through gritted teeth. A flick of my wrist, and a blade appears in my free hand, ready to be deployed. "She could be a spy."

"Gods save us, haven't you got a courteous bone in your body?" Rosie glares ferociously at me before addressing herself to my captive. "I do apologize for my, erm, *friend.* He's a brute and a lout, but he can't help it. It's just his way; we're working on improvements. In the meanwhile, no offense intended, I'm sure."

"None taken, lady," the elf responds in a faraway sort of voice, as though she weren't even now suspended like a scruffed kitten in my grasp. "I beg your pardon for happening upon you in this . . . inopportune moment. I thought perhaps I should make myself scarce for a short while, but when I moved to retreat, my foot caught a stray leaf. It was that, I trust, which alerted your *friend* to my presence."

"Oh!" Rosie flushes brilliantly, even by green hellfire glow. "Oh, you saw . . . ? I mean that wasn't . . . we weren't . . ." She stops herself and holds up one finger. "I'll just get dressed now, shall I?" She turns that finger and points it at me. "Put the woman down, Valtar! And put a shirt on," she adds, before gathering up her garments and darting into the bushes nearby.

As if I didn't already have reason enough to skewer this spy on the spot, the sight of her long, bare legs disappearing into the foliage nearly breaks my fragile restraint. I drop my scowling gaze to the elf, who, twisting around in my grasp, looks up at me blandly. She raises apologetic brows and contrives to shrug while still suspended.

Growling softly, I drop her in an ungraceful pile of gray limbs. She pulls herself together with some dignity, a spare, bony little creature, with skin like papery tree bark and blueberry-bright eyes. She's clad in very little, garments woven of winding leaves and vines, scarcely more modest than Rosie's small clothes. But on her old, wizened frame, the effect is rather different.

She smirks, as though reading this thought in my face. "You could have left me be," she says primly, crisscrossing her knobby legs and resting long-fingered hands on her knees. "Finished up your business with the lady. No one would've blamed you, and I'd have happily returned at a more discreet opportunity."

My teeth set on edge. "What are you doing prowling out here in the middle of nowhere?"

"Don't interrogate her, Valtar!" Rosie's voice pipes up from among the trees. "She has just as much right to wander these woods as we do."

The elf's smirk grows, and she tilts her head a little to one side, green-grown hair wafting over her bony shoulders. "Strange it is," says she, "to find a dragon and dracori in these parts, far from others of your kind."

My pulse quickens. That she should know what I am is no surprise, considering the burn scar emblazoned across my chest. But I would not have thought Rosie's nature would be apparent, even to her elfin senses. Once more my knife hand twitches, the urge to solve this problem with a quick thrust of a blade far stronger than I like to admit. The elf eyes me closely, as though reading my mind. That wry smile of hers never wavers.

"Tell me what you want, elf," I say, keeping my voice low so as not to be overheard. "I'll know if you lie."

"Oh really? Are your heightened dracori senses so attuned to falsehood?"

"If you mean any harm against her, I'll—"

Before I can state the crux of my threat, Rosie emerges from the bushes in a loud rustle of leaves and crackle of branches, her garments rather haphazardly donned, her laces all askew. She looks first at the elf, as though checking for puncture wounds, then turns to me. "Are you trying to intimidate her? It won't work, you know."

My lip curls, my gaze fixed on the intruder. "I don't trust elfkind."

"You're in luck then. She's not an elf; she's half elf. And didn't I tell you to put a shirt on?"

"What difference does it make?"

"Well, you might catch a chill, for one. For another, not everyone will be as accommodating about that scar of yours—"

"I mean about her being half elf."

"Oh. Not much, I suppose. But if, for whatever reason, you don't trust elfkind, that needn't apply to her, because she's half human."

"I don't trust humans either."

Rosie tosses her hands despairingly and turns to address herself to the elf—or half elf—once more. "I'm Rosie Harpwood," she says, and—because the gods, when they formed her, never thought to bless her with either sense, subtlety, or self-preservation—holds out a hand in greeting.

"Viessa." The half elf places her twiglike fingers in Rosie's grasp and shakes politely. "Truthseer of the Glynrieth kintribe."

"Oh, you're a truthseer?" Rosie's eyebrows rise with interest. She looks as though she wants to query further but stops herself. Apparently it is impolite to question the half elf. She hesitates, licks her lips, then follows up with "I would offer you refreshment, but unfortunately, we have none to share. The lake water is fresh, if you are thirsty."

"Not at all, Rosie Harpwood." The half elf holds Rosie's hand a little longer than necessary, strange gray fingers tightening when Rosie tries to withdraw. "It is you I have come to find."

Rosie shoots me another warning glare when I take an aggressive step forward. I hold myself back, but only just. Fire burns in my veins, urging me to take control of this situation. But I promised to join her in her quest, not to control her choices. Though she might easily enter my mind and turn me into her puppet if she cared to, she has never once so much as made the attempt. Perhaps this is due to ignorance . . . but having slaved so many years under the thrall of both her mother and her sister, I cannot help reveling in this unexpected freedom. How could I now betray that freedom by exerting control over her in turn?

So I restrain the impulse to slit this stranger's throat on the spot. Instead I turn away from the two of them and go to fetch my shirt and jerkin, as bidden. Though it kills me to do it, I put my back to them, even as they fall into a quick and easy patter. Rosie, familiar with elfin dialects, slips in and out of her own language and that of the half elf, the result a confusion of sound to my untrained ear. I don't try to follow it, but simply stand with my back to them, every muscle in my body alert for even the smallest trace of threat. My blood still pulses with the heat of a fire hotter even than the hellflame dwelling in me.

Almost reluctantly, I turn to look at them again. At the elf, still cross-legged and solemn faced, speaking in low, unhurried tones. But my gaze cannot remain focused on her. It is drawn inexorably back to Rosie. The way the green fire glow plays on her skin makes her look more Draconan than I've yet seen her—more like Mhoryga. The sight should disgust me, but it doesn't. All I feel is a deep and terrifying well of longing opening up inside me, down in my core. Gods damn me, but I ought to be thanking that half elf for the slight stirring of a leaf which alerted me to her presence. Were it not for her intrusion, I don't think I would have had the strength of will to stop myself from running headlong down the path of pure desire. I would have taken Rosie. Ravished her. Had her trembling on the ground beneath me even as she cried out my name to the wild, lonely sky. I would have consumed her with my fire until we both lay burnt in ecstatic cinders.

My eyes linger on her lips, on the curve of her neck and cheek, the line of her shoulder still visible beneath the lopsided chemise and bodice. Memory of her skin warms the palm of my hand, and I feel again the point of her nipple under my thumb. How could it be that she would react to my touch with such eagerness? I am a creature of death; the fires of destruction flow in my veins. And yet she responded to me with such *life*. This woman—this being—of light and joy and goodness and sweetness, who won't even contemplate stealing a horse under the direst circumstances. Who gives her trust so willingly to a monster who could never in a thousand lifetimes deserve it.

She makes me feel something I never thought I would feel again. She makes me feel . . . *hope*.

No sooner does the thought flash through my mind than it's replaced with a sudden stench of sulfur. For an instant, so brief it's over in a blink, I am back in that night sixteen years ago, striding down the street of a burning village. I stand before a cottage, and green hellfire licks through the windows. I hear a woman's screams as that fire consumes her, trapped within those walls.

My eyelids flare open. The dancing green flames in my head resolve to a simple campfire. Rosie kneels before the half elf, still prattling on animatedly, unaware of the turmoil in my soul.

If she knew . . . if she knew what I did to her . . .

I turn away once more, marching down to the lakeshore, leaving Rosie with her guest. There I stand for some moments, gazing out over the water. Evening has fallen heavily by now, and the stars begin to emerge overhead. They do not reflect on that dark surface, however. The lake looks like an endless black pit, yawning with eagerness to claim me, to drag me into its depths.

What was I thinking, allowing myself to feel what I'm feeling for this woman? She is not my salvation; rather, I am her damnation. The death in my soul cannot help but ultimately overwhelm her, dousing that light of hers forever. Unless I am careful, unless I maintain some distance between us.

Besides, how can I accept what she so eagerly offers me, when she doesn't know the truth? When she doesn't know who it was who gave her those burn scars.

"Valtar?"

I don't turn at her voice, speaking suddenly behind me, but ease a tight breath through my teeth. She moves to stand at my side, gripping her skirts with both hands. Away from the fire, she shivers slightly, and it's all I can do not to draw her into my arms.

"She needs our help," she says at last.

"What?" I look down at her sharply.

She won't meet my gaze. She merely contemplates the lake, her face uncharacteristically serene. "The truthseer," she says. "She's not a particularly powerful one, half-blooded as she is. But she saw me in a vision and came to find me. The eldrin of the Glynrieth kintribe is dying."

"Eldrin?"

"It's an elfin word." She purses her lips, considering how to explain. "It means *father.* Or *elder.* Or *leader.* All of those, and none, and something more as well. It's difficult to translate." She shrugs then, tossing her head a little to one side. "The point is, he's dying. But Viessa saw me in a vision, and she believes I can save him."

I don't answer. I grind my teeth hard, biting back the initial response that roars up my throat, ready to be spewed like a blast of fire.

Rosie, sensing my tension, glances sideways up at me. "She's been traveling for over a month searching for this very spot. Can you believe it? A month ago, I'd not even arrived at Stromin Palace yet." She laughs softly. "The gift of sight is a powerful thing."

I don't care about sight gifts or truthseers or dying elfkind elders. I want to take Rosie by the shoulders and shake some sense into her skull, force her to see the reality of our situation with the same clarity I do. But my hands curl into fists at my sides, and I say only, "We've nearly four hundred miles yet to go before we reach Cyran."

"Oh, we aren't giving up on the journey to Cyran," she answers lightly. "This is just . . . a detour."

"We cannot afford detours."

"See here." She turns to face me directly now, arms crossed over her carelessly tied laces. "Cyran was *your* idea. You're the one who wants to plunge us into the depths of dragon-held territory on the off chance I'll be able to master some sort of mind control between here and there. Truth is, I'm not convinced I can."

"But you are convinced you can help this eldrin person?"

"Yes."

"Why? Have you treated whatever ails him?"

She pauses here, her gaze flicking away from mine, and chews her lip uncertainly. "Well, no," she admits. "What Viessa described . . . I haven't heard of anything quite like it. But she saw me in a vision. Me, specifically. She even saw my scars. She knows who I am, knows *what* I am. And she believes that, dragon or not, I am the one her eldrin needs. She is a truthseer after all."

"Truthseers can be wrong."

"No," she answers forcefully, "they cannot."

It's my turn to cross my arms. "What about Alderin's truthseer? He warned no one of my true identity. Even when directly asked, he did not say that I was dracori."

Rosie smiles. "That doesn't mean he did not see the truth. He simply chose to relate what he believed to be pertinent information. And," she adds, jabbing a finger at my chest, "he did say that without you, my mission would fail."

I stare down at her. Down at those sunbright golden eyes of hers, sparkling and animated, convinced she's just won some contest of wills. She smiles, and though I once saw myself as an unassailable citadel, my heart fortified against all this world could throw at me . . . that smile alone is my undoing.

"What's it to be, Valtar?" she asks. "Do you plan to hog-tie me and carry me to Cyran on the back of a stolen horse? Because if not, I will follow Viessa back to her people and try to help the eldrin if I can. I hope you'll join me, but . . . but I understand if you cannot."

The smile vanishes as she speaks this last, as though she truly fears I will abandon her now. As if I could do anything of the sort. As if I could bear to leave her presence. Everything in me fights the urge to grab her, to kiss her again. I want to pick up where we left off, carry her into the trees and away from that damnable half elf. Back into a world where there is room for no one else, just the two of us. But that is not possible. There is no such world.

"Where you go, I go," I say at last.

Her lips part to answer, but I don't wait to hear it. I turn from her, leaving her by the lakeshore, and march back to the hellfire blaze. Without a word or a look at the half elf, who watches me with some trepidation, I pick up my cloak from where it lies in a heap. With a shake and flick, I throw it over the fire, smothering the flames, and plunge our world into darkness.

THE FOLLOWING DAY, the half-elf woman leads us away from the little town and deeper into the wild.

Elfkind have their own ways of navigating the forests of this world. Not fully bound to the constraints of our reality, they bend and warp it in subtle ways, opening doorways through Utherlynd which allow them to cross whole continents in a single stride. Half-elfin as she is, Viessa cannot fully access such paths herself. Nevertheless, she possesses the ability to distort reality around her, condensing a dozen miles into a few feet.

She cannot do it frequently, however—not with a dracori and a dragon spawn in tow. While we are both possessed of innate magic, it is of a kind hostile to elfin magic. A wrong breath emitted at an untimely moment could spoil the enchantment and leave us stranded in the un-space between realities. So we travel in fits and starts, mostly trudging behind the little gray-skinned woman, who darts and springs through the forest like a creature of the wild. Rosie stays between us, and I bring up the rear guard, my eyes ever alert for potential threats.

My comfort is that Nyxia could never follow an elfkind trail. Even if that scout of hers detected us down by the lake, she will be totally baffled by our progress from that point on. From the very first time the half elf opened up one of her strange, reality-warping paths, Nyxia will have lost our trail entirely. By now, multiple such jumps into our journey, we have certainly left her far behind.

I am relieved to note that we are still journeying vaguely in the same direction as Cyran. If we can reach this old elf person and do whatever needs to be done quickly, we might not end up wildly off course. At most, we may add only a day or two to our overall journey, and that means that maybe . . . if we are extraordinarily lucky . . .

I shake my head, trying hard not to let the image of a tortured, eyeless face fill my mind. The dense forest growth seems suddenly to solidify, transforming into stone. The stink of sulfur sears my nostrils. And before me is a man, hung on the wall with iron fetters, his body broken, his features all but unrecognizable.

Arun.

Is he still alive? My brother, held captive in the dungeons of Heleris Stronghold. For years now, Mhoryga has used him to influence and manipulate me, to force me to do her will even from afar, beyond the range of her mental link. She's inflicted innumerable wounds upon his flesh, taken both his eyes, mangled his hands, severed one foot entirely. She's chipped away at both his body and his dignity, rendering him little more than a ruin of what once was a noble man.

And yet, somehow, she has yet to destroy his spirit.

I grit my teeth, pulling my mind back to the present, focusing on Rosie's form moving through the trees before me in the green-filtered light of midday. A few steadying breaths, and I continue after her, forging on step by bitter step. Arun must still be alive. Nyxia, for all she hates me, will delay reporting my defiance until the very last minute. She won't want Mhoryga to know that she's lost control over me. The Dragon Queen is not above inflicting terrible punishment on her daughter—I've seen her do dreadful things to Nyxia for far slighter infractions. No, no, Nyxia will hide the truth as long as she can, which means Arun is safe. For the time being.

Whether or not I can keep him that way remains to be seen. Rosie's idea of journeying to Inamaer and visiting the shrine of the phoenix strikes me as almost certain to fail. But if she is able to get into the minds of the dragons of Cyran, we might have a chance. Mhoryga is not as strong as she once was. Without a daughter's fiery heart to feast on, the full force of her demonic power has been compromised. She is still wildly powerful and dangerous, the most dangerous entity in this world, but . . . she's not *absolutely* unstoppable.

If Rosie can control the dragon spawn, even just a portion of them, we might be able to fight our way through to Drathoridan and kill the Dragon Queen. Not Rosie, of course—she is not the person to commit that deed. But if Mhoryga is stretched too thin, distracted with trying to regain control of her lost dragon spawn and defending her territory, what might an assassin's subtle blade accomplish?

Part of me knows it's impossible, a lunatic's dream. But then I think of Arun, strung up in the dark, blind and crippled and yet so defiant. I think of my father, King Travarn of Inithana, refusing to submit, even as he stood at that stake and flames ate his flesh. What more can a man of this world hope for than to die in flames fighting against Mhoryga?

Only . . . I must find some way to protect Rosie in all this. Which is difficult when Rosie herself is so bound and determined *not* to be protected.

We march on through the long, silent hours of the day. Even Rosie has given up trying to make conversation with our guide, which is a relief. Viessa is fully concentrated on her task of guiding us across this lonely countryside. Here and there, I spy signs of *ravara*, far more than I would have expected this far from Cyran. They seem to be drawn to the half elf; something in her magic resonates with their wicked souls. They loom out of tree hollows, rise suddenly from brambles, ripple across the surfaces of puddles—none particularly strong, all hungry, all eager to feast.

Viessa avoids them deftly enough. At each sign of a new demon, she opens another little pathway through realities and ushers us hastily into it. A few steps and we leave the would-be assailant many miles behind, no doubt blinking and wondering what became of its luncheon.

Thus the day passes, and evening draws on. I find myself wondering how long it will take to reach this woman's kintribe. If she took the better part of a month to find Rosie, does that mean we have an equally long journey before us?

No sooner has the thought crossed my mind, however, than Viessa pushes back a thick pine bough and declares, "Here we are!" in that cheerful, faraway tone of hers.

Rosie and I crowd close behind her, peering out into a clearing. Seven painted wagons stand in a circle, and in the midst of them is a cook fire with a large copper pot. A dozen or more individuals drift around the space. Some wear clothing akin to human garb, complete with jerkins, laced bodices, and leather shoes. These tend to be of standard human height and look, though there is often a telltale sign of their half-elf state. One man, for instance, could pass for any country yeoman, save for the bright yellow dandelions that grow in place of eyebrows.

The other folk are shorter, like Viessa, and dressed like her as well, clad only in bits of leaves and trailing vines. Some seem to have branches sprouting from their heads, others trail roots from the tips of their fingers. But all, whether human or elfkind in appearance, interact with a familiar ease that bespeaks their familial bond.

"Welcome to Glynrieth kintribe," Viessa says, turning to smile at the two of us. Even as she speaks, two yellow-eyed little urchins—children, I would guess, but am not altogether certain—emerge from under one of the wagons, letting out great whoops of joy. They charge our grove, and instinct urges me to reach for a knife. Rosie's hand finds mine, however. She catches my eye with a stern glance and a shake of her head.

I grind my jaw, watching as the little creatures throw themselves into Viessa's arms, chattering at the tops of their high voices in pattering elfkind dialect, which I cannot begin to follow. The truthseer accepts their aggressive affection, then nods in greeting to several of the taller elfkind, who approach more sedately, hands lifted in greeting. One of these, a large fellow with arms like young tree trunks, points at me and growls something soft but threatening.

Viessa casts me a short look and shrugs. But Rosie takes a hasty step forward. "Oh, don't mind him!" she says hastily. "He's my . . . erm. He's my *luric.*" She glances back at me and mouths the word *brother.*

Our half-elf guide begins to cough rather loudly into her fist. She looks at Rosie and repeats dubiously, "*Luric?*"

"Yes," Rosie answers and gives her a forceful stare. Viessa sighs and tosses up her hands but doesn't offer any contradiction. Rosie catches my gaze again, and I could almost swear I hear her voice in my head, whispering, *"Just go with it, please."*

I scowl. Perhaps claiming kinship affords me some protection here . . . but that doesn't mean I like it. Rosie turns away from me, however, and addresses the elfkind once more. The big one with the tree arms seems to be a leader of sorts. He casts me one more suspicious look before focusing his attention entirely on Rosie. He studies her with an intensity I do not like, and I find my hand twitching for a knife once more.

Viessa, however, seems to have some sway with her kintribe. She speaks in a final, imperative tone, and even the large leader backs up a step, head inclined. Then Viessa takes hold of Rosie's hand and begins to lead her toward the circled carts.

"Where are you taking her?" I demand.

"It's all right, Valtar." Rosie tosses me a quick smile over her shoulder. "They're bringing me to their eldrin."

"I'm coming with you."

Apparently the elfkind have no difficulty understanding me. They all begin speaking at once, sharp words of protest. Even the two small ones join in the chorus, shaking little birch-bark fists at me.

Rosie chews her bottom lip. "They don't trust you. Because you're dracori."

"So?" I look around at the gathered throng, scowling, then meet Rosie's gaze again. "You're a dragon."

"Yes, but their truthseer saw me in a vision, so they trust me. Also there's the added little fact that I've not manifested."

"Was I not in the vision?"

"Unfortunately no."

"That's too bad. Because I'm coming with you."

"Valtar—"

"You're not going out of my sight with these strange folk."

She huffs a little laugh. "What exactly do you think they'll do to me?"

My gaze shoots to the tree-armed leader once more. He is not the only large fellow in the gathering; there are several ferocious-looking specimens. Though I've had few dealings with elfkind over the years, I've learned enough to hold them in wary regard.

But I turn to Rosie and say once again: "Where you go, I go."

Rosie sighs. "That's all very well, but I didn't expect you to mean it quite so literally."

5

ROSIE

The *urira* wagons are so small and poky on the inside, I'm not sure how Valtar will fit within. I manage well enough, climbing the fold-out steps and ducking through the low, curtained doorway in the back into the dim space within. Tiny Viessa leads the way, moving as easily as though navigating a spacious ballroom. I, however, need to be a bit more careful, for fear of bumping unexpected corners with hip or elbow.

I needn't have worried about Valtar, however. Despite the small confines, he follows at my heels, ever silent and graceful. I suppose he did live among dwarves at one point in his childhood; he must be used to navigating tight spaces.

At least my dragon sight swiftly adapts to the gloom, my pupils dilating to take in the low light offered from a small, pink-hued *scintil* hung from the low ceiling. A long but narrow wooden bed takes up much of one side of the wagon, and on this the eldrin reclines, covered in a blanket of *luxisys* leaves and *yllahorn* blossoms, a combination meant to promote healing vibrations in the soul.

The eldrin himself is as long and narrow as the bed, quite a shockingly tall person, especially compared to the diminutive Viessa. His features are hard as rock with a chiseled quality, the skin stretched so thin one can see the smallest indentations of the skull beneath. Rather than hair, tufts of dry, brittle, browned grass emerge from his head, and I suspect that in full health it is a much greener, lusher crop. Even with this strangeness considered, he is undeniably beautiful, with that otherworldly beauty I have glimpsed among full-blooded elfkind on the edges of Inamaer Forest.

As I suspected, the eldrin is a full-blooded elf, the only one I've seen among the Glynrieth. While Viessa has not shared the story of her kintribe, I can fill in the blanks for myself: A young elf in an age long ago—before any of the six kingdoms of Belanor were founded and the world was not as it is now—ventured out from Utherlynd looking for adventure in the mortal realm. There he fell in love with a mortal maid, married her, sired children by her, and buried her in the long-ago mists of time. Rather than return with his broken heart to his own kind, he lingered on in the world which had become his home, with the children he begat and their children and their grandchildren and their great-grandchildren, all the long-lived half-elfin folk of his line, until memories of the woods and glens of his own realm were all but forgotten.

I gaze down at that emaciated face. How could anyone endure such heartache over so many centuries? Yet he must have continued to find reason to live and love and remain in this world, accepting each loss as it came and went. His face is lined with pain from the sickness which eats at him, but there are other lines as well: lines of sorrow, which, somehow, only enrich his already unnatural beauty.

I look up at Viessa, who stands at the head of the bed, her aged eyes focused on her eldrin. I wonder who she is to him. A granddaughter or great-granddaughter perhaps. "Where is the source of his sickness?" I ask softly.

Her bark-like face is difficult to read, but there's something in her expression that sends a shiver down the back of my neck. She reaches out and deftly brushes away some of the leaves and flowers.

I gasp in horror.

A tumor bulges from the eldrin's neck. Mottled black and red and faintly pulsing like a living thing. Now that the *yllahorn* blossoms no longer mask it with their perfume, a stench of sulfur bellows up and hits me in the face. I recoil, stomach churning, and back into Valtar. His hands grip my upper arms, warm and steadying, and for a moment, I allow myself to stay there, to be comforted by his large, solid presence.

Then I step forward again and look more closely. Aside from the visible outer tumor, I can just see dark strands, like grasping fingers, spreading from that central place up to the eldrin's jaw and down to his shoulder. How deep this cancer truly goes, I cannot guess.

I meet Viessa's solemn gaze. "What happened?"

Before the half elf can answer, however, Valtar speaks behind me: "Dragon poison."

"What?" I turn to look up at him. His face is oddly strained, a tightness around his eyes. The grim line of his mouth is somehow grimmer. It's as though, looking on the plight of the eldrin, he is reliving some dreadful memory of his own.

"I've seen this before," he says without meeting my gaze.

"When I was a boy. My brother and I were sent to the Magjor dwarf tribe in the Evindal Mountains. I saw this same sickness strike the dwarves as dragon smoke, filling the atmosphere in the air above, sank down to poison the roots of the world." He takes a step nearer, staring at that pulsing mass. "Dwarves, like elves, are naturally born Utherkynd. The Magjor Tribe made their home in our world, but their bodies and beings were still of Utherlynd. The very reality of Utherlynd exists in antithesis to Dracor—the two cannot overlap, cannot coexist. Just as dragon spawn and dracori cannot enter Inamaer, so beings of Utherlynd cannot endure the poisons of Dracor."

I think suddenly of the empty passages and cavernous halls of Stromin Palace where I spent much of the last month of my life. Did the dwarves of Stromin flee back to Utherlynd once it became apparent that Mhoryga's hold on this world was expanding? I never thought to question how it was that such a mighty edifice came to be abandoned and fall into the hands of Alderin Aumanus.

I try to look at that awful tumor again but shift my gaze quickly. "Is anyone else in your kintribe affected like this?" I ask, addressing Viessa once more.

She shakes her head.

"Their human blood protects them," Valtar says, "to a degree. In time, they too will fall prey to this sickness if Mhoryga is not defeated and her poison spreads."

"Can they not flee to Utherlynd?"

Viessa speaks up at last, still in that faraway, far-seeing tone she always uses. "Utherlynd is not welcoming to half-elfkind." *Scintil* light gleams off a shimmer of tears in her eyes. She blinks, and they run in greenish streams down her otherwise expressionless face. "When the human city on the coast was taken, and dragon poison choked the air, we of Glynrieth begged our eldrin to leave, fearing what it would cost him to stay. But he refused to abandon his children, his *iliphar*."

I recognize that word: *beloved*. Tears fill my eyes now as well. Which is not like me—working at Iliyani's side, I've seen many kinds of death and much suffering. Crushed bones, burnt flesh, bite wounds improperly treated that fester with gangrene, not to mention all the various fevers and bad humors which plague humankind, young and old alike. I've learned to save my tears for private moments. But something in the nobility of the eldrin's face stabs straight to my heart.

If only Iliyani were here. Iliyani with her ninety-plus years of knowledge and experience, with her hands so steady and her nerves of iron. Perhaps she would know what to do. She might have seen this evil phenomenon before. But I haven't a clue.

Swallowing against the lump in my throat, I say softly, "I'm sorry, Viessa. I . . . I don't have anything in my pouch that will help your eldrin. I can give him a little feverfew for the pain. And if we can find it, perhaps some *holabella* to deepen his sleep. Other than that . . ."

But Viessa holds my gaze, that inscrutable face of hers hardening almost imperceptibly. "I saw you, Rosie Harpwood," she says. "I saw you heal our eldrin. Heal him you must."

Though I'm not one to easily doubt the word of a truthseer, I shake my head. "I don't know what you saw, but . . . but you must have been mistaken. There's nothing I can do here. Not to heal him. Not to save him."

Viessa will not release my gaze. She continues to look at me in a silence so firm, so stubborn, I can almost feel it in my bones.

I'm beginning to think I will simply have to turn and march out of the wagon without another word and hope the peaceful-looking Glynrieth won't turn on me and Valtar in sudden fury.

Then Valtar speaks abruptly, breaking the silence: "It must be cut out."

I turn once more to look at Valtar by the pinkish glow of the *scintil*, my brow knotted.

"It's a matter of knife work," he says darkly. "I've seen it done. King Hagra of the Magjor fell ill. A tumor grew out from his stomach, twice the size of this. The *molal*—the healer—cut it out using a *meorise* blade. He had to cut deep enough to make certain it was all removed. But Hagra survived. He lived to face the dragon spawn and the inferno of hellfire that destroyed his kingdom and wiped out the Magjor." He pauses a moment, pressing his lips together as his throat constricts. Then, in a low voice: "But he died fighting. Not . . . like this."

I don't have to ask if Valtar was among the invasion force that ultimately overwhelmed the dwarf folk who were once his hosts. I see the truth burning in the depths of his eyes, a fury and a pain he can never escape. No words I might say seem right, so I keep my mouth shut.

Finally Valtar looks at me. "It would require a *meorise* blade."

"We have three," Viessa says softly.

Valtar nods. "They would need to be heated so that they may cauterize as you make the cuts. Also, the location of the tumor is difficult, as you might easily nick the artery."

"Me?" My mouth drops agape. Hastily I shake my head. "I can't do it." He regards me silently, and I feel the eyes of Viessa fixed on me as well. I turn to glance at her, then shift my gaze swiftly back to Valtar. "I've never done anything like what you're describing. I assisted Mistress Iliyani in an amputation once, and that was . . . It was . . ." I can't finish, can't bear to think back on the horror of that experience. Even with a liberal dose of *holabella* to send the poor miller deeply under while we worked, the sight of his mangled arm, crushed by the millstone, and the sound of the saw against bone will haunt my dreams forever.

"This won't be like that," Valtar says, as though reading my thoughts. "It's more subtle."

"I can't do it." I wrap my arms around myself, squeezing tight to keep from coming apart at the seams. "I don't have a steady hand for that kind of work." An idea strikes, and I lift my gaze, catching Valtar's eye. "You will have to do it."

"What?"

I'm not certain it's possible for a man to look more shocked than Valtar does in this moment. I press on, taking an eager step toward him. "You *are* the knife expert, aren't you?"

"I've always used my knives for a very different purpose."

"Do you have a steady hand?"

"Yes."

"Of course you do. And you know where all the vital organs and arteries are located, correct?"

He hesitates, jaw grinding. Then: "Yes."

"So you're the man for the job!" My breath eases as conviction settles more firmly on my shoulders. "I will make a poultice of yarrow and *anlyth* to slow the bleeding, and *holabella* to deepen his sleep, then, when you're done, a tincture of elderberry and calendula to help prevent infection. I believe I have some calendula in my pouch, and elderberry is common enough in these parts. I have to hope my treatments will work on a full-blooded elf; I've only ever treated half elves before. But I'm fairly certain I can adjust the dosages accordingly."

Valtar backs away several paces under this verbal barrage. He turns to Viessa, seeking an ally. "You saw *her* in your vision, not me. Is that not so? Speak sense to the woman!"

Viessa offers no response.

Valtar curses softly before finally addressing me again. "I'm not a healer," he says. "I'm a killer."

There's such a dreadful weight to those words. Like a mantle of iron draped over his shoulders, inescapable and ever present. The spirits of all those lives he's ended with abrupt and efficient precision haunt him day after day, night after night, breath after breath.

Suddenly, this isn't just about my fear of harming the eldrin anymore. It's about Valtar too. About something he needs to prove to himself.

"You've already begun to walk a different path," I say. Slowly, uncertainly, I reach out and take his hand in mine. Strange that, for all our breathless moments down by the lakeshore, this one little gesture feels suddenly so intimate and so vulnerable. I press his fingers, which for the first time feel cold to my touch. "You were born for so much greater than death, Valtar. I know it."

It takes some courage to look up into his black eyes. To stare into those mirrorlike pupils and see in them a reflection, not of the *scintil* orb, but of a fire from long ago. Green flames, devouring, all-consuming. I feel the souls of all his dead gazing back at me through those flames: his father and the Magjor king. The victims Mhoryga sent him to dispose of. So many, so varied, all carried in his shadow-wrapped heart.

I squeeze his hand a little tighter, moving to press my palm to his. I wish I could impress upon him my own belief in the goodness at the center of his being. The goodness to which he was born, but which Mhoryga has sought with all her demonic power to annihilate, leaving behind something twisted and empty to better serve her purpose. But strong though she is, the Dragon Queen hasn't fully crushed the true man.

"Please, Valtar," I whisper.

He curses and drops his gaze at last, staring at our joined hands. "Very well," he growls. "I'll do it."

WHEN TOLD I need *holabella* leaves, *anlyth* buds, and elderberries, the Glynrieth kintribe is quick to respond. All the smallest folk disperse into the surrounding forest like so many silent shadows. Within a quarter of an hour, I have everything I need and then some. The large, tree-limbed leader, Ayre by name, gave orders for the large cook pot to be removed from the central fire and a smaller pot set in its place.

I've soon got plenty of boiling water, a mortar and pestle, charcoal, red clay, rock salt, a bottle of clear *xilor*, a liquor favored by elfkind, and cloths of loosely woven linen. In short order, I've got a poultice prepared, along with my elderberry-and-calendula tincture. This would be stronger and more effective if given a few weeks to sit in the sun, but it's better than nothing. The *holabella* is fresh, rather than the dried leaves I'm used to working with, but I know roughly how to adjust the dosage. Mixed with a little warmed goat milk, hopefully it will slide smoothly down the eldrin's throat. Unless the tumor itself prevents ingestion.

I shake this thought away hastily, focusing on the tasks before me. It's a relief to throw myself into these familiar activities, drawing on the knowledge I've earned over sixteen years under Iliyani's guidance. I feel more myself in this space of chopping, grinding, measuring, stirring, sifting, and boiling than I have in many weeks. Here I needn't pretend to be Roselle Pandracor, End of Dragons—I am simply Rosie Harpwood, apothecary's apprentice, once more.

With all my brews, tinctures, and poultices prepared, I return to the *urira* to find Valtar also making ready. He's removed his jerkin, rolled his shirtsleeves up to his elbows, and secured them with twine. His hands and arms are scrubbed nearly raw, as though mere cleanliness were a protection against that evil growth. Viessa has brought a little brazier filled with hot coals into the wagon, and the three *meorise* knives, collected from various members of the kintribe, are warming on the grate even now. I nearly asked why Valtar didn't use his own dracori flame to heat them, but remembered that *meorise* is the only known ore found in this world which is resistant to hellflame. This might also be why it is effective against a tumor grown from dragon poison.

Valtar greets me with a curt nod. I answer with a smile far more confident than I feel and set to work preparing our patient. With Viessa's help, I tip back the eldrin's head and drip my *holabella*-and-milk concoction down his throat. I give him more than I would a half elf and can only hope it will be sufficient to keep him under for the entirety of the operation.

This done, I set aside my poultice and tincture to be used after the fact and rummage in my pouch for one more treasure picked up during our previous three days of travels: three slightly crumpled but still vibrant and pungent-smelling ralodithas. These I place into cloth masks and hand to Viessa and Valtar. "For the smell," I say in answer to the silent queries on their faces.

My next task is the most onerous. Using calendula paste and water, I wash the area around the tumor. It's grim work, for the growth is disgusting. But I never let my stomach get the better of me when attending sickbeds with Iliyani, and I maintain control over it now. The eldrin deserves the best I have to offer . . . even if it is ultimately not enough.

Finally I look up at Valtar once more, meeting his eyes over the line of his pale mask. "Ready," I say.

For a moment I fear he will back out. An expression of pure dread seems to pass over him like a shadow. But then he bends, retrieves the first of the *meorise* blades from the brazier, and steps up to the eldrin's bedside. Viessa gathered more *scintils* and suspended them directly overhead to give him the best possible light in this small, dark space. His dracori eyes will have to do the rest.

He stands for a count of eight breaths, blade hovering in the air above that growth, above the eldrin's throat. If I didn't know any better, I'd think he was sending up a prayer.

Then he sets to work.

His initial cuts are extremely small, delicate even. I would call them tentative, but I see no hesitation on Valtar's part, only great precision. Bit by bit, he severs the clinging outer layers of the growth, parting it from healthy skin. The first cut alone releases a noxious stench that nearly breaks my resolve and sends me screaming from the wagon. Thank the gods for the ralodithas! Without it, I may have passed out.

The eldrin stirs slightly. Valtar hastily withdraws the knife. "He must stay perfectly still," he says, voice tense. "Otherwise, I cannot vouch for his life." He flashes me a look. "Can't you give him more of that sleeping brew?"

"I'm afraid if I do, he'll never wake again. Men have gone under and died on far smaller doses." I chew my lip inside my mask, then say, "Wait a moment. What about this?" and plunge my hand back into my pouch. There's one more raloditha, larger than the others. Carefully I pull back the triangular petals to reveal the center and stamen, then place the whole blossom over the eldrin's nose and mouth. He inhales deeply, his emaciated chest expanding. He holds this breath for some moments before releasing it in a long gust. After that, his breathing levels out, and he does not stir anymore.

I nod to Valtar. He lifts a brow but takes a new knife from the brazier and sets to work once more. From where I stand, I could watch every step of his process . . . but choose instead to focus basically anywhere else. Mostly I watch the eldrin's face. It's strange how peaceful he looks. And it's not just due to my *holabella* dose; he looked that way before as well. How could someone maintain such a serenity of spirit in the face of such suffering? I suppose when one has lived as long as this being has—losing countless loved ones along the way to the ultimate decay of mortality—one learns to face whatever comes with courage.

I lift my eyes to study Valtar next. He is focused on his work, oblivious to my scrutiny. That lock of black hair has fallen over his forehead again, wafting against the scar which cuts through his eyebrow. A dangerous gleam sparks in the depths of his black eyes. It would be terrifying indeed to be an object of prey to a man like him. And yet I was that prey not so long ago. Even in the first moments of our meeting, he was intent on killing me . . . only I kissed him before he got the chance. What would have happened if I hadn't given in to that wild impulse, dragged him from that alcove, and planted my lips on his? Would he have gone through with it? Used one of those hidden knives of his and carved out my heart?

Suddenly Valtar rubs his forehead with the back of one hand.

"This is the critical part," he says, his voice slightly muffled through his mask. "The tumor has taken hold right alongside the carotid artery. The smallest slip, and . . ."

He doesn't need to finish that sentence. I wish I could offer some word of encouragement, but everything sounds so trite and hollow inside my head. I simply nod, hoping he'll read my confidence in his abilities in my eyes.

Valtar hands his blade to Viessa, who cleans it and places it on the brazier to reheat. Meanwhile, Valtar takes up the smallest, most delicate of the three blades and bends down to his work.

I wonder how much time has passed. It feels like both moments and many, many hours since we started. The raloditha I hold over the eldrin's face is fading, and I don't have any more in my pouch. But he doesn't stir again. His breathing is very shallow and light. Gods help me, but I hope I didn't give him too much *holabella*.

"That's it."

Valtar takes a step back from the bed and holds up the gross mass of the tumor, which fills his large palm. The stink redoubles, and even Viessa suddenly covers her face and turns away. I can scarcely bear to look at the thing. I look at the eldrin's neck instead. "Did you get all of it?" I ask, eagerly. The hot blades cauterized as they went, so there's no need for my yarrow-and-*anlyth* poultice, but I would like to apply my disinfectant tincture as soon as possible.

"I think so," Valtar says. "It's impossible to know without cutting deeper into the eldrin's neck and shoulder, but I think I got the entire mass."

Even as the words leave his lips, however, I frown. "Something doesn't look right."

Valtar dumps the growth into the jar Viessa holds out for

him. She slams a lid in place, but the stink lingers. Valtar turns from her and joins me back at the eldrin's side, bending to study the wound.

As though responding to his presence, there's a sudden flare of green light down inside the eldrin's flesh. Smoke rises in little coils, and the stink of burning flesh fills the air. Valtar reels back. "It's too late," he says, his voice choking. "We didn't get here soon enough. It's already too strong. Look!" He points. And despite the steadiness of his hand while performing the operation, his finger now trembles. "It's re-forming."

I don't want to look. I don't want to see. But I can't help myself either. What I took at first to be coils of smoke now look like creeping black tentacles, protruding from the eldrin's wound. They multiply before my eyes, gripping the edge of the cutaway area, forming a knotted, pulsing mass. Horror churns in my gut, momentarily smothering every other feeling, even despair.

Then, something happens. Something deep down inside of me, down in that place where I've only ever felt hellfire burn before—a spark.

"No," I breathe.

The next moment, it's rushing, roiling, bursting up from inside me, an explosive and all-consuming *burn*. But it isn't hellfire. It's something hotter. Something bright and white, a force of tremendous power, and unlike the hellfire, it doesn't frighten me. Unlike the hellfire, I know what to do with it.

"No," I say again, firmly this time. And I reach out and place three fingers against the writhing mass of tentacles and the hard center knot of the regrowing tumor. My fingertips begin to glow white.

"Rosie, don't!" Valtar cries. But his voice seems to be coming from a million miles away.

The tentacles react to my touch, hissing and recoiling like snakes. Then they dart out, catch hold of my hand, climbing up my wrist as though to claim me as well. For a moment, the white heat beaming from the tips of my fingers turns green, and it seems as though the skin of my hand and arm flakes away, revealing black scales underneath.

I set my jaw and turn my hand sharply, wrapping the tentacles around my fingers and gripping them hard. Now, even when they pull, they cannot escape; I've got them fast. The furnace inside me fountains up, erupting from the depths of my soul, from those deepest wells of repression inside me. White flame bursts from my hand, a great, glaring light that fills the whole wagon. There's a scent of burning—not a sulfurous stench, but a sweet perfume, like a million exotic flowers bursting suddenly into flame.

The white glow spreads from my hand down into the tentacles, burning them away in little sparkling puffs of nothing. It continues to spread, to pulse beneath the eldrin's flesh from his neck to his shoulder, his chest, down one arm, pursuing every cancerous vein. Light and heat glow out from inside him, flooding his body with radiance.

"Rosie, stop!" Valtar cries, reaching out as though to grab my arm. But I put out my other hand, press it to his chest, and he lets out a surprised yelp before staggering back, the front of his shirt singed. I don't turn to look at him, but maintain my focus on that wound, on that white fire coursing from me into the elf man.

And I feel awakened.

The eldrin stirs. Just as the last of the blackness burns out from his flesh, his eyelids flutter, and he looks up at me through that white, pulsing glow. His eyes shine with the light I bring, full of ancient depths, knowledge, and revelation. He moves his lips, struggling to speak, and though I cannot hear what he says through the roar of fire in my veins, I recognize the elfin word: *Valindra.*

Fire Angel.

6

Valtar

Rosie turns without a word and flees the wagon, trailing white sparks in her wake. They dance behind her like fireflies in the night before winking out and leaving us behind in darkness.

I try to follow her at once, but before I manage more than a step in her direction, the eldrin lashes out and catches my arm. He yanks me back to his bedside with surprising strength. Turning to him sharply, I find his strange, pale eyes staring up at me, and they seem still to reflect the white fire which had radiated from Rosie's soul.

"Who was she?" he gasps. "Who was that angel?" In the moment, I'm too overwrought by everything I've just seen, too overcome with the urgent need to pursue Rosie, I scarcely realize he speaks in my own language, the tongue of Inithana. Later on, I'll consider it; not now.

Viessa springs forward, speaking rapidly in her half-elfin dialect. But the eldrin refuses to release me. His grip is ironhard, not what I would expect from a man only just plucked from the brink of death. "Who was she?" he demands again, more vehemently. "Tell me!"

"She's . . . Rosie," I answer and twist my arm, trying to break free.

But the eldrin shakes his head. He blinks, and the white fire in his eyes vanishes for a moment. Then he stares up at the *scintils* hung from the ceiling above his head. "*Valindra*," he whispers, the second time he's uttered that word. In a softer voice but choked with emotion: "Savior of the world."

I cannot bear to hear more. With a ferocious wrench which nearly dislocates my shoulder, I break free of his grasp. Ignoring Viessa's voice calling after me, I spring out of the wagon into the waiting night. It isn't difficult to see which direction Rosie has gone; little white sparks float in the air in her wake. The elfin kintribe stand gathered outside their eldrin's wagon, heads turned in the direction she fled. At my sudden appearance, all those strange, otherworldly faces whip about sharply, fixing me with frightened eyes. Someone speaks with a questioning lilt, but I don't understand the words and haven't the patience to try to discern them.

Leaping from the wagon steps, I spring after Rosie, calling her name even as I plunge into the forest. In my mind's eye, I see again that dark cavern in Stromin, see her fleeing before me as the fires of hell seek to rise in her veins. It nearly consumed her then, and that fire was nowhere near as strong as what I just witnessed shining out from inside her. Her mortal form had appeared ephemeral, like nothing more than a thin paper lantern, only just containing the blaze inside. If the fire grew any brighter, any hotter, her body would simply crumple to ash. I've got to find her, got to pull her back from that inferno while I still can.

So I plunge through the underbrush, following those little sparks and the burnt patches in the ground. It doesn't require any tracking skill to follow that trail. Part of me is convinced it will be too late by the time I reach her, that I'll find nothing more than a burnt-out husk, far beyond all help or healing.

Then suddenly, I spy her up ahead. She's come to the edge of a riverbank and collapsed on the ground beneath the boughs of a listing poplar. She's still glowing—pulsing with light from the inside out. It's no longer as fierce and bright and burning as it was in the wagon, but a softer aura. Almost . . . heavenly.

"Rosie?" I call hoarsely.

She turns, looking up at me over her shoulder. Her eyes are still white, and little flames lick from their corners. The sight is eerie, and though I cannot remember the last time I was truly afraid, I take a step back. She blinks, however, and the flames dissipate, revealing once more the golden orbs I know so well.

I hasten to her, drop to my knees at her side. But when I reach for her, she draws back. "Careful! I'll burn you."

I withdraw at once. Were it hellfire which burned inside her, she would not worry for my safety, as hellfire burns in my veins too. But this . . . this is something new. Something I've never before experienced. I look her over, searching for signs of damage. There are burnt patches in her clothes, places where her skin shows through. But though her old scars are still readily visible, I see no indication of other hurt. "Are you all right?" I ask.

"I think so." She looks down at her body, turning her hands and arms, almost wonderingly. Little pulses of light shoot up her wrists and gleam in her fingertips, there and gone again in moments. She bites her lip and folds her arms around her body, shivering, but not with cold. Then she looks at me again, her eyes wide. "The eldrin?"

"He's fine," I answer shortly. But the concern in her face urges me to elaborate. "I think you purged the poison from his body with that . . . with whatever that was you did."

She nods and drops her hands into her lap. Then, slowly, she lifts her right hand between us, palm cupped. There's a moment of stillness, then with a faint *whoosh* of air, a little burst of white flame dances to life in her hand. I stare at it in amazement. It smells sweet, intoxicating, like . . . I'm not certain what. It's a familiar scent, something from my long-ago existence, back before the holy places of Inithana were razed to the ground by dragon spawn, and the worship of the old gods forbidden in favor of our new dark goddess, Mhoryga. Like the ghost of a past life, I seem to recall kneeling in a place of sacred song and silence, breathing in the sweetness of incense. This scent is like that, but fuller, deeper. Wilder.

Rosie turns her hand. The fire shifts from her palm, springing to burn from the tips of her fingers and thumb, five delicate flames, like talons. "I suppose," she says, moving her fingers and making those flames dance, "you'll have to believe me now." She catches my eye. "I *can* manifest after all. Not in hellflame, but in . . . this. The fire of renewal." She licks her lips, and it seems as though tiny sparks drop from her tongue. "Phoenix flame."

I cannot speak. I've not believed in her phoenix fire theory, but now? This sort of fire wielding is exactly what one would expect in the preliminary manifestation stage of a young dragon spawn. I've never seen anything like this flame, however. Could it be that she was right all along?

But what about her hellfire? I've felt it inside her. Whether or not she wants to believe it, the flames of Dracor are still very much part of her nature. This fire may be dominant for now, but that doesn't mean the other won't try again to fight its way to the surface.

Rosie closes her fingers into a fist, dousing the flame. Her eyelids lower, and she breathes out slowly. The white light inside her dissipates, the glow fading away. Soon the world around us is dark again, and even with my dracori sight, I find it difficult to see her clearly. But she turns her head toward me, and her voice, when it touches my ear, is firm with resolve. "I must go to Inamaer, Valtar. I must find Bald Mountain and the Shrine of Lorayarus."

I shake my head. "It's too dangerous."

"It cannot possibly be *more* dangerous than venturing into Cyran and a nest of dragon spawn."

"It's not that," I insist. "It's the transformation itself. What if you cannot survive the phoenix flame?"

She holds up her hand, emitting another little gout of white fire from her palm. "It would appear I can survive it."

I grind my jaw, fighting back the sharp answer I want to give. I can only stare at her, hoping she'll see the truth in my eyes and understand.

"Isn't this how it's supposed to work for dragon spawn?" she persists. "First they manifest the flame in their blood and learn to wield it. Then they enter the Dracor Flame and acquire their true dragon form. Maybe if I hadn't already manifested this fire, then I couldn't survive Lorayarus's pyre, but since I have, does it not follow that transformation is now within my grasp?"

"I can't have you taking such a risk." My voice comes out heavy, like stones hauled up from the pit of my chest.

Rosie tips her head, her lips quirking slightly in a wry smile. "It's my risk to take, isn't it?"

I bow my head. All my hopes and plans seem to wither and die around me. They were wild hopes and foolish plans, but . . . they were better than the fate Rosie seems determined to march herself into. If she enters Inamaer, if she goes to the Shrine of Lorayarus, I will lose her forever. I know it with the certainty of death and damnation.

And even with the fate of the entire world at stake, I'm not certain I can bear that loss.

But I say only, "Even with your fire manifested, it's a perilous journey to Inamaer, with far too many enemies on our trail. We should still make for Cyran, try to secure allies. Your ability to enter the dragon-spawn minds should be stronger now that you have fire of your own. Stronger than Nyxia's, certainly."

Rosie nods, turning from me to gaze out at the river, flowing gently beneath the moonlight, ancient and uncaring of our small, mortal troubles. I find my gaze captivated in study of her profile, noting subtle changes which had not been present even yesterday. There's a stern line in her brow, a hardness in her jaw. A firmness of resolution and courage, which I hate to see. I hate the burden she bears which forces her to become this person, to become something other than the bright, lively, impulsive creature I met two short weeks ago. The person I . . . for whom I've come to feel so strongly.

"All right, Valtar," she says at last, her voice soft. "We will still go to Cyran and see what allies we can claim. But," she adds, turning to me and pointing an imperious finger, "as soon as we've done so, we set out for Inamaer. Understand?"

I nod. Internally, I hope I'll be able in the meanwhile to convince her of the foolishness of her plan, to compel her with reason and sound argument to pursue the invasion I've envisioned, without any transformation involved. But just now, I'm simply glad she's not going to change course. Not yet, anyway.

"The eldrin wishes to speak with you both," Viessa's voice speaks abruptly behind us.

I startle. A flick of my wrist, and a knife appears in my hand, but Rosie catches hold of my arm firmly. I flash a glance at her, and she shakes her head. With a grimace, I turn to face the half elf, who appears out of the forest like a materializing phantom. She casts me a cold glance before turning to Rosie, her hard expression softening into a smile. "He wishes to express his thanks."

Rosie nods. Then she rises, brushing leaves and dirt from her skirts, and it's such a normal, such a mortal sort of gesture, my heart wrings at the sight of it. "Of course, Viessa," she says. "Lead the way, please."

THE KINTRIBE HAVE built up the central campfire to a bonfire blaze. There's a spirit of festivity in the air which was not present before, and the figures moving here and there about the clearing seem almost sprightly in their excitement. They've produced quite a large chair from one of their wagons and placed it before the fire like a throne. There the eldrin sits, frail but upright, his wasted body already much improved from how it looked less than an hour ago. He wears a mantle of woven oak leaves on his shoulders, which does not hide the cauterization scars left by my heated blades on his neck. Rather to my surprise, the sparse tufts of brownish grass hair on his scalp have already begun to thicken and green.

He raises a hand in greeting to Rosie as we emerge from the forest. "*Vyrendil*," he says, the elfish word trilling from his tongue like music.

Rosie bobs a little curtsy and answers rather less musically but competently, "*Vyrendil*, eldrin."

Then, to my surprise, he turns to me as well. This time, when he speaks in perfectly legible Inithanan, I realize it enough to be taken aback. "Welcome, Son of Fury," he says, "fire hewn and faithless. May you find your faith restored at last in the new crucible you must face."

For a moment, gazing into those ancient, ageless eyes, I feel as though the eldrin is seeing straight down to the heart of me. Down to that place where I first began to betray who I am, the man my father strove to make me. I say nothing in response, merely bowing low, eager to break that point of connection between us.

The eldrin turns to Rosie once more, falling back into that musical rhythm of speech. I watch her from the corner of my eye, see her face light up with enthusiasm over whatever the elfkind is saying. Finally she clasps her hands. "Thank you!" she cries, then, "*Hyldarr nor, eldrin!* Oh, thank you so much, it is too kind of you." She turns to me, eyes dancing in the bonfire light. "The eldrin has promised his people will take us as close to Cyran as they dare. They have paths which will bring us not sixty miles from the city! We'll have to make the rest of our way on our own, but he's promised us horses as well."

A shadow falls across my soul, and I feel suddenly cold. "No," I say. "We cannot accept."

Rosie frowns. Then she looks back at the eldrin, holding up one finger, and says, "One moment, please," before grabbing my arm and dragging me off to the edge of the firelight. "Why not?" she demands in a fierce whisper. "We have certainly earned a horse or two. And isn't this what you wanted? To go to Cyran?"

My throat is tight. "Not like this."

Her frown deepens. She shakes her head fiercely, and for an instant, I glimpse a flash of white fire in her eyes once more, there and gone again. "What exactly is your problem, Valtar Skylock? The kintribe will be using elfin paths. What would take us weeks and weeks should now be only three days, maybe four. We'll be at Cyran in a fraction of the time it would take us on our own." She tilts her head, narrowing her eyes. "What's going on? Tell me the truth."

I can't. Because the truth is, I *do* think we should hasten to Cyran with all speed. But . . . I also want more time. Not just time to train, to prepare her for entering the heads of the dragon spawn. Just time. With her. This version of her, the version who has not had to become anything other than the woman she's always been.

I know what lies ahead. Long before she makes the choice to take her dragon form or not, her very spirit will be forced to alter before the horrors we will encounter. What she sees in Cyran, what she discovers in the heads of the dragon spawn and the dracori . . . . what she discovers inside *my* head . . . it will change her. She will have to grow harder, sterner, more vicious simply to endure it.

There is no hope of preventing these changes, of protecting her from the future self so fast approaching to consume her. Already she's begun the metamorphosis, right before my eyes. And while I admire the strength I see in her, I fear it as well. Because it won't be long before she has gone beyond my ability to protect. She will be something far too great and terrible.

Bowing my head, I turn away from her, stare into the darkness of the forest around us. Arun's face appears before me like a specter. Eyeless, gaunt, defiant in the face of suffering. There's so little time left to save him. Perhaps this offer of the eldrin's is the very miracle I need. But—though I hate myself for thinking it—for the first time since I can remember, Arun is no longer my primary concern.

I close my eyes, unwilling to meet Rosie's questioning gaze. Slowly I breathe in and out, searching for a space of stillness deep inside.

"Valtar?" she says at last.

"Very well." I grind the words through my teeth. "Very well, we'll travel with the kintribe. We'll accept the horses."

"Excellent!" With a joyous little bounce on her toes, Rosie reaches out and catches my hand, squeezing hard. "Things are looking up, Valtar! Truly. The gods are on our side, just you wait and see!"

I hold her hand in mine and silently meet her gaze. The truth is, even if the gods do favor her, they have never favored me. And after all the sins I've committed, they never will.

I can only hope no one else will pay for my sins in the end. Just me.

7

Rosie

We travel with an escort of five. Not a large party, to be sure, but the eldrin would not risk more of his people venturing so close to Cyran. Viessa was quick to volunteer for the task, along with Ayre, the tree-limbed man. The eldrin offered the use of one of the seven *urira* and supplies aplenty for Valtar and me for after we reach the point of parting. There are horses for both of us as well, but I'm not much of a horsewoman, and therefore elect to ride in the wagon. While certainly not the most luxurious mode of transportation known to man, the *urira* of the Glynrieth kintribe is preferable to hiking on my own two feet for endless mile upon endless mile. So, as I cling to the side bar of the driver's seat beside Viessa, I try to remember to thank my gods with every bone-rattling rut and divot we manage to hit. And I'm fairly certain we hit all of them.

Whether by miracle or magic, Viessa drives the wagon team through dense forest without hesitation, finding paths for the large *urira* and its wheels where I am certain there can be none.

Every so often, the kintribe works together to wrinkle reality, and with a little shiver and a shudder, we emerge dozens of miles from where we were moments before. Though I am certainly no expert on half-elfin magic, I gather that, working together, they are able to create larger wrinkles and cover greater distances than Viessa could manage on her own.

By midday, we come at last to smoother ground, and the *urira* rolls gently behind the two powerful gray horses. I breathe a sigh of relief, leaning back in the wagon seat. After hours of exhausting jostling, it's a relief to relax my muscles. Tilting my head back, I enjoy the warmth of the spring sunlight filtering through the green-leaved branches overhead. Viessa is not a talkative soul, but for once, I don't mind letting silence dominate the atmosphere. Every now and then, thoughts try to intrude, worries and concerns and far too many impossible questions. But I don't want to bother with those. Not yet. Right now, I want to enjoy what might be my last opportunity to purely *exist.* Every time I catch myself starting to venture down one of a dozen mental pathways, I pull back and focus on the *clop-clop-clop* of the wagon team's hooves and the *creak-creak-creak* of the *urira*'s wheels and frame.

Now and then, however, I cannot help when my thoughts reach for Valtar.

He rides on a dark chestnut mare, mostly out of my sight behind the *urira*. Occasionally, when the trees around us aren't too dense and the path too narrow, he'll urge his horse up alongside the driver's seat on my right, but never once catch my eye. After a few moments, he simply reins in his mount and falls back behind the wagon with the other riders once more. He's putting distance between us. In more ways than one. I know he's not pleased to be traveling with the kintribe on these strange paths of theirs, but . . . well, I didn't think it would make him be quite so cold.

I purse my lips into a line. We've barely spoken to each other since that moment down by the river. We were given separate places to sleep last night, my "brother" with the unmarried men on one side of the camp, while I bedded down with the maiden women. Gods blight me, why had I not thought to name him my *druin*—husband—instead? Not that we would have had much more privacy. Not with all those keen half-elfin eyes and ears surrounding us.

But in three days—two and a half now—we'll part from these new companions and be just the two of us again. Will Valtar want to pick up where we left off? Is he thinking about that moment we shared on the lakeshore as much as I am? Or rather, trying *not* to think about it as hard as I am trying not to? Perhaps it was just a mistake. A moment of lust brought on by nakedness and proximity, not to be repeated.

What would he do if I were to throw myself at him the moment we're alone?

All unknowingly, I slip into this line of musing as the rumble and roll of the *urira* rhythmically rocks me in my seat. *What is he thinking?* I find myself asking over and over again. *What is he thinking? If only I could somehow know his thoughts . . .*

And suddenly I see myself.

Naked.

Or all but naked—clad only in my small clothes, my flesh prominently displayed. I'm straddling his lap once more, and I feel the sensation of my skin pressed against his, or . . . no. I feel his skin pressed against mine. And I smell my own scent of fresh soapweed and wildflowers, and it's absolutely intoxicating, thrilling my senses. My gaze trails down the line of my throat, over my scars, and lowers to my own breasts. I watch with fascination how those soft curves rise and fall with quick breaths, and a deep, throbbing urgency erupts inside me, low in my gut, and—

I blink.

For a moment, I no longer see myself, but am back in my own head, my own perspective, staring into Valtar's black eyes. He looks at me, the lust and longing wiped from his gaze, replaced with an expression of pure shock.

Oh gods!

With a yank of both spirit and will and a little dizzying whirl in my chest, I jolt back into the present. Facing forward in the wagon seat once more, heart pounding, I grasp the handrail tight and suck in a little breath before casting Viessa a short glance. The half elf appears oblivious to my distress. A ruse, most likely. Something tells me not much gets past the truthseer.

I swallow hard, staring out at the countryside before us. Did I just . . . ? Gods spare me, did I just accidentally get into Valtar's mind? Read his thoughts? Was he reliving that moment down by the lake in such vivid detail?

My stomach knots. Though I try to stop it, a little smile pulls at my mouth. Breathing out slowly, I turn, grip the handle of the wagon seat with both hands, and lean out over the side, trying to catch a glimpse of Valtar riding behind. He's not within my range of sight, however. Instead I catch the eye of one of the other half-elf men, the one with the dandelion eyebrows. He smiles, friendly. I blush, offer a short nod, and sit upright once more, biting my lips.

Maybe Valtar's right; maybe I do need to spend a little time honing this ability of mine. It had been easy with Rhyo, but perhaps that's because he is dragon spawn, not dracori. He is my brother, or half brother at least, which possibly makes the mental connection between us stronger.

With Valtar, however, I only recall feeling his mind two other times. The first was when I strolled the gardens of Stromin Palace in company with Lord Elis Balxidon, one of my other champions. I'd sensed Valtar's presence close by, watching the two of us, a truth he'd later confirmed.

The second time was during the third trial. I shudder, not liking to recall that terrible day, the day Lord Elis lost his life. The day when my four surviving champions had ventured down into the dark depths below Stromin, into the pressure of the underearth. I'd been so afraid for Valtar, so fixated on whether or not he would return, I believe I somehow entered his mind. The experience of heat and compression and darkness was far too real to be mere imagination.

Ever since that dreadful day, I've not sensed him, not even once. Could it be he has been consciously keeping me at bay? And if so, what changed?

I look down at my hands. I feel the fire inside them, inside my soul. That white-hot heat, latent, waiting. It frightens me, and yet I'm almost certain I could summon it if I tried—which seems odd. Should this not be another skill to be trained? But it feels more like bending and stretching out my own arm. Strength training can only improve it, but the ability is already there. I clench my hands into fists. It must be this new fire which has opened up the pathways between Valtar and me once more. But I can't help wondering: What became of the hellfire? This white flame felt so all-consuming when it burned through me, but did it purge the hellfire from my soul? Or will I feel that green inferno again the next time my life is threatened?

Shaking my head, I sit upright, focus my attention on the rolling green countryside and the lonely dirt track before me. So much for enjoying simple existence while I still can!

Abruptly I draw a deep breath, and without looking at Viessa, ask, "Why did the eldrin call me that name?"

From the corner of my eye, I watch Viessa turn her face toward me, inscrutable as ever.

"*Valindra*," I murmur. "I know what it means. *Dra* is fire, and *valin* means angel. So he called me an Angel of Fire. But why?" I shake my head. "He must know I am no angel."

"Then what are you?" Viessa asks with that imperturbable, faraway dreaminess which colors her every tone.

"I'm human," I answer shortly, then frown and look down at my hands again. "I am . . . dragon."

"And what are dragons?"

An odd question. It should be self-explanatory, and yet I puzzle how to answer. Finally I say, "They told me Mhoryga is a being of Dracora, a demon of the Tenth Realm. Which means her children all carry demonic blood."

"And you?"

My stomach pitches. I'd never thought about it in such bald terms before. "I suppose that makes me half demon."

"What else?"

"What do you mean? I'm half dragon, half human. That's it. That's what I am."

"But the dragon queens are different, are they not?"

I lapse into silence, turning this question around in my mind. According to what I've been told, Mhoryga would take and breed with any number of human males to create her male dragon spawn. By the hundreds and thousands she's hatched them, human-shaped offspring who later manifest their dragon form.

But the dragon queen eggs are different. They cannot hatch in ordinary hellfire, but require the heat of the Dracor Flame, the pure fire of Dracora, the Tenth Realm. Something about that birth must make them *more* dragon than human in some way, enabling the queens to grow far larger, far more terrible—far more like Mhoryga—than the dragon spawn ever could. They are true demons, entities of evil and chaos.

My heart shivers in my breast. When I think of all the horror Mhoryga has wreaked upon this world, I do not doubt her ultimate goal is to make it into another Dracora. Some have theorized that she intends to grow an army of dragon spawn great enough to reenter the Tenth Realm and overthrow her father, Dracoris, once and for all. In the meanwhile, she will crush, burn, and destroy everything that gets in her way.

"Demon," I whisper, the word soundless on my numb lips.

But that is not what the eldrin called me. He said *Valindra*: a being of light and power, a restorer of order and ultimate goodness, born of the gods themselves.

I look down at my hands again, seeing once more the white, healing flame which had burned from them last night. The flame of renewal—the flame of Lorayarus. What exactly is the great phoenix? An angel? I'd never considered him in those terms, but it does make sense. The priests who keep his shrine view him as something sacred, something close to deified.

And if I was born in his flame as Alderin claimed, what does that make me?

Fire Angel. I don't feel angelic. Not in the least. Not that I feel particularly demonic either. I feel completely human, even now, even after all the revelations of the last few weeks. And when I think of Valtar . . . then I feel more human than ever.

I lapse back into silence, grateful yet again for Viessa's quiet nature. But no matter how the long hours roll by, I cannot seem to find a space of peace within my tumultuous soul.

WE PASS THROUGH seven little reality wrinkles throughout that first day. Though it doesn't feel as though we traveled any extraordinary distance, by the evening, we are a hundred miles or more from where we started in the morning. I sniff the air from my perch on the wagon seat. Is it just my imagination, or do I smell sulfur? Suddenly Cyran feels much closer than it did before. Too close.

The half elves set to work making camp for the night. For once not ravenous, thanks to the well-provisioned supplies in the wagon, I feel a bit useless and full of nervous energy as I climb down from my perch. And stiff. Gods, am I stiff! All those hours of jostling over rough terrain take it out of a girl.

I'm just stretching out my back, hands planted on my hips and chest jutted forward rather inappropriately, when Valtar appears like a silent phantom at my side. "We need to practice," he says.

I yelp and stagger a sideways step then shoot him a glare. "Well, hullo to you too." I find myself suddenly working very hard not to think about that little glimpse I'd had into his mind earlier today.

As though guessing my thoughts, Valtar turns away quickly, suddenly transfixed by the sight of the tree-limbed Ayre hauling fuel for a campfire out of the back of the *urira*. His throat constricts, but when he speaks again, his voice is level, nearly expressionless. "You need to prepare. We will be in Cyran far sooner than anticipated. There's little time to train."

"Oh, you mean in . . ." I wave my hand vaguely at my head.

Then, my mouth quirked in a grin: "I don't know if I need as much training as all that. Didn't seem to have any trouble earlier today."

His black eyes swivel, briefly meeting mine before darting away again. A faint flush stains his pale cheeks, confirming what I already suspected. It really did happen. I really did see into his mind.

A warm flood races through my veins. "Valtar—" I begin.

He interrupts sharply. "You'll find it far more difficult to enter the minds of the dragon spawn in Cyran."

I blink and look down at my feet. "And why is that?"

"For one thing, they won't be thinking about you."

Immediately my smile springs back into place. I look up at him again, trying to catch his eye. "Do you think about me often, Valtar?"

His profile is stone hard, but I know him too well by now not to spot every minuscule tightening of his jaw, flare of his nostril, narrowing of his eye. He wants the world to see him as an impervious force. But I can't. I never could.

Finally he looks at me, holds my gaze. There's something burning in those dark depths, something hotter than hellfire. I want to call it forth, to see that heat erupt the way I believe it wants to. "You must practice entering a resistant mind," he says. "You must learn to find weaknesses in their barriers and break through them in an instant. Then you must learn to take control."

Something cold knots in my gut. Suddenly I don't feel all pleasantly warm and tingly, just sick. I wrap my arms around my middle. I don't want to take control of anyone, least of all Valtar. I want him doing whatever he wants to do. Preferably to me.

The smile has fallen from my face once more. "Very well. How do you propose we begin?"

"You still have the knife I gave you."

It's not a question. I touch the sheath strapped to my waist. I haven't used the blade since I cut Prince Taigan's arm during my frantic escape from Stromin. Part of me had hoped I would never need to again.

"Take it out," Valtar says.

"Why? What does knife work have to do with this mental link?"

"The focus that comes from weapons drilling is not unlike the focus you will need to enter minds and work influence."

Resisting the urge to sigh, I slip the knife from its sheath. It feels foreign in my hand; I've had a grand total of two lessons, and I doubt I'll ever be much of a weapons enthusiast. At Valtar's injunction, I assume first position. "Widen your stance," he says, touching my ankle with the toe of his boot, then moves to raise my arm slightly. I try not to notice how my skin thrills in response to the touch of his fingers at my wrist. "Concentrate," he growls.

I give my head a short shake and firm my brow. The half elves have paused setting up their camp and watch us curiously from a little distance. I smile at Viessa just as Valtar snaps, "First maneuver."

I perform the first block and riposte Valtar taught me what feels like an age ago now, back on that lonely mountaintop above Stromin Palace, beneath the eye of the moon. My muscle memory isn't bad—I'm able to go through the motions well enough.

"Again," Valtar says.

I oblige, moving a little quicker this time.

"Again."

We go through it a third, fourth, tenth time. I'm soon warm and glistening with sweat, but my wagon-sore muscles are loosening up. I remember more than I thought I would and am able, without prompting, to recall several more forms he'd previously taught me. It feels good to move, to grip the knife in my hand, and—

Suddenly Valtar lunges at me, a sharp, violent gesture, coming at my side. I pivot, managing to get my arm up just in time and partially block his blow. But I don't deflect him completely, and he takes another quick step, catches hold of my wrist, twists my arm behind me, and pins me in place.

"You must focus," he snarls, his voice close to my ear.

"I'm trying!" I snap back, twisting in his grasp. He lets me go, and I whirl to face him, my breath quick and tight. I toss a lock of hair out of my eyes. "How'd you like it if I summoned up a fireball and blasted you in the stomach?"

"Can you?"

My brow puckers uncertainly. Truth is, I haven't felt much of that white fire which had come over me last night. Is it something I can use in battle, the way the dracori wield their hellflame? I'm not sure.

Before I've completed that thought, Valtar lunges again. I let out a little squeak of surprise but manage to block his blow and even successfully perform the retaliatory slice, though it doesn't come close to grazing him. Still, if he hadn't known it was coming, if he hadn't expected it, I think I might have gotten him. Like I did Prince Taigan.

Valtar backs away, not even winded, damn him. "Good," he says grimly, not quite a compliment but close enough. "You're ready to learn the next form."

I want to ask again what this has to do with mental control, but I'm honestly too tired just now. Instead I watch as he demonstrates the maneuver, the play of his feet, the extension of his arm. And when he asks me to repeat it, I manage a fair mimicry. He calls out for adjustments, and I try again, then again. "It feels like a dance," I say.

He grunts an acknowledgment. "It's not unlike."

"I don't see how dancing will help me in a real battle."

"The important thing is to train the muscles so that, in the moment, you needn't act on thought, trusting your body to know what you need before you know it."

I nod and perform the series of movements yet again. Sweat clings to my chemise, soaking through my back to dampen my bodice. I finish the form and pause, wiping my brow. I'm tired. The campfire is blazing, and I can smell a hearty stew heating in the cook pot. Stomach growling, I turn to Valtar. "I still don't see how this is going to help me enter minds. I'm so busy concentrating on not tripping over my feet, I can't very well be bothered with anything else."

Valtar's face is shadowed in the evening light, beneath his low hood. Even my dragon eyes struggle to discern his features. "Getting into the minds of the dragon spawn is like knife work. It has to be a reflex, as natural to you as breathing."

"I can't imagine that."

"What about when you got into the dragon boy's mind?"

I shrug one shoulder. "That just seemed to . . . happen. The closer I got to him, the clearer it was. It was more a matter of trying *not* to enter his mind."

Valtar nods. "That was, in large part, because Rhyo was so young and so afraid. You will not find that to be the case with most dragon spawn. Certainly not with the dracori."

"Then what am I supposed to do?"

Before the question has fully left my lips, Valtar is in motion. He moves with such serpentine swiftness, a creature of pure muscle and focus, and it's only by virtue of the many repetitions he's made me practice that I get my arm up in defense. It doesn't matter. He knocks the knife clean out of my hands and deftly hooks my leg with his boot. I go down hard, landing flat on my back, breath knocked from my lungs. He's on top of me in an instant, a blade pressed to my throat, and—

And suddenly, I am inside his head, staring down into my own fear-widened eyes.

"*Stop!*" I command.

The knife instantly drops from his fingers. I feel the hilt hit my shoulder before it lands on the ground beside my face.

I stare up at him, only . . . I simultaneously stare back down at myself. Two perspectives, concurrent and equally clear. And somehow, in a way I cannot fully describe, I understand that he . . . he *belongs* to me.

"*Get off*," I growl. The voice traveling between our minds doesn't sound like mine. It is a voice of simmering heat and rage.

Valtar backs off, rises, and stands to one side. There's a strange emptiness to each move he makes, like his powerful body is some sort of stuffed dummy, maneuvered by another's will. By *my* will.

I sit upright, breathing hard, and rub the small of my back. It's strange, because I see myself doing it, see my own rumpled garments and wild hair, see my own angry face scowling up from where I sit in the flattened grass. I see it all so clearly, just as clearly as I see Valtar's hard features, his hooded eyes watching me closely.

"*Once you're through the outer defenses*," he says, "*you'll have to fight to keep from being ousted again*."

It takes me a moment to realize his lips didn't move, that I heard his voice in my head. In the same moment, my vision begins to fracture, the two perspectives flattening, turning sideways, pushing back into each other. It hurts, like a stabbing between my eyes. With a little growl, I concentrate, forcing my awareness back into his mind. This time I take a firmer hold, and the colors become more vivid, the edges crisper even than reality.

When Valtar speaks again, his voice is fainter somehow: "*Impressive. Now, command me to do something.*"

"*I don't want to.*"

"*You must learn.*"

"*This doesn't feel right.*"

Actually it feels very right. Too right. Too easy. Now that I'm here, my own awareness of power expands. It's all right here, the ability to make this man whatever I will, to morph him into the version of himself which best suits my immediate needs. It's an intoxicating, destructive feeling.

Green fire burns in my gut. Hellfire, not trying to rise, but suddenly very present. When I search for it, the white flame I'd manifested last night is nowhere to be found.

"*Command me,*" Valtar urges again.

But I resist, afraid. Then I think of Rhyo, trapped and afraid in that dungeon cell in Stromin. If I hadn't commanded him against his will, he would be dead. Doesn't that matter? Doesn't that make me different from Mhoryga? I remember the memories which flashed through Rhyo's head, the horror of his own transformation, the pain of becoming the very monster he most feared.

I look at Valtar again, this dark specter of a man. A dracori. He too was transformed. He too was made what he feared and hated. After watching the dracori march through Inithana, after watching his father burned alive in hellfire, he was forced to become one of them, and . . .

And suddenly I see him. Not the Valtar I know, but a boy,

scarcely more than twelve or thirteen years of age. Dragged between two bare-chested dracori, his small, thin body weak with terror. Green flame burns from torches all around him, and the air is thick with the stench of sulfur and death. Before him is a stone chair, a cruel-looking thing, all sharp edges and blackened with scorch marks.

"*What are you doing?*" Valtar demands, his voice suddenly sharp, angry. And frightened. Terribly frightened. But I can't help it. I'm here now, here in his mind, delving deeper into places in his memory. Unable or unwilling to look away, I'm not certain which.

"Rosie, stop!"

The boy lifts his head and sees the chair toward which he's being dragged. I feel the jolt of terror shoot through him, mingled with a strange resolve that feels out of place in one so young.

From somewhere near, a voice cries out, young and frightened: "*Valtar, no! Just let her kill me! Valtar, don't do it!*"

I turn and see another boy, a little older than the first perhaps, tied to a stake on a wooden platform, surrounded by bundled sticks. His arms are chained over his head, his waist bound with an iron band. He writhes in his bonds, his face both fierce and desperate.

The first boy casts him only a brief look, shudders. But when his dracori captors release his arms, he walks to the chair himself and takes a seat. The scarred men bind his arms down, turned to expose his wrists.

It is now that I see her for the first time: the Dragon Queen.

I have heard her described on numerous occasions, both as a great world-covering shadow wreathed in flame, descending upon kingdoms in apocalyptic wrath, and as a woman-shaped demon, glorious beyond the reckoning of mortals. But nothing prepares me for this first sight of her. The woman—the monster—the entity who has wreaked such suffering in this world.

My heart jolts with love. With loathing.

Mother.

She is, as they said, beautiful. With skin of golden scales, gleaming like jewels, she walks with the great stride of a giantess. Black hair flashing with tongues of green fire falls nearly to her heels, and bladelike talons gleam from the ends of her long fingers. She is naked, and yet this is somehow not shocking. Why should such a being clothe itself? What could modesty possibly matter to one like her? No, more shocking by far is the sheer power which radiates from her inmost being, a majesty uncontested anywhere in this world.

She approaches the boy where he sits, bound in that chair, and gazes down at him from flashing golden eyes. For a moment, I feel as though it is I who looks back at her, trembling in my seat, all my desperate courage shredding away in ragged tatters.

"*You are mine*," Mhoryga says. Then she smiles like the final burst of a dying sun. With lightning-fast speed, she lashes out and pierces both the boy's arms with her talons. I feel the vicious jolt of his life's blood pouring out from him. I feel his pain, his agony.

"*Rosie!*" Valtar's voice roars somewhere in the background of my mind. "*Get out of here! Leave this place!*"

But I don't leave. I can't leave the boy, not here, not in this pain. And not just him—there's the other boy too, the one bound to the stake, struggling and screaming his brother's name.

Just as the boy in the chair begins to fade, just as blackness closes in on his vision and eternal darkness yawns to claim him, Mhoryga slashes her own wrist, opening a vein. Burning, green-molten blood gushes forth. She holds it to his mouth, and it scalds him. He screams and chokes as it burns down his throat, down to his gut, and he—or I, for I feel it with him, vividly, viscerally—*we* believe it will burn us alive from the inside.

Mhoryga grabs the top of his head, forcing him to hold still as she feeds him more. "*This is your blood now, child,*" she hisses. "*You will survive and become my creature. Or you will burn. There's no going back.*"

"*Valtar!*" the boy at the stake screams.

"*Valtar!*" I cry out, stretching out both arms as though to catch him from that chair, to drag him away with me to safety.

SUDDENLY I AM back on the ground in the middle of a forest clearing. Staring up at a distant evening sky, even as my voice bursts from my lungs in a shout: "Valtar!"

"I'm here."

I blink, gasp, struggling to draw a full breath into my lungs. Valtar kneels beside me, his hands supportive as he helps me to sit upright. Apparently I'd fallen over at some point during this little mind venture. I shake my head, choking on my own inhaled air. Part of me is aware of the watchful gazes of the five half elves, keeping their distance but curious.

Most of me, however, leans into Valtar's large, solid presence. The strength of his arms wrapped around me. The breadth of his chest under my cheek. The beat of his heart, strong and alive and present. I cling to him, shuddering hard. For a long while, I cannot speak, cannot think. It's all I can do just to be.

Finally I pull away from him a little, just enough to look up into his face. He looks paler than ever, almost gray. "Valtar," I whisper. "I'm sorry."

He shakes his head hard. Do I imagine it, or are his arms trembling?

"I shouldn't have made you relive that moment," I continue, my voice rough in my throat. "I was curious, and then . . . and then I simply couldn't stop."

He closes his eyes, the lines around his mouth deepening into hard slashes. Still he does not speak.

"I shouldn't have made you go back there," I say again. "I . . . I forced you. I commanded you. Didn't I? Tell me, Valtar. Is that what happened?"

After what feels like an eternity, he nods.

Oh gods. I place a hand against my stomach, feeling again that dull throb of hellfire, unrisen but present. Simmering. "I'm sorry," I say softly. "Valtar, I am so, so sorry."

He bows his head, breathes out slowly against my hair. Then: "It proves you can do it. That memory was locked down fast, but you broke through my defenses without even trying. If you can do that, you can be trained to take on older and more mentally fortified dracori than I. And the dragon spawn." He shrugs. "I don't think you'll have an issue with them."

It doesn't sound comforting in this moment. I bite my lip, hands clenching into fists even as I grip the front of his jerkin. "I don't want to do that. I don't want to make anyone do anything they don't choose for themselves."

Valtar pushes me gently from him, just to arm's length. Just so that he can look me in the eye at last. "You've got to," he says firmly. "Neither of us may like it, but this is what must be. It is our only hope."

How can what he says be true? How can this be what the gods have ordained for me? This power of mine, real though it may be, is the antithesis of the healing fire I wielded just last night. I drop my chin. "It feels so wrong."

"It won't be all wrong," Valtar replies. "If you can break

through barriers like that, you should be able to break through any compulsions as well. You can undo whatever commands Mhoryga has placed upon her creatures, return their free will to them." He places a finger under my jaw, forcing me to look up, to look at him once more. "You can use this power for good, Rosie."

He sounds so confident. I simply don't know that I believe him.

"Promise me," he urges, "you will keep trying."

I swallow hard. Then nod, once. "I promise."

"But Rosie?"

"Yes?"

"In the future, if I ask you not to press on a memory . . . listen to me."

Tears spring to my eyes. I nod again and hastily dash a hand across my face.

He rises now, drawing me to my feet before him. Despite the watchful eyes of the half elves, I find I want very much to step forward and wrap my arms around him, rest my head against his chest and simply breathe him in. When I dare to meet his eyes once more, I think perhaps I see that same desire lingering there. It would be easy. So easy, in fact. I could snap my fingers and simply make him give in. Make him hold me. Make him kiss me. Command him to forget his inhibitions and make love to me.

A knot twists in my gut, sick and painful. Is this what Mhoryga does with all her plaything husbands? Is this what she did to my father? To Alderin? Oh, gods spare me, I don't want to force Valtar to do anything, but . . . what if that's what I've been doing all along? From the moment I first kissed him against his will and, inadvertently, stopped him from going through with his planned assassination. Have I been, all unknowingly, manipulating him from the beginning? Making him feel something he doesn't actually feel?

I pull away from him. Suddenly it's too hard to breathe in his presence.

"Rosie?" Valtar says, his brow wrinkled with concern. "Rosie, are you—"

"I think we've put on enough of a show for the kintribe, don't you?" I say briskly, turning my back on him. "Come on. I've had my fill of training for one evening, and that stew is smelling better by the moment. Though no doubt I'll be pining for one of your raw wood pigeons soon enough!"

Blithe words ringing in the air behind me, I march away from him, hastening into the camp circle. I can only hope Valtar didn't detect the tremble in my voice.

8

Valtar

Each day we travel with the kintribe, the stink of dragon smoke grows stronger in the atmosphere. Were we journeying by foot or horse, not using these strange elf paths, it wouldn't be so jarring. As it is, every time we step out of one of those cursed reality wrinkles, I feel as though I'm being hit in the face with a spiked mace, so pungent is the stench.

It's for the best, I remind myself every so often. For one thing, though we even now hurtle closer to dragon-held territory, I haven't caught so much as a glimpse of scale or wing since we fell in with the half elves. That close encounter by the lake, which had seemed to foreshadow certain disaster, has faded to nothing but a vague uneasiness.

As for Rosie . . . I have to give her credit. She is not a natural fighter, is in no way suited to the training I put her through each evening. Violence and aggression run in opposition to her very nature. Yet she throws herself into both the knife sparring and the mental training with as much vim as she can summon. And, because it's Rosie, she can summon quite a lot of vim.

Some part of her is holding back, however. Ever since that first entrance into my mind, when she peered into my past and saw that torturous memory, she's been afraid of going deeper, of violating my free will. Part of me appreciates that hesitation; another part of me knows it will be her undoing if she doesn't work through it. Soon.

"I think you might have been right, Valtar," she says with a heaving breath on our third and final evening with the Glynrieth kintribe. We've left the small camp for a nearby field, where I've just put her through a rigorous series of forms, including mental work. She's darted into my mind successfully four times in the last hour and twice made me do her bidding. First, she made me scratch my nose and rub my stomach simultaneously. Then she made me drop my knife and pick a handful of bluebonnets, which I was then obliged to present to her with a flourishing bow. Her wicked giggles almost made up for the ignominy of each act.

She sighs now though and tosses her arms in a helpless gesture before dashing a lock of sweaty hair from her face. The sight of her flushed and panting like this stirs my blood in ways she cannot begin to guess, but I force my face to maintain a stoic facade when she turns a doleful expression my way. "Really?" I say dryly, and raise an eyebrow.

"Oh, don't look so surprised." She wrinkles her nose at me and shakes the point of her dagger in my general direction before finding herself a little grassy knoll and plopping down on it. Sighing heavily, she sheathes her blade and plunks her chin in her hands, watching the half elves across the field making their little camp beneath the shelter of a family of young oaks. Her brow puckers, and I can't tell if she's sad or worried.

I sheathe my own blades and move to sit near her, elbows resting on propped-up knees, my hood fallen back over my shoulders. "And how exactly am I right, if I may be so bold?"

She shakes her head, chin still cupped, and turns to eye me. "Maybe we shouldn't have been so quick to accept the help of the kintribe. Now we're close to Cyran, and I don't feel remotely ready for . . . anything."

She isn't. She can't be. Even if we'd had a year of training, nothing could prepare her for everything that's to come. But there's no point in mentioning that now. "Don't forget," I say instead, "we are still a good sixty miles off from the city. Even with horses, we've got some time before we arrive."

She curls her lip, not comforted.

"You're doing better than you think you are."

"Well, that doesn't mean much since I *think* I'm downright pathetic."

The corner of my mouth pulls, but I hastily stifle any telltale smile. "If it's any comfort to you," I say earnestly, inclining my head toward her, "I believe that, even if Nyxia should catch up to us now, you would be able to keep her out of my mind. Our link has strengthened dramatically, and you're doing more unconscious work than you realize."

She shifts uncomfortably in her seat, wrapping her arms around her stomach as though the very idea makes her sick. "Is it harder to do on a larger scale?" she asks after a lingering silence. "With more minds?"

"I don't think so. As I understand it, once you learn how, the compounded minds don't compound the effort. It's like . . . like vapors filling a chamber. You yourself are the chamber, and you yourself are infinite. All the minds of all the dragons and dracori will simply fall into your infinity and become part of your expanded conscious."

Her brow knots as she considers my words. For once, she doesn't have a smart remark. Her lips purse, and she turns her head, staring off into the northern horizon. Toward Cyran. Can she feel the city? Can she, even from this distance, begin to sense all those draconic souls now inhabiting it? Perhaps she's not even fully aware of the feeling, but that doesn't mean it isn't there, growing inside her.

"Have you been able to call up the white flame again?" I ask.

She half turns back to me but doesn't meet my eye. Instead she holds out one hand. A little flex of her fingers, and a small gout of fire springs to life in her palm. It lasts maybe five seconds, dancing in the evening breeze, before extinguishing, leaving behind a faint scent of strange perfume. "That's it," she admits. "Not exactly a blaze of glory."

"It will grow stronger."

She shrugs. "Maybe." Then she lifts her head a little, attention focused on the kintribe folk once more. I glance idly in the same direction and see Viessa fetching some strange contraption out from the back of the *urira*. It's almost as large as she is, and from this distance, I have no idea what it could be.

"I'm going to miss them."

I glance at Rosie. Her eyes are sad, her mouth downturned, but I say nothing. I'm no more comfortable with the elfkind than they are with me. Other than their swift paths, the only value they hold in my eyes is the buffer they've provided between me and Rosie. Because the truth is, I need that buffer. I need a clear and definite reason to keep my distance from her when everything inside me is drawing me to her. Sometimes it's all I can do not to grab her by a handful of that glorious golden hair, pull her head back, and kiss her with all the violent passion pent up inside me. Even now, my gaze lingers on her lips, and the memory of their softness, their eager pliability sheer torture to my soul. How vividly I recall the taste of her skin, the sweet mewling of her voice when I touched her just so . . .

"Oh, listen!"

I jolt back to the present and yank my eyes away from her face, staring down at the ground between my feet. Rosie, unaware of my thoughts, sits up a little straighter, head craning toward the kintribe camp even as a rumbling melody fills the evening air. Begrudgingly, I look up from under my heavy brow and cast my gaze back across the field. Viessa sits on the back steps of the *urira* wagon, her strange contraption unfolded and supported in her lap and over her shoulder. It sports multiple pipes and some sort of bag which expands and contracts as she blows into the mouthpiece. The sound it utters is multitudinous and deep, like a chorus the surrounding oaks themselves would make if they suddenly learned to sing.

One of the other half elves begins to play a smaller reed instrument, which lilts along in counterpoint with Viessa's droning. Ayre moves to join them, taking a seat on the ground near Viessa's feet. He produces an upright doff drum, props it in his lap, and beats out a dancing rhythm, which ties the other two instruments' voices together. The result is a melody that runs, jumps, leaps, and swoops in unexpected patterns, all while keeping time with the dancing campfire flames.

Rosie jumps to her feet and holds out her hand to me. "Come on!" she says with such excitement, I don't think to question whether or not it's a command. I simply place my hand in hers, let her drag me across the field back to the camp. The other two half elves have begun dancing to the song, moving together and apart again in sprightly patterns, their shadows flashing by firelight. Rosie watches them for some little while, her face aglow with delight.

Then she turns to me. "Dance with me, Valtar." This time, I feel the tentative almost-pull of control and my own immediate urge to obey. Realizing what she's done, however, Rosie retreats at once from my mind and says in a more tentative tone, "Please?"

I want to. Gods above know how I want to! Any opportunity to have her in my arms is a temptation almost beyond resisting. I must restrain myself. I cannot give in to this impulse, this need for her. If I'm going to protect her from all the terrible forces out there in the world, I must protect her from myself first. So I shake my head.

Rosie's smile crumples. For a moment, I feel her again scratching on the edge of my mind, but the sensation retreats again almost before I'm aware of it. Part of me wishes she would push through my defenses, would command me to do her will. But she doesn't. Instead she turns and watches the dance once more, swaying softly in time to the doff until the song comes to an end.

The laughing kintribe dancers applaud the three musicians, who take half bows from where they sit. Then the man with the dandelion eyebrows—Orijor, I believe his name is—calls out something in their language, which I take to be the name of a song. Ayre nods and begins to beat a new rhythm. The other two musicians join in, first the delicate pipes, then Viessa's large bag-and-bluster contraption. This song is more haunting than the last, the sort of melody which sighs and moans and gets down into the listener's bones.

Orijor appears suddenly at Rosie's side, speaking a few quick words in his pattering tongue. Rosie laughs, tossing her head back in a tumble of wild curls. When the young half elf holds out his hand, she places hers in it and allows him to lead her forward and whirl her into a dance.

And suddenly my whole body is hot with inner fire.

It's worse, somehow, than when I watched her dance with the other champions back in Stromin. I'd felt then more than I'd been willing to admit at the time—a bitter, burning jealousy which ate at my insides. But that was before I'd come to admit the truth. The truth which had sprung into being the very instant that odd, impulsive, spirited young woman pressed her lips to mine in a hidden alcove above a back stairway.

That was before I knew that I loved her.

I catch a breath, nearly staggering at the weight of that revelation bearing down on my shoulders. It's the first time I've allowed myself, even in the privacy of my mind, to admit it. I can only hope Rosie is too distracted with her dance and her partner to notice the turmoil erupting inside me. Because this is dangerous. I've learned the hard way how destructive love can be. What has my love for Arun brought about other than suffering? Both for him and for the people whose lives I've destroyed, all simply because I could not stop loving my brother.

This feeling is more dangerous by far. The way I feel for Rosie . . . I would topple kingdoms and slaughter masses for her sake! For the mere chance that she might be well, that she might be able to keep on dancing and laughing as she is right now.

With a wrench of will, I take this thought and press it down deep into the lowest, most hidden places inside me, places even Nyxia would not think to look. Down to where it might as well not exist at all, beyond reach of my own awareness. It's better this way. For Rosie's sake, for the world's.

And yet . . .

As I watch her spin out and then back again, caught in the arms of that damnable elf, the burning in my veins redoubles. The way she moves, the way she laughs, intoxicates my senses. Firelight plays in her hair, transforming it into gold almost as pure and shining as her two flashing eyes. She smiles in that way which makes me want to move mountains, and her hips sway as her tattered skirts swish about her calves. She's kicked off her shoes, and her bare feet spring about the trampled grass, light as feathers. I want to take those feet in my hands, feel the gentle curves and delicates bones. I want to cover them with kisses like the unworthy slave I am, then let my kisses trail up her calf to the curve of her knee before sweeping my tongue along her inner thigh. I want to hear her gasp out loud as I find her secret places and teach her the true meaning of desire.

Rosie's laugh bursts in my ears, yanking me back to the present. She spins again, claps her hands, and I can bear no more. A growl in my throat, I turn away from the scene. Half mad with mingled longing and fury, I march into the deepening darkness, uncertain of any path, only certain I need to put distance between myself and her. My blood is racing too wildly, and I cannot trust my impulses. Maybe it's better if I go, better if I leave her.

I stalk away a good ten paces. But then the music shifts abruptly, leaving the dancing song behind and moving into a new melody. Just one instrument at first—that grumbling, multi-voiced instrument of Viessa's. It reaches after me like beckoning, singing a refrain which stops me in my tracks.

My heart catches in my ribs and seems to forget how to beat.

The song plays on, gentle at first, but swelling in power, awakening something inside me. Something I'd thought I'd forgotten.

"Valtar?"

I startle and turn to find Rosie beside me. She's left her dance partner to hasten after me and now peers up into my face, studying me by moonlight. "Valtar," she says again, "isn't this the song you sang to me? The other night, when . . . after the *ravara* nearly drowned me?"

"Yes." The acknowledgment is like a stone in my throat. Damn me, how does Viessa know this song? It's an old Inithanan ballad, not something a half elf of Belanor should ever have heard, much less learned to play. I look back over my shoulder to where Viessa sits with her instrument cradled between her knees. The other two musicians glance at each other, uncertain. Then Ayre shrugs and begins to beat his doff, finding a rhythm that complements the song. The other fellow lifts his pipe to his lips and trills out a delicate harmony.

"Sing for me."

I startle and turn back to Rosie, eyes widening. She tips her head, her mouth tilting in a smile. "Won't you, please? Like you did the other night?"

Once more, the faintest trace of compulsion vibrates on the edge of my mind. But she pulls it back hastily, leaving only her eager voice, her pleading eyes. And suddenly, in this space, in this moment, with the stars turning overhead and the stink of dragon smoke heavy in my lungs, poised on the brink between the freedom I've known in her presence and the horror we must soon walk into . . . my reservations crumble to dust.

Half despairing, I turn to the musicians. To my surprise, my gaze is caught by Viessa's as she plays. There's something frightening in the truthseer's eyes. Somehow I know she has seen my future. And Rosie's. She knows what's coming but has chosen not to speak. I cannot guess what she has seen, only that it is inevitable. I feel the pull of destiny like the gravitational draw of the moon itself.

I bow my head as the music of my people and my past soaks down inside me. In that song I see again their faces—Father and Mother, both alive, and Brother, whole and near. I see the world of my childhood, full of possibility and adventure. I don't remember who sang this song to me back in those days. Mother perhaps, though the voice in my head is more like Father's. Indeed, it may have simply been a court musician or passing minstrel, come to entertain the court of Inithana. It doesn't matter; the song is there, pulsing in my blood.

I open my mouth and begin to sing in the old tongue of Inithana, a language no longer spoken in this world: "*Dri e lastri devorilae, Sar an dromel tu norlie.*"

As the stars pour down from heaven,
I sit alone with you in my mind.
Day to night, night to day, my love,
Even to the dying of the moon.
Alas, we are not side by side.

Drawn almost against their will, my eyes seek out Rosie. She watches me, her expression rapt, one hand pressed against her heart. The wind stirs her hair, blowing strands across her face. Even as I sing, I reach out and brush those strands gently back behind her ear.

Turn your eyes to me, my love.
I'll be there. I'll be there.
In the still of the night, I will dream of the time,
When my land and my love are mine.

Something moves in my mind—Rosie. She does not touch me with her physical body, but I feel her presence inside me. Closer than an embrace, her spirit moves with my voice, dancing with my song, becoming part of the music, a living harmony. I close my eyes again, allowing the song and the dance and her sweet presence to fill me.

When at last the tune comes to an end, I look down at her, my gaze hard and solemn. But though the moon is mostly hidden behind a thin film of smoke, her face glows with radiance.

"You really do have a lovely voice," she says at last, breaking the silence.

Without a word, I turn and walk away. I simply cannot bear it, cannot bear that she should look at me like that. Like there's some great good inside me, a treasure she wants to unearth and bring to light. So I distance myself from her, from that song, from all that it evokes, only just keeping from breaking into a run.

My footsteps carry me blindly across the field, all the way to a place where the ground breaks abruptly. I find myself overlooking a night-shrouded vista of the Albhian countryside. Well-tilled fields, little towns and hamlets, winding roads—whether in my imagination or in truth, they all seem to appear before my eye. But I can feel the dread holding this nation captive. Though Cyran is still many miles from here, the calamity which took place has rippled across the land. There is no escape; where can anyone turn now that death may fall any moment from the sky?

Behind me, the kintribe folk begin playing another one of their trilling songs. But the music of my own people continues to echo in the hollow of my chest. I see Inithana in my mind, blasted beyond all recognition, her people burnt, transformed, or scattered. I know what's coming for this country. Soon enough, whether in this century or the next, all the world will be covered in Mhoryga's flame.

I feel Rosie's approach long before she appears at my side, just visible in the tail of my eye. Her burning, living presence is like the sun in my life, and I long to turn to her, to soak in her brightness. But I stand firm, keep my gaze fixed before me. She is silent for a while. It might be the longest she's gone without speaking since I've known her. Then she simply reaches out, touches my hand. I almost recoil but then . . . don't. I allow her fingers to close around mine and squeeze softly. After a few breaths, I squeeze back.

"Do you think Arun is still alive?"

Her voice is soft, but the question is like a knife to my heart. I drop my chin to my chest. "I don't know."

She looks up at me, but I don't meet her eye. "We're going to save him, Valtar. We're going to save him and restore your kingdom."

How confidently she speaks the words. Can she even believe them? How? Only days ago, she resisted the very idea of her identity. Has so much changed in so little time? Has the advent of her strange new flame inspired this confidence?

I turn to her at last. For a long moment, I simply hold her gaze. She doesn't blink, doesn't back down. She looks back at me with quiet strength, so resolute, I feel the stone in my heart begin to shift. I still know without a shadow of a doubt how impossible it all is, but . . . if there is anyone, in any realm or world, who can find a way to do the impossible, it's this woman. This mighty, ferocious, effervescent woman with her enormous heart and her unfailing kindness and her sheer, stubborn refusal to give up. The only force in the universe who might be Mhoryga's equal. And opposite.

I want to kiss her. Painfully, achingly, overwhelmingly. The way she looks at me now, this very moment between us, will linger in my dreams for whatever time I have left breathing in this world. And when my life is over, and my soul is banished to any hell willing to claim it, still will this vision of filtered moonlight shining in her eyes haunt me.

I look down at her hand still clasped in mine. "We should go back," I say softly, though it kills me to utter the words. "We have a long journey tomorrow. You need to rest."

Her face breaks a little. She bites her lower lip and drops her head, then nods. Turning away, she begins to move back toward the camp but continues to hold my hand for three paces. Then she quickens her footsteps, pulls her fingers free, and hastens on ahead. I watch her go and feel the foreshadowing of the moment she will slip away from me. Forever.

9

Rosie

I wake in the early dawn light beneath the oak trees, my travel blanket pulled up to my chin to ward off the chill. With a groan, I roll onto my side, only for my eye to be caught by a gleam on the ground beside me. Bleary-eyed, I blink several times before my vision clears enough to see what it is: a leaf. A shining, gold leaf.

A sudden sense of aloneness washes over me. With a little gasp, I sit up, push back the blanket, and look around the sheltered place beneath the oaks where, only last night, an *urira* wagon had sat, a campfire had burned, and elfkind musicians had played their strange instruments. It's all gone now: wagon, kintribe folk. Even the campfire has been kicked away, the ashes scattered so thoroughly, I can't discern exactly where it was anymore. Viessa, Ayre, and the others must have packed up in the predawn, moving soundlessly so as not to disturb my sleep. As promised, they've left behind two satchels of supplies, which sit nestled among the roots of the oak tree nearest me. Two horses as well, both fully tacked and ready to ride, are picketed close by, idly nibbling at the short-cropped grass within their reach.

I turn my gaze to where Valtar bedded last night. He's not there. Of course he isn't. There's no way even half elves could slip off silently enough not to wake him. No doubt he was up well before they, going about some mysterious business of his own.

A glint of sunlight shines off the gold leaf again. I reach for it, catching it in my palm and holding it up for closer inspection. It isn't naturally gold but gold dipped, every delicate vein caught in a shimmering eternity. A token of some importance, unless I'm much mistaken, though I don't know exactly what for. Something tells me Viessa left it, and she doesn't do anything without reason. It's strung from a delicate chain, so I slip it around my neck.

Then, rising, I stretch and take another look at the world around me. Despite the morning sun and the layer of spring dew sparkling in the grass, the atmosphere feels heavy somehow. Dirty. I sniff the air and catch a distinct trace of sulfur. Turning my head, I peer through the mist to the northwestern horizon—the direction where, instinct tells me, Cyran must lie. I feel a certain pull. It's a subtle sensation, deep down in my bones, but it's been growing every day. An unsettling and yet undeniable sense of . . . *belonging*, somehow.

I frown, fingers curling into fists. The last thing I want is to feel as though I belong anywhere near a dragon nest.

A crack of twigs behind me and a soft *shush* of leaves. I spin in place to see Valtar approaching through the oak trees. He must have purposefully stepped on those twigs to alert me to his presence. A little smile pulls at my lips; sometimes, for a brutal assassin, he can be quite thoughtful. He carries his outer jerkin over one arm, and his shirt is all unfastened, revealing glimpses of both hard muscle and harsh brand scarring. Judging by the dampness of his hair and the gleam of his skin, he's just come from washing himself in the nearby creek.

Something warm stirs in my lower belly. Suddenly I'm very aware of how alone we are for the first time in days. Save for the horses, of course, but they don't seem particularly interested.

"Well," I say, planting hands on my hips, "don't you look fresh as a daisy."

Valtar stops, his brow puckered slightly. Even in this disheveled state, a dark and dangerous aura clings to him. Something about the set of his broad shoulders, the powerful musculature of his towering frame, always gives off the impression of a panther, all latent energy and predatory focus. Not the sort of person any sane individual would compare to a flower. Least of all, a daisy.

He grunts, shakes his head a little, eyes darting away from me. Stepping over to the travel packs, he opens one and begins to rummage through it for I know not what. I breathe out a little huff of air, then clasp my hands behind my back and drift toward him, chewing my lip. Now that we're alone, I find I'm not terribly eager to make a start on the day's travels. Horses have never been my favorite, and besides . . . he does smell nice. I washed last night with Viessa and the other female half elf in our company, using their sweet-scented soaps, a blessed change from soapweed. I'm confident that I don't reek of travel at the very least. And with the memory of our encounter by the lakeshore still fresh in my mind, I can't help wondering if now would be a prime opportunity to pick up where we left off.

"Valtar?" I say softly and reach out to him.

My fingers have not yet touched his arm, however, when, with a vicious snarl, he whirls on me suddenly, grabs me by the arm, and yanks me to him. His other hand grips the front of my bodice, tearing the laces in a single rough gesture. I choke on a little cry, but the sound has barely vibrated in my throat before his lips are roughly against mine, hungry and demanding, while his hands bruise my body with need, ripping my sleeve, reaching under my skirts, and—

I blink and stagger back three paces. My breath is tight, my lungs heaving, but when I clasp both hands to my chest, I find my bodice is fully intact. No torn laces, no ripped sleeve. Nor are my parted lips bruised with burning kisses. I suck in a painful inhale and shake my head to clear the fog. It was a vision. An image . . . from his mind? Did I just inadvertently jump through his defenses and see his inner thoughts?

A brisk wind blows across the field, pulling at strands of my hair but failing to cool my fiery cheeks. "Valtar?" I say again tremulously, lifting my gaze to him. I catch his eye for half a second before he turns sharply away from me, his back a solid wall. He stands still for ten breaths; I watch the heaving expansion of his rib cage. Then, with brisk, almost militant movements, he shrugs into his jerkin and begins to fasten the buckles. "There are travel wafers in your bag," he tosses over his shoulder. "You should eat before we ride. We've a long day ahead of us."

Without another word, he picks up his own bag, slings it over his shoulder, and strides toward the picketed horses. I watch him go, my breath still short, my eyes wide. I could call him back, of course. Even now, if I sent out the command, he would pivot on his heel and run to me, and the moment I'd just witnessed might still play out between us, real this time. But how can I know what he wants? How can I know the difference between my own lustful urges and his true feelings for me?

"Damn," I whisper softly, wrapping my arms around my

shivering body. I stand like so for some moments before finally, with a short, frustrated exhale through my lips, I bend to pick up my bag.

WE TRAVEL THROUGH more populated countryside than we've known since our escape from Stromin. There are plenty of dirt trails, paths, and even proper paved roads leading in the general direction of our destination. We make good time.

I will never understand what some people see in horses. I get that they have their uses and certainly earn their keep, and I'm happy to offer them my wary respect. But riding is such a miserable experience, and you won't convince me it's any more enjoyable for the horse. I much prefer donkeys—Mistress Iliyani's old brown ass, Bruni, was so fat and docile, riding him was like straddling a furry pumpkin. Horses are a different matter altogether. But I am at least competent enough to stay in the saddle, and Viessa seems to have picked a plodding old mount for me, bless her. My gray gelding wants nothing more than to walk nose to tail behind Valtar's more elegant chestnut mare. As long as he doesn't take it into his thick head to bolt suddenly, I suppose we'll manage well enough.

We pass by several small hamlets in the morning. By noon, we see a proper town in the middle distance. All around us are people going about their businesses, their lives. But there's tension in the atmosphere, a pervasive dread. We pass close to a field where a farmer and his crew are tilling the soil in preparation for planting. They pause in their labors to watch Valtar and me ride by, eyes distrustful. One of the young men grips his hoe aggressively. I hope he won't be foolish enough to try anything . . . and if he is, I hope Valtar won't be too quick to retaliate. We continue down the road quietly enough. When I turn in the saddle to look back, the men are watching us still but make no move to follow. Frowning, I face forward but cannot shake the feeling of being watched until our road takes us over a little hillock and out of sight.

Is it my imagination, or is the sky darkening much earlier than it should this late into spring? By a little past noon, there's a distinct gloom in the air. Every now and then a wind blows, sometimes with fresh air from the sea; other times, it carries a sudden stink that makes me gasp and causes my horse to pin back his ears and toss his head nervously. We ride on, however, wordless and determined, our faces set northwest.

By midafternoon, we come to a quiet stretch of lonely countryside. Valtar reins in his horse abruptly, twists in his saddle, and looks back at me contemplatively. Then he says, "We'll stop here."

I lift my heavy head, catching his eye. "Like hells we will," I say. "There's a whole day ahead of us! Ride on, I say, ride on. The sooner we get this stretch of our journey over with the better."

Valtar narrows his eyes. Then, in lieu of an answer, he simply swings down from his saddle and leads his horse off the trail into the short grass and a grove of poplar trees, which offer shade and a little filtering protection from the stink in the air. I fight the urge to command him back. Sometimes his way of simply overpowering any given situation is too galling. But truth be told, I do want a break from this cursed saddle.

With a sigh, I dismount. The distance to the ground feels greater than it did before, jarring to my very bones. I groan loudly, and the gelding swings his head around to look at me with mild concern. "Not your fault, old fellow," I say and offer the beast a pat on the shoulder.

We follow Valtar off the path, making our way through a

clump of weeds on the roadside into the shade offered by the trees. He's ventured in far enough to be out of sight from the road. By the time we catch up, he's already prepared two feed bags for the horses. We picket them, remove their bridles, and he slips the bags into place. Soon the homely sounds of munched oats fill the air, and I'm already starting to feel a bit better.

Before I can spread out my bedroll and collapse for a nap, Valtar turns to me and says, "First form."

"*What?*" I throw up my hands and huff a breath that's tantamount to a curse. "You're joking, right? The last thing I want is to go swinging a knife about after all those hours in the saddle!"

"You need to limber your muscles," Valtar says placidly. "Trust me, you'll feel better if you move a little before resting."

I want to argue. No, I don't want to argue—I want to command him to go munch a bag of oats himself! I could do it too; we both know it. But he continues looking at me in that way of his, so damnably patient. "Fine," I growl at last, and whip my knife from its sheath. I assume the first form stance, ready to gut him if he gets too close.

"Now," Valtar says, and I perform the initial series of maneuvers. I can tell my footwork is sloppy; my legs are so stiff and aching. "Again," Valtar says.

I go through the first form five times, improving slightly with each iteration. Valtar begins to call out other forms, and I perform these as well. Damn him, if he wasn't right! My body does feel better as my limbs stretch, and my muscles remember they're good for more than keeping my bum planted in a shifting saddle. I'm exhausted almost to the point of tears but grit my teeth and perform each maneuver he asks of me to the best of my ability.

"Good enough," Valtar says at last. Immediately I collapse to the ground, spread-eagle, and simply stare up at the sky through the poplar branches. I'm fairly certain I could nod off here and now and sleep right through the afternoon and all night.

Valtar's shadow falls across me. I squint one-eyed up at him and ask coldly, "Can I help you?"

He crouches and offers a wafer cake. I look at it for a long moment, uncertain if it's worth the effort of sitting up, much less chewing and swallowing. "Come," Valtar urges. "You must keep up your strength."

"You know," I growl, pushing up onto my elbows, "I've come to appreciate why nobody likes you."

His eyebrow lifts slightly. "Ah, but remember? Like me or not, we're friends now. You said so yourself. You can't take it back."

"Don't try me," I mutter, but accept the wafer and take a bite. Even the delightful sweetness of elfin baking isn't enough to bring a smile to my face. It's better than scorched rabbit, I'll give it that.

While I eat, Valtar rises and moves away from me. Because remaining in my proximity seems to be anathema to him these days. I glower at his back as he moves to stand between two trees, gazing out from our sheltering grove. Ordinarily I don't struggle this much to find a cheerful spirit, but ordinarily I haven't just spent eight hours in a saddle, damn it.

"If we continue at this pace," Valtar says suddenly, breaking the silence between us, "we'll reach Cyran in about a week."

I grunt. He'd said three days last night, but that was before he knew what kind of a horsewoman I am.

"Judging by the smoke in the air," he continues, "we should begin to see signs of dragon presence by tomorrow." He turns finally and looks at me where I sit, munching wafers. "That's why we've stopped early. I felt you should rest before encountering the first dragon spawn."

The mouthful on my tongue turns to ash. I swallow it with difficulty, but cannot manage another bite, appetite gone.

"They are likely to be drawn to you," Valtar says, his voice relentless. "Even as you become aware of them, so too will their awareness of you grow. We have one advantage though—most of them have no idea another dragon princess exists. You may be able to use this to your advantage."

"How?"

"If you can get into their minds before they set eyes on you, you can simply command them to leave. They may, as a result, think you are Nyxia and not question the order."

This sounds reasonable enough. I've not yet tried to issue a command from out of sight and am uncertain how that would work. Theoretically, it should be possible. "What about your plan for us to assemble a dragon armada of our own?" I ask, waving my wafer vaguely.

"That is still the plan. But you should practice simple commands before you try to take them for our side."

Something about the way he says it makes my skin crawl. "What about simply breaking Nyxia's compulsion over them," I say. "Wouldn't that be enough?"

Valtar doesn't answer. Not in words at least—his frown speaks volumes.

"I don't like the idea of *controlling* anyone," I persist. "I'd rather set them free. Isn't that possible? Isn't that what I've done for you?"

I want him to tell me it's true. I want to believe he's not so hell-bent to help me, to guide me, to protect me, to train me, simply because I'm the new controlling influence in his life. But he doesn't answer. He continues to look at me with that inscrutable face of his.

"They've only ever known Mhoryga's will." I turn the wafer over in my hands, crumbling it at the edges. "If given the chance to do otherwise, who's to say they won't join our side willingly?"

"They might," Valtar speaks at last. "Or they might become unstoppably destructive rage beasts and burn everything in sight."

"You didn't."

"I'm dracori, not dragon spawn. Besides, I . . . I . . ." He looks away quickly, setting his jaw hard. I desperately want to know what he was going to say. Almost unconsciously, I reach out to his mind, feeling tremulously along the edges of his vulnerability. He shoots me a sharp glare, however, and I retreat at once, embarrassed to be caught breaching his privacy even slightly.

I look down at the crumbled wafer in my hands. "All right," I say at last. "I'll send the dragon spawn away. Though I'm not sure how."

"We need to practice."

My stomach knots. "What? Now?"

"Yes. I need to know you can reach into minds from a distance." He moves across the little clearing, his footsteps quick and sure. "I'll walk up the road a piece. You count to a hundred—no, make it five hundred. Then try to find me. Bring me back to you."

A little chill crawls down my spine. I don't care for the idea of being alone here, so close to dragon country. But neither do I want to let him down. "If that's what you think is best. Go on then. Take a walk."

Valtar looks at me long and hard. There's something unreadable in his face, something I wish I could discern. He opens his mouth as though to speak, then closes it again. Turning away, he marches from the grove without another word. The two horses both lift their heads, and the three of us watch him disappear among the trees, making for the road.

"One," I begin, and sigh. "Two. Three."

A count to five hundred feels like a small eternity. I suppose he needs time to create some distance between us, but my stomach knots harder with each passing second. I may rush the last hundred a little before eagerly stretching out my awareness in search of him. A moment of panic thrills through my veins. He's not there. I can't find him, or anything, for that matter. There's just a big *nothing* feeling all around me.

My chest constricts. "*Valtar?*" I call out in my mind.

Almost immediately I hear his voice: "*Rosie.*"

"*Oh, thank the gods!*" I place a hand over my thudding heart. "*I thought I'd lost you.*"

He's silent for a long moment. I begin to wonder if our connection is lost again. I concentrate harder and begin to see a picture in mind. At first it's fuzzy, nothing but a vague assembly of lights and shadows. Then one shadow begins to take more definite form and solidity. I focus on that one, watch it clarify slowly into a human shape. Bit by bit, the details come into focus, until I see Valtar himself—Valtar, striding swiftly down the roadside, his black cloak swirling in his wake, his hood pulled low over his face. It's so vivid, I almost feel as though I'm walking beside him.

"*I wouldn't leave you, Rosie,*" he says suddenly. The mouth of the image doesn't move, but his voice is crystal clear in my head.

I breathe out in relief. I know he wouldn't abandon me, of course. Not purposefully, not willingly. A smile breaks across my face, followed by a flood of warmth. Not since Durona died have I felt such confidence that another soul in this world truly cared about me, would truly do anything for me.

Valtar stops abruptly. He doesn't turn, continues to face down the road. But his expression hardens.

"*Valtar?*" I say through our mental link. "*What's wrong?*"

"*That name,*" he answers, his voice a growl. "*What was that name you just thought?*"

I blink, surprised. I didn't realize he could hear my thoughts as well, not if I didn't directly speak them to him. Perhaps the mental link is stronger than I realized. I bite back a little smile, relieved that I wasn't thinking anything . . . inappropriate.

"*Durona?*" I say. "*She was my mother. At least, I thought she was. She raised me until I was about seven years old. But she died.*" I'm silent for a moment, then add: "*Dracori.*"

As though the word acted as a summoning spell, the world around me erupts in sudden flames and screams. My heart leaps, my blood rushing with terror as I spin in place, utterly shocked by this abrupt change to my reality. I'm no longer on a quiet roadside, walking beside Valtar; nor am I seated cross-legged in a poplar grove.

Instead I am running down the middle of a village street. I feel the rough paving stones through the soles of my boots and the heat of hellfire flames against my bare skin. Houses loom on either side of me, green flames bursting from doors and windows, devouring thatched rooftops. Overhead, dragon spawn swoop in wide, destructive circles, raining fire from above.

I stagger to a halt and spin in place, taking in the hell around me. A small piece of my mind recognizes this street—that's the chapel house where Mother used to send me to learn my prayers. That's the meeting hall, where important events and feasts were hosted. That's the square, where we gathered on feast days for dancing. There's the crab apple tree I used to climb each spring, searching for a snack. All ablaze.

Screams and shouts fill my ears, but suddenly a figure appears through the smoke, striding toward me down the center of the street. A tall, bare-chested figure with a black hood over his head. The hellfire glow illuminates the ugly dragon brand emblazoned across his torso. "*Get out of here!*" His voice rolls through the heated air, hits me like a blow. "*Get out!*"

I stare at him, paralyzed with fear. He draws nearer, looming with terrible menace. When he lifts his arms, balls of green hellfire appear in his palms. "*Get out! Get out!*" he roars.

I turn on my heel and run. Run with everything I have in me, feet slapping the paving stones, hair flying in my wake. "*Rosie!*" the voice behind me shouts. I don't stop to question how that monster, that dracori, knows my name. The world is hot and burning, and I feel my flesh beginning to blister, but some instinct drives me down the center of that street, propels me in the direction my heart tells me safety lies. I see it ahead of me. A remote cottage, set a little apart from the rest of the village. My heart leaps. Home! I'm almost home! There I will be safe, surely. There is protection and love and comfort and . . .

I skid to a stop. My eyes widen. For the cottage door opens, and a child appears, staring out at the world gone mad. A child with masses of golden hair and bright gold eyes.

Before I can come to grips with what I'm seeing, another figure appears—a woman with fierce gray eyes and a jaw like granite and shoulders strong enough to carry a young ox. "*Mother!*" I try to cry, but the name dies on my lips.

The woman picks up the little girl, swings her onto her hip. In her other hand she grasps a sword—a big, notched blade, sharpened to a razor's edge. Brandishing this weapon high, she rushes out into the cottage yard and the screaming night. Before she's gone ten paces, however, five figures emerge from the shadows all around the cottage. Dark, hooded figures with fire in their hands and dragon brands on their chests. The woman flashes her teeth. For a moment, she takes an aggressive stance, as though she will hurl herself at them, even knowing how useless her sword is against the hellfire they wield. Then she looks down at the child in her arms.

Pivoting on her axis, she drops her sword and clutches the child to her breast, racing back for the cottage. She leaps inside and slams the door behind her against a vicious blast of hellfire.

"*No!*" I cry, and take a lunging step forward. "*No, no, no!*" This will be Durona's final mistake. I know it; I know it too well. She will burn alive inside that cottage. I watch the fire devour the mud-and-wattle walls, creeping to the thatch, even as the dracori close in.

A surge of hatred fills my veins. I look down and find green hellfire simmering between my fingers. For once it does not burn me. Gritting my teeth, I take a stance, prepared to hurl my flame at the nearest dracori, determined to break their ranks, to give Durona and my childhood self a chance to escape.

A hand falls heavy on my shoulder.

The next instant, I'm whirled about and find myself face-to-face with Valtar. He looms large over me, hellfire burning in his eyes. When he opens his mouth, the back of his throat is alight with flame.

"*Get out of here, Rosie!*" he roars. "*Get out!*"

Then he lifts me off my feet and hurtles me through the air.

I LAND ON my back in the poplar clearing, wind knocked from my lungs. Hellfire roars in my veins, and when I hold up my hands and stare at them, I expect to see them wreathed in flame. But there's nothing. Not on the outside at least.

Inside is a different matter. Heat burns inside me, even as it has before, searing through my bones, my soul. This isn't the white, healing fire, but the true inferno of hell, seeking yet again to escape and be free in this world.

Moaning with pain, I roll onto my side and grip my stomach where the crucible burns hottest. Where is Valtar? Where are his comforting arms, his soothing voice? I need him—gods, I need him more than ever!

But he doesn't come. I'm alone. Burning alive.

Closing my eyes, I reach desperately down inside. Down beneath the scorching hell, down to that deeper place in my soul. And there—I find it. The white fire. It's small, but still present, still alive. Can I call it to me? Will it answer my summons?

Please, I whisper inside my head, and imagine extending my arms. *Please. I need you.*

The flame flares, responding to my voice. I feel it grow, swell, and finally leap to my outstretched hands. I catch it, draw it to my heart. I don't know what I'm doing; none of this is anything within my range of experience. But I've got to try something or I will die, right here, right now.

I press the white flame into my heart. It hurts, but it's a good hurt. A hurt that feels right. Slowly the fire begins to spread, as though with each beat of my heart it pulses out farther and farther, moving through my veins into every extremity. Wherever it goes, the green hellflame retreats, either absorbed in the white fire or extinguished by it, I cannot say. My physical body lies in a tight ball of agony beneath the poplar trees, shuddering, whimpering. But it's working. White fire flows through me, wave after wave, until finally the last trace of hell is driven back down, down, down into the deepest well of my being.

I breathe out slowly through parted lips. It's done. I'm safe once more—clean. While I know the hellfire isn't gone for good, the sense of reprieve is as good as a cure. I lie for a long while, simply breathing, simply glorying in the sense of my fire-free limbs. After what feels like hours, I open my eyes, only to find the sun has set. The shadows under the poplars have grown long and dark, and even with my dragon sight, I struggle to discern the horses and their pickets.

"Valtar?" I whisper. My throat is rough and thick. I cough painfully, trying to clear it. "Valtar?" I call again, a little louder this time. Surely he must have come back by now. He must have realized I wasn't doing as he asked, wasn't reaching into his mind and drawing him back to me. But when I lift my head and peer at the night-darkened world around me, I glimpse no sign of him.

Arms shaking, I push myself up into a seated position and tuck my legs under me. I ought to . . . what? I shake my foggy head, try to order my thoughts. I ought to make a fire. Set up camp. Prepare for Valtar's return. I ought to eat something, replenish my strength following this ordeal. But I can't move. I feel like an old, hollowed-out tree.

Surely Valtar will return soon. Any moment now. Then I can apologize to him, tell him I accidentally slipped back into an old memory. Maybe he'll even put his arms around me, offer me comfort as he's done before.

Then, very quietly, the thought whispers in the back of my brain: *That wasn't* my *memory.*

I frown. What am I thinking? Of course that was my memory. How many times have I relived that terrible night when the dracori rode in on dragon spawn and attacked my home village? I've heard the screams of the villagers echoing in my dreams these last sixteen years. Over and over I've gazed into my mother's face for the last time, just before she pushed me up that chimney, made me climb up and escape without her.

But . . . that wasn't what I saw this time. This memory was different. Like watching all the same events from the outside.

I bury my head in my hands, pressing the heels of my palms against my eyes. None of this makes sense. And I'm too tired and still in too much pain to *make* it make sense. Valtar will explain it. When he returns. I just need to wait for him to get back, and he'll put it all right again. With this comfort cradled close to my heart, I lie down once more and wrap my arms over my head, as though to block out my own careening thoughts. Tucking my knees up to my chin, I coil into a small, tight ball. And I wait. For Valtar.

He will come back.

He will come back.

He must come back.

10

Valtar

I come to myself just as I fall to my knees. My breath is short, my heart stabbing like a knife in my throat. Violent convulsions quake my limbs even as sweat pours down my face, my back, soaking my garments. Terrible heat builds within my flesh vessel, mounding from a space deep in my innermost being. I've kept it at bay for nearly two weeks now, channeling only small bursts of hellfire every so often. Now all that pent-up energy seeks an exit, and the need is too intense, a pain beyond bearing.

Arching my spine, I throw out my arms, throw back my head. A great roar breaks from my lips and, with it, a gout of hellfire from the pit my soul. It burns my throat, across my tongue, lashing from my eyes, my hands, my chest. A fountain of flame, shooting straight to the sky. All this pain, all this fury, all this rage which Rosie's presence has kept at bay now escapes in one tremendous burst.

Because Rosie is out of my mind. Out of range. Leaving me utterly lost and alone.

Emptied at last, I collapse forward onto my forearms, brow pressed into the hard ground. I breathe in agonized gasps, my scorched lungs shivering with each inhale and exhale. What happened? Something must have driven me to this breaking point, but in the moment, shuddering with the aftermath of expulsion, I can't order my thoughts clearly. I remember running. Running and running, as hard as I could. Seeking escape. From what? Or whom?

From Rosie.

No. No, that can't be it. Why should I flee Rosie? I . . . I love her. I need to be with her, need to protect her.

But Rosie was in my head. She was in my memory.

In *that* memory.

"*Rutt*," I hiss, closing my eyes. Sweat falls from my forehead and foam from my gaping mouth, turning the dust of the road into mud. For some moments, I can do nothing but try to remember how to breathe. The cold air is a welcome torture as I draw it down my throat. Pain is better than thought just now.

But eventually, thought must return. I see again those moments in my mind—the sight of her within my memory space, running down the street, burning buildings on either side. I did not want her to see what was coming, did not want her to learn the truth. Not like this. Not before I could confess it with my own tongue and, simultaneously, beg her forgiveness. Desperately I'd pursued her, determined to oust her from that corner of my mind if it was the last thing I ever did.

I grit my teeth, thinking back on the violence with which I'd thrown her. Her power over me was so strong, it had taken all the strength I could summon to fight back, but . . . what if I hurt her? Oh gods, what if, when I sent her mind flying, it impacted her physical body as well?

I've got to get her. I've got to make certain she's not harmed by my wild impulse of self-protection. And then I will tell her the truth, damn me. The whole truth. About that night and my presence there. About my role in the death of her mother. She deserves to know. I should have told her long ago, and I tried to, but . . . ultimately, I was a coward. Such a damnable, worthless coward.

Arms trembling, I push myself upright. A puff of sulfurous smoke blows through my lips. I'm exhausted, hollowed out inside. It's been a long time since I expelled that much hellfire flame; I haven't felt the need for it, not with Rosie always so near.

I get up onto my knees, the most I can manage just yet. Closing my eyes, I try to reach out, to find her with my mind. Nothing. I've run too far, out of range. Or else . . . or else . . . What will I find when I return to that poplar grove? Images of her broken body, burnt from the inside out, dance before my mind's eye.

I surge to my feet, staggering hard to keep my balance. My body threatens to fold up on itself, but I force it to obey my will, to stand and find its equilibrium. When the world finally stops tilting wildly around me, I turn, face back up the road down which I ran. She's back there. Suffering maybe. I've got to get to her. Now.

I take a few stumbling steps. My limbs scarcely seem to belong to me, as though my soul has been partially disconnected. My head is so heavy, I cannot lift it, cannot look at anything but my own two feet. Gritting my teeth, I force myself to focus on just the next step, then the next.

A shadow flickers across the ground.

My heart jolts. A thrill of fear lances through my veins, calling to the hellfire inside me. But that fire is too deeply subdued after the expulsion. I won't be able to wield it again for hours yet.

I yank my head up, staring into the empty sky. Clouds have gathered, growing thicker and denser by the moment. But those aren't rain clouds. They're smoke.

"Gods damn it," I growl.

Though my limbs still don't want to obey me, I start to run, moving in jerking, lurching strides like an animated corpse, propelled by pure adrenaline. The ground seems to shift under my unsteady feet, and several times I nearly fall on my face. But I keep going. I've got to get to Rosie, now, now, now—

Another shadow. Then a third. Again, I look up. This time I see them, spiraling in descent through their smoke screen. Dragon spawn. Three of them. I narrow my eyes and hiss through gritted teeth. Those are dracori mounted on their backs. My mind recoils out of reflex, expecting any moment to feel Nyxia's voice inside me. But it doesn't come. I'm still free of all influence, both Nyxia's or Rosie's. But that won't help me, weakened and outnumbered as I am.

My hands move unconsciously, reaching for knives. But wait . . . I stop myself, fingers tense. This can't be Nyxia's crew. There is no way she could have followed us, using the elf paths as we did. These must be dragons from Cyran. Which means they don't know who I am.

I curse the weakness in me that could not repress that gout of flame. It must have been that green beacon shooting to the sky which alerted them to my presence and brought them straight to me. I should have swallowed it back and let myself die! But at least I'm nowhere near Rosie. If I can't sense her, they shouldn't be able to either. And maybe I can brazen my way out of this.

I look down at myself. My clothes are hellfire-proof, but they don't look like a dracori uniform. Hastily I strip off my jerkin and open my shirt to display the burn scar, an obvious sign of allegiance.

The dragons are circling lower now, obedient to their dracori riders. They seem wary of approaching me, uncertain whether I am friend or foe. Finally one of them lands. This dragon is the largest of the three, a big, battle-scarred brute with scales that might once have been green but are now nearly blackened with scorch marks. The dracori himself is a match for his mount, a hardened warrior with a face like a smashed brick. Like the other dracori, he is shirtless, his brand prominently displayed.

He slips from the dragon's back and strides toward me, a handful of hellfire at the ready. Green flames spark in his eyes. It can be difficult to guess nationalities of origin once the dracori transformation process has taken place. The influence of hellish blood drains life and vitality from the skin, leaving all dracori equally colorless, like myself. But judging by his features, I would guess he is not Khylmirian. Which would make him one of the recently transformed dracori of Cyran. I don't know if this will play to my favor. Newly transformed or otherwise, he will still be under Nyxia's compulsion and, through her, Mhoryga's slave.

"Are you dracori?" the man calls out, his accent confirming him as Albhian born.

"I am."

"Show me your flame," the dracori says.

I grit my teeth. "I cannot. As you may have observed, I just purged my flame. It has not yet replenished. But you can see for yourself the brand of our goddess on my flesh, same as yours."

The dracori narrows his eyes. The other two have landed now, their dragon spawn fractious and tossing their ugly heads. They both have that look about them, which many older dragon spawn acquire, of having not transformed back to their human shape in a long, long time. My heart constricts at the sight of them. This could be Rosie's fate. Or worse. If she manifests as a dragon queen, there is a distinct likelihood that . . . I shake my head, unwilling to finish that thought.

"Where do you hail from?" the first dracori demands. "You are not of Cyran."

I meet his searching gaze and hold it hard. "I came over with the invasion force."

Though this man is thoroughly Mhoryga's creature, reborn with hellfire in his blood, I don't think I imagine the slightest shift in his expression at my words. A glimmer of hatred that should not be there, should not be possible. Perhaps there is still something of the true man down inside, underneath the compulsion.

"That was a year ago," the dracori says. "What of recently? Where is your dragon spawn?"

"It was killed."

"And it was just the two of you? What are you, a scout?"

"Something like that."

One of the other two dracori steps forward, whispers in the first man's ear. The man turns to listen, his brow tightening. Then his gaze sharpens, knifing into me. "Are you Valtar Skylock?" he demands.

My stomach plunges. "No," I answer coldly.

"What is your name?"

"What does it matter? I am a servant of Mhoryga, same as you."

"That is not an answer."

I hold his stare. Then, wondering again if what I glimpsed in his face was true, I take a chance. "Does the name Elis Balxidon mean anything to you?"

I'm not sure what possessed me to say it. An instinct, perhaps, but one born from many years of learning to read people in a blink and act accordingly. That instinct has kept me alive for a long time now, and I've learned to trust it. The name has an immediate impact on the man. For an instant, the dracori mask falls away, and I glimpse the person beneath—a man of Albhia, a man of Cyran City. A man who would certainly know the name of the brave young lord of Albhia, cousin to the prince, defender of his people.

That momentary revelation vanishes in a blink, however. The dracori's eyes flare with green fire once more. His lips curl back in a snarl. He raises one hand, snaps his fingers, and the other two dracori move in to flank me, their eyes hooded. "You're coming with us," he says.

I flick my wrists. Two knives appear in my hands, and I sink into a defensive crouch. "I think not."

Without hesitation, the dracori on my right raises his hand, emitting a blast of hellfire straight at my face. I cross my arms and blades before me, absorbing the flame, even as the force of the blast seeks to knock me off balance. When it ends, I don't wait for a second assault. Teeth bared, a roar ripping from my throat, I lunge.

11

Rosie

I wake to the sound of horses nickering and stomping impatiently from their pickets. A layer of dew covers my body, a poplar root digs into my hip bone, and everything both inside and out hurts with a dull, aftershock ache that makes me want to curl up into a tight ball and try to escape back into the safety of unconsciousness.

Instead I groan and cover my face with both hands. My limbs feel positively hollow following my near burning . . . When was that? Yesterday? Did I truly sleep through the night? I must have, judging by the chorus of birdsong and the pale light making its way through the branches to dapple the ground where I lie. It must have been the heavy, dreamless sleep of the near-broken soul, like a little slice of oblivion. I remember nothing, not even—

Valtar.

I pull my hands back and sit up abruptly, searching the little grove. He isn't here. Gods damn it, he isn't here! I begin to shake. Harder and harder, until I think I'll fly to pieces. Squeezing my eyes shut, I wrap my arms around my middle, desperate to hold myself together. *Just because he's not here right now doesn't mean he didn't return in the night*, I remind myself desperately. He may have come at any point and chosen not to disturb my sleep. How many times have I awakened to find him gone? It's not unusual for him to vanish like a phantom. But he always looms suddenly back into existence, all silent and mysterious. It's just his way.

Somehow these reassurances fail to calm my racing heart.

I get up at last, force myself to tend the horses, filling their feed bags. Birds chatter in the branches all around me, but their voices don't feel like song anymore. They sound like warnings, battle cries. That terrible tension which I'd sensed on the road yesterday has deepened. But perhaps that's just my imagination. Or my anxiety over Valtar.

Where is that dragon-eaten man anyway?

I perform my morning ablutions, using some of our drinking water to splash my face, and run my fingers through tangled hair. These tasks complete, I force myself to choke down half a travel wafer. And still, no sign of my broody assassin. Did he leave? My stomach knots. Though I've been trying not to think of it, I allow my mind to look back on what happened. On that memory. Not my own memory . . . but Valtar's.

I draw a shuddering breath, fingers squeezing the remaining bits of wafer into crumbs in my lap. Valtar was there that night when Durona died. He was there. Among the other dracori, when they trapped us in the cottage, and she burned alive saving me. When I nearly burned as well, my flesh scorched in a hellfire blaze. That's what he didn't want me to know. That's what he didn't want me to find out. That he was part of that assault, and . . . and . . .

A sudden sob breaks my steeled spine. I bend over, weeping,

my body shaking harder than ever. At first I can't think why—it's such an absolute eruption of emotion, without thought. I give in to it, let all that feeling flood through me, body and soul. At least it isn't fire. It's sorrow, deep and drowning and dangerous, but I know I can survive it if I simply ride the wave through the caverns of my heart and out into the open air beyond.

At length the torrent eases. I find myself washed up on a rocky shore of calm. Shaken, battered, but still whole. I use a fold of my skirt to rub my nose and wipe tears from my face. The truth is, this sorrow isn't for me. At least not *only* for me. I've had sixteen years to mourn Durona's loss, and while I know I'll never fully get over the horror of that night, I've learned to live with it, to hold space for it inside myself.

But these tears are for the boy. The boy I saw taking a seat in that stone chair, his arms strapped down, even as his brother screamed at him from where he stood chained to a stake. The boy who became a monster. The monster who marched under compulsion in company with other monsters, obeying the orders of their goddess queen.

Valtar is ashamed. I felt his shame pulsing through every part of that memory. But it's something he can never undo. Like my loss of Durona, he must make space within himself to live with that sin. Otherwise it will destroy him.

"You should have told me," I whisper, sitting up a little straighter and speaking my words to the murmuring poplars, the birds, and the silence. "You should have told me, you blessed idiot."

Then I remember—the brush of his fingers against my scars. I remember that moment down by the lakeside, his voice, rough with urgency: *Rosie . . . those scars. Rosie, I've got to tell you something.*

He was trying to tell me. He wanted to, he meant to. It wasn't his fault I kept interrupting him with kisses, poor man! A little smile breaks across my face. With a shake of my head, I laugh softly. It's going to be all right now. When he comes back, I'll tell him that I know. And I'll apologize for invading that memory. I'd thought it was one of mine and not realized why he was so desperately trying to get me to leave. Now I understand. And I am sorry for the invasion of his privacy.

We'll make peace. All will be well again. Maybe this agonizing distance he's been putting between us will finally disintegrate, and then he will . . . and then we will . . .

But he doesn't come.

Hours pass. The sun glides across the hazy, smoke-filmed sky.

And Valtar doesn't return to me.

Something must have happened. I know—I *know*, damn it—that he would not abandon me. Something must have happened to stop him. Did I hurt him? I don't know the full extent of my powers, don't know what fighting me out of his mind might have done to him. Dracori are not meant to resist the influence of dragon queens. Maybe doing so harmed him in some terrible way? He might even now be lying in a ditch by the side of the road, vulnerable and . . .

I spring to my feet. Enough waiting around. I'm going to find him. He can't have gotten far. I only counted to five hundred, after all. No, he's got to be close but unable to reach me. I'll find him, I'll help him. I'll summon up the healing fire inside me if I have to.

I take three strides through the trees before stopping. A curse grinds through my teeth, but I force myself to turn about and fetch the horses. I can't just leave them. Someone might come along and take them, and then where would we be? Begrudging every moment it takes, I pack the bags, tack up the beasts, and somehow manage to scramble up into the saddle of my gray gelding. He does not care to lead the way, and it takes all the ferocious kicking, nudging, swearing, and cajoling I can muster to get him in motion. The chestnut follows at a sprightlier step, and I half wonder if I ought to have mounted her instead. But I'm not sure I dare. I might be a dragon, but I don't imagine myself a match for a red mare, especially one with turned-back ears like that.

I manage to get the three of us out of the grove and back onto the road. There I pause, looking first back the way we've come from, then forward in the direction we're journeying. Which way would Valtar have gone to perform his little experiment? There's no sign of footprints on the paving stones.

I close my eyes, reaching out with my mind for some sense of him. A prickling of awareness answers me almost at once. Valtar! It must be him, surely. There's a sense of heat, of fire, an impression of hellflame. I stretch out further, deeper, and—

And suddenly, I find myself viewing the world from high in the sky. A patchwork landscape of fields and rolling hills unfolds below me, while chill wind rushes over my hot scales, and updrafts buoy my outstretched wings. I open my mouth, and smoke billows forth in a black cloud.

Startled, I draw back. Just a little, just enough that now I find my awareness floating in the air alongside . . . a dragon. A massive, battle-scarred dragon. His face is turned away from me in profile, and I see the ugly gash where an eye should be.

As though conscious of my scrutiny, he pulls up in midair, churning his wings to maintain a hovering position, like a hawk preparing to strike. His heavy head swings back and forth, his one gold eye searching. A voice of fire appears in my mind: "*Nyxia?*"

I choke and yank my awareness back into my body so hard, I nearly tumble from the gelding's back to land sprawled on the road. A quick grab for the pommel, and I manage to steady myself. My heart tumbles over in my breast. Oh gods. Oh gods above, I should have expected that. And yet somehow I just . . . didn't. The truth is, for all Valtar has been so anxious about pursuit, I simply haven't sensed any dragon presence since Rhyo left. I suppose there's a small part of me that simply didn't believe they were so near.

Shading my eyes, I search the sky. The smoky film is thicker than it was yesterday, but not so thick that I cannot discern the cumulous clouds drifting overhead. No sign of a dragon. Not yet at least. But one could swoop down on me from those clouds at any moment.

I bite my lip. No use in sitting here like a rabbit, waiting to be caught in the hawk's talons. I've got to find Valtar. Now.

I don't dare attempt another mind sweep, however. Instead, gritting my teeth, I turn the gelding's head back the way from which we've come. I simply can't bear the idea of going any closer to Cyran and dragon-held territory on my own. If I don't find Valtar within half an hour, I'll turn around. I'll just have to trust that he stuck to the road and didn't break out into the countryside at some random point along the way.

My stomach knots with dread, tighter with each hoofbeat. Once, a vulture soars overhead, and I choke on a scream. Even when I find the source of the shadow which passed over the road in front of me, I simply can't calm my racing heart.

When I judge that we've come to the half-hour mark, I rein

the gelding in. There's a rise in the road ahead of me, and I can't see what lies beyond it. What if Valtar is just over that rise? After all, his long legs and quick stride could easily outpace this plodding beast I ride. If I don't look, I won't be able to stop thinking about it. I dig my heels into the gelding's sides. The poor animal heaves a heavy sigh and takes a few resentful steps, but he's so slow it infuriates me. "Fine!" I snarl, and slip from the saddle, thudding hard to the ground. "You wait here then."

Not bothering to secure their reins, I leave both horses in the middle of the road, gather my skirts, and spring forward on my own two feet. I'm panting hard by the time I reach the top of the rise. The road stretches on before me, through the valley. I see farmed fields on either side, lined with low stone walls. Nothing else. No sign of any black-cloaked assassin as far as the eye can see.

"Where's your friend?"

Startled, I whirl to my right. There is one of the low walls of stacked stones bordering a newly tilled field. Three men lean against it in various attitudes of repose, smoking long pipes. They wear broad-brimmed hats which cast deep shadows over their features. One stands a little straighter. He's got a sharp-toothed hoe propped against the wall beside him.

I rest one hand against the knife sheath at my belt. "Good morning, gentlemen," I say, forcing a bright smile. "I should like to ask you the same thing, actually. Did you happen to see a fellow come this way yesterday afternoon? Tall, dark, and dangerously good-looking? A bit on the menacing side?"

"Only when he rode by with you," the man with the hoe says. The other two are straightening as well now. One of them knocks his pipe against a stone to empty it. Their eyes never stray from mine. "I remember you," the man adds.

I swallow. Suddenly, my impulsive choice to leave the horses behind strikes me as singularly foolish. Deep down in my gut, fire simmers low, but I'm still so raw from my near burning yesterday, I can't let it rise. Not now.

I force another cheery grin. "Well, if you've not seen him, I'll bid you good day."

As I turn to go, the first man says, "I know what you are."

I stop. *Don't look back*, I tell myself, but the prickling along my neck is too intense to ignore. I turn to discover all three men climbing over the wall.

I don't wait to see more.

Heart in my throat, I break into a run, feet slapping hard against the stones. The men shout behind me, and I know they're giving chase, tools in hand. I need to get to the horses. I need to somehow mount quickly and efficiently . . . which, let's be honest, is not likely to happen. But I won't think about that. I grit my teeth, force myself to run harder.

The horses, however, have their own ideas. At the sight of me and my flying skirts and the three men pursuing, they throw up their heads, uttering little squeals. The dragon smoke in the air has already made them jumpy, and this is just one terror too many. They bolt up the road, leaving me in their dust. I stagger, almost stop, eyes widening and heart thudding in my temples.

"No use trying to run, dracori!" one of the men shouts behind me.

Whirling to face them, I go for my knife, even as another surge of hellfire tries to bubble up inside me. I gasp with pain but manage to force it back down. Drawing my blade, I hold it up between me and the first of the men approaching. "I am *not* dracori!" I snarl as ferociously as I can. Which I suspect is about as effective as a fluffy kitten staring down three hungry wolves.

But the men do slow, their faces wary. One of them, a little younger than the others, says, "Maybe you're not. But your friend certainly is."

I shrug, unable to deny it. Valtar simply looks like a dangerous villain. "It's not his fault," I say. "He didn't choose to be made what he is. And he's fighting it."

"Do you think we care for your excuses?" the first man growls, stalking toward me, that vicious-looking hoe gripped in both hands. "You betrayed all humankind when you turned to the dragons. Dragon spawn, dracori, dragon friend . . . it makes no difference to us."

Another jolt of hellfire in my veins makes me stagger. I nearly drop the knife. My eyelids flutter, green flames licking on the edges of my vision. No, no, *no!* These men won't even get a chance to do whatever it is they have planned. If the fire rises, they'll watch me erupt in flame from the inside and burn alive right in front of them. "Please," I say, my voice choking. "Please, you don't want to do this."

". . . Nyxia?"

"Oh, don't we?" the third man says, his teeth flashing in a grimace.

"Open up your bodice." The first man is close enough now that I can see the pockmarks on his cheeks, scars from a long-ago illness. "Show us your scar, dracori."

I gnash my teeth. "I don't have a scar."

"Then show us what you do have."

I draw a long breath. My wide eyes blink once, and—

I'm up in the sky. Soaring above fields and a winding, snakelike road. My heavy head turns this way and that, searching. I see myself down below, from this disembodied distance, a small figure with bright gold hair, waving a knife at the three large figures lurching toward me.

I see my hand tremble.

See the knife drop.

Suddenly I slam back into my own body, sprawled flat in the middle of the road. My head spins, and hellfire burns up from the depths of my soul. I scream with the pain, more aware of that heat than of the hands grabbing me, tearing the laces of my bodice, rifling under my skirts. I writhe, flail, struggling to suppress the swelling destruction inside me.

"Rutt, she *is* dracori!" one of the men cries. "Look at her eyes!"

"No, she isn't," another replies, ripping the front of my gown open. "No scar, see?"

"Maybe we should let her go."

"Are you a man or aren't you? She's a friend of dragons. We saw her with that dracori yesterday. She deserves what she—"

An enormous rush, like a boulder flying from a siege engine, passes overhead, so fast my confused senses cannot comprehend it. The weight of the first man pinning me to the ground vanishes abruptly, and screams burst in my ears. Off to one side somewhere, there's a gout of hellfire flame. I cannot heed any of this, however. The hellfire burning inside me is too hot, too much. And it's too soon since the last time.

But wait.

I know what to do.

I've done it before. Surely, I can do it again.

Curling into a tight little ball, shuddering, screaming, I reach inside my spirit. Down to that place where white flame burns in the center of my heart. It answers immediately, more ready and willing than last night. I gasp in relief as it floods through me, body and soul, overwhelming the hellfire flames with its purity. The scent of flowers fills my head, and my breathing eases.

It's all over in a few moments. But I continue to lie where I fell, eyes closed, limbs shivering. Slowly, dully, I begin to be aware of other things in the world around me. First, that the men are gone. I don't know where.

Second . . . I'm not alone.

There is a presence. Not just physical, but mental also. Someone is right here, inside my mind with me.

"You're not Nyxia."

I force my eyes open. Paving stones fill my immediate view, but when I lift my gaze a fraction, I see cruel, arched talons.

"And that was not hellfire."

I close my eyes again as a large, hot head lowers toward me, nostrils sniffling curiously.

"What are you?"

I've got to answer. Now. I must pull myself together and face this moment. But I'm still so weak and shaking, and Valtar isn't here to help me. But this is it. This is the moment when I find out . . .

Swallowing painfully, I force my eyes open and look up at the dragon. He's much older than Rhyo; that is obvious from first glance. Bigger too, with powerful muscle definition beneath his hide of reddish-brown scales. His horned face should be terrible, but it has a sort of nobility about it, despite that gash and the gaping eye socket. Tattered wings arch from his shoulders. He's an old veteran of many campaigns. And yet, in that one eye of his, I see open curiosity. Not something I would expect to find in the eye of a dragon.

"I don't remember the last time she wasn't in my mind," he says,

tilting his great head as he contemplates me. "*She's always there—Mother. Even when she's far away. Nyxia keeps the connection alive. But now they're gone, Mother and Nyxia both. And you are here.*"

He lowers his head, and there's threat in his voice when he speaks again. "*Who are you? What are you?*"

I try to speak, but my throat is too raw. So I answer into his mind instead: "*I am your sister.*"

The dragon reels back. His heavy body lumbers awkwardly when not in flight, his spiked tail lashing. He stares down at me with that one eye, shocked speechless. I feel the reverberations of that shock from his soul like pulsing waves.

Slowly, I push myself into a seated position. "*I am Mhoryga's daughter,*" I say, "*but I wasn't born in Mhoryga's flame. I am new. I am different. And . . .*" This is the part that scares me, but it must be said. "*And if you will let me, I will set you free of her.*"

His eye blinks.

Then, suddenly, his dragon form melts away. It's a strange, jerking series of images, painful to behold. He roars as his body convulses, shifts, bones breaking and reknitting in new shapes, while hellfire licks across his flesh, burning away the scales. His roar transforms into a human's bellowing, and when the fire and smoke clear away, a man stands before me. A large, broad man, several decades my senior. His hair is black, and his features remind me vaguely of Valtar. His father was Khylmirian, I suppose. But that one eye of his is gold. Like Mhoryga's eyes. Like mine.

He shakes himself and drops his head to look at his own body. His throat tightens, and he turns his own hands, staring at them wonderingly. "I . . . I have not worn this form in . . . in a long while." His voice shakes, still growling, green flames flashing from his tongue. After a fraught silence, he adds, "I thought I'd forgotten."

I take a moment to glance around. Not far from us, smoldering corpses lie in the road. I quickly turn my head away again, stomach knotting with horror at the vicious deaths those men died. I don't quite know how to feel. They were afraid of dracori . . . but they were more than willing to harm me, whether I was dracori or not. Did that make them monsters equal to the fiery fiend which slew them?

Finally I turn to the man—my brother—again. "What is your name?" I ask, speaking the words out loud.

"Dragon," he answers at once. Then he frowns and shakes his head. "No. No, I am . . . I was . . . Rhangyl. Rhangyl Oladithas." He speaks the name as though he hardly believes it.

"I'm Rosie Harpwood," I answer. "Or Roselle Pandracor. I'm still not certain which."

"Pandracor?" he repeats, his gaze sharpening.

And suddenly I hear another voice in my head, a memory. *Pandracor*, King Alderin had said, smiling at me when he spoke. *It means* end of dragons. *That is what you will be, my child. The end of the terror which has gripped this world for two centuries.*

I draw a slow breath, straightening my shoulders, and meet the dragon's eye. "Rhangyl," I say firmly, "I intend to overthrow Mhoryga and set our brothers free. But to do so, I'm going to need help. A lot of help. More help, I suspect, than I even know. I think *you* know, however. I think *you* know exactly how powerful Mhoryga is, how great are her forces. How impossible overthrowing her may be. So let me ask you this: Knowing what you do, will you help me?"

He gapes at me, as though struggling to understand my words. Finally he says, "How many do you have on your side?"

"I have . . . had . . . will have . . ." I clench my fists tight. "One dracori."

Rhangyl's lip curls. I feel a rush of hatred ripple out from him. For the first time, I understand how the dragon spawn feel about the dracori, who ride them and abuse them and treat them like animals. After all, the dragon spawn had no choice in their making, but the dracori chose to undergo transformation. Rhangyl, now that he's free to feel anything at all, hates them.

"He's not like that," I say, answering his unspoken thought. "He's on our side. He's risked everything to help me, and . . . and . . . and I'm not sure what happened to him." I swallow hard and force myself to add, "He might be dead."

Another rush of thought bursts from Rhangyl's mind: "*Betrayal, betrayal, betrayal!*"

"No!" I get to my feet, holding the ripped laces of my bodice closed with one hand. My knees try to buckle, but I brace myself. "He would never betray me. Something has happened to him. I've got to find him." I bite my lip then, afraid to ask even as I know I must. "Will you help me?"

Rhangyl looks around at the lonely countryside, then up at the sky overhead. When he looks at me again at last, he says, "There are dragon spawn and dracori everywhere. It won't be easy."

"Are there others like you? Who wish to be free of Mhoryga?"

"I don't know. I've been so deeply under her compulsion, I didn't know how badly *I* wanted freedom until . . . almost this very moment." He moves his broad shoulders in a half shrug. "The others might feel the same if given the chance."

I reach out to his mind again. He flinches, and I realize suddenly how easy it would be—to slip into his head, to make him join me. To force him into my service. But I don't want that.

"*If you cannot help me, Rhangyl,*" I speak into his head, "*I understand. But I must find my friend. I cannot delay.*"

I withdraw now and physically turn away from him. Staggering on unsteady feet, I begin to make my way up the road in the direction we traveled yesterday. Toward Cyran. There's a burst of heat behind me, and my heart leaps. I wonder momentarily if my brother is about to blast me to oblivion, now that my back is turned. After all, to him, I must seem like any other tyrant.

But the final eruption of fire does not come. Instead, the ground vibrates as a heavy body lumbers up the road behind me. Soon Rhangyl, once more in dragon form, falls in at my side. He does not speak for some while, and I'm still too frightened to find any words. We walk together in silence.

Then he says, *"I could carry you, if you like. We could search for him from the air."*

I bite my lip. I remember riding Rhyo when we escaped Stromin. Even wrapped in Valtar's hellfire-proof cloak, it was almost too hot for me to bear. But I didn't have phoenix flame at my disposal then.

The dragon swings his head, peering at me with his one good eye. I grin up at him, a sudden rush of hope in my chest, and say, "I've got an idea."

12

Nyxia

Seven days. Seven long, excruciating, pointless days since her scout returned to her, claiming to have spotted Valtar and her dragon sister. Seven days since she flew with her small contingent of dracori and dragon spawn to this very lake, only to find the remnants of a hellfire blaze and . . . nothing else.

Seven days since every scout she's sent out has returned without so much as a glimpse to report. It's like they vanished from this world entirely.

"Rutting *hells*," Nyxia snarls. With a powerful but poorly aimed kick, she sends a shore stone flying across the lake to splash harmlessly in the midst of a flock of geese. The birds honk and flap in their haste to retreat from an unseen attacker, but when no more dire threat appears, swiftly subside into the same paddling calm, unconcerned by what they cannot see or sense.

Nyxia's lip curls. She stands on the edge of the lake, murky water lapping at the toes of her boots. Lifting one arm, she points her talon-tipped fingers, imagining a bolt of pure hellfire shooting straight from her palm. In her mind's eye, she can just about see it, the funnel of flaming destruction, channeled with deadly accuracy. Taking out first one, then the next, then the next of those offensive fowl, until the air stinks with burnt flesh and feathers. No fire leaps in response to her summoning, however. Not even the faintest simmering of heat in her gut.

Footsteps sound on the rocky shoreline behind her, moments before an arm drapes with casual affection about her shoulder. "Too bad, sister mine," a deep voice growls close to her ear. "Craving a little goose dinner, eh? I can get that for you, if you like. What's your preference—slow roasted or charred?"

Nyxia turns to the young dragon man beside her. Zoar—her brother. He wears his human form just now, revealing his youth. At nineteen, four years her junior, he's much younger than she would usually choose for personal dragon-spawn mount. His features are only just beginning to harden from boyish roundness into manhood, and his mouth has not yet acquired that line of ferocious cruelty common in his kind. But despite herself, Nyxia has developed a certain fondness for him, something she's never felt for any of her other brother beasts. Perhaps it's his determined refusal to ever show fear in her presence. He does fear her, of course; they all do. As well they should. But sometimes it's nice to pretend.

Meeting his teasing gaze now, Nyxia scowls. Zoar is the only person in her life permitted to even subtly reference her lack of manifested flame. He knows she could punish him severely for this disrespect if she so chose, but he continues to grin at her in that lopsided way of his, one brow slightly upraised.

In lieu of an answer, Nyxia shrugs off his arm, crouches, swipes up a small, smooth stone, turns, and hurtles it across the water. Her precision is lethal; the stone strikes the largest of the geese dead in the eye. It drops in the water without sound or flutter, while the other geese go on swimming nearby, unaware of the murder which just took place in their midst.

Nyxia turns a simpering smile at her brother. "I can manage my own geese, thank you." She then turns to another dragon, lounging nearby. This one is a bit younger than Zoar, a boy on his first deployment, little more than a child. "You," Nyxia calls sharply.

The dragon spawn lifts the arm he's flung over his face to ward off the sun and peers at her warily. Nyxia casts about momentarily for his name. Rhyo was it? She's never made a point to learn most of her brothers' names. There are so many of them, and they simply don't interest her beyond their basic function as beasts of burden. "Go fetch that goose for me."

Immediately, the dragon boy gets to his feet and sets out at a trot around the lake. Nyxia sighs. She probably should have specified that she meant for him to take dragon form and fly, but then again, they don't want to be too conspicuous.

"You know, sister mine," Zoar says, crouched on the shore and picking up stones, testing their weight and shape for skipping, "you're fooling yourself if you think a little goose slaughter is going to work out what ails you. There's a nice town just a few miles thataway." He tosses his head in indication, then shoots Nyxia another of his sly grins. "What do you say to a spot of cottage burning? There's nothing cheers your soul more than the sight of a thatched-roof bonfire."

Nyxia shoots him a dark look. "You know as well as I, we're too deep into enemy territory and too far from reinforcements to make it worthwhile." While the town certainly didn't look as though it had much in the way of defenses, one never could know for certain. While she could bear the loss of a handful of dracori and even a dragon spawn or two, she must be careful with her own life. She is too important to Mother, serving as her eyes, ears, and mind channel on this side of the ocean. Were Mhoryga at the height of her strength, she wouldn't need to use a surrogate to hold sway over her children and creations. But since Nyxia proved such a disappointment, failing to manifest and provide the burning heart Mhoryga required, the Dragon Queen's powers are not what they might be. She needs her daughter, using her like an extension of herself, and Nyxia is only too glad to be useful. But that means she can't take unnecessary risks.

With a sigh, Nyxia turns from Zoar, gazing out across the lake once more to where her murdered goose bobs forlornly on the waves. "Do you think they were really here?" she asks musingly.

Zoar doesn't have to ask whom she means. "We did find signs of hellfire," he says. "Unless some other dracori bastard is out enjoying a solo cross-country trip, I would bet good money it was them."

Nyxia worries her bottom lip. Ever since that last communication with Valtar, she's been sending scouts hunting after him, desperate to catch both him and her damnable sister. At first they'd struggled to pick up any trace of them, but then one of her scouts returned, claiming to have glimpsed both Valtar and a golden-haired girl bathing in this very lake. Finally it seemed she was going to get the break she deserved. No such luck.

Golden hair . . . Nyxia turns the idea around in her head, oddly discomfited by the idea. All these years, she's never imagined Naevya with golden hair. When she was little, she used to make dolls to represent her long-lost sister, always black haired like herself. They were twins, after all—two eggs born in the same clutch. A never-before-heard-of occurrence for dragon princesses, who were always hatched solo. When picturing Naevya, Nyxia had envisioned her ideal companion, as like to herself as a reflection. The missing piece of her half-formed self. *Two hearts, one flame.*

But no. She's nothing but a cursed little golden-haired foreigner, taking after their damned father, no doubt. No wonder she too has proven a failure, incapable of wielding hellflame.

"Where did they go?" she grits between her teeth. Her gold eyes scan the sky, searching for the thousandth time that day for a glimpse of her scouts. It's been more than a week now since they had any trace worth pursuing. How did Valtar manage it? How did he make her sister simply *vanish*?

Nyxia's fingers curl into fists. Damn him. Damn that man to the fieriest depths of hell. Sometimes she wonders if he cares about Arun at all. If he did, he wouldn't keep failing Mhoryga like he does.

She closes her eyes—and for a moment, she's back sixteen years earlier, a small child once more, crouched just inside the doorway of her mother's throne room. Her ears are filled with Arun's screams. In that moment, Nyxia came the closest to hating Mhoryga that she ever has before or since. It was a terrifying thing for a child, whose very existence was founded on being her mother's daughter. In the aftermath, her soul wrestled with her own blasphemy. In the end, she could only cast herself upon the knowledge that there was nothing else Mother could have done. She *must* punish Valtar for his disobedience, mustn't she? But she couldn't very well damage one of her own dracori, not when she'd poured so much of her own fiery blood into him. He had a purpose to fulfill, a purpose which would be compromised if he weren't well and whole.

So Arun was forced to suffer. There was no other way.

But why couldn't Valtar ever learn? Damn him, why did he continue to hesitate, to falter, to stumble? Why did he cause Arun pain upon pain? Arun doesn't deserve it. He's never done wrong in his whole life. Nyxia presses a hand to her heart, an unconscious gesture in reaction to the sudden stabbing pain there. The last time she'd seen Arun was just before the invasion of Cyran, a year ago. Mother had permitted her to visit him in his cell, down in the dark holdings beneath Heleris Stronghold. She'd pushed open the door, stepping into the darkness where the blind man was kept, her dragon eyes only just able to discern his crumpled shape.

And yet, though she did not speak a word or give any sign to betray her identity, Arun had lifted his eyeless face and called out, "Is that you, little fierceness?"

It was the nickname he'd given her, back when she was still a child living in the same prison tower where he used to be kept captive. She'd begun to visit him often after their first encounter, making the perilous climb down the tower wall to his balcony. There they would sit together, legs outstretched, and watch the green fires of Mount Dracor burning from across the Rothomir Wastes. Those were Nyxia's happiest times, basking in the presence of the only kind soul she'd ever met in her life. He told her stories, made her laugh. They shared little jokes between them.

And every time Mhoryga ripped away some other part of his body, it was Nyxia who found him, bandaged him with bits of her own clothing, and sat with him for days and nights on end until the shudders passed.

She draws a long breath through her nostrils now, opening her eyes and staring out across the lake once more. She would give anything to protect Arun. Anything at all. She wouldn't be like Valtar. She would spare him all hurts, ensuring that the rest of his existence was free of suffering. Why couldn't Valtar be like that? Why must he continue to fail so miserably? Rutting hells, but she'd like to tear *his* eyes out with her own talons! And what will happen if Valtar doesn't return soon? If he doesn't bring Naevya's heart as commanded? Will Mhoryga follow through on her final threat? Will she kill Arun at last?

"No," Nyxia whispers. "I can't let that happen. I won't."

She will find Valtar. She will find both him and her damnable sister. She'll rip out Naevya's heart herself, if only . . . Oh gods, if only she can get her to manifest her flame first! A flameless heart won't help Mhoryga. If they bring home a heart as useless as her own proved to be, Mhoryga will probably kill Arun anyway.

"Come on, you worthless, half-formed thing," she mutters in a voice so akin to Mhoryga's, one might think her mother spoke through her mouth. "Prove your worth. Make this right. Bring home a prize fit for a goddess. Then maybe—"

"Well, look what the demon dragged in," Zoar says abruptly.

Nyxia turns sharply to see her brother pointing to the sky. She looks up. A little thrill of dread knots in her stomach. It's a dragon spawn: not one of her contingent but one of those she'd left behind in Cyran. Her brow setting with concentration, Nyxia sends a bolt of thought streaking out from her. "*What are you doing out here?*"

The dragon spawn flinches and drops low in the sky before recovering his balance and a little altitude. He begins a wide circle of the lake. "*I have news from Cyran,*" he answers, his voice shrinking with fear. "*Valtar Skylock has been captured.*"

"*What?*" The word bursts from Nyxia's head like a knife into the dragon's skull.

The dragon spawn utters a cry of pain, once more dropping

in the sky. With a powerful surge of wings, he manages to keep from falling entirely and continues soaring over the lake. "*He is being held in chains by the Lady of Cyran. She sends her greetings and would like to know if—*"

"*Does he have my rutting sister with him?*"

The dragon hesitates, and in that hesitation, Nyxia guesses the answer to come. "*No.*"

A scream of rage and frustration bursts from Nyxia's throat. She shoots another bolt along the mental connection, stabbing the dragon spawn's mind with such violence, his wings fold up, and he drops like a stone. His large dragon body splashes into the lake, wings flapping feebly as his own weight drags him down.

"Get him," Nyxia barks, motioning to two of the dracori standing on alert nearby. They exchange short glances. "*Get him!*" she repeats, sending a mental lash their way. "I can't afford to lose dragons right now."

The dracori leap into motion, diving into the frigid water to reclaim the fallen dragon, who has already taken human form now, but continues to struggle. Trusting they'll drag him out before he drowns, Nyxia turns to Zoar, still lounging on the shore beside her. "It's time we paid a little visit to Cyran," she says.

Zoar answers with a grin, green flames licking through his teeth.

13

Rosie

A thin film of white fire covers my body from head to toe. At first it was difficult to maintain the proper balance; it kept snuffing out in slight breezes, or else blazing so bright and hot, I couldn't see through the flames. A few hours of practice, though, and I seem to have gotten the knack of it. Wrapped in this flame, I am far better protected from hellfire heat than I was when shrouded in Valtar's dracori cloak.

Rhangyl doesn't like it. The big dragon had flared his nostrils and stamped his big, clawed feet uneasily when I first demonstrated my unique form of fire and presented my idea to him. Dragons do not fear burning, but he looked very much as though he thought this fire of mine would scorch right through his scales. Upon tentative experimentation, however, we found that, while my flame protected me from his searing heat, it did not seem to have any negative effect on him. Reluctantly, he allowed me to climb onto his back.

And so I find myself, for the second time in my life, flying through the sky, high above the world. Were I not so anxious about finding Valtar, I would say this experience is far more pleasant than the last one. Then, I was both too overcome with the pain of Rhyo's radiating heat and the shock of Alderin's startling revelations to pay much attention to the flight itself.

Now, I'm aware of a certain strange sense of *rightness.* The sensation of wind blowing through my hair, tossing little tongues of white fire behind me like banners, feels natural somehow. I'm half tempted to spread my arms wide, to leap from Rhangyl's back, and see where the air currents may carry me. A rational side of my brain, still clinging to reality, knows what the answer would be: straight down, bringing an abrupt end to all my heroic plans and this pathetic little saga in which I find myself a central figure.

But another, wilder side of me whispers, *You were born to fly.*

Rhangyl performs broad sweeps of the countryside. His wings tilt into the updrafts, soaring and easy, but I feel the tremendous power within him. He is all muscle and fire, a true fiend incarnate. Yet this side of him is no more real than the man who'd stood before me down on the ground below, gazing at me with such shock. It's difficult to fathom our connection. *Brother*—the word is so strange to an orphan like me, bereft of all family. After all these years, it's nice to know that I share blood with another being in this world. Even if the blood we share happens to be of demonic origin.

Clinging to spines, I straddle Rhangyl's back and peer over his shoulders, searching the landscape below us for some sign of Valtar. The optimism with which we began this venture has slowly faded over the last hour. Rhangyl has covered so much territory, and yet I still cannot seem to catch a trace of the man.

After what feels like forever, Rhangyl suddenly speaks in my mind: "*I smell hellfire. Below.*"

Eagerly, I sit up a little higher on his back to get a better angle over his shoulder. At first I spy nothing, just the winding road below us. Then I spot it: a patch of ground scorched black from some great conflagration. A stink of sulfur rises to my nostrils, causing my stomach to turn. No sign of Valtar anywhere. Nor any dracori or dragon spawn.

"*Fly a little lower*," I urge. I'm not sure what I'm looking for, but I can't get a strong impression of the site from this height. Rhangyl obliges, easing into a wide, circular descent. I crane my neck as we swoop past the burnt ground and blackened paving stones of that portion of the road. Something gleams, catching my eye.

My heart leaps to my throat and lodges there.

"*Down, Rhangyl!*" I command, forgetting in that moment to maintain his option for choice. The need to get closer, to discover the truth of what I think I'm seeing is simply too great. Rhangyl tosses his head, distressed at the sharpness of my voice in his head, but obliges at once. He alights on the road several yards from the edge of the burnt patch, and I slip from his back at once. Still wearing the sheen of white fire, I hasten forward, drop to my knees, and reach out to claim the small object I'd spied from above.

It's a knife. One of Valtar's knives. I've seen his collection many times by now, both in practice and in moments of violence. While some part of me tries to insist this knife could belong to anyone, somehow I *know* it is his. But Valtar would not leave behind one of his knives so carelessly. Never. Which means . . . which means . . .

I clutch the hilt of the blade, press it between my breasts. Feel the line of steel lying against my sternum. It's still hot, heated through with hellfire in the midst of some confrontation. Valtar fought here, valiantly. But did he win? Or was he . . . is he . . . ?

A snort of hot breath against the back of my neck. I close my eyes but do not turn to face Rhangyl. Shudders of dread rack my body. It's all I can do just to hold myself together.

"*Is it his?*" Rhangyl asks inside my mind. "*Your friend's?*"

I nod.

Rhangyl is silent for some moments. Then, in strangely gentle tones for one who speaks with a voice of pure fire: "*Who was he, exactly? This dracori who means so much to you?*"

I bite my lip. "*His name was . . . is . . . Valtar Skylock.*"

A spark of interest communicates from Rhangyl's soul to mine. It's so bright, I lift my head and turn to the dragon. He peers one-eyed down at me, his gaze fixed on the hilt of the blade. "*Nyxia sent a dragon to Cyran three days ago,*" he says eagerly. "*She gave orders that if anyone encountered a dracori by the name of Valtar Skylock, he was to be taken prisoner, and word sent immediately to her.*"

My blood runs cold. Even the phoenix flame, which I have sustained for more than an hour now, flickers out of existence, abandoning me in this space of frozen dread.

Nyxia.

She's coming. The dracori of Cyran have taken Valtar prisoner, and now Nyxia is coming for him. And what will she do to him when she gets here? How will she punish him for his failure to obey her and, subsequently, Mhoryga? I may be new to this mind-control power of mine, but I've inadvertently caused Valtar pain even so. How much worse must it be when this power is wielded by someone who knows how to use it and has no reason to hold back the hurt she inflicts?

"I've got to find him." I speak the words out loud, a whisper but full of force. Then I meet Rhangyl's one eye and say more firmly, "You've got to take me to him!"

The dragon shakes his ugly head, his expression almost human. "*I can't.*"

I get to my feet, Valtar's dagger still clutched in my hands. Temptation burns inside me with a force akin to hellfire—temptation to give commands, to take control. I could do it. I could force Rhangyl to my will here and now. I could forget that he is my brother and make use of him as the beast I see before me.

I drag a slow breath into my lungs, hold it there. When I breathe out, it isn't the heat of hellfire which licks across my tongue, but the healing warmth of white flame. I won't give in. Not now. Not yet. "You know where they would take him," I say. "If they have indeed captured him, you know where he would be brought."

Rhangyl hesitates, waiting, perhaps, for compulsion to come over him. When it doesn't, he gives his head a little shake. "*They would bring him to the Lady of Cyran.*"

"Who is that?"

Another pause followed by another flicker of surprise. Then, abruptly, Rhangyl's dragon form melts away, and the man stands before me once more. He staggers a little to catch his balance, unused to this smaller, lighter form, though for a man, he is quite large and broad. He turns a solemn look upon me, studying me closely with his one gold eye. Finally, he answers: "When we invaded Cyran last year, we took prisoners among the humans of higher rank. They were forced to undergo the dracori transformation, drinking Nyxia's blood in lieu of Mhoryga's. Not many survived. But the Lady of Cyran did and subsequently succumbed to the compulsion of the Dragon Queen. When Nyxia quit the city some months ago, she left the Lady in charge."

"In charge?" I repeat. "What does that mean exactly? Are not all the dracori and dragon spawn under thrall to Mhoryga via Nyxia?"

"Yes," Rhangyl acknowledges. "But when neither is present to enforce specific commands, the thrall is left rather . . . generalized. Mhoryga cannot maintain absolute control over all of us from across the ocean. When Nyxia is present, Mhoryga's access to our minds is stronger, but without Nyxia, the link is fainter than ever. Instead, she channels tremendous power into a single mind—the Lady of Cyran. While my fellow dragon spawn and the dracori are under a broad compulsion to obey the Lady as we would Mhoryga herself, the Lady receives more specific commands and acts as Mhoryga's avatar in Cyran."

I mull over this information. It's difficult to focus with the need for action bubbling in my veins. But I must not act rashly if I'm going to save Valtar. "The dracori of Cyran," I say at last, "those created after the invasion . . . they were not willingly transformed, were they?"

Rhangyl shrugs. "There are always some more willing than others. In the case of the Lady, I truly don't know. You must understand, I'm not a figure of any consequence in Cyran. I am little more than a pack mule." The bitter words fall from his lips with a shower of green sparks.

I look down at Valtar's knife, turning it in my hands. The beginnings of an idea are forming in my mind. Not a good idea, I suspect. In fact, I'm almost certain it's a bad one. Very bad indeed, something to make Valtar throw up his hands in despair. But it's all I've got . . . and if this Lady of Cyran has indeed sent for Nyxia, we don't have much time. I've got to find Valtar, break him free, and flee this place before her arrival. Unless . . . unless . . .

"Could you get me to this Lady of Cyran?" I ask, looking up at Rhangyl.

He shakes his head. "I am not permitted anywhere near the Lady's stronghold."

"But you know where it is."

I sense something in his mind in response. Though I hate to invade his privacy, I can't help pushing a little deeper. A picture appears before me of a great palace on a hill, a long hall with a tower at the western end, and a huge rose window facing east. Within that hall, seated on a lonely stone chair is a figure—small, upright, grasping the arms of the chair with ironhard fingers. She sits in rigid concentration, trapped in a mind link with a monster an ocean away. Never moving, never resting. Perpetual subjugation. Green fire burns in her eyes, sustains her body, and drives her ever deeper into madness.

I pull back from the dreadful vision, shaking my head. Panting a little, I raise my gaze to Rhangyl's once more. He looks at me with tremendous sorrow and solemnity. "That's where she is?" I whisper. "In that hall?"

"Always," Rhangyl replies. "Her connection to Mhoryga is tenuous. She must remain in a constant state of concentration to maintain it."

"Then we can reach her."

But here my dragon brother shakes his head vehemently. "She is guarded at all times. Did you not see it? There are scores of dracori lining the walls of that chamber, and dragon spawn patrol the skies above."

I set my jaw against the force of his words and, more powerful, the wave of fear pulsing from his very soul. I don't want to let his fear drag me down. Valtar is counting on me. And unless some sudden burst of inspiration strikes soon, this is the only plan I've got.

"How close do you think you could get me before anyone began to question you?"

Rhangyl considers this, his brow knotted tight. "If you think you can keep the dragon spawn out of my mind, I may be able to get you as far as the hall itself before they realize what is happening. Once we're inside, I can make no promises."

I turn from him, pace a little way down the road. My eyes gaze ahead, off to the northwestern horizon, in the direction I know Cyran lies. A haze of smoke lies thick on the rim of my view, but I can feel it nonetheless—that sense of drawing, that pull toward others of my kind.

If I make it into that stronghold, if I breach the Lady's mind, will I be able to shatter Mhoryga's tentative control? And if so, what then? I cannot guarantee that the dragon spawn and dracori will turn to me instead. Perhaps, under their compulsion of obedience, they will continue to obey the Lady herself. But if I cannot win her over, all will surely be lost.

She's only one mind, I tell myself, desperate to bolster my courage.

But she's a mind in direct link to Mhoryga, another part of me whispers.

Mhoryga. The great queen. The devouring force, come into this world with fire and devastation, intent upon ultimate dominion. I am not ready to face her—neither in person nor in the realm of the mind. I've had just a few days of lessons with Valtar and didn't fare particularly well in any of them. How could I possibly hope to wrestle with a spirit as old and steeped in flame and malice as the Dragon Queen?

But the moments are slipping away, and each moment brings Nyxia closer. Once my sister is here, wielding her confident control over dracori and dragon spawn alike, we will be lost indeed. Breaching the stronghold of the Lady of Cyran may be next to impossible, but as long as there's a chance, I've got to take it.

"Rhangyl," I say, turning to him once more. I look him in the eye and, very carefully, purposefully, refuse to let myself enter his head even the slightest bit. "Rhangyl, will you carry me on your back to the stronghold of the Lady? Will you take this risk with me?"

He lifts his chin slightly, his expression forbidding. But when he speaks, he says only, "This dracori . . . he means that much to you, does he?"

I nod. I dare not trust my voice.

Rhangyl breathes out through his nostrils, emitting two streams of black smoke. "Very well," he says, his voice a low growl. "I'll bear you to Cyran. If we die in a blaze of glory, so be it. At least we will die free."

A JOURNEY THAT would have taken days on horseback is but a few hours by dragon wing. Maintaining the constant protection of the phoenix, I soar with Rhangyl high above the Kingdom of Albhia, taking in whole towns at a glance before leaving them behind in the smoky atmosphere.

I crouch low, holding tight to two protruding horns, and wish I could take back every negative thought I ever had for that poor gray gelding of mine. Whatever discomfort I may have experienced in the saddle is nothing compared to the bizarre experience of sitting astride a dragon's back. Various knobs and spines dig into my flesh. I don't know how the dracori make it look so easy!

Though they do have their leather suits for protection. I wonder if they utilize some sort of flying saddle; I've never been close enough to see.

Far too soon, the towers of Cyran City appear on the horizon, wreathed in dragon smoke dense as fog. The city sits above the River Cy and is a grand sight indeed, dazzling to my countrified eyes. It's built sprawling along the river, with the great stronghold Eirbalar—our destination—perched on a cliff overlooking the lower, lesser buildings. The architectural lines are graceful, but a black cloud of poisonous fumes hovers over all, transforming this little mortal paradise into a hellscape.

My heart turns over at the sight. I remember how fondly Lord Elis spoke of his home, the sorrow in his voice when he told me of the invasion. *My sister was killed during the assault*, he'd said, his words limned with mourning. *Enya is her name*—was *her name.* Though he had held on to his lively and audacious nature, full of smiles and mischief and a readiness to laugh at the world around him, the occupation of Cyran weighed heavily on Elis's soul. He volunteered to participate in the champion trials in hopes that I, of all people, would prove the means to liberate his home.

Now here I am. Flying toward Cyran on the back of a dragon. What would Elis think if he could see me now? If he hadn't lost his life in the dark caverns below Stromin, struggling with his last breath to prove himself worthy as my champion? Would he cheer in the face of my audaciousness or beg me to stop, to consider? Not to let my feelings for Valtar drive me too soon into a confrontation for which I am wholly unprepared.

I set my shoulders, bowing lower over Rhangyl's sinuous neck. My course is set now. I won't turn back.

The dragon-spawn voices begin to appear on the edges of my awareness. I felt them at a distance hours ago. Now, as we draw nearer to the city, and I begin to discern the dark bodies of my brothers patrolling the air above the towers and along the river, they grow more difficult to suppress. In dragon shape as they are, their minds are filled primarily with fire, little trace of their human personalities to be discerned.

Valtar and I have not practiced shielding my mind against their awareness, but Rhangyl claims that he would not have noticed me had I not reached out with my mind, accidentally touching him in my search for Valtar. He believes as long as I keep very quiet and still, we can slip through most of the airborne force without drawing undue attention. It will seem to them as though he is merely a scout on his way to give report to the Lady.

The nearer we come to the stronghold, however, the tighter security will grow. Those dragons nearest to the Lady's seat will certainly question Rhangyl . . . and will notice the rider on his back. I'm keeping my white flame as low as possible, but I won't be able to hide it from overt scrutiny. And what will we do when they inevitably move to interfere with our progress?

Rhangyl's voice burns in my memory: *Then we fly like hell itself is on our heels.*

I tuck my soul in tight, trying to block out the voices of the dragon spawn. There are so many of them—an overwhelming number. The most I've ever seen at once were the dragons which attacked my home village on the night Durona died, but that was only a small company. This is an entire invasion force, flown across the ocean to carve out Mhoryga's first solid foothold in Belanor. There are hundreds of dragons here—both up in the sky and down in the city below. All burning, all raging. All filled with hatred for their own existence. I fear them and I ache for them simultaneously. My brothers—my poor, enslaved, hopeless brothers.

We are drawing closer now. Rhangyl turns slowly, aware of my presence on his back and my lack of experience with flight. Were I a trained dracori, I would crouch and even stand as he performed the wildest maneuvers, never once losing my balance. I am not dracori, however, and though I do not fear heights, neither do I particularly care to fall to a splattering end on the peaked rooftops below.

I focus my eyes on Eirbalar Stronghold up above the river, picking out the long hall and the tower on its western end. That is our destination, so close and yet still so far. And at least a dozen large dragon spawn circle directly above it, a threatening formation.

One of these takes note of our coming. He peels out of formation and flies toward Rhangyl. I feel his mind reaching out, both curious and threatening. He has not noticed my presence yet, but it's only a matter of time. Another joins him, and they angle their wings until they flank us, one on each side. I peer over Rhangyl's wings and find one of them looking directly at me.

A fiery voice scratches on the edge of my mind: "*What is that?*"

Rhangyl doesn't answer. He redoubles his pace. The dragons speed up, keeping pace with him, and the larger one moves to force Rhangyl off course, turning him away from the stronghold. I hear dragon voices roaring in my head, but for the moment cannot understand them clearly. Is it possible for me to do what Valtar said? To reach out and simply order them to leave? If I do, I'll betray my true nature. Perhaps I could undo the compulsion binding them? My mere presence in his mind was enough to free

Rhangyl. Surely it wouldn't take any more for these dragons, and I could—

Suddenly the smaller of the two dragons rolls, opens his mouth, and shoots a bolt of green fire. As though he expected it, Rhangyl banks abruptly, and only the death grip I already had on his horns prevents me from being flung out into midair. My stomach left somewhere behind me, I cling with all my might, choking on a scream. Rhangyl moves with dizzying agility for a creature of his size, eluding the blast of flame which would not hurt him but would burn right through me. Our stealthy approach is at an end, however, so there's no further need for me to keep my phoenix flame suppressed.

With a wrench of effort, I pull the white fire up around me, burning brighter than before. Not a moment too soon—the second dragon opens fire, a great wall of green flame that engulfs Rhangyl and would certainly have scorched my flesh down to the bone. Even through the protective shield of white flame, I feel the heat of it.

"*Rhangyl!*" I cry desperately. He roars in response and takes another sharp angle. I cling to his back like a spider, my senses so overwhelmed, I cease to feel anything, even fear. There's nothing but the need to hold on and hold on and hold on some more.

Another dragon appears on our right, streaking toward us, his mouth gaping, green fire mounding in his throat. In a moment of impulse, I lash out with my mind: "*Stop!*"

To my surprise, the dragon spawn jerks. His flame flies wildly over my head, missing Rhangyl entirely. Our attacker's wings seem to fold up, and he drops. I try to turn my head, to see where he went, but Rhangyl banks again, and I'm carried far out of sight.

More dragons are closing in. Too many for Rhangyl to elude.

He rolls and pivots miraculously, more nimbly than I would have credited for such a large beast, but hampered by my presence on his back. We're not going to make it through this throng, unless . . . unless . . .

I reach out again, wildly, and catch hold of the largest mind close at hand. A big, old, silver-scaled dragon, who bears down upon us with mouth agape, as though intending to snap Rhangyl's spine and swallow me whole while he's at it. Hardly knowing what I'm doing, acting on instinct more than thought, I throw out a command.

The silver dragon never hesitates. He angles his wings ever so slightly, altering his course. He crashes into two other dragons, grappling with them both, claws tearing, jaws ripping. Have I sent him to slaughter his own brothers in a fount of fiery blood? Too late to second-guess my decision—Rhangyl has already carried me beyond them, through the gap I've effectively created in defense of him.

A vision of pink and gold flashes before me. Vaguely I realize that we are flying down, aiming straight for a huge window of stained glass in an elaborate design. My eyes widen briefly, and only an impulse of self-preservation causes me to close them at the last second and duck my head down under my own arm. Rhangyl crashes through the panes. Shards of glass whip past my skin, tearing garments and flesh alike.

Then we're tumbling to the stone floor. Rhangyl hits it hard, body coiling and crumpling as his wings slap against marble. I fly from his back, hit the ground, and roll in a tumble of limbs and glass and tongues of white flame. For a few moments, I'm too stunned to think. My head is full of dragon voices—roaring, screaming, wailing, raging. Blackness dances on the edges of my vision, and when it starts to clear, it's replaced with green flames. Somewhere behind me, I hear Rhangyl's voice, but I don't understand what he's trying to say.

I pull myself upright. Everything hurts, but nothing seems to be broken. The white fire surrounding me must have protected my limbs, which otherwise should have shattered along with the window. More bursts of hellfire erupt on the edges of my vision, but when I manage to get my head up, to look straight in front of me . . . I see a face I know.

Elis?

But no. I shake my head and look again. It isn't Lord Elis before me, though the mop of light brown curls and the wide-set hazel eyes are terribly familiar. It is a young woman. Younger than Elis, but not by much. Despite the disturbance in her hall, she sits on her chair of red marble stone, clutching the arms with white-knuckled fingers, staring down at me intently, with no regard for anything else.

She blinks—and green fire sparks in her eyes.

I realize suddenly that Elis was wrong when he told me his sister had died in the invasion. Or perhaps he knew the truth and simply didn't want to admit it. Didn't want to acknowledge that Enya Balxidon had become what he loathed and feared most in this world: dracori.

The Lady unfastens her fingers from the chair and rises, standing over me where I crouch. Her hands twist, and hellfire appears at her fingertips. I pull myself upright, vaguely aware of Rhangyl behind me. But he is fighting for his life against three dragon spawn, who have pursued him through the broken window. He cannot help me. I am alone here before this woman. Before Enya, the Lady of Cyran.

"Who are you?" she demands in a voice of fire and brimstone, scarcely human. Green sparks fall from her lips. "Who are you that you dare breach the sanctity of my hall?"

"Enya," I gasp, and push up from my knees onto my feet. My legs are trembling so hard, I can scarcely keep upright. But at the sound of that name, the woman stops. Her eyes widen.

Then hellfire bursts from her eye sockets, and flames pour from her tongue. The blast shoots directly at me, and I only just have time to put up both arms, wreathed in phoenix flame, in defense. The bolt of hellfire strikes hard, but my white flame deflects it. Then we stand again, facing each other. The young woman breathes hard, nostrils flaring.

A fiery voice appears directly inside my head: "*I know who you are, my child. You've come back to me at last.*"

I reel back a step, the breath knocked from my lungs. That voice . . . I've heard it before. In Valtar's memory, when he sat bound to that chair, and the demon goddess he both worshipped and loathed towered over him and dug her talons into his exposed arms.

Mhoryga.

"*You know me, I see,*" the voice of fire speaks again, crackling in my mind. "*That is good. For you must know as well how fruitless this little rebellion of yours must ultimately be.*"

I stagger back another step, heart pounding, hands trembling. The white flame of the phoenix flickers in my hands, but I'm too frightened in this moment to know what to do with it.

"*Now,*" says my mother, speaking through her avatar, "*surrender to the hellfire. Manifest your true flame at last and prepare to fulfill your purpose.*"

The Lady raises both hands. Green fire sparks to life between her fingers, then surges toward me in a funnel of fury. I get my arms up just in time, crossing them before my face. White fire and green clash in a cataclysm of fury. "*What is this?*" Mhoryga's voice demands, shocked and angry to find me not defenseless. "*What is this fire? What is this flame?*"

I do not answer. All my concentration is fixed on keeping the phoenix flame alive against that onslaught. I don't know how long I can hold it. Minutes? Moments?

But then I feel a tickling just on the edge of my perception. A little prod of spirit, curious and uncertain. I know who it is. I don't know how I know, but the conviction is there and it is right. "*Enya!*" I cry out again, reaching for the mind of the woman still trapped inside that body alongside the possessing fiend. "*Enya, help me!*"

That little awareness of soul struggles, fades, struggles again. She's there. She wants to help. But she's weak. If I can only find some way to reach her, if I can only push through this hellfire heat.

Summoning up an image of Lord Elis, I hurl it past the blazing fire. It's a memory, one of the moments we shared together in Stromin—our first dance. He made me laugh that night, despite my fears. Laugh and, momentarily, forget everything but the delight of being in company with someone young and alive and full of charm. Someone who still had hope, however foolish it may have been.

Somehow the image gets through. Enya gasps, her body jolting so hard, the hellfire abruptly snuffs out. She stands before me, panting, eyes round and staring, even as remnants of green flame drip from her fingertips. For a moment, her eyes are clear . . . and once more I'm struck by how much they remind me of Lord Elis.

"Who are you?" she asks. And it's her own voice which speaks, a human voice.

Before I can answer, however, she utters a terrible scream and drops to her knees, clutching at her own head. Mhoryga. Her hold on her dracori slaves is terrible, and she won't let go easily.

Stumbling on unsteady feet, I hurtle across the space between us and drop to my knees before the other young woman. "Enya!" I cry again, and grab her by the head, forcing her to look into my eyes. Leaping green flames shoot out at me, and her mouth opens, ready to emit a greater blast. But my phoenix flame surrounds me, protecting me from the worst of it.

"She's here!" Enya screams, shaking her head between my hands. "She's inside me—" Her voice breaks in another hideous scream of pain. In her head, I hear the Dragon Queen's voice, roaring with fury, with power.

Behind me, the dragon spawn battle, their flames burning up the walls of this once-noble hall. Any moment, they will tear Rhangyl apart and set upon me, and there will be nothing I can do to stop them. But for now, I push that awareness down deep and gaze into Enya's eyes, searching for her soul inside. It's there—huddled with terror, all but completely suppressed under the might of the greater possessing spirit. But still, somehow, with unmatched tenacity, holding on.

"*Enya, you are no longer compelled,*" I say. "*Be free.*"

Mhoryga shrieks in my head, even as I pour white phoenix flame out from my fingertips into Enya's mind. My fire envelops her, matching the rising green hellfire flame in heat. Hotter and hotter we burn, two opposing forces, our souls locked in battle. I gaze into Enya's eyes and see my mother staring back at me.

"*Get out of her,*" I command, white flame lashing from my mouth. Then I squeeze her head tighter and send jolts of fire straight into her brain. "*Get out!*"

A two-part scream bursts in my brain, followed by an eruption of fire—green and white—exploding through my senses. I hold on, refuse to let go, refuse to back down. Then, with a last, terrible shudder, Enya collapses to the floor in front of me. I blink hard, desperate to clear the fire from my vision, and stare down at the fallen lady. Have I killed her? Was this struggle of wills simply too much for the battlefield of her mind to endure?

"*Look out!*" Rhangyl's voice echoes against the stone walls behind me.

I whirl just in time to put up a shield of white flame as a dracori in a Cyran uniform strides toward me, blasting hellfire in quick, repeated bolts. Another blast from a different angle misses me by inches. I shift position, getting another hand up in protection. But it's not enough. All around me, dracori flood the hall, summoned from every corner of the stronghold in defense of their lady. There are too many of them, and I am too weak following my struggle with Mhoryga.

I turn my gaze desperately to Rhangyl, pinned down under three other dragon spawn. His one good eye catches mine, filled with regret, with remorse. He fought so bravely for me, against impossible odds, and now—

"*Stop!*"

The voice rings through that space, speaking both to minds and ears simultaneously. The dracori obey immediately, dropping their fiery hands and stepping back, heads bent. Even the dragon spawn cease their vicious battle, though they keep Rhangyl pinned beneath their claws.

I turn slowly and find the Lady of Cyran slowly pulling herself to her feet. Her eyes are clear. Hellfire still courses in her veins, but her mind, for the moment at least, is her own. And the dracori are still compelled to obey her.

She looks down at me, studying me with an intensity that

borders on mania. "You're the one," she gasps, her voice a whisper of heat. Smoke trails from her parted lips. "You're the dragon princess." She shakes her head, her curls flopping over her forehead in a manner so like Elis, it makes my chest ache. "I didn't believe it. There were rumors about you, stories, tales, and . . . and Elis believed. But I did not think you were real." To my great surprise, she drops to her knees before me, hands outstretched as though in supplication. "Roselle Pandracor," she says, in a voice like a prayer. "End of Dragons."

I ease a long breath out through my lungs. Everything inside me aches, burns, but for the first time in I don't know how long, some of the knotted fear in my gut relaxes. I gaze into the eyes of one who was supposed to be dead, and suddenly find I have the capacity to believe in miracles once more.

I lick my dry, cracked lips. There are any number of things I should say, any number of responses I ought to give. But when I speak, there are only four words I seem to be capable of uttering in this moment.

"Where is Valtar Skylock?"

14

Valtar

They beat me within an inch of my life. First when taking me captive; again when they brought me before their Lady.

When thrown at the feet of the Lady of Cyran's chair, I'd looked up through swollen eyes . . . and found Mhoryga gazing back at me. Her connection to her avatar was tenuous, not enough to question me as she wished without Nyxia present. But her will to see me suffer was strong enough to communicate from across the ocean. The Lady, acting on the impulse of her goddess queen, gave the signal, and her dracori closed in on me once more.

When they were through at last, and I lay in a bloody pulp in the middle of that floor, the Lady said coldly, "Chain him below. And send word for Nyxia. She will question him further and discover just how deep his treachery goes."

Dracori gathered me by the arms, wrenching me upright. One eye was swollen shut, but with the other I could just discern the stern features of the Lady and the green flame of her mistress shining through from within. She smiled—and it wasn't a human smile.

"*Your brother sends his greetings, sweet prince.*" Her voice appeared inside my head, a whisper of searing flame.

Then they dragged me away, jarring my broken bones and my dislocated shoulder until the pain all but overwhelmed me, and I fell into a semi-swoon. But I could not pass fully into unconsciousness—that was a relief I did not deserve. Fighting with everything I possessed, I gripped the edges of awareness and held on. Even as I hold on now, down here in the dark below Eirbalar.

I won't give up. I won't give in. Rosie needs me. I must . . . I will . . .

My body sags in chains. They've hung me from the wall, my arms overhead, having first forced my dislocated shoulder back into its socket. I'm bleeding from my nose, my mouth, from numerous gashes across my body where their sharp boots and gauntleted fists struck and tore flesh. Multiple ribs are broken, and I suspect one of my legs as well, judging by the intense agony radiating up my hip.

Nonetheless, I twist my arms, seeking some means of escape. The chains are *meorise*, of course; Cyran must have collected whatever *meorise* objects it could in preparation to defend against dragon invasion. The dracori, having found them, are happy enough to make use of them now against a fellow dracori. The rare ore is resistant to hellfire. Even if I could summon up my flame—which I have not managed since my last expulsion—I couldn't melt these chains as I might ordinary iron. But what if I found the right leverage, and managed to break my wrists? Then I could slip free and . . . what? There are multiple dracori guards just outside my low cell door. Will I take them down on a broken leg and two broken wrists, with no fire and no knives? It hardly seems likely.

I bow my head, unwilling to admit defeat and yet, in the moment, incapable of anything beyond mere existence. Pain has a marvelous way of keeping one very much in the present. I breathe through it, as I learned to do long ago, counting out evenly between every inhale and exhale. If I can still my mind enough and come to a space of awareness beyond the pain, perhaps there I will discover what I need to get out of here. To get back to Rosie.

Hours pass. I don't know how many. I may have been down here for days already, forgotten, left to starve. But no—Nyxia was sent for. She will surely come, and then the true pain will begin. I know what torture Nyxia is capable of inflicting; I've suffered it before. If necessary, she will grind me into fine powder, extracting every bit of information from me she can before she scatters my remains to the winds.

And Rosie will be left to face what is coming alone.

This thought hurts worse than the prospect of pain. For Rosie to believe I have abandoned her . . . it's unbearable. I can endure any other agonies, but not that. I've got to reach her. Somehow, I've got to let her know that she isn't alone, that I will stand with her no matter what, unto the bitterest end.

With renewed force, I struggle, seeking again for leverage that will allow me to break my own bones. I'll figure out the rest once I get free of these chains. Eventually they will have to come for me after all. Surely my fire will renew, and I'll blast my way through throngs of my foes, steal a dragon, take flight. Fanciful images play out in my mind with the convoluted vividness of hallucinations. Perhaps that is all they are—the product of my half-mad mind, desperate to escape this hell.

Exhaustion claims me sooner this time. I sag again, hanging

in the darkness like a sack of meat. Oblivion dances on the edges of my mind, and I let it toy with me, a tempting mistress. When consciousness returns, however, it isn't Rosie's face I see hovering before my mind's eye. It's Arun. Arun as I last saw him, strung up very like this, deep in the darkness below Heleris. Only his darkness was deeper by far, a never-ending blindness.

Gods, how I've failed him! Again and again. And perhaps the greatest failure was ever letting myself believe I could save him. Had I not deluded myself, Arun's suffering would have been over long ago. Instead, in my combined hubris and fear, I've forced him to endure a living hell, year after year.

We're going to save him, Valtar, Rosie's voice whispers phantomlike in my memory. *We're going to save him and restore your kingdom.*

How did I let myself begin to believe once more? No matter how viciously I quashed any foolish ideas, still that optimism of hers continued to make its way through my defenses, working its way to the very marrow of my bones. Knowing better, I nonetheless began to hope once more. I shouldn't have done it. I should have known the only way to save Arun would be for the rest of the world to burn. A price I was willing to pay until . . . Rosie. I hate myself, hate this weakness in me. But if forced to choose between them now, what would I do?

In the end, there isn't any real choice. The answer is always her. Always Rosie. From now to the end of my days.

What's more, I know Arun would choose her as well. What was it he'd said so long ago, at our final parting? *I would rather die in flame than be the reason that hope is stricken from the world.*

But Arun could not have guessed that Rosie would be like the sun shining into the midnight of my black soul. He couldn't have known she would become my very reason for drawing each new breath. Or maybe he did know . . . It had seemed to me sometimes, after all those years of torture and suffering, that my brother had acquired an uncanny level of perception, verging on prophetic. Maybe he guessed what would happen when I crossed the ocean on this last mission for my goddess queen.

I breathe out slowly, counting to ease my heart rate. I need to get out of here. Nyxia is coming—I can feel her approach even now. If she gets here before I am free, it will all be over. For me, for Arun, and for Rosie too. For the world. I've got to free myself, got to find her. But though I rattle my chains and scream at the top of my lungs, there is no change in the darkness around me, no sudden light or revelation.

Desperation crushes me like a fist. I drop my head to my chest. Then I do something I've not done in many, many years. Closing my eyes, I whisper softly, "Please."

It's a prayer. A pathetic nothing of a prayer, but the best I have to offer now. I send it out to every god I can remember, and some I'm almost certain I'm making up. "Please," I say, running through the pantheon of Khylmirian gods to whom I once knelt and offered worship. "Please, please, please." I move on then to the gods of Belanor, whom I have never worshipped, but used to hold in solemn reverence. "Please. Hear me, please." From them, I progress to the gods of the Magjor Tribe, dwarf deities who receive rough dwarfish prayers hewn from stone. They may not like to hear from me, who betrayed their worshippers to certain death. But I'm not praying for myself. I do not matter. After everything I've done, if they wish to crush me with divine retribution, I don't blame them, nor will I resist.

But I pray for Rosie.

Please.

Let me go.

Let me find her, let me save her, let me serve her.

Kill me however you wish. Torture and dismember me, flay the flesh from my bones.

Only let me see Rosie again.

Let me make certain she's safe.

Eventually my prayers run out. I hang again in silence, with nothing but darkness for company. Perhaps it was foolish of me to reach out to the gods. They abandoned me and all my people long ago.

Suddenly, my awareness quickens. At first, my dulled senses are too numb to know what I am perceiving. A sound, a sight, a smell, a vibration—it's all one and nothing here in the dark. But something has changed. Something . . . is coming.

Then a voice whispers inside my head: "*Valtar?*"

"Rosie," I murmur through swollen lips. Even as I try to tell myself it's not real, it's just another dream ready to turn nightmare, I lift up my head and bellow with everything in me, "Rosie! Rosie!" My voice slams against the walls of this close chamber, beating like fists on the door.

Sound bursts in my eardrums, followed by an eruption of light in my eyes. The door to the cell creaks open, and a *scintil* appears, a glowing orb held in a small hand. Its light illuminates the face of an angel, and somewhere in the back of my head, I seem to hear an ageless voice whisper: "*Valindra.*"

Then Rosie rushes across the cell to me. She drops the *scintil* unceremoniously and puts both hands on me, touching my chest, my neck, my swollen face, my side. "Valtar," she says, and the sound of my name on her tongue is the sweetest song I've ever heard. "Oh gods, Valtar, what have they done to you?"

It doesn't matter. All the pain, the breaks, the gashes . . . all melt away at sight of her face. I can scarcely hear her words, caught as I am in rapt study of her features. I'm not convinced she isn't a dream.

Rosie looks up at me, tears on her cheeks. "I'm sorry it took me so long to get here. I came as fast as I could."

My heart swells, threatens to break. "It was my fault," I croak out, spitting blood with the words. "I should never have left you."

Her lips quirk to one side even as tears continue to fall. "Maybe this will teach you to give your training exercises a bloody break now and then!" She turns and barks at the figures standing in the doorway. "Get him down from these chains at once."

I lift my heavy head, finally aware of other souls in the chamber. The first is the Cyran dracori leader whom I met on the road, the one who'd taken particular delight in shattering my ribs with the toe of his boot. The second face illuminated in the glow of the *scintil* is the Lady of Cyran. I jolt in my chains, straining with rage, and roar inarticulately.

"Oh, Valtar, don't be such a grump," Rosie says, patting my bare chest with one hand.

"You don't know who she is!" I snarl, visions of Mhoryga's eyes still vivid in my mind. "That woman, she's—"

"Elis's sister. I know," Rosie says, and looks up at me, her face serious. "She's free of Mhoryga's influence. For the moment at least."

I gape down at her. "How . . ." I begin to ask but cannot manage more. The questions are too many, too impossible, piling up in my throat all at once. How did she get into Cyran and somehow breach the seat of the Lady herself? How did she oust Mhoryga from the mind of one of her avatar hosts? How did she manage all of this, alone, while I've been chained up useless in the dark? Maybe it's time I rethought my former opinions of this woman. Maybe she is better suited to the task of world saving than she at first appeared.

Rosie turns to the Lady again and repeats her command to have me let down. There is no compulsion in her voice, however. The Lady flicks a gaze my way then back to Rosie again. "He is dracori."

"As are you," Rosie replies.

The Lady folds her arms. Her features—which, now that I recognize them, are indeed very like the cheerful face of Lord Elis—are hardened into stern lines. "That one is not like my dracori," she says, her lip curling. "He came with the invasion force. He's been dracori for a long time, steeped in dragon poison. He is Mhoryga's creature."

Rosie, however, draws herself up a little straighter. "If Valtar is *anyone's* creature," she declares, "he's *my* creature. Now let him down!"

The Lady's gaze moves from Rosie to me and back again. I feel her resistance . . . but I feel her gratitude as well. Rosie could easily force her to obey her commands, and yet she leaves the ultimate decision up to the Lady herself. Enya knows it. And she can't help positively worshipping the ground Rosie walks on just for the sake of that freedom. But she's suffered much in the last year, and her hatred for me and my kind runs deep.

In the end, she nods to one of her dracori guards. The man steps forward with a key in hand and unfastens my manacles. When the iron grip around my waist springs open, I simply collapse to the ground, my broken leg stuck out at an odd angle.

Rosie drops beside me, arms around my shoulders. "Oh, Valtar! Valtar, what have they done to you?" she croons, drawing my head to her shoulder. I collapse against her, breathing in her scent, her presence, her very existence. It's better balm than any medicine her apothecary skill might concoct. "I'm so sorry," she murmurs into my hair. "I searched for you, but I didn't know where you were. By the time I figured it out . . ."

I want to tell her to stop apologizing, to remind her that this is entirely my own fault. I deserved that beating and worse for ever letting her out of my sight. Just now, however, I can't do anything but breathe her in. A flare of white flame catches my eye. Startled, I begin to pull away, but she presses one hand into my back, holding me against her, even as the other hand raises the dancing flame. "It's all right, Valtar," she says. "I've been learning the trick of it. I'm actually fairly adept."

She places her glowing hand on my various injuries, one after another, beginning with my wrongly bent leg. Fire sinks from her palm, through my skin, down into muscle and bone. The burn is painful, the reknitting an agony. I groan and press my head into the curve of Rosie's shoulder. She doesn't stop. She moves from breaks to cuts, from cuts to bruises. By the time she's done, I feel hollowed to my very core.

But when I look down at my body, I find it healed and whole. Everything except that hideous dracori scar. Even her flame cannot undo an old hurt like that.

I look up, catching Rosie's eyes by the *scintil*'s glow. "I should never have left you," I say, my voice low and cracked with emotion. "I should never have let you out of my sight."

She pushes the lock of hair back from my forehead. "You couldn't have known what would happen."

"I should have known," I say, urgently. "I should have guessed. And I should never have walked away."

She meets my gaze. Her lip trembles slightly, but she bites it and smiles. "It's over now, Valtar. We're together again. Don't you see? Nothing can part us, not for long at least."

"About that night, the night the dracori attacked your village—"

"Hush." She places a finger against my lips. "We don't need to talk about it now. I know. I understand."

I bow my head, suddenly too overcome to speak, to hold that golden-eyed gaze of hers a second longer. Instead I grab her hand, draw it to my mouth, kissing it with more passion than any kiss I've ever dared steal from her lips. She continues to stroke my hair gently, and for a few moments, nothing and no one else exists.

Then the Lady of Cyran's voice speaks from the shadows beyond the *scintil*'s glow: "Much as I hate to interrupt so tender a moment . . . Nyxia has been spotted across the river. She'll be here within the hour. Does that interest either of you?"

THE NEXT HOUR is a storm of confusion. Lady Enya summons all the transformed Cyran dracori to her hall, along with the freed dragons willing to answer her call. Not as many as I initially hoped—we've got threescore dracori and fifty dragon spawn. What has become of the others, I do not know. The Khylmirian dracori are presumably freed of their enthrallment like the rest, but they have disappeared into the city streets. Many of the dragons simply fled Cyran in a mass exodus, taking flight for the sea. Only time will tell if those who remain will bow their heads to Rosie, their long-lost sister. In the meanwhile, Nyxia must be faced. Before she crosses the river into Cyran, if possible.

"It doesn't have to be you," Rosie says, even as she helps me into the dracori gear the Lady provided from among her own crew. "Enya's people are with us now, and some of the dragon spawn as well. Once Mhoryga's hold on Enya was broken, the compulsion dropped from their minds. They will fight."

I pull on the cuirass and fasten the buckles hastily, half afraid to meet Rosie's searching eye. "It has to be me," I answer, my voice hard as stone. "When they get close to Nyxia, she will claim their minds once more. She's too strong and too practiced in the art. No." I shake my head firmly. "It has to be me."

Rosie's hand lands atop mine. I freeze in the act of fastening the last buckle, my breath suddenly tight. "How do you know?" she asks, her voice tremulous. "How do you know she won't get into your head too, Valtar? That she won't turn you against me?"

"She can't." Gently I run my finger down to her jaw and tilt her chin up, forcing her to meet my eyes. "She can't, Rosie," I repeat with conviction. "There is no room for anyone else in me now. Only you."

She holds my gaze for a moment before dropping her eyelids and nodding. But we both know the truth. We both know I have yet to be tested. Whatever I may believe, it is unproven until I face Nyxia. Now that the moment has come, I don't want to shrink from it. I will find out if I am as strong as I believe I am.

"I want you to take Rhangyl." Rosie removes her hand from mine and takes several steps back, watching as I finish securing the cuirass. "He is my . . . my brother. A dragon spawn. He helped me get into Eirbalar and defended me from the dracori while I confronted Mhoryga in Enya's mind. He has proven true."

I nod. The dragon in question suffered some damage in his efforts to protect Rosie, and for that he has earned my gratitude. Her healing touch repaired the worst of his wounds, as it repaired mine, and we are both fit enough for battle. A grim smile turns the corner of my mouth. It will be good to fly again, to feel the power of a dragon spawn beneath me. To match my strength and cunning against a foe like Nyxia is a fate of which I never dreamed back when I lay deep in her thrall.

"It doesn't seem right," Rosie says, crossing her arms, "for you to leave me like this, when we only just found each other again."

I want to reach for her. I want to take her in my arms, pull her to me, and crush her in my embrace. But if I do so, I won't be able to let her go. I won't be able to do what I must. "If there was anyone else—" I begin, but she shakes her head sharply.

"I don't need excuses." She draws back, nostrils flaring with a deep inhale. I can see the tears she's struggling to keep at bay shining too bright in her eyes. "I just need you to come back to me in one piece. Understand? I can't keep putting you back together."

"Rosie—"

Before I can say anything more, she turns and steps from the small antechamber, leaving me to finish and follow in her wake. I hurry, strapping on bracers, boots, knives, and donning a black dracori hood. While I hate to wear the vestments of my former enslavement, there's a chance it will help me get close to Nyxia without her realizing who I am. I'll need whatever element of surprise I can get. Nyxia is without hellfire, but she commands the dracori and dragon spawn who surround her, manipulating their actions with the nimble alacrity of a puppet master. While I may not be susceptible to their fiery blasts, a fall from great height will smash my bones the same as any other man, and my flesh is vulnerable to talons and teeth.

Worst of all, however, is what Nyxia can do to my mind. Not just the compulsions, but the pain. She has used her powers to bring me to my knees before. She won't hesitate to do so again if she gets half a chance. But that half chance may be the only opportunity I have to end the threat she poses to Rosie once and for all.

I stride from the antechamber back into the glass-strewn long hall, where Lady Enya has gathered her dracori and the dragon spawn, who all wear human form. Rosie has gone to stand beside her, the one-eyed Rhangyl hovering close behind. Rosie sees me coming but looks away immediately, as though afraid of betraying some emotion in front of all these watching eyes.

"People of Cyran," Lady Enya says abruptly, her young voice filling that echoing space with surprising power. She steps forward into the center of the hall, drawing all eyes to her. "We cannot unmake what we have become, nor can we undo all that we have done. But now we have a chance. A chance to strike back, to defend the honor of our fair city, of Albhia, and all of Belanor."

She goes silent now. I believe she speaks into their minds, communicating via the link which remains unbroken, though the compulsion is gone. The dracori exchange glances, and I catch the eye of the brick-faced man who dragged me here in the first place. He shoots me a vicious look. Neither of us left that altercation unscathed, and though I came out the worst, he still sports an ugly gash along one cheek where my blade caught him.

"Now you know what we are up against," Enya concludes, once more speaking out loud. "I need five volunteers to fly with Valtar Skylock and intercept Nyxia and her dracori before they cross the river."

"Why only five?" the brick-faced dracori demands. "Nyxia has twelve mounted dracori with her."

Enya acknowledges this with a grim nod. "Until we know for certain that she cannot penetrate your minds, we cannot risk more."

Silence grips the hall as every dracori and dragon spawn here contemplates the reality that their freedom may be so short-lived. In the end, however, Enya gets her five volunteers, including my brick-faced menace. His name is Tanyl, and he was once captain of the guard in Eirbalar. While I won't fault his courage in this crisis, it doesn't endear him to me. But I make no protest when he falls into formation beside me and the other four.

The dragon spawn are more hesitant to step forward. Cyran is not their city, after all, and fear of Nyxia is embedded in their very bones. Rhangyl, however, steps forward and speaks to them in the growling language adopted by dragon spawn across Khylmira—a language no dracori would waste time learning any more than we would learn the language of dogs. When he is through speaking, five more dragons step forward, their faces pale but resolute.

Rhangyl turns to Rosie now and, to my surprise, goes down on one knee before her. He takes her hand in his and presses it to his forehead, a symbol of abject loyalty. Rosie gazes down at him, shocked to her core. Tears spring to her eyes, and she rests her other hand on top of his head, murmuring something I cannot hear from across the chamber.

He rises, bows once more, then turns and marches across the hall to me. "Time to fly, dracori," he says.

15

Rosie

Enya takes me up the winding stairs to the top of the western tower and the large balcony there. From this vantage, we watch the six dragon spawn take flight, dracori on their backs.

"We can enter their minds, you know," Enya says, looking at me with that odd combination of respect, fear, dismay, and hope which seem to muddle together into an all-new, never-before-named emotion in her eyes. "We can watch what happens and know better how to . . . prepare ourselves."

She means if Valtar cannot get close enough to Nyxia to stop her, if she gets into his mind or the minds of the other dracori and dragon spawn, it will mean the worst for us. At best, Enya and her people will have to flee this place, try to keep out of range of Nyxia's influence. As for me? Well . . .

I face the balcony rail, gripping the stone hard beneath my hands. I don't have to face that question. Not yet. Not while Valtar is still out there. Gods, but I wish I possessed half that man's confidence! The way he throws himself into the fray with scarcely a thought, fully believing both in the security of his mind and the ability of his body against foes that would make lesser men wet themselves with terror. I can only pray he's right and his mind is truly as fortified against my sister's influence as he seems to think.

He should have kissed me before he went.

The thought prickles in the back of my brain, even as I worry my lower lip to the point of blood. He should have kissed me . . . kissed me like he did that day by the lakeshore. I don't know if it would have made a difference. But it couldn't have hurt. It might have strengthened whatever bond we share and whatever protection my influence offers.

But he didn't. He wouldn't. He wouldn't even meet my eyes when he strode past with Rhangyl at his side. Perhaps he didn't want to jinx this mission with goodbye embraces. Perhaps he means to kiss me upon his triumphant return. Oh gods, let him triumph! Let him return! Let him get back to me and rutting kiss me black and blue!

Drawing a deep breath, I close my eyes and concentrate, casting my mind out. I'm not used to reaching minds from a distance yet, but I'm already better at it than I was. I find the cluster of dragon spawn almost at once. The dracori are available to me as well, but their minds are foreign, not so open as those of my own kin. Rhangyl's mind, especially, looks welcoming, so I slip inside it, nestling behind his single eye. He's aware of me; I sense the small jerk of his head when I appear. But he doesn't complain, rather he seems to scoot his own consciousness a little to one side, making room for me. He trusts I'm not here to take control and, therefore, offers no resistance.

I gaze out from his eye to see the rooftops of Cyran passing underneath. It is a great city, the pride of Albhia, one of the finest centers in all the Belanor continent. Even stained with dragon smoke and cast under a pall of hellfire fumes, its former glory is readily apparent. I wish I might have come here in a more peaceful time and wandered those winding streets, visiting the sights of interest, learning of its people and its ways.

Instead I raise my gaze to the River Cy up ahead. It's three miles wide at this point in its journey to the sea, dotted with little islands on which rich Albhian lords have built charming pleasure-houses, abandoned since the invasion. Beyond its far shore stretches the countryside of Albhia, through which Valtar and I traveled so recently.

And there—small dots on the horizon of my vision, appearing no larger than vultures, but swiftly growing—Nyxia and her twelve dracori, mounted on dragon spawn.

My heart lurches. I've not yet seen this sister of mine. Until recently, I'd not known she existed. Apparently we shared a nest, but when Alderin took my egg, he attempted to smash hers. I don't know what prevented him from finishing the job. Did the knowledge that his own child lay cradled within stay his hand? Either way, she and I were meant to be together, born of the same clutch. Only a trick of fate separated us, made us into enemies.

I find myself curiously drawn to that approaching dark silhouette. A small part of me unconsciously reaches out.

"*Beware, little sister,*" Rhangyl's voice snarls in my head.

I hastily pull back. He's right. I don't want to alert Nyxia to my presence or give her reason to suspect the dragon spawn even now flying to meet her are anything other than a greeting party. One wrong move could spell disaster for us all. So I crouch within Rhangyl's mind, curled into a tight little ball but observing still.

They are getting closer. I can detect the distinct colors of their scales flashing in the late-afternoon sun. Soon my farseeing gaze can pick out the features of each stern dracori rider, all Khylmirian born. Nyxia didn't bring any newly transformed Cyran dracori with her on this mission.

Suddenly a presence scratches on the edge of Rhangyl's mind. Nyxia! She's already seeking entrance, expecting to find the approaching dragon spawn open to her. When Rhangyl does not immediately give her access, she reacts with swift vengeance. Pain explodes through Rhangyl's mind. I don't feel it myself, but Rhangyl's response is unmistakable. His body jerks violently in midair. His wings falter, and he drops, plunging a hundred feet. I feel the stomach-flipping vertigo, and stagger on the balcony, putting my hands out to catch my balance. And what of Valtar? Did he hold on through that drop?

Worry driving me, I leap from Rhangyl's mind, searching for my assassin. I find him immediately, balanced on the back of his mount with practiced ease. There's no trace of Nyxia in his mind, not yet at least. He doesn't seem to be aware of my presence either, focused intently on the job at hand. I hear him shout to Rhangyl, "*Fight her! Fight her off, damn you!*"

Rhangyl roars, his wings outstretched to recover an updraft. His mind is clear for the moment, but only because Nyxia is now probing the minds of the other dragons. The two parties approach each other swiftly, and a clash is imminent. Back inside Rhangyl's head, I gaze out through his eye at the centermost figure in that formation. For the first time, I behold my sister.

Nyxia is a strong woman, clad in dracori-style armor, but unhooded. Her bounteous black hair tosses freely behind her, whipping in the wind of her flight. Dragon scales speckle her jaw and brow bone, catching glints of sunlight like drops of gold. She does not sit on the back of her mount; she stands. Balancing as gracefully as a dancer, now and then crouching to grasp a horn, she flies in perfect synchronization with her beast. It's as though her body, long practiced in this art form, performs the feat unconsciously, even as her mind searches out, skipping and dancing from dragon spawn to dracori, holding the reins of their wills in her iron fist.

Enya gasps.

Ripping my gaze away from the wild image of my sister, I see one of our own six dragon spawn roll suddenly. His mouth drops open, and hellfire gouts straight at Rhangyl. The flame passes over him and Valtar, causing harm to neither, but now the dragon is bearing down upon them, roaring in ferocious attack. Like a reflex, I leap from Rhangyl's mind, seeking entry into this other dragon, thinking I might call off his attack. I crash against the edge of his awareness, blocked by a sudden, wild, manic presence that fills up his head to overflowing. Nyxia.

No sooner do I realize the truth than another of our dragons turns and streaks straight at Rhangyl as well. With Valtar clinging to his back, Rhangyl dips, rolls, eluding one, but receiving a long gash from the claws of another. It's not enough to bring him down. He bursts free of their convergence, out into open air. By now, a third dragon spawn is already in motion, responding to the call of his mistress. It swoops just over Valtar's head, and the dracori rider on his back, also under Nyxia's influence, aims a blow with his sword, which misses by mere inches.

No, no, no! This was not supposed to happen! Nyxia's dragons aren't even upon us yet, and we're already engaged in a death brawl. Dragon spawn and gouts of hellflame spin wildly through the air in confusing patterns my mind cannot follow. I see one dracori fall from his saddle, and though my mind reaches for him, I'm not fast enough. There's nothing I could do anyway. They're too high up; that fall is his death.

Wrenching away, I leap from mind to mind, seeking a place of rest in the frenzy. Everywhere I turn, I find Nyxia again and withdraw at once, afraid of catching her attention.

Finally I sense Valtar. I'd hardly realized he was the one I searched for in the madness, but the moment I find him, I breathe a little exhale of relief and leap into his mind like a rabbit down a bolt-hole. Only this time, there's a snake lurking within.

I see her. In a space of madness and mania, she stands across from me. A presence taking form as the image of the woman I glimpsed balancing on a dragon's back. Only here she is alone—a formidable figure, a true daughter of dragons. In this space inside Valtar's head, she looms large, and her black hair flows about her like a storm cloud, blotting out the sky.

She holds Valtar in her grasp. My mind creates pictures to understand what I sense in spirit only: I see him kneeling at my sister's feet, panting hard. Her long talon fingers grip his skull so that rivulets of blood pour down his face. Valtar struggles, screams, but cannot break her hold.

"*Let him go!*" I roar.

Nyxia looks up from her prey. Looks straight at me. "*So,*" she says, "*you are here after all.*" She shakes her head, smiling cruelly down at her victim. "*You see, Val-Val? If you'd just given me a straight answer, we wouldn't have had to bother with all this mess.*"

So saying, she flings him away from her and, without pause, springs like a wildcat at me. I startle, jolting back, and find myself adrift in the tumult outside of any one mind. I search for a clear space, find Rhangyl. Gasping with relief, I dive into him, peer from his eye . . . just in time to see Valtar falling through the clouds below us.

"*Rhangyl!*" I scream. "*Save him!*"

My dragon brother is already in motion, streaking like an arrow away from the vicious dogfight. Nyxia appears, eager to penetrate his mind and turn him from his course. She's not expecting me to be there, however.

"*No!*" I cry. Grabbing hold of her violently, I fling her out. But Nyxia is so strong, and the force I exert to expel her so great, I knock myself out of Rhangyl's head, out of that space of mind entirely. My physical body lands flat on the stone balcony floor back in Eirbalar. I stare up at the peak of the western tower and the smoke-churned sky overhead.

Enya's face comes into focus. "Princess?" she asks nervously. "Princess, I couldn't stay with them. What's happening? Did you see?"

I can't speak. My lungs seem to be collapsing in on themselves. Valtar! Did Rhangyl catch him? Did he manage to fight off Nyxia long enough and . . . and . . . ?

"She's breached the river." The hard voice of a dracori speaks somewhere out of my tunneled range of vision.

Enya looks up, nods once. Then she turns her gaze to me again. "Come, Princess," she says, clutching my shoulders and pulling me upright. She's not much older than me, but stronger, tougher, hardened to the life she's been forced to endure. "We must get you out of here." She barks commands to the nearest dracori: "Mount up and fly! Get away, and—"

"No," I whisper. Then, more forcefully, even as I struggle against her hold, "No!"

Still grasping my shoulders for fear I'll topple over, Enya looks down at me sharply. "We can't stop her, Princess," she says. "We've got to get away from this place before Nyxia gets into our minds again. Unless you think you can prevent her?"

I don't. I wish I could, but what I just experienced out there in the aerial battle tells me I'm nowhere near strong enough to contest Nyxia. Not on that battlefield, at least. But what if I've been thinking about this from the wrong direction? I've been trying to fight her over individuals, when she herself is trained to wield hundreds of minds at a time. That's not a contest I can win, not with my painfully limited training. But what if . . . ?

"You go," I say to Enya, then turn to address the dracori and dragon spawn with us on the balcony. "Get away from here, as far as you can." My eyes catch Enya's once more. "I stay."

"No!" Enya grips my arm, her fingers ironhard. "How can we protect you?"

"You can't. No one can. I've got to face Nyxia. Alone."

Enya shakes her head fiercely. "You won't be facing Nyxia alone. You'll be facing all of them—all twelve of Nyxia's dracori and their dragon spawn and everyone she just took back under thrall. She'll recall the dragons who fled and summon the dracori who vanished into the city. Anyone left within her range will run to her when she beckons."

The enormity of what Enya is saying threatens to crush my fragile resolve. But I throw back my shoulders and face her bravely. "It ends here, Enya. If it ends in my death, so be it. I find out now what I am and what I may become." I fling out my arms, igniting my white phoenix flame. It rushes over me, covering me from head to toe. Enya backs away, her expression awed and frightened. "Go," I tell her. "Lead the others to safety. Now!"

For a moment, I fear the Lady of Cyran will argue with me.

But she offers a curt nod, turns, and orders the remaining dragon spawn and dracori into the air. A small gold dragon bows its head to her, and she leaps gracefully onto its back, clutching horns for balance. She casts one last glance my way, her expression grim. Then she takes to the air.

I'm alone on the balcony, gazing out across the city to the river. Through the haze of smoke, I cannot discern the results of the dragon battle. Then Nyxia appears, riding in on her blue-scaled mount. Nyxia and twelve—no, sixteen dragon spawn. She took them then. She took all those I sent out to her, except one. She didn't take Rhangyl. He's still out there, either dead or free. Did he dive fast enough to save his rider? Did he rescue Valtar? I shake my head hard, sucking a shuddering breath through my nostrils. I can't think about that. Not now. Not yet. I must focus. If there's going to be a chance for any of us, a chance for our world, I must be brave. Valtar would want that.

Granted, Valtar would also want me to have mounted a dragon spawn and fled this place at top speed. But Valtar doesn't always get what he wants, does he? I set my face in a grim smile, blinking back the tears which try to rise. My white flame burns around me, and as the dragons bear down, I let it grow hotter, brighter.

Only just in time. As the first of the fifteen dragons arrives, its jaw drops open, and hellfire rains down on me. Nyxia knows I used to be vulnerable to hellfire. She doesn't know about my phoenix flame, however, or how I've learned to employ it to protect myself. No sooner does the first dragon flit past than the second comes, spewing hell with tremendous force. One after another they strafe me, but standing in the center of my flame, I am safe. Though the stones at my feet blacken and melt, still I remain untouched.

"Come on, Nyxia," I murmur. "You know you want to. Come play with me yourself."

I swipe my arm, using tongues of phoenix fire to cut through the roiling smoke and fumes before me, clearing space. The barrage has momentarily paused as the dragon spawn circle the tower. Is that uncertainty I sense vibrating on the edges of their minds? Not their own uncertainty, but Nyxia's within them. She doesn't understand this white flame of mine. She's never encountered anything like it, cannot comprehend it.

My vision unable to penetrate the intense smoke screen, I throw out my mental voice, trusting her to detect it. "*Nyxia!*"

An answer appears in my head immediately: "*Hullo, Naevya.*"

Billowing smoke parts, and Nyxia appears. Not a vision of her, not an image in my head—the real Nyxia, in the flesh, standing on the back of her great, blue-scaled dragon. His powerful wings pulse hard, keeping them suspended on a level with the balcony. She walks from between his shoulders, across his neck, down his broad brow, his snout, and steps lightly onto the balcony rail. There she stands, heedless of the dizzying drop at her back. She looks at me, taking me in slowly where I stand in my white-flame shield. Her expression is frankly curious and mildly revolted. I study her in turn, taking in the wildness of this creature, this broken monster who, by chance alone, was left behind in hell itself, with a demon for a mother, while I was carried off to safety. She is the person I could have become—would have become—if not for a single twist of fate. If Alderin had snatched her egg instead of mine.

"You're not what I pictured," Nyxia says at last, speaking the words out loud. "You're not only half formed, you're . . . mutated." She juts her chin, indicating the fire suffusing my limbs. "What is that?"

Rather than answer, I take a stance, not unlike the first position Valtar taught me long ago on that moonlit mountaintop. I do not hold my knife, but I angle my hand, long talon fingers gleaming with fire. "You don't have to do it anymore, Nyxia."

She lifts an eyebrow. "Do what exactly?"

"Serve Mhoryga."

Nyxia looks at me blankly. Then she bursts out laughing, tossing her head back so that her unbound hair flows with the twirling coils of black smoke all around her. "What are you talking about, sister? Would you tell an eagle it need no longer honor the god of wind and sky? *Of course* I must serve Mhoryga. It's what I was born for, what we both were born for."

Her feverish voice sends a chill to the pit of my gut. "Every living thing is born to fulfill the purpose ordained for them by the gods alone."

"The gods alone?" Her eyes sharpen, gleaming with green flame. "Don't you know? Mhoryga *is* god. She is the only god of any worth in this world. Soon she will be the only god left, and all will worship at her altar, all will breathe her incense, all will cast themselves gladly into sacrificial flames at her pleasure." Her wild eyes rake over my body once more and narrow with contemplation. "So you have manifested flame of a kind. That's good, that's good. Your heart should be ripe. In fact"—she draws a wicked knife from her belt, long and curved and cruel as a talon—"I'll take that heart now, if you please."

She leaps from the balcony rail and rushes me, teeth bared in a rictus smile. She has no manifested flame, but she does not need it. Her untamed ferocity is Draconan to its core. She lashes out, a downward blow, meant to pierce me through the throat, draining my life's blood while leaving my valuable heart whole.

My feet move almost of their own volition. Though I do not

hold a knife in my hand, I perform the block and riposte with that unconscious response of muscle memory which Valtar worked into my very bones. I knock her arm to one side, just enough to make her miss, and my long talon nails lash out, cutting through the leather and fabric of her dracori uniform, deep into flesh.

A soft jolt of air escapes Nyxia's lungs. She staggers. I don't let the opportunity pass me by. Lunging, I grab her head in my hands and plunge deep into her mind.

Her defenses are strong, but her shock is so great, and the sudden eruption of my white fire is more than she expects. One by one, I burn through each barrier she desperately tries to erect, driving down deeper, deeper, into the darkness and the mire and the ever-burning hellflame, which she cannot manifest but which dwells inside her even as it dwells in me.

"*Nyxia!*" I call to her. She flees before me, a rabid, desperate flight, seeking the confines of these twisted places in her mind which have been her refuge all these years. Suddenly I burst through a layer of fire and find myself suspended in open air before a great, smoke-blackened stronghold built into the side of a cliff, standing desolate and proud before a great stretch of wasteland. In the distance, so massive that it can be seen even by mortal eyes from more than a hundred miles away, is a mountain spewing green fire and black fumes. The sight of it fills my heart with a powerful sense of inevitability. I almost change course and start toward it, my spirit eager to speed across that blighted landscape.

With a firm grasp of will, I focus instead on a tower close at hand. I see a balcony and, above it, a solitary window, opening and closing in the rough wind, its glass panes shattered against stone. Somehow I know that what I seek is within. Using my phoenix flame, I propel my awareness closer until I can peer into the little chamber. It's a prisoner's cell: a pallet bed, a cold hearth, a straw-strewn floor. Nothing by way of small luxuries, a space meant for containment, not comfort. And yet it is here to where Nyxia's mind has fled.

I see her in the corner by the door, curled up in a tight ball, shivering with terror. Her long talon nails scrape at the door, dragging long grooves through the wood, even as her small voice whimpers, "*Let me out. Let me out. Mother, let me out.*"

I know suddenly what I am seeing: the dragon princess, valued only for the beating heart in her chest. Caged and held in waiting until she should mature to ripeness. This was how my sister lived then. No mother's love, only imprisonment. Ignored and forgotten, abused and neglected . . . and yet, still, somehow adoring of the one who harmed her most.

"*Nyxia*," I say.

At the sound of my voice, the little creature tucks into herself, becoming a ball of skeletal limbs. Her protruding backbone looks like nothing so much as dragon spines, ready to burst through translucent flesh.

"*Nyxia*," I say again, my awareness floating through the window and into that chamber. "*You don't have to remain here anymore. You can leave. You can come away with me.*"

A hiss erupts from the corner. The child turns, her emaciated face ferocious, teeth bared. I almost retreat; it requires all my courage to remain firm. I take a more solid form, standing in that prison cell with her, and hold out one hand. "*You don't need Mhoryga.*"

The child shakes her head, snarls of black hair falling over her face. But when she speaks, it is a woman's voice which emerges from her mouth: "*You're a fool if you think that, Naevya.*"

Then she lunges, screaming. As her little body uncoils from itself and leaves the floor, it grows into the adult Nyxia. Suddenly we're not in the tower chamber, nor in the space of mind. Back to the physical world, I stagger across the balcony, one of Nyxia's hands tearing into my shoulder, the other hanging useless at her side, blood streaming from the wound I dealt her. But she is strong, even wounded—far stronger than I am and far better trained. She knocks me from my feet. I land hard, breath driven from my lungs. She pulls back her left arm, talons flashing.

Desperately, I put up one hand and send a blast of white flame into her eyes, back down into her mind. My soul encounters a wall of green hellflame—superheated and coursing through her spirit. Even unmanifested, she is a true dragon, but, like me, unable to grasp the full strength of her dragonness. I feel an inexplicable sense of *pull*, as though her flame is trying to draw my own hellfire into itself. When I resist, the pull reverses, and I'm struck by how easily I might drag all that power, green and seething, into my soul. What's more, I feel that, were I to do so, it would not destroy me. Rather, there's a sense of wholeness, of completion here. If I were to take this fire from Nyxia, would I finally, truly, be able to manifest the hellflame that is my birthright?

But no. No, that is not what I want. The white flame of the phoenix is mine; I will take no other.

With a roar, I plunge deeper and deeper still, a white bolt of energy shooting through the green inferno. There! At last, I feel it: Mhoryga's pulsing presence, a tangled web of malice, entrapping Nyxia and all the minds over which she wields control. It's not like what I found inside Enya, where the Dragon Queen peered through the eyes of her captive. It's more insidious, for there is a trace of free will in this binding. A choice made again and again. Made in fear, perhaps; made in confusion and loathing and a poisonous, self-destructive love. But chosen.

But every choice can be unmade. I believe that to the depths of my heart.

I look upon that tangle of spirit threads, all the collected minds of dracori and dragon spawn gathered here and grasped in a tight fist of control. Raising both hands, I send twin streams of white fire straight into that pulsing mass. A roar shakes my mind, threatening to shatter my protective walls of sanity and send me straight into raving lunacy. Mhoryga's voice or Nyxia's, I hardly know. What I do know is that I have found the center of Nyxia's control. If I can undo it, she will lose her power over dracori and dragon spawn alike. They will be free.

Nyxia lunges at me, manifesting suddenly in this mind space, more draconic here than she is in the physical realm. She hurtles toward me, but I shift one hand, blasting her with a stream of white fire, driving her back. Nyxia writhes, thrashes, seeking to push through, but cannot resist the stream of power pouring out from me. I hear her calling to the dragon spawn, to the dracori, but they are as paralyzed under this assault as she is, unable to move by either her will or their own volition.

The massive knot of minds begins to break. Strand after strand snaps, disintegrating in luminous sparks, until there is nothing left but the pulsing snarl at the very center. Two strands, two souls: Nyxia's and Mhoryga's, inexorably entwined. I set my teeth. I've got to break it. The need is so strong, I forget Nyxia and channel both hands, both streams of fire, straight at that black tangle. Summoning everything in me, I pour more energy into the flames, until—

A burst of light and darkness combined sends me flying out of that mental space, crashing against the tower wall. I collapse to the floor and lie stunned, even as my brain fills up with a hundred minds and more, all screaming, roaring, and—strangely enough—laughing. It's the dragon spawn. Freed of thralldom, they take to the skies around the city, wings pulsing, scales flashing. Not just the twelve Nyxia brought with her, or the four she collected on the far side of the river. Every dragon in Cyran. I feel how wide open their minds are, how easily I might slip in and take them over if I so choose. But I don't. I simply watch and feel their strange mingling of terror and gladness.

"What have you done?"

I turn, find Nyxia pulling herself to her feet, clutching her wounded arm. She staggers to the balcony rail just as a streak of blue scales soars past, up into the sky. "*Zoar!*" she screams, both with her voice and her mind. The dragon spawn does not pause, does not look back. She stands there alone, watching him fly into the swirling smoke above the city, vanishing from sight.

Then she whirls, fixes her gold eyes on me. "You don't know what you've done."

"I've freed them," I answer, still not quite able to get to my feet.

"And you've condemned *him*." Burning tears gather in Nyxia's eyes, trailing scalding lines down her cheeks. "She'll kill him. She'll burn him alive!"

The next moment, she hurtles toward me. I'm too stunned by the tremendous exertion of power I've just put forth to do more than lift my hands in defense. There is no fire in me, not now. I'm helpless as her talons grip the front of my gown, wrench me to my feet, and slam me again against the wall. Her wounded arm will not serve her, so she puts up her knee, jamming it into my stomach to pin me in place as she rears back her left hand, prepared to slash my throat.

A shadow falls across us. Large, winged. Full of flame.

Nyxia's eyes widen. She turns. We both look up into the one-eyed stare of Rhangyl, hovering over the balcony. His wings pulse hard, even as the black-clad figure on his back leaps into open air, descending on us like a bolt of the gods.

Valtar slams into Nyxia, knocking her to the ground. He pins her under him, his knife at the ready, prepared to slice her open on the spot.

"*No!*" I cry.

I can't say for certain if I sent a compulsion with that command or not. Either way, Valtar's hand freezes. He looks back at me, black eyes brimming with hellfire. "She must die," he snarls. "Now."

I shake my head, pushing away from the wall and staggering toward him one step, two. "She's been compelled. It's not her fault. Not entirely."

Valtar gnashes his teeth. "She's made choices aplenty in her life."

It's true. I've seen the reality of that knot in her mind, that tangling up of her life with the will of our mother. But I shake my head and turn my gaze to Nyxia, pinned under Valtar's powerful grasp. "You don't have to go back to her," I say, addressing my sister. "Stay with me. Help me. Together we can face her. We can overthrow Mhoryga, liberate this world."

Even with Valtar's blade poised at her throat, Nyxia utters a dreadful laugh. "Is that what you think, Naevya? That our mother is some edifice to be toppled? She is the Queen. The only god of this world. You and I? We are nothing to her, half formed and worthless. Our only choice is to worship."

Valtar stares at her, hatred radiating from his very soul. An inarticulate growl rumbles from his throat, and Nyxia's gaze darts back to him. "You've done it now, Val-Val," she growls. "You've killed him. You've killed Arun."

"Not if I kill you first," he answers. "Not if you can't carry your tales back to Mhoryga."

"It's already too late. Don't you understand?" Tears pour down Nyxia's cheeks, even as she utters another of those lunatic laughs. "She knows. She knows everything—your betrayal, my failure. And she *must* punish us for it. There is no other way." She drags in a shuddering gasp. "Arun will die. And it's your fault."

"No," Valtar whispers. His limbs shudder with sudden weakness.

As though sensing her chance, Nyxia moves violently, gripping him by the back of the neck and twisting just at the point of leverage. Valtar goes over on his side with a grunt of pain, and by the time he gathers his limbs under him, Nyxia is already on her feet, already running for the balcony rail. "Nyxia, wait!" I cry.

But my sister hurls herself wildly out into open air, arms outspread, as though to embrace the bone-shattering stones below. I feel the sick plunge in my own gut, as though I'm the one who plummets. I take two staggering steps, a vain need to reach for her driving me.

A powerful pulse of wings. A wave of hellfire heat. The blue-scaled dragon slices through the smoke, appearing like a nightmare. One instant I see him descend. The next he rises again, wheeling up and up, back into the smoke screen and out of sight. But before he vanishes, I glimpse the little figure clutched in his claws.

Desperately I reach out with my mind, trying to catch hold of that retreating soul. I can't reach him—not quite. Not burned-out as I am. And yet, somehow, I can't shake the impression that, though his compulsion was broken, he returned to Nyxia by his own volition.

16

Valtar

"The time is *now*," Lady Enya Balxidon declares, standing at the head of the long, stone council table. She has gathered the dracori and a handful of dragon spawn into the war room antechamber off the great hall. There's a sadness at the sight of one so young standing in that position of power which, by rights, ought to be occupied by a seasoned warrior. But though she is tender in years, her experiences have aged her, and the hellfire flowing in her veins burns bright.

She looks around at the grim faces seated before her. Those of high rank who were not slaughtered during the invasion were transformed into monsters like her. They wear their new liberation uneasily. While under thrall, they had no need to face the reality of what they'd become. Now that all compulsions are broken, and the immediate threat of Nyxia dealt with, each has a personal war to rage in their heart.

But there is no time to accommodate all these souls in crisis.

Lady Enya knows it. So she steels her face before them and urges with fiery vehemence, "If we are to take down Mhoryga, there is only one thing to do."

She turns to Rosie now, who sits opposite her at the far end of the long table, illuminated by the glow of low-hung lanterns. The golden light, so different from hellfire blaze, flickers through silver filigree, casting delicate patterns across her cheeks. Her face is uncharacteristically solemn, and though she holds herself upright in her seat, it doesn't take an expert eye to see that she is exhausted from her recent ordeal.

An ordeal which is but a small taste of all that is to come.

"You have broken Nyxia's control over the dragon spawn," Enya continues, leaning forward, knuckles planted on the tabletop. "Now, Princess, you must gather the scattered dracori and dragons here, secure them under your own thralldom. There have to be nearly five hundred dragon spawn alone on this side of the ocean. With a force like that, we can cross to Khylmira and set upon Mhoryga in her own country."

I stand on the fringes of the room, keeping to the shadows, my hood pulled low over my head. I've chosen my position well; from here, I can keep a close eye on everyone in the room, not to mention all exits and entrances. My nerves are all on edge, my veins jumping with readiness to fight, to kill. One wrong move from any of these dracori bastards, one flick of an eye or twitch of a finger in Rosie's direction, and I will leap into action.

But it's been hours now since Nyxia's departure. In all that time, I've spotted no sign of her presence in the minds of any of her former slaves. Though I don't want to believe it—afraid of letting my guard down too soon, too easily—I'm beginning to believe her hold over Cyran is truly broken.

My heart sinks deeper into my chest, as though every beat transforms it slowly into stone. I watch Rosie's face as Enya continues speaking, detailing her plans. Though her phoenix flame protected her from the worst of the hellfire barrage, the effort involved in keeping that level of flame alive has sapped her strength. It will be some time before she can summon up more. In the meanwhile, she can't even heal the hurts she received in the altercation. There are burns and cuts all over her body.

But when Lady Enya subsides at last, Rosie speaks with quiet firmness: "I will not gather the dragon spawn."

Every eye in that room snaps to her face, some wide with flashes of fury, some narrow with suspicion, all deeply curious.

"If they come, they must come of their own volition," she continues. "If I force them to return, if I force them to fly with me, how am I any different from Nyxia?"

Captain Tanyl, my personal dracori nemesis, growls and leans back in his chair, arms crossed. "You're different from Nyxia in that you want to overthrow Mhoryga. If that means temporarily possessing the minds of Mhoryga's creatures and turning them against her, so be it."

Rosie catches him with her golden-eyed gaze. "Don't forget, Captain, you were one of Mhoryga's creatures but a few hours ago."

A flush of rage stains his cheeks. "I am a man of Cyran."

"Yes. And you are here in this council of war because you choose to be. You and those like you are who I want at my side in the coming conflict, not mindless slaves."

"There aren't enough of us," another dracori asserts, one of the five who flew with me against Nyxia. He is still shaken from his experience of being repossessed, something he won't forget anytime soon. Having tasted freedom, the idea of enthrallment sits uneasily in his mind. "We can't hope to stand against the might of Mhoryga. Not in Khylmira, not in her own territory."

Now those are the truest words I've heard spoken this day. I catch Rhangyl's eye across the chamber. The dragon spawn was surprised to be included in the council; he's used to being treated as a beast of burden. But he, like me, has seen Khylmira, has seen Drathoridan and lived under the glare of the Dracor Flame. He has beheld Mhoryga with his own eyes and knows the vastness of her power. These Cyranian dracori cannot comprehend it. Though they carry hellfire in their veins, though they have suffered under thralldom, they don't *know*.

My gaze shifts to Rosie once more. I wish I could force her to heed Enya and the others. Her powers have already expanded tremendously since she and I began training. With practice, she would soon be able to summon all the dragons and dracori this side of the ocean. Even then, it would be a small armada compared to what Mhoryga commands in Khylmira . . . but if Rosie continued to grow her powers, she might be able to start overtaking swaths of Mhoryga's dragons as well. Soon we would accumulate an aerial force that swept like a shadow of doom across the continent.

In my mind's eye, I see us flying high above the Rothomir Wastes, sights set on Mount Dracor and the citadel of Drathoridan. Rosie herself would not be with us—she would remain safely behind in Heleris Stronghold, commanding her host from afar but remaining out of the worst conflagrations. I am the one who would lead the charge, mounted on a great dragon spawn, blade in hand and hellfire at my fingertips. Mhoryga would see our approach and, for the first time in her ancient existence, tremble with dread.

But . . .

If Rosie insists her brothers and the dracori must retain their autonomy, the vision falls apart. Her mere presence was enough to break Nyxia's hold on me, so long as Nyxia herself wasn't near. The same was true for Rhangyl. But mere proximity hadn't been enough when she got into Cyran, not with Mhoryga reaching out through her avatar. And though she managed to break Lady Enya free and temporarily liberate the slaves, Nyxia's arrival undid everything in an instant. Even I, for all I believed I could not be taken by Nyxia again, found myself fighting with all my strength to keep her out of my mind, to the point of losing my hold on Rhangyl. If the dragon spawn hadn't obeyed Rosie's command and swooped to catch me, I would now be lying in a broken heap of bones and dead meat.

And all this happened with an entire ocean between us and Mhoryga. She is simply too powerful, even reduced as she is, without a daughter's heart to feast on to renew her flame.

Finally, Enya throws up her hands in a severe gesture for silence. All eyes turn to her, and she turns to Rosie. "Very well," she says, and hellfire snaps between her teeth, her dracori nature asserting itself in a moment of frustration. "If you will not gather the dragon spawn, what then? What do you propose? Are we to go back to the way things have been these last two hundred years? Do you expect Albhia to defend the coasts of Belanor, staving off the inevitable tide of Mhoryga's forces? Because I can assure you that won't work. My people have battled long and hard, holding the gates against overwhelming onslaught. We can't hold them much longer. Mhoryga keeps breeding more of her spawn, creating more of her damnable dracori. And she has something we don't have: time. She never ages—she simply grows in strength and malice, accumulating more power with every passing decade. What does a defeat like today matter to one such as her? In a year, two years, a decade, a century, it will be as though it never happened. She will crush us."

"And it won't be long," Rhangyl says quietly, his deep voice filling the space, "before she comes back into cycle to generate another dragon princess egg. When that happens, when she has another daughter's manifested heart to devour, her power will swell to even greater strength than the world has yet seen. Nothing will stop her then."

Shadow grips the room, like a hand squeezing a heart until it can no longer beat. All are aware of the small sliver of opportunity presented to us. But everything hinges on one person. One small person, who sits now so quietly, hands folded in her lap, eyes downcast. One by one they look to her, hopes, fears, dreads all hanging on the next words she will speak.

The lantern light flickers. To my eye, the filigree patterns cast on her skin seem to emphasize Rosie's scars. Those terrible burns, those visible reminders that she is not what her mother intended her to be. She has never been one to fulfill others' expectations of her. She is her own person, and she must and will always pursue her own path. Any effort to crush her into compliance only makes her indomitable spirit burn all the brighter.

In this moment I fear her. Not *for* her but *her*—her own terrifying self. Because in her, all the hopes of this world have come to rest. But if she does what I know she has already proposed in her heart, my own selfish hopes will be shattered forever.

At last she speaks. Her voice is so soft, but all in the room strain their ears and hold their breath, so that the silence is thick, and her words seem loud in this shadowed chamber.

"I am going to manifest," she says.

I feel the shock wave pass through those assembled. Through every one of their minds passes an image of a creature like Nyxia taking dragon form. Nyxia's nature is so draconic, so wild and ferocious, if she were able to pass through the Dracor Flame, she would only become more of what she already is. But Rosie? Nothing in her reveals the dragon inside. No, not even those long, unfiled talons, stained with Nyxia's blood. Those seem, not a true part of her, but a strange grafting-on of some foreign creature not akin to Rosie herself at all.

Rosie lifts her head. Slowly she turns, her golden gaze meeting and holding each pair of eyes at that table for a long moment. She doesn't turn to me, but I feel her awareness of me where I stand close by in the shadows. "I must become a dragon," she says. "I must become something strong enough to break through Mhoryga's defenses and face the Dragon Queen herself. And then I will kill her."

No one here can believe it. No one can imagine it. She won't even call the dragon spawn against their will. How can she possibly turn killer? It is simply incomprehensible.

Enya breaks the silence first. "That settles it. We must travel to Khylmira anyway. You cannot manifest without the Dracor Flame."

But Rosie shakes her head. "The fire I require is something very different from the flames of Dracor." She lifts one hand. A small, pale flicker of white flame dances to life in her palm.

"What then?" Enya demands.

Suddenly I find I cannot bear to stand here and listen anymore. Though every single particle of my body urges me to stay in Rosie's proximity, I peel away from the wall and silently slip from the chamber. Darkness has fallen in the great hall, but I cross it in long strides, avoiding the shards of glass strewn across the floor. At the far end of the hall, I find the stairway leading up the western tower and ascend it, three treads at a time, coming at last to the open balcony overlooking Cyran and the River Cy. I walk out onto the hell-blackened stones until I stand over the very place where, just hours ago, I'd had Nyxia pinned down. At my mercy. Gods, I could have killed her then! After all those years of torture, I could have driven my blade into her throat and watched her bleed out, choking on her last breaths. But I didn't.

Even now she flees to Mhoryga. She will tell her mother everything . . . everything she doesn't already know. The Dragon Queen will have her retribution.

You've killed him. Nyxia's voice echoes from the stones around me, whispering on the chill wind. *You've killed Arun.*

There was a part of me which had hoped Rosie would be convinced to abandon this manifestation plan of hers. That she would succumb to the pressures of Enya and the Cyranian dracori, call the dragon spawn to her, and set out at once across the ocean. Then we might have caught up to Nyxia. We might have been able to take her down before she got her cursed message back to Drathoridan. I should have known she would not be swayed. Not Rosie. She is a force of nature contained in that small frame. Gods damn me, but I've never feared anyone the way I fear her! Not even Mhoryga. With Mhoryga, loathing dominates all other feelings, including fear. But with Rosie . . . I love her too much. And love can only ever fan fear's flames.

I move across the balcony, stand at the balustrade, cast my gaze across the rooftops of the city down below. The smoke, which clung so close to Cyran for the last year, has begun to clear, blown away by a fresh gale from the sea. I can just about discern the line of the ocean on the horizon from this vantage, and my heart leaps in my chest. It feels in this moment like the ocean is a portal back to my brother, a gate I dare not step through. Because to do so would mean abandoning Rosie.

I sense her approach well before I hear her, that awareness in my mind keenly attuned to the very vibration of her soul. She climbs the tower stairs, steps out onto the balcony, and hesitates a moment in the doorway, watching me. Then, on soft, padding feet, she moves to stand behind me, within arm's reach.

"Valtar?" Rosie says quietly.

I don't turn to her. I can't. I bow my head, my body bent heavily over the balustrade.

She is silent for a little while, debating her next words. "Rhangyl has agreed to carry me to Inamaer," she says at last. "We set off tomorrow at dawn. I hope . . ." She hesitates. "I hope you will come with me."

When I don't answer, she moves to my side, leans her elbows against the balustrade, and peers up into my face. I turn away sharply, unable to look at her. "Valtar?" she says again. The quiver in her voice cuts me to the heart. She reaches out, touches my arm gently.

All the strength seems to go out of my legs. I collapse on myself, right there, one hand still gripping the balustrade, the other covering my face. To my surprise, there are tears on my cheeks, scalding my skin with hellish heat. In this moment, I am utterly broken.

"Valtar!" Rosie cries. She kneels beside me, takes me in her arms, pulling me to her slim shoulder. I cling to her, even as silent sobs rack my body. "Are you hurt? Please tell me. I can help you, I can heal you."

She can't. She can't heal everything I have done to make myself into this monster. She can't bring back the lives I've stolen, all in desperate hope of saving the brother I have ultimately betrayed. For her. Because that's what I've done—traded his life for hers. And for what? Whatever happens, she will be lost. The inevitability of that loss threatens to crush the very life from me. She doesn't know, she doesn't realize. If she did, would she go through with this plan of hers? I think so. I think there's nothing in any world that will stop her, now that her purpose is fixed. Which means there's nothing more I can do to protect her.

I must and will fail her. Even as I failed Arun.

She pushes me from her a little, just enough that she can look into my eyes. Her trembling fingers gently move a lock of hair back from my forehead. I feel her tentatively touch the edge of my mind, but when I flinch, she retreats immediately, honoring my privacy. And that act in itself, after everything I've been through, is more than I can bear.

My arms close around her back, spasming with a sudden shock of need. She responds, acting on an impulse of instinct entirely beyond thought, locking her arms around my neck. My mouth gropes for hers, finds it, takes it. Claims it as though I might claim her very soul, pull her into me, and hide her from all this mad, mad world. She clings to me, but I feel how easily she will slip away. She seems to lose all sense of solidity, an ephemeral dream passing through my fingers and out of my life. I growl with the desire to hold on to her, taking everything she offers with a ravenous hunger that can never be satisfied. Oh gods! Oh Rosie, my Rosie! I would sell my soul were it enough to make you mine. But we are too late. My soul was sold long ago.

I wrench her arms, break her hold on my neck, and thrust her from me. "Valtar?" she quavers, but I drop my head so that her searching eyes cannot see my face.

"I can't do it, Rosie," I say. "I can't watch what you will become. I've borne much in this lifetime, but . . . I cannot bear that. Not that."

I rise before she can speak, turn heel, and flee her. Flee everything she makes me feel and want and need. Everything I should have suppressed long ago. Most of all, I flee the future, which even now bears down upon us, jaws open to devour.

17

Rosie

The problem with growing up in the back of beyond, I soon discover, is that it's difficult to locate on a map when one needs to find it again.

Enya produces a large stack of scroll maps from her war room, each offering detailed studies of the Unified Kingdoms of Belanor. She finds a particularly good one of Anfalen; when unrolled, it covers most of the tabletop, and my eyes are overwhelmed by the wealth of detail, down to the delicate patterns of scales decorating the fish which leap from the winding river at various intervals. Towns and cities are depicted in strong, broad strokes of black ink, and roadways are carefully drawn with landmarks and conversion metrics to give one a proper understanding of mileage.

What it does not boast is a single reference anywhere to Gartsworth Village.

Inamaer Forest is clear enough. That big patch of ink and green paint dominates much of the top right portion of the map, like a looming cloud just on the verge of overcasting the entire kingdom. There are a handful of towns and one city noted around the borders. But no villages. Certainly not one as tiny and inconsequential as Gartsworth.

Finding Mistress Iliyani's cottage is going to be harder than I thought. She hid us well over the sixteen years I was in her keeping—better than Durona did. I wonder how quickly Iliyani figured out who and what I am. Was it right away? Or did the suspicion grow in her over time? Perhaps she spoke to a truthseer about me or is a bit of a truthseer herself. It would explain a great deal about my intractable mistress.

Well, I decide at last, sitting back in my seat and rubbing one eye with the heel of my hand, I'll just have to hope I spy familiar landmarks from the air. I don't know what I'll do if I can't find Iliyani. Plunge into the forest all on my own? Not a pleasant thought, though I have done it once before. When the dracori attacked our home village and killed Durona, I fled into Inamaer, for they could not follow me there. I have no memory of my time in the forest . . . it's a great blank in my head. When at last I staggered out again, I practically fell into Iliyani's arms, seemingly by accident. That's all I remember.

I sit back on my chair, stretching my stiff shoulders and rolling my neck. I should sleep. Enya had a cot set up for me in the corner of this chamber. I should make use of it while I still can. It's not as though I can spend the whole night poring hopelessly over these maps for something I won't find. I should lie down, close my eyes, and . . . and . . .

And somehow not think about Valtar Skylock.

About that kiss on the balcony.

About what it meant, about what *he* meant when he said he can't bear to watch what I'm to become.

Will he not be coming with me tomorrow? My stomach knots

with bile. Part of me is tempted even now to send out a mental cry, to demand that he come to me and explain himself. To order him to fly with me at dawn.

But no. I don't want Valtar to come with me unless he wants to, only . . . oh gods, how I *want* him to want to! I don't know what to expect once we reach Iliyani's. I don't know if it will be safe to enter Inamaer, if I'll be able to find the Shrine of Lorayarus. And if I find it, I don't know if I'll be able to transform. So many unknowns, each more terrifying than the last, but all of them would be easier to bear with Valtar at my side.

"Come now, don't be sappy," I mutter, dashing a traitorous tear from the end of my nose. "You did manage to infiltrate Cyran and rescue that gods-damned idiot on your own merits, didn't you? You are capable and strong. You can do this. Even if he decides to back out now. You *will* do this. You *must.*"

But all the stern talk in the world can't silence that part of me which just wants to curl up and die at the prospect that Valtar has finally had enough and abandoned me.

It is a long and sleepless sort of night. I manage to catch a few hours' sleep but wake well before the sun. When I emerge from the antechamber into the long hall, a dark figure stands in the passage. My heart leaps, and my lips start to form the name: "Valtar?"

But then the figure steps forward into the light of the candle I carry. Not Valtar—Rhangyl. I bite back my disappointment and force a little smile. "Good morning, brother. Did you stand watch over me all night?"

He bows solemnly, his long black hair falling in a sheet over one shoulder. "It was my honor, sister Pandracor."

My heart shivers at the name. I've asked him and the other dragon spawn to call me Rosie, but they seem to have fixated on that other title and the hope it signifies. I don't bother fighting it now. "You won't be very fresh for flying now, will you?" I say instead.

Rhangyl grins. "Dragon spawn need little sleep. In fact, I feel more energetic than I have in ages."

He escorts me to the long hall. There I find Enya has ordered a table set up with a small but nourishing breakfast. While I eat, Enya herself shows me the supplies she's prepared for the journey, all packed in convenient satchels, just the right size for a dracori saddle. She's been more than generous; there's enough here to last me for weeks, plus gold and silver, should I need to stop in a village to purchase necessities. I shall be far better prepared for this leg of my quest than when I fled Stromin Palace with nothing but the clothes on my back. Though I did have a quite useful assassin on hand that time.

"I wish you would let me go with you," Enya says, closing the last satchel and buckling it tight. "Or let me send Tanyl and some of the other dracori."

I shake my head, certain in my answer. "I don't want to be conspicuous, and one dragon spawn is already pretty difficult to ignore. Rhangyl and I will manage well enough."

"And what would you have us do in the meanwhile?"

I blink at her by the candlelight. Horror slowly dawns in my head—horror that Enya Balxidon, Lady of Cyran, looks to *me* as some sort of leader. A terrifying prospect! I have no military training, no strategy, no experience from which to draw. I'm not meant to lead. I'm just a weapon. A fiery arrow to be aimed and shot in Mhoryga's general direction.

But Enya continues to watch me with those serious eyes of hers. Eyes which are so like her brother's, it makes my heart hurt. Somewhere in the back of my mind, I seem to hear his voice again, speaking to me with earnest entreaty: *Never forget, Princess Roselle, the hope of all Belanor rests on you. I pray, when need arises, you will find fire aplenty.*

I swallow the knotted lump in my throat and force myself to draw a breath. "The important thing," I say, "is to keep out from under compulsion. Set a watch for Nyxia, and at first sign of her return, evacuate the city. Otherwise . . ." I hesitate. What I'm about to say doesn't sound like something that belongs to me somehow. But I force myself to finish. "Otherwise I want you to be ready. If I manifest, I will return here first, and we will fly together to Khylmira."

Enya nods solemnly. There's something in her eye, something I recognize as clearly as though I'd jumped suddenly into her mind and read it there myself. Enya was not meant for a world like this, for a destiny like the one which lies before her. She was brought up to be a lady—like Philippa, so very put together and elegant, with knowledge of how to dress, move, and comport herself. She was not brought up for war. She was certainly not brought up for hellfire in her veins. But everything has changed. The transformation she has undergone is as stark in its way as anything I am about to face.

I look at her now, this quiet pillar of strength in the face of the hell unleashed upon her world. She is a true leader, whether or not she wanted this role. And I know, if I should survive my own manifestation and return this way, Enya will join me in the final fight against Mhoryga. She and her people will do as they have always done—strive and suffer and never yield until their last breath is spent.

We step out together onto the balcony, where Rhangyl has already assumed his dragon form. Experienced dracori do not often use saddles, but one has been found and adjusted to make the journey more comfortable for me. The supplies have all been loaded as well, and Rhangyl paces, eager to be off.

I bite my lip, subtly casting about for some glimpse of Valtar. He isn't here. My gaze lingers a moment on that place by the balustrade where we'd shared that kiss just last night. Was that his way of saying goodbye? Painful as it is, I understand if he doesn't want to come with me. He made it clear from the start that he does not approve of this plan of mine. And I have Rhangyl now; I'm not alone. He needn't feel responsible for me anymore.

But I would have thought, after everything we've been through, that he would at least come to see me off.

"All right then," I say brightly, nodding to Enya. Closing my eyes, I summon up the phoenix flame. It's not as hot or powerful as what I summoned yesterday. That was such a tremendous exertion of power, and I suspect it'll take time before I'm able to wield on that level again. But it's enough to cover my body in a protective layer so that I can mount the dragon spawn and ride without slowly roasting. Rhangyl crouches, and I climb up into the saddle, find the stirrups, and grip two horns in front of me. Rhangyl sends a wordless query back to my mind. "*Yes*," I answer. "*I'm ready*."

He spreads his wings. A powerful surge of muscle, and he springs into the air. I feel like I've left my stomach somewhere behind me, but once we're up and clear of the tower, that strange sense of rightness settles over me once more. As though I'm finally in my proper element, the place I've belonged all this time without knowing it.

Rhangyl circles the tower. Craning my neck, I look down to the balcony where Enya stands alone, looking small and rather forlorn. I risk letting go of one of the horns to wave, and she waves in response. A simple gesture, but it makes me feel better. It's good to know I've got a friend in this world.

Rhangyl is just choosing his course, heading east toward Anfalen, when a shadow passes overhead. Yesterday it would not have been visible, with the light obscured behind so much smoke. Now the hellfire fumes are clearing, and the sun shines through, casting shadows of all who fly across its disk. I look up, shading my eyes. My heart lurches at the sight of a dragon's silhouette, performing a lazy arch overhead. My gaze follows its flight as it plunges lower, pursues a turn around the tower, then, with a surge of wings, catches up to Rhangyl, drawing alongside him. The dragon is the same golden-scaled beast Enya rode yesterday, but I scarcely notice him. It's the rider who holds my attention.

"Valtar," I whisper.

He cannot hear me. Not with the wind stealing whatever sound I've managed to make. But he turns even so and looks at me, and my heart flips over in my breast. Has he come to say goodbye? Or is he joining me after all? It almost doesn't matter which, just so long as he is here, now, in this moment.

He offers a salute, one hand pressed to his heart. Then he bows low over his dragon's neck, and it puts on a burst of speed.

"*After him, Rhangyl*," I urge. My one-eyed brother tosses his head, a roar bursting from his throat. So we streak through the sky in pursuit of both dragon and assassin.

WE FLY THROUGH the day and well after sunset, dragon eyes being as capable in the dark as they are by daylight. I use one of the maps Enya gave me to decide our route, sending commands directly to Rhangyl's mind as necessary.

Valtar and his mount keep pace with us. The young dragon, spry and full of eagerness in its newly liberated state, seems to burst with the need to expend energy. Valtar gives him his head, and he darts off here and there, circling and looping back, but always ultimately falling into formation beside Rhangyl again. There is no doubt who is the true leader.

Two hours after sunset, Rhangyl speaks into my mind: "*You are exhausted. We must stop.*"

I am exhausted. Not from the flying—that's been quite wonderful, honestly. As much as I hate being on horseback, dragon riding is perfectly to my liking. But the effort required to keep my phoenix flame alight and protecting my body from the natural hellfire radiating from Rhangyl's being . . . that takes its toll. I've let it slip a few times, only to find my skin beginning to redden and blister. Hastily I've pulled it back into place, but I'm beginning to feel drained. I hate to stop, though; according to the map, if we pursue this same course and same speed, we'll come to the general area where I hope to find Gartsworth Village by sunset on the fourth day.

Well, no use in arriving at Inamaer too worn-out even to dare enter the forest. "*All right, Rhangyl,*" I reply. "*See if you can find us a soft place to land.*"

Not long after, Rhangyl alights in an orchard white with apple blossoms under moonlight and smelling sweetly. I fairly tumble off his back, stagger three paces, try to hold my balance, then simply give up and allow myself to sink spongy-legged to the ground. The fire I've maintained all this while snuffs out in an instant, and the world suddenly feels much darker and colder than before.

The golden-scaled dragon lands not far away. I watch idly as the figure on its back slides off. No spongy-legged wobbling from

Valtar, no indeed. He moves with the same alacrity as ever, damn him. Without a word or look my way, he unloads the supplies from his dragon's back, then turns and does the same for Rhangyl. While Valtar goes about making a small campsite, Rhangyl and the young dragon confer together in dragon tongue. I feel their voices but choose not to lean in and overhear, allowing them some privacy. They both take human shape, and I see that I was right—the golden dragon is indeed quite a lot younger. He's not much older than Rhyo, though much broader and fiercer eyed. A boy destined to be a warrior, had not a crueler destiny caught up with him first.

"Sister," Rhangyl says, leading the boy over to where I sit in my ungainly heap. "Allow me to introduce Rathal. He has been most anxious to make your acquaintance."

"A pleasure, Rathal," I say a bit dully.

To my surprise, the boy takes my hand and kisses it gallantly. "Sister Pandracor, it is an honor to serve you in any way I can."

My heart warms. Somehow it still shocks me to realize that all these dragons are in fact my brothers, that I share a kinship with them unlike any other in this world. It makes me wonder about the dragon spawn, who have haunted my dreams since the night of Durona's death. They too were my brothers. If I were to meet any of them, would I feel this same strange bond? Possibly. I've always thought of them as monsters, demons, but . . . the truth is, they never asked to be born, never asked to be our mother's slaves.

Rhangyl and Rathal help Valtar gather wood for a fire. No hellfire blaze, I note—nothing to draw undue attention our way. Soon they've got a cheery and quite ordinary fire dancing. Though a few minutes ago I was roasting hot, now I shiver in the spring night chill and gladly draw a little nearer.

"With your permission, Sister," Rhangyl says, "Rathal and I will hunt. We saw cattle a few miles back the way we've come."

My lip curls. I don't love the idea of them stealing some poor farmer's cows. But they are dragons, and dragons need more sustenance than travelers' wafers, especially after the long flight they've just made. "Try not to be seen by anyone," I caution. Rhangyl nods, and Rathal actually salutes, bless him. That is going to take some getting used to! They step out of the firelight. There's a *whoosh* of hellflame, and two long, sinuous shapes take flight into the night sky.

At last I am alone with Valtar.

He sits on the far side of the fire, one elbow resting on an updrawn knee. He seems to be utterly absorbed in his contemplation of our fire. I watch him for a little while, as the light flickers across his stone-hard features. Crickets sing from the orchard, and the stars turn slowly overhead, and all this while he absolutely refuses to so much as glance in my direction.

Eventually I've had enough. "So, are we going to talk about last night?"

Valtar is silent. I watch the muscles of his throat tighten.

"No." I sigh and, picking up a stick from the pile of kindling, use it to stir the embers. "No, of course not. Why should Sir Valtar the Reticent actually *talk* about anything? Silly things like thoughts and feelings? *Pffft!* That simply wouldn't do. He's a dark and enigmatic brooder through and through, and we can't very well go breaking the character mold, now can we?"

His eyes flick up to meet mine from under his low hood. Then back to the fire again.

I grit my teeth and stir the embers a little more roughly, watching them burst and collapse on themselves in bright sparks.

I find myself thinking about that kiss. It's the first kiss we've shared since our little lakeside interlude. There was something so raw and desperate in his grip, in his mouth, in his soul. Something I didn't understand in the moment but which I wanted very much to alleviate. I'd felt as though, if I could just hold him hard enough, kiss him fiercely enough, I might be able to make whatever was hurting him right, only . . . only now I'm not so sure.

"If we're not going to talk," I say after a little while, "might I ask you for a repeat of last night's performance?"

This time, though his eyes don't glance my way, I see a reaction at last. A faint flush stains his pale cheeks. But there's something wrong in his expression, something that dissolves all my attempts at lighthearted banter and makes me ill. I don't want to ask, but I know I've got to.

"Valtar," I say, the teasing note gone from my voice. "Valtar, did I . . . did I *make* you kiss me?"

"What?"

His voice is so sharp, I flinch. I find it difficult to look at him and drop my gaze to my lap instead. "It's just," I say so softly, I fear he won't be able to hear me over the snap and crackle of the fire, "I've been wanting you to kiss me. Oh, so much! But I'm afraid . . . I'm afraid that my wanting may have seeped through our mind link. That I forced you to do things you don't actually want to do. Down by the lake, you kept trying to tell me to stop, but I wouldn't listen." A tear escapes, races down my cheek. I swallow with some difficulty and force myself to continue. "I didn't stop to think I might be . . . controlling you." With a little sniff, I sit up straighter. "I've been practically throwing myself at you since the literal moment we met. But Valtar, I . . . I couldn't bear it if . . . if I made you feel something that wasn't true. If you tell me that's what happened, I'll never forgive myself, but . . . but I need you to tell me. I need to know. I need to know if . . ."

I can't finish. I can't ask him to tell me if my feelings for him are one-sided. If it's all been nothing but an invention on my part, and he was forced to play along. But if it's true, I must prevent any further damage from being done. Because the last thing I would ever want to do is hurt this man.

Though I wouldn't have thought it possible, Valtar has somehow gone stiller than before. Like a statue carved out of marble. I shut myself up at last, blinking hard and, with an effort of will, lift my gaze to look at him over the fire. To my surprise, he's watching me. Staring. His lips slightly parted. Oh, if only he would say something! Reassure me or curse me or *anything*. Temptation urges me to tap into his mind, but that would be too hypocritical. So I hold myself in check and do the only thing I can: I wait.

Abruptly he rises. His footsteps soft and graceful, he stalks around to my side of the fire until he stands over me. I lift my head, looking up at him, my brow puckered. For a long moment, we remain like this, staring at each other by firelight.

Then he bends down, grabs my arms, and yanks me to my feet. A wild hope that he's going to kiss me shoots through my heart, but he doesn't. He holds me with a painfully tight grip, staring into my eyes. Fire reflects in his black pupils and highlights the expression of terrible pain twisting his features.

"What have you done to me?" he growls at last through clenched jaw. My stomach plunges, thinking this is the confirmation I feared. But his fingers only tighten, and he says, "Rosie, can you not understand? Everything you do, everything you are, fills me with longing beyond anything I can bear. You don't have to *compel* me; I am already compelled. Driven to madness with the need to be with you, to breathe your air, to bask in the light of your spirit. Knowing you has been like knowing life itself, and the thought that you should leave me is hell. Hell, Rosie! Worse by far than any torment to which the fire in my veins must damn me. That hell I could face, because I had not yet tasted heaven, but now . . . after you . . ."

He wrenches one hand from my arm and clasps my cheek, fingers trembling. I gasp a shuddering breath, lean into his touch, tilting my head. I want to kiss his palm, want to draw his lips down to mine and kiss those too. "Valtar," I say through the tears choking my voice, "you can have me. All of me. I'm yours for the asking! Surely you know that."

His teeth bare in an agonized grimace. "But you're not mine, Rosie. Don't you see it? You belong to the world. You are *Valindra*. The Angel of Fire. You were sent by the gods themselves, bound to fulfill your holy purpose. And what can I do but stand by and watch?"

He tears away now, marching from the fire, and stands with his back to me. His broad shoulders form a forbidding wall, and his head bends low. I suck in a ragged breath, touching my cheek where his palm heated my flesh. "Valtar," I say softly, "it doesn't change anything. Maybe I do have a destiny to fulfill but . . . what after?" I move toward him, touch him gently on the shoulder. He flinches. I tighten my hold, as though I can somehow keep him from slipping away from me into the darkness which calls him.

"There's hope yet, Valtar," I say, though I know I must sound impossibly naïve. I can't help it; I believe it. "I may be able to defeat Mhoryga. Heliar almost did it, didn't she? That's what they taught me. And she was just another dragon, while I will be something new! A fire Mhoryga has never before faced. It may truly come out all right in the end, the world saved, your people and mine spared. And then we'll have the rest of our lives to—"

"Don't you understand?" Valtar slips free of my grip and strides five paces away before he turns and looks back. The expression on his face is dark and dreadful. "You speak of Heliar, but do you not remember the whole story? A dragon queen is not like your common little dragon spawn. She is a supernatural force, a power beyond this world. A creature of Dracora and the Tenth Realm." He lowers his head, looking at me from under the heavy ledge of his brow. "When you manifest, Rosie, you won't be able to take human form again. Not for a long, long time."

My blood goes cold. "How long?" I whisper. "How long before I'll be able to . . . to come back? As myself, I mean?"

He shakes his head. "Heliar is the only dragon princess who lived beyond her transformation. It was twenty years before Mhoryga finally killed her. She never reverted to human form in all that time."

"Twenty years?" I breathe out slowly, bowing my head. My voice is shaky. "Twenty years is a long time."

"Rosie."

I look up. He meets and holds my gaze, hard.

"Rosie, you might never come back. Not in my lifetime. Not ever."

18

VALTAR

The great expanse of Inamaer Forest looms on my left, like a monster lurking, patient for its moment to devour. The demonic blood in my veins is simultaneously attracted and repelled by the fresh air of Utherlynd, which wafts from those green depths. If I were to try to plunge into that forest, to enter the Utherlynd, it would destroy me, for the magic of that realm exists in antithesis to the fires of Dracora.

I look over my shoulder at the dragon spawn flying just in my blind spot and the little, white, flame-wrapped figure perched in the saddle on his back. Rosie is dragon spawn, a creature of Dracora, which ought to mean she cannot enter Inamaer any more than I can. A small part of me hopes she will be thwarted in her plans at the last minute when the very air of the deeper forest repels her, forces her back into her own world.

But I know better than to dwell on that hope. I remember all too well that night, sixteen years ago, when the burnt and terrified child tumbled from the thatched roof of her cottage home and landed on the ground close to where I stood. When I told her to run, she'd fled straight for Inamaer, vanishing into its depths where neither I nor any of my dracori cohorts could pursue. She is truly unique among all dragon and dragon-born kind.

Which means, sooner or later, she will enter that forest and be lost to me all over again. Only this time, the loss will be complete.

It's been seven days now since I told her the truth of what her transformation will mean. I'd half expected the next morning for her to tell me and her dragon brothers that she'd decided to forgo this quest after all and return to Cyran. Instead, she was uncharacteristically quiet, preparing for her day, mounting and setting off, all with scarcely a word. That silence has continued for the week of our journey. She's ever polite, but withdrawn, and I've not pressed her. I'm afraid if I do, I'll only drive her harder into pursuing her own determined course. If I've learned anything at all in the short while since meeting Rosie, it's that she cannot be forced to be anything other than what she is.

So I follow. Hoping, wishing. Silent.

On the fourth morning since setting out from Cyran, we reached the borders of Anfalen Kingdom. By sundown, we'd come within sight of Inamaer. Even from the air, there isn't much of the forest to be discerned. A heavy mist obscures anything beyond the first mile or so of its borders. Utherlynd, the Realm Beyond, stands apart from this world and the Ten Realms of the Ilemanti, a plane of pure magic and mystery, close to the borders of heaven itself. This physical manifestation is vast. We've spent the last three days flying its borders, searching for some landmark Rosie might recognize from the sky. Gartsworth Village, our destination, doesn't appear on any map, and I can't help wishing the whole town has simply fallen off the face of the world.

But I suspect if Rosie cannot find her former mistress and seek her help, she will plunge into Inamaer all on her own. I grit my teeth into the wind. No, it's better if she can connect with elfkind and have an escort to Bald Mountain and the Shrine of Lorayarus. I don't want her friendless in the vastness of Utherlynd.

The day grows late, the sun beginning to plunge toward the horizon. Rosie doesn't show any signs of stopping, no more than she has any of the previous nights. She drives us on and on until she is on the verge of collapse, and Rhangyl insists we stop for the night. Her control over her flame has grown over the last week, along with her endurance, but it is still a tremendous effort to keep that fire wrapped around her body for protection. She's going to wear herself out.

An unexpected plucking appears suddenly on the edge of my mind. I shake my head, startled. Rosie has been extremely careful not to go anywhere near my mind in days. But now she's here, and I find my heart jolting in response to her presence.

"*Down there*," she says.

I look but don't see much. My dragon tilts forward, however, and begins to descend alongside Rhangyl. Lower down, I spy an insignificant little cart track leading beneath overshadowing trees, which my eyes would certainly have failed to discern if I weren't already looking for it. Rosie leads the way on Rhangyl, and we follow that track for some minutes before she urges both dragon spawn to land.

Once we touch down, Rosie slips from Rhangyl's saddle, a little unsteady on her feet. She looks my way as I dismount, her expressive face carefully masked. "This is the way to Iliyani's cottage," she says, then turns to the two dragon spawn. "I'm afraid you wouldn't be very welcome visitors. I think it best if you take human shape and wait here." Another glance my way. "You can wait as well if you prefer."

"I'm coming with you."

She nods. Without a word, she turns and starts walking, leaving the cart trail and branching off onto a little dirt track, even smaller and less noticeable. I hasten after her, convinced only those born and raised in these parts would ever be able to navigate all the secret little highways and byways. It's like its own tiny world.

"The main road," she tells me, in a strangely disconnected voice, "leads all the way into Gartsworth proper." It takes me a moment to understand that she means the cart trail; it requires a stretch of imagination beyond my abilities to call it a *road*. "But Mistress Iliyani prefers to keep to herself," she continues. "Everyone knows where to find her if they need her, of course. Unless she takes it into her head that she doesn't *want* to be found. Hopefully that won't be the case this afternoon, for I think she dabbles in enchantments now and then, which can be so inconvenient."

I nod even as my lip curls. The air here, lower down and so close to the edge of Inamaer, is thin and a little difficult to breathe. Strange that Rosie seems entirely unaffected by it.

We come within sight of a little cottage sitting in a patch of late-afternoon sunlight, surrounded by a riotous crowd of irises. Out from the greenery and frilly purple heads streak two creatures, long and low. They yowl like demons escaped from some netherworld, evil fire alight in their eyes. I flick my wrists, knives appearing, one in each hand, but Rosie drops to her knees, arms extended.

"Tiger! Shadow!" she exclaims with delight. "Don't be rude to my guest, or I'll douse you both in holy water, so help me!"

The demonic creatures stop their infernal racket and become, rather to my surprise, a pair of stripy cats. Purring and rubbing against her knees, they flick their tails and lift their haunches to accept scratches. "Who are my good little progeny of evil, then?" Rosie croons.

"You are aware they are both possessed," I say, fingering my knives.

"Oh yes." Rosie smiles up at me, and my heart hitches against my sternum. "It happens all the time around here. They're only First Realm demons, you know, *vathana*. They like to hang out on the borders of Inamaer, but can't get in, so eventually they're obliged to find hosts. Cats are prime targets for demon possession, but you'll get the occasional piglet, chicken, or even chipmunk. They don't cause trouble, though we usually slaughter the pigs before they get too big."

I watch in silent wonder as Rosie makes much over the little hellbeasts. I feel as though I'm seeing a whole new side of her, now that she's back in her own world. And I find myself strangely jealous of both Tiger and Shadow, who revel in her caresses, losing all dignity and rolling on their backs to display striped bellies.

Tearing my gaze away, I discover a strange little figure standing in the doorway of the cottage, watching us. She stands no taller than my belt buckle and has the face of a walnut, all wrinkles and crevices. A ratty lace cap adorns her head, but she wears it with all the solemn dignity of a royal diadem. At first glance, she appears positively ancient, but I suspect she might be older even than that. I have no doubt, in the first instant that I meet her gaze across the yard, that she is, in fact, a truthseer.

"Took you long enough," she says by way of greeting, her voice like a rusty hinge.

Rosie, distracted from the demon cats at last, looks up and

smiles at her former mistress. She jumps to her feet, hastens across the yard, and, despite the woman's forbidding expression, kisses her on one wrinkled cheek. "Hullo, Iliyani! Have you missed me?" she asks with that irrepressible brightness I've missed these last seven days.

Mistress Iliyani grunts. "I've had the Perharice boy up from the village to run errands for me, so we've gotten by."

Rosie looks a bit hurt but shrugs it off. "Well, I've had quite a time of it, let me tell you! How about you make us a pot of chamomile tea, and we'll tell you all about it?"

"What's there to tell?" Iliyani contrives to somehow widen herself, using every square inch of her tiny frame to block the cottage entrance. "You're a dragon. I can smell the fire on you, so I take it you've finally manifested. Hadn't you ought to be off to destroy your mother by now?"

Rosie shoots her a narrow look, which Iliyani deftly ignores. Instead she turns to me. "So here you are then. Hmmm. Bigger than I thought you'd be. The noble champion, favored by the gods."

I slip my knives back into hiding and cross my arms.

"Technically Valtar didn't win the championship," Rosie says. "But he did well enough, and there's lots more to tell you, if you care to hear it."

Iliyani snorts. "I've always been of a mind that if people tended their own business, the world would be a better place. That said"—she looks at Rosie, her glinting little eyes taking her in slowly—"what are you doing here, girl?"

Not getting the hoped-for invitation to enter, Rosie looks deflated. "I'm here because I need your help," she admits.

"Help?" The old half elf makes a face. "I've got nothing to do with dragons and dragon business. I keep to my little part of the world and try to do more help than harm. That's it."

"Yes," Rosie says, "but you know elfkind who live in Inamaer. I've seen you dance with them every solstice night."

Iliyani's face neither acknowledges nor denies this. Her mouth forms a tight knot of wrinkles.

"I want you to talk to them," Rosie persists. "Ask them to help me."

"Why?"

In answer, Rosie holds out her hand, and a burst of white phoenix flame erupts in her palm. Iliyani may be a truthseer, but she is not an all-seeing one. She gasps and takes a little step back, even as the demon cats yowl and streak for the nearest tree, disappearing up into its branches in a heartbeat.

"I manifested fire," Rosie says, "but not hellflame. And I don't believe hellflame is what I need to achieve my final form either."

She goes on to explain the circumstances of her birth and her own speculation based on that information. Iliyani listens intently, interested despite herself. When Rosie is through, the old half elf is silent for a long, contemplative while. "I may know an elf or two of the forest," she says reluctantly at last. "I don't have much clout with them, though. I'm half-blood, and they don't think much of me as a result. I can't ask them to guide you to the Shrine of Lorayarus."

Rosie nods. Then, to my surprise, she says, "Would this make a difference?" and pulls something out from the neckline of her gown. It's a little gold-dipped leaf, obviously elfin in origin. A gift from Viessa, I suspect, as she's worn it ever since we parted with the half elves.

For the first time, Iliyani looks truly surprised. Her gnarled hand extends, and Rosie hastily slips the necklace off and drops it into her mistress's curling fingers. The old woman holds the leaf up close to her face, watching it spin slowly. "Where did you get this?" she asks, her voice strangely awed.

She doesn't even attempt to hide her fascination as Rosie relates our adventures with the eldrin of the Glynrieth kintribe and the moment when Rosie's fire abruptly manifested. When Rosie comes to the end of the tale, Iliyani shakes her head, the laces of her cap wafting gently against her withered cheeks. "This necklace belonged to Llamyril Stargaze, a long-lost prince of the elves. It carries a great deal of weight." She sucks on her gums for a thoughtful moment. "It may be the gods directed your steps more intentionally than any of us might have guessed."

She closes her fingers around the necklace now and fixes Rosie with a firm stare. "Very well. I'll take this with me to the edge of the wood and speak to my cousins. It may be . . ." She shakes her head, unwilling to commit. "It may be they can be prevailed upon to help you after all."

Rosie nods her assent, and Iliyani hastily stashes the token inside her bodice. Her gaze flicks from Rosie to me and back again. "You can wait inside the cottage if you like," she says, begrudgingly. "But under no circumstances are you to let those two dragons of yours cross my threshold. Yes, I know you flew in on dragons—wasn't born yesterday, was I? And don't go drinking my good chamomile. Dandelion tea is good enough for dracori."

With that she stumps from the porch, through a patch of irises, aiming straight for the forest without bothering to find a path. I watch her hunched little figure disappear into the shadows before turning to find Rosie's gaze upon me.

"Shall we?" she says, indicating the open doorway.

I don't particularly want to enter the old woman's cottage, but follow Rosie like the loyal dog that I am. I stand near the door, arms crossed, as Rosie goes about stoking the fire and putting on the battered old kettle. She takes a little packet down from a shelf on the mud-and-wattle wall, shooting me a mischievous grin. "I'm using the chamomile," she says.

I make no comment. Of all the risks she intends to take in the near future, this one seems mild enough. While Rosie busies herself, I glance around the cluttered little space. There are signs of Mistress Iliyani's occupation as apothecary everywhere: drying herbs, sacks of minerals, and tinctures stashed in dusty bottles. A long worktable dominates most of the primary living space, unexpectedly overseen by a battered but recognizable marble bust of Glorindal, the legendary Hunter King of Anfalen.

I take a step in that direction to get a better look, but Rosie utters a little "Oh!" and leaps across the room, wrapping her hands around the eyes of the bust. "I can't have the two of you meeting," she says. "He might get jealous." She turns the bust away then laughs at my baffled expression. "Dear Glorindal here was my first kissing partner," she says. "I was rather lacking for options, you see, and figured I needed to start getting some practice in."

My eyebrows tilt. She's looking up at me, the reticent woman she's been this last week gone, replaced by the sweet, winsome, ridiculous Rosie I know so well. My heart feels suddenly leaden, sinking down to my gut. How much longer will this version of her exist? Now that Iliyani has gone to speak to the elves, I feel the moment of our inevitable parting creeping up much faster. I should be ready for it, but I'm not. I want to beg her not to go with the elves, to stay with me instead. To return to my original plan of simply fleeing into the wilds, running away from everything and everyone.

But I know she won't. She can't. And I can't ask it of her.

As though reading my mind, her smile fades a little. Then she draws a little breath and, still clinging to Glorindal's severe visage, says, "Valtar, I've been thinking—" A piercing whistle from the kettle interrupts with a vengeance. Startled, Rosie leaps to the fire, covering her hand with phoenix flame to protect it from the hot handle, which she grasps and pulls from the hearth rod. She pours steaming water into a waiting pot, her attention apparently absorbed in the task. The delicate scent of chamomile fills the space.

Then, without looking up at me, she says, "Valtar, I've been thinking that perhaps . . . perhaps you could marry me."

The floor beneath my feet pitches abruptly. I reach out and grasp the edge of the table with one hand. "What?"

She finishes pouring and sets the kettle to one side. Her hands tremble as she puts the lid on the pot and covers it with a cloth to retain heat. With a little shake of her head, she looks up and catches my eye. "If all goes well, I'll be setting off into Inamaer soon. Tomorrow, most likely. I know you can't go with me. I know dracori cannot enter Inamaer. Which means . . ." Her lashes lower, covering those golden eyes of hers again for a moment. Her voice quavers. "Which means we must say goodbye. Soon. But Valtar, I . . ." She steels her spine and makes herself look at me again, this time more firmly. "I love you." She laughs helplessly, tears in her eyes, and tosses her hands. "I love you! There, it's easier to say a second time. I love you, and your brooding silences, and your unfailing courage, and the way you always seem to understand me, even when I don't understand myself, and—let's be honest—those broad shoulders of yours aren't the worst thing I've ever seen in my life. But I love so much more than that. Knowing you are there when I need you. Knowing if

I fall, you'll be waiting to catch me. You push me to be better, stronger, braver than I ever knew I could be. You have protected me, guided me, held me when I thought I was going to come all to pieces, and . . ."

She seems to run out of words. Silence hovers between us, and I wonder if I need to answer, need to fill it, now, before the moment is lost. But then she continues in a softer tone: "If these are my last days, last hours perhaps, of life as *me*, myself, as Rosie Harpwood . . . I want to spend them with you. I want to be with you, to lie with you. To have you on me and in me and through me. I want to be one with you, to know that I am yours and you are mine, body and heart and very soul." She looks me in the eyes, courage burning like fire in her gaze. "I want to be your wife, Valtar Skylock. If you will have me."

I feel as though my feet have turned to stone. I want to stay in this place, anchored, rooted, so that the world itself cannot turn and take me away from here. But the moments are passing, whether I want them to or not. There is no time to waste.

I start toward her around the table. She draws a quivering little breath, tilting her head back to meet my eyes, and there's a trace of fear in her face. "It doesn't have to be forever, you know," she says all in a rush. "You won't be held to any vows you made to me when I'm not *me* anymore. I'm saying, you don't have to consider yourself married to a dragon! But if you wanted me now, if you thought you might—"

I place two fingers on her lips, silencing her. And I look into her eyes—drinking in the sight of those golden irises which once filled me with such dread and now are the very light of my existence. I feel in this moment the absolute height of joy to which I now know I can and will rise, and, as a result, how much harder and farther the plunge into despair will be. I fear that plunge—

fear I will not be able to endure the agony of shattering from so great a height. But I cannot bear to miss the glory she offers. The chance to soar to the very brink of heaven itself, wrapped in her arms.

"I will marry you, Rosie Harpwood," I say, my voice rough and low. I bend down, let my fingers drift away from her lips so that mine can hover just over them. "It will be my honor."

Then I catch her mouth in mine, tasting her tears even as a little whimper of joy vibrates in her throat.

19

Rosie

Iliyani returns from her tramp into the forest at sundown. She stomps up the porch steps, pushes the door open, sniffs loudly, inhaling the telltale scent of chamomile, and shoots me a withering glare. I meet her gaze with a bland smile. I'm seated demurely at the table, across from Valtar and completely out of reach.

But I feel so aware of him. We've restrained ourselves, waiting for my mistress to return . . . in part simply because we knew she would return, and abruptly. The last thing I want tonight is to be rudely interrupted in the middle of whatever Valtar and I might get up to. Best settle one piece of business before we begin another.

The awareness of him is alive in my senses, however. As though even now, his hands are on my body, his lips pressed to mine. Something in my face must betray my thoughts too, because Mistress Iliyani takes one look at me, and her expression somehow manages to sour even more.

"Well," she says, taking a heavy seat in her chair by the fire, "you're all set. My cousins will meet you at dawn tomorrow under the old willow. They'll take you as far as Bald Mountain, but you'll have to make the climb to the shrine on your own. It'll be . . . oh, about a three-month journey to get there, if you want to go by mortal standards of time."

"Three months?" I echo, surprised. "That long?"

"Oh, not out here, it won't." Iliyani pops her feet up on a stool and pulls a pipe and tobacco from the depths of some pocket. "If you return at all," she continues, stuffing the pipe with deft fingers, "it'll probably be no more than an hour or so for those of us on this side. Though I suppose, if things go strange-like, a dozen years might slip by. It's hard to predict the ways of Utherlynd."

I cast Valtar a quick look, suddenly sick in my gut. Though he looks back at me levelly, I can tell he's biting his tongue. He knows what I need right now isn't resistance but courage.

That's not all I need.

"Mistress Iliyani," I say, turning to the half elf, "you've done so much for us already—"

"Gods-spitting right, drinking my best chamomile," she mutters, lighting a piece of kindling at the hearth and holding it to the pipe bowl.

"—but I was wondering if we might beg one more favor."

She lifts a grizzled eyebrow. "Beg away, girl. Not saying it'll do you much good, but you can beg if you like."

I cast Valtar another look, which he meets with the same level calm. I've learned to read the smoldering heat burning in the depths of his eyes, however. It's there now, a simmering flame that makes my stomach flip and dive. Emboldened, I address Iliyani once more. "I was wondering if you could marry us."

The old half elf seems to freeze in her chair. The kindling

burns down right to her fingers, and even now, she hardly seems to notice. Her little eyes dart from Valtar back to me, bright as twin sparks.

"You see," I continue, "we'll have to say goodbye tomorrow morning, and . . . well, tonight we thought . . . we'd like to . . . I mean, since it's our last chance and all . . ." I lick my lips, flushing under Iliyani's stare. "I'd just like it to be official. It'll feel more . . . complete that way."

"Gods spare us, the girl wants to go and marry a dracori!" My mistress tosses the smoldering kindling to the fire at last and takes a long draw from her pipe. Then, speaking through a cloud of exhaled smoke, "We haven't any witnesses. Unless you count Tiger and Shadow."

"My brothers," I reply. "They're down the road a piece. They'll bear witness."

Iliyani curses softly. "Dragon spawn bearing witness to dracori nuptials. Who ever saw the like?" Then she shrugs. "But I suppose you are a dragon yourself, ain't you, girl. I never thought dragons would be sticklers for convention like this, but who'm I to judge?"

"So you'll do it?"

"Saints and angels, girl, do I look like a priest to you?"

"No. But you're the only real authority in my life, and . . . and somehow, I think it would be all right in the eyes of the gods if it was you." I tilt my head, and though I know pleading has never once worked on my irascible mistress in her long, crotchety life, add, "Please?"

Iliyani casts Valtar an evil look and mutters a stream of dark things under her breath. Then she tosses up her hands. "Fine then! I suppose it's the least I can do after all the fetching and carrying you've done for me over the last sixteen-odd years. But don't you let those dragon-spawn brothers of yours anywhere near what's left of my good chamomile!"

ROSES BLOOM IN a snarl of delicate pink buds and tiny-but-vicious thorns around the back door of Iliyani's cottage. Valtar harvests a handful for me to carry, as is right for a bride on her wedding day. I stick a few in my hair for good measure, hoping the thorns won't tangle too badly. It certainly dresses up my travel garb, though the overall look is not, perhaps, the picture a girl dreams of for her wedding day. Only I find I don't care two straws—I'd marry Valtar in a potato sack, roses or no roses.

Rhangyl and Rathal, looking both surprised and abashed, step into Iliyani's yard with some trepidation. I'm not certain what exactly Valtar told them when he fetched them from the cart trail, but neither of them tries to talk me out of anything. Rhangyl, bless him, salutes me with a kiss on the cheek. "For your happiness, sister," he murmurs.

I flush, turning the bunch of roses around in my nervous hands.

Iliyani assumes a commanding position on the porch steps, claps her hands for attention, and calls out in stentorian tones: "Get over here, you two."

Valtar and I move to stand before her, my dragon brothers at our backs. Even up several steps, her bent little head is about on a level with mine, and she's obliged to crane severely to look up at Valtar. She manages it, however, her lacy cap flapping in the breeze. "I ain't much for speeches and ceremonies," she says. "And I'm not altogether convinced dracori have it in them to love or possess much by way of hearts. But this girl of mine . . . well, she means the world to me."

I suck in a short breath, looking up from my cluster of roses to gape at my mistress.

"Now don't go taking on about it!" Iliyani snaps, her wrinkles sinking into deep scowl lines. "But you've been something like a daughter to me, and I find I would like nothing more than to help you steal a little happiness in this life. Gods know, there's not much happiness to go around, so who's to blame you for reaching out for a handful? If your heart's set on this man, so be it. Do you vow before Vialth, Eidolo, and all the Divine Hosts to love, cleave, honor, and all that for as long as you both draw breath in this world?"

I glance up at Valtar. While I've been nervously bouncing my gaze from my flowers to Iliyani to my feet, he has remained focused on me with absolute intensity. My heart leaps with the knowledge that, whatever may come, that focus of his will remain, a steadfast constant on which I may rest in any storm.

My lips break into a smile. "I do."

"And you, dracori?"

"Valtar," he says coldly, without shifting his gaze.

"Sure. Do you, Valtar, likewise vow to love this girl, honor her, protect her, and devote yourself to her good and happiness while the gods see fit to make her yours?"

Fire burns in the depths of his eyes, warming me straight to my toes. "I do," he says.

"Then I suppose that about does it," Iliyani says, and while I could be imagining it, there might be the faintest tremble in her voice. She covers it with a brisk clap of her old hands. "Kiss her, why don't you? Then take her into the house for the night. I'll bunk down with the donkey. Call it a wedding gift." With this pronouncement, she stumps down the steps, bustling between us, and sets off across the yard to the donkey's stable at a brisk waddle.

I don't quite know where to look or how to react. But Valtar takes a step forward and draws me into his arms. Suddenly, there's just the two of us. Somewhere far away, I hear my dragon brothers offering up an awkward cheer, and the demon cats yowling from their perch up in the tree. But those voices seem to be part of another world.

Valtar bends his head and plants a chaste kiss on my lips. Just the barest brush of connection, but it sends a delicious shiver down my spine. When he pulls back, he murmurs, "Shall we?"

I don't dare cast a look back into the yard. Ducking my head to hide a sudden flush, I hasten up the porch steps and into the cottage. I walk to the worktable and set down my bouquet, even as Valtar shuts the door behind us and drops the bolt. My heart begins to race like wildfire. Which is silly . . . I've been practically naked with this man before, felt his hands and lips on parts of my body no other man has even glimpsed. But there's something about this moment, this space. About the knowledge that tonight is all we have. It makes me feel afraid. And a little dizzy.

I turn to face him, gripping the edge of the table for support. The interior of the cottage is dim now that the sun has mostly set, illuminated only by the low fire on the hearth. Valtar, moving with silent grace, adds a log to the fire. I swallow and look around the little space. It isn't much by way of a honeymooners' nest. My own bed is up in the little loft among the rafters, and Iliyani has a simple pallet tucked into an alcove, with doors to shut her in nice and snug. It's not even long enough for me to stretch out in, much less someone of Valtar's great bulk.

I lick my lips. "I'm sorry. This isn't, um . . . I maybe didn't think this through completely."

Valtar, crouched by the fire, turns and looks up at me.

Then, for the first time in I don't know how long—possibly ever—he smiles.

It's so strange, to watch those stern, stone-carved features of his shift, to see the latent sorrow which clings to his very soul suffused suddenly in pure joy. My heart melts, and my knees go a little weak.

"Oh, Valtar," I breathe. "Please kiss me. Now."

He rises, steps across the room, and pulls me into his arms. This kiss is not like the little peck on the lips outside. No—this is our first true kiss, as man and wife. A kiss of claiming and cleaving. I feel something inside me opening up to him, like a doorway in my chest has just unlocked and swung wide, bidding him enter in. He kisses me long and hard, his lips firm as they manipulate mine, and when he breaks away at last, I lean against him, clinging and rather boneless.

When I catch my breath, however, I know what I want. Without a word, I begin to fumble with the fastenings of his jerkin. My fingers tremble so hard, I can hardly manage them, but he moves to assist. Between us, we strip off his jerkin, and then, rather than bothering with the laces, he pulls his dark undershirt over his head and discards it on the floor. Firelight plays across his muscles, gleaming against the ugly darkness of his dracori scar.

I stare at his chest, at that scar. Slowly, I let my fingertips brush over it, running lightly from where the Draconan head arches over his heart down to the tail curling below his navel. Funny how something that used to frighten and repulse me now holds no such power. It's all part of Valtar, and I love every part of Valtar. Even the scars.

I lean forward and kiss his torso. He draws a shivering breath.

I kiss him again and again, running my hands sensuously across the hard muscles of his chest and down his abdomen, reveling in the great strength and masculinity of this man I have married. Shyness forgotten, I tilt my head back at last and say, "Well, Valtar? What would you have me do next?"

Without a word, he pulls at the front laces of my bodice. He doesn't rush, not like I did. He lingers over each lace, slowly parting them to expose the low dip of my chemise. I laugh softly, reminded suddenly of our first meeting, when my bodice laces tangled with the buckles of his cuirass. He'd been so careful then when freeing me, his fingers precise, his gaze fastened everywhere but on the display of flesh presented before him. Not this time. Now he drinks in the sight of me. The laces unfastened, he brushes one finger slowly along the lacy neckline, gently tugging it lower, lower. Then, a growl in his throat, he bends and kisses the swell of my breasts, his mouth hot and trembling against my flesh. My breath ratchets faster, my chest rising and falling in quick pants under his lips.

"Oh," I gasp, fingers slipping up the back of his neck, threading in his hair. "Valtar, you'll drive me mad!"

He grips my overskirts and yanks them down to a pile at my feet. The chemise follows shortly after, along with corset and stockings. His hands hot against my skin, he grips the bare patch at my waist between breast wrap and pantalets, turning me and pulling my back against his chest. Then slowly, slowly, he glides his hands from waist to stomach, then up over my breasts. I moan. An embarrassing little squeak bursts from my lips as his mouth bends to hungrily kiss the curve of my shoulder.

"This doesn't seem to be doing much good anymore, does it?" he murmurs, plucking at the laces of my breast wrap until it falls away entirely. I gasp at the sudden feeling of nakedness, gasp again as his thumb finds and plays with one nipple, all while his mouth excites bursts of sensation across the sensitive skin behind my ear.

By the time he turns me to face him again, I'm quivering from head to toe, uncertain how I can bear so much pleasure. He presses my bare breasts against his chest as he kisses me harder than before. I wrap my arms around his neck, clinging to him as though for support in a storm. His mouth is rough, demanding, hungry, and yet somehow reverent, and I drink him in, parched for more.

Slowly, he begins to lower himself, his lips exploring down my neck to my collarbone, my breast. I grip handfuls of hair as he takes my nipple in his mouth, gently manipulating with lips and tongue. "Oh!" I whimper, struggling for breath which seems utterly stolen from my lungs. "Valtar, that's . . . that's so . . ."

Words fail entirely. I rock into him, my back arching into the sensation he gives. But he's not through yet. He continues his journey down, kissing my stomach, my navel. His fingers slip along the edges of my pantalets. With a sudden tug, he pulls them down to my thighs, even as his head tilts back, looking up at me.

"What are you doing?" I pant. His breath is hot against my stomach, igniting a deeper, wilder heat lower down, between my legs. I have no experience from which to draw, no understanding of what is taking place in my own body. On a practical level, I know how coupling is supposed to work, but . . . nothing I've picked up involved anything like this! The feeling of his lips against the delicate skin at the transition between abdomen and loins . . . oh gods, what is he doing to me?

"Rosie," he commands, "widen your stance."

"What is this?" I grin. "Another knife lesson?"

But at the firm pressure of his hands, I obey, and then—he's there! Between my thighs, at my crest, his tongue toying with me in ways I never imagined. I stagger back against the table, my buttocks hitting the edge, my hands gripping for support. I shift one hand to grab his hair, adjusting my balance even as he slings one of my legs over his shoulder. The change of angle undoes me. A gasp of raw pleasure bursts from my lips, followed by a long groan as stars explode in my head and waves of delight pulse through my body.

When the peak is finally achieved, and I begin to ease back down the far side, I toss loose hair and rose petals back from my face and look down at Valtar. He is still crouched before me, his cheek against my thigh, gazing up at me from those black eyes of his.

"I have wanted to do that from the first time you kissed me," he says in a husky growl. "I've dreamed of it. Of being right here, with you."

"Really?" I reach out, brush a dark lock of hair back from his forehead. "Well, why didn't you have at it? I suppose it might have been a bit shocking at first, but . . . Oh gods!"

I let out a little squeal when he turns and nips my inner thigh. Tangling my fingers in his hair, I pull him up to me and kiss him viciously, forgetting everything except that dance of lips and tongue and the friction of our bodies against each other. "You have me at a disadvantage," I speak against his mouth. My fingers tug at the waistband of his trousers. "Is it not grossly unfair that I should be naked as a baby bird in front of you, while you remain all virtuously clad?"

"Not so virtuously," he remarks wryly, looking down at the front of his trousers where the signs of strain are becoming more undeniably evident.

In moments, I've got him stripped down. Then I step back, and for the first time, gaze in awe at his naked form. Gods, but he truly looks as though he were carved in marble! "It's a good thing I already turned old Glorindal's face away," I say, slowly lifting my admiring gaze back to his face. "Otherwise, he'd smash himself to the floor in jealousy!"

Valtar chuckles—a dangerous, delicious sound, one I'm not sure I'll ever get used to—and wraps me close. His largeness is both intimidating and exhilarating. He grips my hips and lifts me off my feet, setting me on the table. I wrap my legs around his waist, drawing him to me. I've heard the first time is often painful for women but soon find this is not so for me. Perhaps it's thanks to the miraculous work he's already done, preparing my body to receive him. Other than a little unfamiliar pressure, there is no pain. Only a sense of rightness, of completion that I hadn't realized I craved. I cling to his shoulders as he thrusts inside, desperately kissing his neck, his ear, his jaw, everything I can reach.

He pulls back a little and cups my face with one hand. When he thrusts again, I gasp. He runs his thumb along my quivering lips in a slow, savoring touch. His own mouth is parted as he draws breath in time with mine. My dragon sight can see him clearly, even in this half-lit gloom, and I tell myself to remember this—exactly this. This moment when he is so completely mine. My lover, my protector. My husband.

Pressure mounts to a fever pitch between us. When it bursts at last, our strangled cries emerge simultaneously from panting mouths. He bows over me, leaning me back and back until I am flat on the table beneath him, his heavy torso pressed against mine. We lie like so for some while, shuddering in the aftershocks of what we've just made of each other. At last he lifts his head, looking down at me. His hand strokes my cheek gently and pushes strands of hair away from my eyes.

"I love you, Rosie Harpwood," he says solemnly. "For so long as the fires of the sun shall rage and the waters of the moon ebb and flow, I am yours."

And I know now that, regardless of what was said or promised on the porch steps, this is his true wedding vow. And he means it. Forever.

Only forever suddenly feels much too brief as the hours carry us inevitably toward dawn.

I wrap my arms around his neck, pulling him down to me once more. "Hold me close, Valtar," I whisper. "Don't let me go."

He cradles me for some little while before beginning to kiss my neck again. I moan at the renewal of pleasure igniting across my skin, then catch his face between my hands and pull his mouth to mine. I have him now. I won't let anything—any fear, any dread, any future—ruin this night.

20

VALTAR

I dare not sleep. Not tonight. Even when Rosie, exhausted, slips at last into a peaceful doze, nestled in my arms, her head pillowed on my shoulder, I remain awake. Looking at her. Drinking in the vision of her face. There are so many details to impress upon my memory. Those golden lashes lying soft against her cheeks. The pattern of burn scars down her neck, across her lovely shoulder and her arm. Silken rose petals are scattered through her hair and a few small thorns as well, but I don't mind those, even when they bite into my skin when she shifts. Everything about her is perfection, both the softness and the bite.

If only a single night could be made to last a thousand years.

Her brow puckers in sleep, as though some dream plagues her. But I can't allow that, not tonight. I stroke her arm soothingly, not to wake her, merely to reassure her of my presence. I promised not to let her go, didn't I? I want her to know all the way down to her bones that I will keep that promise, keep my vigil, even into the darkest, loneliest hours, when my soul cries out to all the gods for mercy! Mercy . . .

Why must they take her from me? Why must I be made to give her up?

But no. I cannot let myself dwell on such questions. Surely it will anger the gods, and I don't want that. I want them on Rosie's side. I cannot have them punishing her for giving her heart to a gods-forsaken wretch like me. For her sake, I must wrestle my soul into submission and gratitude. From this day to the end of my worthless life, I must bow down on my face in thanksgiving for this one perfect, beautiful night.

The floor makes for a hard bed, but we've piled up our discarded clothing and the blankets from Iliyani's alcove. I've slept worse many times in my life and certainly won't complain. Not with this sweet being curled up against my side. Strange that she is so small and yet she fits me so well, as though we were made for each other. My Rosie. My wife.

She begins to stir, her hands uncurling and curling again like a cat's. Pain jolts in my chest. Dawn is not far off now; I can feel the change in the air, the pressure of a new day ready to spring into being. If I had the strength, I would force the sun back down behind the horizon, subdue the whole world under a cloak of night for another few hours at least. But there can be no turning back. The joy I experienced last night must soon be paid for with the agony I always knew would come. All that's left for me to do is face it.

Rosie blinks. I watch with both delight and unending regret as her lashes flutter and her gaze relearns to focus. She gives a kitten-like mew and stretches, her lovely, naked body arching against me. Tilting back her head, she looks up at me and smiles. It's like a knife's thrust to my heart.

"So," she says, running her hand over my chest, "husband. Did you sleep well?" She reaches up then and tussles my hair, nose wrinkling. "You look terrible. All hollow eyed."

"You look perfect."

She snorts. "Sweet talker. But just for that, I'll kiss you again if you like."

I roll on top of her, taking the offer with enthusiasm. Perhaps dawn can wait a little longer as I lose myself in the glory of uptilted breasts and upthrust hips and the soft folds between her thighs. All so exquisite, fashioned just for me. When we part at last, it's only to lie side by side. Her hand presses against her panting breast, and she shakes her head. "If I'd known everything you were capable of, Valtar Skylock, I'd have married you long ere now!"

The bright teasing of her voice. The musical lilt, the flirtatious angle of her head as she peers up at me. I know how valiantly she fights even now to keep at bay what the next hour will bring. And I love her for her courage, more perhaps than I've ever loved her before.

But it's time. If I do not rise to face my doom, I will run out of courage myself, forcing her to bear it all on her own two shoulders. I cannot do that. Not to her.

Rising, I offer her a hand, help her to her feet. For just a moment, I allow myself to pull her body against me, to breathe her into my soul and being. Then, silently, I help her dress. Her face loses some of its smiling determination, and her hands tremble as she fastens buckles and secures ties. Gods, how badly I want to rip each garment off her once more, to grab her by the hair and buttocks and pull her back down to the floor with me! Instead, I straighten my jerkin, tighten my belt.

Then, by the light of the mostly dead fire on the hearth, I meet her gaze. "Ready?"

She hesitates.

For a single breath, I allow myself the most blinding, terrifying, delicious hope that she will, after all, change her mind.

Then she says, "I'm ready, Valtar. Let's go."

THREE ELVES STAND in waiting on the edge of Inamaer, beneath an enormous willow tree. They seem to waft in and out of view, as though unwilling to be made fully corporeal in this world of mortals. From what I can see of them, they are strangely beautiful creatures—tall and painfully slender, with large eyes and leaf-woven hair. I think perhaps I've never hated anyone so much as those solemn beings, come to take my wife away.

Rosie walks beside me, holding my hand tightly. Iliyani trundles along on Rosie's other side, having emerged from the donkey's shed rather the worse for wear and more mean-spirited than ever. Rhangyl and Rathal appear through the mist, still wearing human forms, their faces wary. They do not like being this close to Inamaer any more than I do.

Rosie comes to a halt a few yards from the willow and the forest's boundary. She turns to Iliyani. "Is there . . . anything I need say or do?"

The old half elf shakes her head. "That token did the trick, child, as the eldrin no doubt knew it would. My cousins here will guide you to the foot of the mountain as promised. They're not a chatty bunch, but I've no doubt once you warm them up, you'll get along famously. After that, you're on your own. They will not dare approach the phoenix's shrine."

Rosie nods. She glances up at me then away again quickly, as though she cannot bear to meet my gaze. Instead she turns to Rhangyl and Rathal. I begrudgingly release her, and she steps over to them. They both drop to their knees, each taking one of her hands and pressing it to their forehead. "Oh, please!" she exclaims. "Don't be ridiculous. Get up and hug your sister, won't you?"

They obey at once, rising and embracing her, as solemnly as though offering up prayers before an altar. Rhangyl holds her a little longer perhaps, and when he steps back from her, there is a spark in his one eye that might be a sheen of tears. "Grace go with you, Sister Pandracor," he says.

"Yes," adds Rathal, bouncing nervously on his toes. "We'll be waiting. Whatever happens, we fly with you now."

She nods, not trusting herself to speak. Instead she turns to Iliyani. The old woman gives her a stern look and, when she approaches, hastily puts out a withered hand. "Don't go trying to hug these old bones, child! Save your embraces for that strong husband of yours; he can endure them."

Rosie swallows, forcing back tears she knows are deeply unwanted in this particular quarter. "Thank you for all you've done for me, Iliyani," she says softly.

"Piffle. It ain't much. So long as the two of you didn't finish off my chamomile." But Iliyani knows she means much more than one night of hospitality. This woman saved a child's life once, then kept her hidden for nearly two decades, better than anyone else ever could, even the valiant Durona Harpwood. Truthseer or not, she knew what she was doing. Rosie accepts the brusqueness, however, offering no more than a simple nod.

Finally she turns to me.

Mist coils between us, parting under her feet as she draws near. The rest of the world fades from my view, my entire existence bound up in this one small person standing before me. She looks up into my eyes, not touching me but reaching for me nonetheless. Already I feel the gaping chasm opening between us, dragging us inexorably apart. My lungs have forgotten how to expand and contract, my heart how to beat.

"I'll be back soon, Valtar," she says, speaking the lie in gentle tones. We both know the truth: If she returns at all, she won't be Rosie anymore. This is the end for the two of us. And it feels like death.

She tries to smile. "If Iliyani is correct, it won't be long! Just an hour or two. You can . . . save some breakfast for me."

I gaze into her eyes, deep and endless, full of the eternities she must now face. "I will wait for you, Rosie," I say softly. "For the rest of my life and beyond."

She bites her lip to stop it from quivering. Then suddenly she launches herself into my arms. I hold her tight, press her close, bury my face in her hair. I feel her fingers gripping my jerkin, those long, talon-like nails of hers digging deep, almost to the skin. I wish she would rip into me so hard that nothing could pull us apart. But when she steps back, I do not resist. Though everything in me fights to hold on, I let her go. Even as I curse myself for doing so.

She turns from me without another look, as though afraid one look more will be too much. She faces those otherworldly beings standing under the willow. Straightening her shoulders, she marches toward them, mist roiling in the path before her, obscuring her footsteps. She doesn't pause, not even when she reaches the willow tree. She keeps walking into the dawn-shadowed forest. One by one, the three tall figures turn and waft behind her.

She vanishes from my sight. Swallowed by Inamaer and the realm that lies beyond.

I breathe out a long exhale. She's gone. Gone from my life. Gone from my world.

Though the sun even now rises, I feel as if everything about my existence has been plunged into unending darkness. Hellfire burns inside me, rage mounting with a need to erupt. How could I have done it? How could I have let her go? The hope of the world has just gone out from the world . . . and it was my fault. Because I could not be strong enough to keep her here. With me.

If only I knew how to pray. If only I could fall to my knees here and now. But it seems as though all those desperate prayers I made while lying with her in my arms have withered away, leaving only my sinful husk behind. The gods could not hear me now, though I pleaded with the tongues of angels.

"Well," Iliyani says, breaking the silence at long last, "I suppose we might as well go have ourselves a hearty porridge and an egg or two. You'll need to keep your strength up for when she returns, dracori. I'll be damned if I don't see my Rosie's husband properly fed while he lurks on my doorstep. You two," she adds, waving dismissively at the dragon spawn, "had best go steal yourselves a goat or two. Be sure you do it from the next town over. Farmer Blotts over in Turrowby cheated me out of a silverbellum brew last winter, and he owes me. Go on then, and I'll—"

Before she can finish, the air suddenly explodes with the sound of thundering hooves and large mammalian bodies breaking through underbrush and foliage. It sounds as though a full company of king's cavalry has arrived in this remote spot in the middle of nowhere. The dragon spawn and I crouch in defensive stances. Their bodies spasm strangely, trying to assume dragon form, but this close to Inamaer, they cannot quite manage it. Rhangyl roars, and Rathal drops to his knees. My wrists flick; blades appear in each hand. I turn in place as mounted horses in battle regalia appear all around me. Lances flash in the new morning light, and hooves churn up mist in a fine frenzy.

"Ah!" Iliyani says without concern. "I'd wondered when he'd get around to showing up. Better late than never."

We're surrounded in moments. I find myself looking at the blades of three lances aimed at my chest. I lift my gaze to the riders bearing them, all helmeted and prepared to do battle. Their armor is laced with *meorise*, repellent to hellflame, but that does not interest me in this moment. I'm more interested by far in the face of the centermost man, who gazes down at me from between two face-shielding cheek plates. But I know those dark eyes.

"Prince Warrick," I growl. "We meet again."

Before the Prince of Anfalen and runner-up competitor for the hand of Princess Roselle Pandracor can answer, another horseman pushes through the rest, jostling aside lances and dominating the space around him. The horse itself is a massive white charger, but one can barely register its existence in comparison to the glory of the figure which sits upon it. Clad in flashing gold armor and a crowned helm, powerful as a demigod and radiating unadulterated majesty, he sits astride his steed like some hero out of myth. He bears no lance but draws a sword from the sheath at his side and points the blade directly at my heart.

"Where is my daughter, dracori?" High King Alderin Aumanus demands.

21

Nyxia

Mhoryga reaches out from Drathoridan, searching across the leagues for those minds she has lost. Nyxia feels her presence, scraping along the edge of her awareness. But though she wants to allow her mother entrance, to feel again that connection to power and truth she has known all her life, somehow she can't. Once Mhoryga gets into her mind, she will know about Valtar. And then Arun . . . *Arun* . . .

Bowed low over Zoar's neck, Nyxia keeps her gaze fixed upon the horizon where even now the Khylmirian shores come faintly into focus. She half hates her dragon brother for the speed and power with which he eats up the miles. The longer she can delay the inevitable meeting with Mhoryga, the longer Arun will draw breath in this world. But ultimately, how can she refuse to cast herself at the feet of her goddess, the center of her being? She must return, she must abase herself. And then she must simply hope.

The crossing is long. Zoar has stopped only a handful of times to rest and replenish his flame, choosing lonely isles lost in the vastness of tossing ocean waves. Otherwise, in silence, he keeps his nose pointed west. Toward Khylmira and Drathoridan and the Dracor Flame. Toward Mhoryga.

Sometimes Nyxia wonders what goes on inside her brother's head. It's strange to be disconnected from him, but try though she might, she has been unable to reestablish her hold. Not since Naevya broke her connection to Mhoryga. Is Zoar as devastated by that sundering as she is? Does he hate it as much as she does? Or—like her—does he secretly revel in this sensation of freedom never before experienced?

No! She shakes that thought away, refusing to dwell on it. Mhoryga is everything. Mhoryga is meaning and existence. She won't let these sinful temptations lure her away from the truth. She needs to get back to her mother quickly and reestablish their connection.

But as they draw near to the Khylmirian shore and the last leg of their journey, Nyxia cannot help shuddering when she feels that nudging of awareness on the edge of her mind. Mhoryga can't get in. For the first time ever, she cannot access the private spaces inside Nyxia's skull. And the knowledge makes Nyxia want to scream. A dichotomy of need threatens to tear her in two. She needs her mother, needs that connection, and yet . . . *to be free*. To have space for her own thoughts, her own ideas, her own desires. Is this not a taste of heaven?

But she is no creature of heaven. No, no, no, she is spawn of hell and proud of it. Proud of the fire in her veins, proud of the dark realm from which she sprang and which she hopes to one day help her mother claim for her own. Yes, they will make this whole world into a new Dracora, and when that is done, they will burst the gates of the Tenth Realm, assault the very throne of Dracoris himself, and . . . and . . .

Why does it all sound so stupid? When Mhoryga spoke of her aspirations in the past, Nyxia felt the lure of volcanic deeds and world-shattering destruction right down to her bones. Now, in the space of her own lonely mind, it suddenly feels so meaningless. Petty and small.

She must get back to Mhoryga. There is no other answer. Before her heart drifts so far astray it can no longer be of use to Mother. She silently urges Zoar on, faster and faster. Though he cannot hear her thoughts anymore, something in him must pick up on her urgency. His wings surge with strength, and they leave the ocean far behind.

Strange, Nyxia considers, that Zoar came back for her, when he did not have to. She didn't know it was possible—that any of her brothers would *choose* to help her if a choice was ever given to them. The others all fled the moment her connection to them was broken. But not Zoar.

Of course, Zoar must serve her. She is a dragon princess, and he a mere dragon spawn. It is his honor that she selected him to be her personal mount, and he knows that. But still, something in her heart aches, a feeling she doesn't know how to name. Gratitude? Affection? Weak emotions, unfit for a dragon—the stuff of human frailty. She's worked all her life to root such weakness out of her soul, and when she couldn't do it, Mhoryga did it for her. How terrifying to realize the moment her mother vanished from her mind, such weakness would flood back into the empty spaces.

Damn Naevya for breaking her bonds. For making her life so complicated. It will all come to nothing in the end. Mother will destroy her rebel daughter, sooner or later. And now Naevya has manifested fire of a sort. Nyxia perks up at this thought. Mother will be so pleased. When they catch Naevya now, Mother may feast and restore her power as she should have years ago when Nyxia failed to manifest. Yes, then everything will be all right.

She just needs to reestablish her bond. Nothing more. Nothing more.

Zoar soars over Khylmira, keeping high above the clouds so that Nyxia only glimpses the scorched landscape below. Towns and old roads, the occasional city, burnt down to rubble. A far cry from the lush green of Belanor, but not to worry! Belanor will soon be made like this. Like Dracora. It is an inescapable fate.

Though Zoar must be tiring, he flies on through the night and into the next day. Mhoryga must be in his head by now, surely. Every so often, the Dragon Queen claws at Nyxia's mind, though she never penetrates it. "Soon, Mother," Nyxia whispers to herself again and again. "Soon, soon."

By dawn of the third day—such a dawn as it is in a land where hellfire fumes block out all sight of the sun—Nyxia sees the Dracor Flame on the horizon. The green glow pulses with the power of the Tenth Realm itself. Nyxia's heart jolts at the sight—not with joy but with terror, with dread. They're close now. They'll be at Drathoridan by day's end, and she will kneel at Mhoryga's feet. What will be her fate then? Will Mother fix this brokenness between them? Or will she leave her daughter cut off, abandoned in this dangerous world with all its dangerous ideas and dangerous freedoms?

They fly on through the long, silent hours. They pass over Heleris Stronghold, built into the side of Mount Helera, standing on the edge of the Rothomir Wastes. Nyxia's heart tugs with a sudden longing to shout at Zoar to land there. She wants to run through those echoing passages, down into the dungeons below. To burst into Arun's cell and see that he is still alive, his soul still burning bright in this world of darkness. But she dares not. If she sees him now, how could she bear to go on to the Dragon Queen? She's too weak, and the temptation is too great.

They soar over Heleris and into the wastes, where demons shamble and death lurks in every crevice and hollow. Nyxia shudders at the sight; she would not want to make that crossing on foot. Innumerable dragon spawn circle the air above, a constant guard set to protect their queen. Nyxia tries to reach out to their minds but finds herself incapable of forming a link with any of them. They ignore her completely. Mhoryga must have told them to let her daughter through.

Heart throbbing, Nyxia drives Zoar onward. Drathoridan looms before them now, standing at the peak of Mount Dracor. The temple to the Dracor Flame is huge, built all around the rim of the volcano. A twisting mass of stone, not shaped by human hands, no—humans could not survive such heat. This edifice was constructed by dragon spawn and dracori, laboring to shape a temple worthy of their goddess. These days, Mhoryga rarely leaves it. Without a daughter's heart to devour, she needs the closeness of the Dracor Flame to keep her strong. But here, in the center of her realm, she is as magnificent as ever.

Strange though—for the first time ever, Nyxia feels a sense of repulsion. It's as though the white fire Naevya hurled into her mind still lingers there, and resists drawing any nearer to that hellish green glow. It's such a strong sensation, Nyxia battles the urge to hurl herself from Zoar's back. Instead, she grips harder, ducks lower, and forces the white fire down deeper inside until she can almost, *almost* ignore the repulsion entirely.

Zoar begins his landing approach at last, aiming for the

eastern platform. Nyxia looks over his shoulder, down into the roil of green magma deep in the maw of the mountain. She feels its searing heat and wonders, not for the first time, what would happen if she were simply to cast herself from Zoar's back into that pit? Perhaps they were all wrong after all. Perhaps she doesn't need to manifest flame before undergoing transformation. Perhaps she could somehow still become what she was meant to be.

But her courage fails her. She cannot make the leap. She turns her head away, focusing straight ahead between Zoar's crowning horns. He carries her nimbly between jutting towers, wings churning the ash-filled air as he descends to the platform. The moment his feet touch down, Nyxia topples from his back. Suddenly exhausted, she fights the urge to simply let her legs fold up beneath her then and there. That last stretch was three days without pause, and though she may be a dragon, she is also—much as she hates to admit it—human. And tired.

A ferocious snarl on her lips, she pulls herself together. "Wait here," she commands Zoar, then pauses. Some small part of her wants to . . . thank him. To tell him what it meant to her that he would come back just when she despaired. To beg him to always do just that. To be there. For her. Ready to catch her when she falls.

But those are not the words of a dragon princess. So she merely looks him in the eye. He looks back, and she wonders yet again if Mhoryga is in him, inside his mind. Well, that's what she wants for him, isn't it? To see him back in the fold?

Now to find out if she can be reclaimed as well.

Turning from Zoar, she sprints across the platform, making for the steps which lead into the temple. She knows the chamber where her mother will be found, the great circular shrine which extends over the middle of the volcano pit, as close to the Dracor

Flame as she can get without actually bathing in its flames. The air inside the twisted walls seethes. Here and there, the black stone cracks and molten green veins are revealed, pulsing with heat. For the first time, Nyxia feels afraid walking these passages. Which is strange, mystifying. She is a dragon! She may not have manifested flame, but she does not fear hellfire. It is in her blood and, unlike Naevya, it does not burn her. And yet pure terror churns in her gut. It takes all the strength she possesses to force herself on through the passages, on to her mother.

She breaks into a run. Suddenly she's like a child again, crying out, "Mother! Mother, I'm here! Mother, I'm coming!"

The door to the shrine stands partially open. Nyxia gasps in relief and flings herself at it. It's heavy and unexpectedly hot under her palms. She feels her skin begin to singe. Gasping, she pushes it wide and staggers onto the open platform above the volcano's mouth. All around her green flame leaps, tonguing the air with greedy eagerness.

Mhoryga stands at the very brink of the platform, gazing down into the roiling mass below, as though she might gaze into Dracora itself. She wears her human form—a seven-foot-tall, goddess-like being, naked save for the golden scales which encase her limbs and the black hair flowing over her shoulders, across her buttocks, and pooling on the floor. Magnificent and terrible, a dragon only loosely clad in mortal disguise.

"There you are, you little half-formed thing," she says in a voice that could sear flesh from bones. "So you've come to me at last."

Nyxia rushes across the floor and throws herself onto her knees in the center of the shrine. "Mother," she gasps, "I came as swiftly as I could. I met Naevya, and she sundered our connection, and—"

"Cease." Mhoryga turns slowly and looks upon her daughter. Her gold eyes, leaping with hellflame, narrow. Nyxia cranes her neck to gaze longingly up at her goddess and notes with dismay a slight withering about her cheeks, at her jaw. She's been too long without a daughter's fiery heart to feast on, and it is still years yet before she will come into cycle to generate a new one. She needs Naevya's heart.

Pulse throbbing with adoration and horror, Nyxia watches her mother's sinuous approach. She feels a wild impulse to rise, to flee. But that's ridiculous! How could she possibly flee? In another moment, she will be enthralled again, and then this foolish fear and all these foolish impulses will be a thing of the past. Yes. That is how it will be. That is how it must be.

"I cannot stand the sound of your human voice," Mhoryga hisses. She stretches out her hand, long talons clacking together. "Give me your mind, Nyxia. I will see for myself everything you have to tell me."

Her palm presses against Nyxia's forehead like a brand, long fingers wrapping her skull. A bolt of fire shoots into Nyxia's mind. She screams as Mhoryga plunges in, plunges deep, dredging up memories and images. But, even through the pain of invasion, Nyxia notices . . . something doesn't quite connect. Some part of her soul holds back in reserve, a spark of white flame. She tries not to believe it, tries to force herself to give up everything. But when Mhoryga fails to notice that one small, shut door in her mind, Nyxia does not voluntarily fling it wide. She keeps it closed, secret. Even as she tries to convince herself that she's ready to be her mother's creature once more.

Finally Mhoryga withdraws. Her lips ripple in an ugly snarl. Her face loses all traces of beauty and becomes, for a moment, purely draconic. "So," she says as smoke curls through her gnashing teeth, "our sweet princeling has forsaken us. Thrown aside all loyalties and cast himself into the thrall of our rebel daughter."

She turns away, leaving Nyxia crumpled and trembling on the coal-hot floor. Her long talons flex, extending and retracting again with the urge to tear and destroy. "Well," she says at last, "since he has treated us so cruelly, we must repay him in kind." She whirls, fixing her golden gaze back on her daughter. "Take your dragon spawn and make all speed for Heleris. I want you to bring me the other little prince. It's high time he paid the price for his brother's sin."

Shivering with pain and dread, Nyxia pulls herself to her feet, staggering to catch her balance. She backs away three paces, unwilling to tear her eyes from her goddess queen. "Mother," she whispers, "would it . . . would it not be better to spare Arun? If he's still alive, perhaps Valtar can be made to—"

Mhoryga draws herself up, growing from seven to ten feet in an instant. Her limbs extend, her neck lengthens, and she becomes a creature of serpentine horror, neither dragon nor human, but somewhere in between. "Do you dare question me?" she demands, hellfire bellowing up in the back of her throat.

Nyxia yelps and cowers away. "Never, Mother! Never! Your will is my joy!"

"Then get you gone from here. Bring me my prize." Her long, forked tongue flicks out, passing over smiling lips. "I will feast on prince tonight!"

22

Rosie

Time in Utherlynd changes one from the inside out. For one thing, it becomes difficult to remember what time really is or was. Days, nights, twilight, and dawn—all seem to blend into one strange state of perpetual existence.

I left behind my own world and entered the vastness of Utherlynd within a mile of walking into Inamaer. I couldn't say exactly when the change happened, for already that sense of timelessness came over me, and it seemed in a way as though I had always walked in these woods, these green-filtered, sun-dappled paths of whispering leaves and birdsong. The very concept of miles ceased to have meaning, and I gave up attempting to keep track almost before realizing I'd done so.

Since then, I've seen things I never could have imagined in my wildest dreams. With my three green-skinned companions, I've walked the edge of a precipice overlooking fire salamander pits, where the incandescent creatures bathed in tar pits and washed their gleaming hides in geysers of rainbow-hued, scalding water jetting up from the depths of this world. I've watched migrant flocks of winged horses, with saffron-colored pinions and dappled flanks that flashed with pure gold in the sunlight—dangerous, wild beasts from which the elves taught me to hide, even as they, along with me, peered out from behind veiling greenery to long after their glorious beauty. I've witnessed a procession of Ettirian giants, striding on the far side of a long valley, their footsteps vibrating the ground in minor quakes so that I struggled to keep my footing.

Best of all, however, was the night we ate the fruits of the *aleena* tree, which gives one dreams of what one longs for most. I dreamed myself back in Iliyani's cottage with Valtar. Back in his embrace, making love which must last a lifetime. In my dreams, it did. For a little while, I believed us to be endless, entwined and inseparable, and if, when I woke, the ache for lack of him was deeper than before, well . . . it was worth it. Worth it to relive those moments which can never be reclaimed.

Sometimes, as we journeyed, I thought about how even now I walk in the footsteps of Durona, the woman I called Mother. Alderin too, of course, but I rarely thought of him. While he may be responsible for my existence, it was not he who reared me, clothed me, fed me, and—I do believe—loved me those first seven years of my life. What must it have been like for Durona, plunging into this strange world, toting a dragon's egg in a sack over one shoulder? Did she believe in Alderin's vision at the time? Or was she simply too devoted to Alderin himself to turn back? I wonder sometimes what the truth of the bond was between them. Durona never once mentioned his name in my presence. As for Alderin? He claimed that he loved her, but not as a man loves a woman. Did she feel the same? Or was her life spent in hopeless devotion to a man who could not return her passion?

Watching as he gave himself away piece by piece for the sake of an ideal she could never hope to understand but must always fight to bring about.

Questions without answers, but they keep me company during the long journey. Iliyani said it would take three months to reach Lorayarus's shrine, but it feels like three years or three centuries. I begin to fear I won't even recognize Valtar if I return. *When* I return—because I will. And as myself. Despite all Valtar's dire warnings, I simply refuse to believe I won't be able to change back and forth from dragon form, the way the dragon spawn do. As Valtar said, only Heliar has ever lived long enough to give some impression of what a newly manifested dragon queen may be like. She was in a constant state of war all her life, particularly after her manifestation. She never had a chance to relax, to remember what it was like to be human.

Things will be different for me. We will take care of Mhoryga, I and the dragon spawn and my faithful dracori. And when we are through, peace will return to the world, and I will no longer feel the need for a dragon aspect. I'll let it go, become myself again. Valtar and I will live—how is it the minstrels put it?—happily ever after.

Yes. I like the sound of that.

So I fortify my spirit for each new stretch of each new day or night or evening—whatever it may be. There's a perpetually purplish tint to the air, and stars are almost always visible, twinkling larger and brighter and more beautiful here than in my own world. I learn to hear their songs; the elves teach me, and teach me as well how to sing harmonies, though my voice is unsuited to such songs. They laugh, delighted at my foolish efforts.

I've become quite chummy with my three companions. They had never met a dragon before and were at first shy to interact, half expecting me to erupt in fountains of hellfire at any given moment. After we each got over our initial misgivings, we found we got along rather well. The eldest of them, an elf man by the name of Qirel, is a bit of a stick-in-the-mud, a somber fellow who sees peril even in a field of wildflowers. (Flower fairies, according to him, are quite a warlike race, and one can never be too careful.) But Faephine and Tanelia, his sisters, are both delightful creatures, prone to laughter and a great deal of song.

So, barring the fact that I miss Valtar with every fiber of my being, I've found this stretch of my quest by far the most pleasant. There was always a piece of me that was drawn to the mystery of what lay on the far side of Inamaer. Perhaps it's because I am Utherlynd born. Some part of my heart is always calling for home.

The first time I see Bald Mountain is a moment that will remain fixed in my mind's eye to the end of my days. It seems as though one morning it simply appears—rising starkly above a valley of lush green, winding rivers, and bounteous flowers, its great blackened crest a stark contrast of destruction. Smoke drifts from the peak, though I know it's been twenty-three years—as mortals count time—since Lorayarus's last self-immolation.

"There," says Qirel, pointing a long finger. "Your destination, Pandracor." Even after all this time, I've not been able to convince the elves to call me Rosie. They insist on my formal title.

"But we don't leave you yet," Faephine trills in her flutelike voice. She pinches my elbow companionably, and I am relieved.

We travel on for days, weeks perhaps. I can't possibly guess. The valley is broader than I initially believed, filled with marvels I could not have imagined if I tried. One night, we startle a coven of vampyr and are hard-pressed to defend ourselves from their shrieking, bloodthirsty retaliation. A few nights later, we happen upon a family of unicorns, dancing in the moonlight. Upon spying us, they immediately invite us to join them, and I learn the pure delight of dancing with a unicorn, something beyond words to describe.

But at long last, the day arrives. We come to the base of the mountain, where all greenery abruptly ends. Nothing but bare rock rises before me. I almost don't see the narrow trail, leading up and up and impossibly higher into those cold regions above. I shiver at the prospect. Good thing I've got my flame to keep me warm.

I turn to my companions, clasping each of their hands in turn. "How can I ever thank you?"

"You saved our brother, Eldaerenth," Qirel replies with an inclination of his head. "It is we who owe our thanks."

"Do be careful, Pandracor," Tanelia sings, while Faephine kisses my cheek, tears shining in her ageless eyes. With those words and nothing more, they fade away, back into the forest. Not a people for long goodbyes, elfkind. I stand for some moments, not quite believing they're really gone. How could companions I've come to hold so dearly simply vanish from my life?

A lump forms in my throat. I choke it back and turn to face the mountain. One more great summit to climb. One more test of courage. And then?

Transformation.

"I'll be home to you soon, Valtar," I whisper even as I take the first step. "Hold that breakfast for me."

So I begin my climb.

23

Valtar

I lift my gaze slowly from the point of the sword hovering over my heart, running up its flat plane to the hand, the arm, and finally the face of the man who wields it. There, in the eyes of the High King of Belanor, I see the truth deep in his soul. The hellfire which burns where it was ignited by Mhoryga, years ago.

I know what Alderin truly is. In essence, we are the same—creatures of hell, fated to love dragon queens. Only Alderin loved the mother, while I love the daughter. But when I meet his eye, I find that I despise him. Because the creature he loved is a demon, whereas Rosie . . . she is something else entirely. Something beautiful and pure, far beyond the deserving of the father she didn't choose and the husband she did.

"You're too late," I say, my voice deep as a moonless midnight. "She's gone."

"Gone?" Alderin lowers his sword, eyes blazing. "Dead?"

Before I can answer, another horseman urges his mount up beside the king's. I turn my sneering attention to Prince Taigan, his arm still bound in a sling from the wound Rosie dealt him. So, he too came on this little cross-country hunt. "What is this, Prince?" I demand with a snarl. "Still seeking to claim your prize?"

"Indeed, as I am her champion, ordained by the gods themselves," Taigan replies. He has forgone a helmet, all the better to toss his curls disdainfully from his handsome brow. "Where is she? If you've harmed one hair on her head—"

"Hold your peace, Nephew," Alderin commands, his voice biting. He turns in his saddle then and spies Iliyani standing to one side, hands on her bony hips. "You there, elf woman," he says. "You are the one who found my child and gave her succor all these years, is that not true?"

She answers with a blank look. Alderin lifts a brow and turns to one of the other horsemen, the notable Captain Norlan with his magnificent mustache. "Norlan," he demands, "is it she?"

"Aye, Your Majesty," Norlan grunts, his eyes wary as he watches the wizened little woman. "That's her all right."

Iliyani tips her head at him, her wrinkles mounding in a nasty grin. "Hullo to you too, sweet captain. It's been a while since last we met, and you stole my best apprentice out from under my roof."

Norlan shudders, and his horse sidesteps nervously, tugging at its bit. Alderin, however, is not so easily intimidated. "And where is your charge now?" he demands. "Our truthseer discerned that she would come here, and we have journeyed hither from Stromin, hoping to save her from her kidnappers." He casts a disdainful glance from me to the two dragon spawn, who stand surrounded by a fence of lance blades, feet braced, hands outspread. I can feel their need to burst into dragon form, but it's no use, not this close to the forest. Which is possibly just as well.

Prince Taigan, even if wounded, is a formidable opponent and a known dragon slayer. Warrick is also capable of handling himself in a brawl. I would not want to fight the two of them together, mounted as they are.

I turn my attention back to Alderin, catch and hold his studying gaze. "Rosie has gone back to Utherlynd, seeking the place of her origin and the flame of Lorayarus."

"Lorayarus?" Alderin looks shocked. "Why? It is the Dracor Flame she needs in order to manifest."

"Rosie seems to think otherwise."

"Princess Roselle," Alderin says firmly, "needs guidance and a champion willing to stand by her side through every trial, not one who would send her into the depths of Utherlynd alone. How can she possibly survive? The greatest warriors and heroes of history have perished beyond that boundary. I myself barely survived, and I—"

I can't stop myself. I toss back my head, uttering a harsh bark of laughter. "You never stepped foot into Utherlynd!"

Alderin's face goes cold, drained of color. "What did you say?"

"You are dracori!" I declare, heedless of the listening ears around us. "The same as me. You could not have passed through Inamaer and entered Utherlynd any more than you could fly. Admit it, Alderin—that story you told Rosie was a farce. It wasn't you who journeyed to Bald Mountain or visited the phoenix shrine. It was Durona—her mother. Just as it was Durona who pulled you from Mhoryga's clutches. Durona who guarded and ultimately gave her life for your child. And what have you done? Nothing more than take the credit."

Taigan gapes in shock at his High King. "What is he talking about?" he demands, his voice thick and a little unsteady. "Uncle, why does he call you dracori?"

Alderin bares his teeth, his gaze never shifting from mine. "You don't know what you're saying."

But now everything seems so clear to me, and I continue relentlessly. "That's why it never occurred to you that she might need another flame to transform. While Durona may have told you what happened, you did not witness it for yourself. You did not realize the power of the phoenix flame, not in the same way you knew and understood the hellfire dwelling in your very soul."

"Enough of this!" Taigan bellows, urging his horse forward. Despite his wound, he clasps the hilt of his sword and half draws it. "I won't hear you speak such calumny of the High King."

"Peace, Nephew," Alderin says, but with less ferocity this time. He appears suddenly much older than he did a minute ago. As though the heaviness of his years and his many burdens caught up to him all at once. But he looks at me steadily nonetheless. "You declare yourself boldly for dracori scum."

I smile without mirth. "If I speak boldly, it is only because Rosie has taught me to live in boldness. She has always been smarter, stronger, and far more capable than any of us realized. It was she who discovered the truth of her own nature, she who made each and every choice which led her to this place. Now she goes alone to meet her fate, walking in the footsteps of the woman who was her true mother."

"And she will enter Lorayarus's flame?" Alderin says, the words uncertain on his lips.

"Yes."

"She will not survive it. No one can. It is the very fire of creation itself. Demonic essence cannot exist in the same plane. She will be rendered naught."

Sickness twists my insides like a gripping fist. I've feared it all along, almost as much as I fear the transformation itself. But the truth is, I don't think that will happen. Though I've felt the hellfire inside her trying to rise, it has always seemed like a foreign element, a disease infecting her, not a natural part of her spirit and being.

"She is *Valindra*," I say. "The Angel of Fire. She will rise, and she will burn, and she will make the whole world new."

Taigan's head turns, his gaze swiveling from me back to his uncle. "I've heard enough of this," he growls. "Let me run this vile dracori traitor through!"

Alderin gives no answer other than to raise a staying hand. Then, breathing out a long sigh, he dismounts and approaches me. We must look a sight—him in his golden armor, I in my assassin's black. I hold myself straight, lifting my chin slightly, unafraid to meet him on any level. There are few men who can bear to look me directly in the eye, but Alderin Aumanus does. He studies me long and hard, searching for something in my face. We each of us feels the pulse of hell in the other's soul.

"So," Alderin says at last, "you let her go in the end. Knowing what must follow. Knowing what you must lose."

I won't let so much as a flinch betray emotion in my face. But Alderin is not easily fooled. He nods slowly. "Perhaps," he continues slowly, "you always were the champion she needed. But will you be able to do what you must in the end?"

I grind my teeth. I know what this man is implying, and suddenly I burn with the urge to thrash him within an inch of his life. "Ah!" Alderin glances down, taking note of how my fists clench. "I see you've thought more on what I said at our last little . . . altercation. But the time for thinking is nearly passed. We are come to the crucible at last and must discover what dross has yet to be purged from our souls."

He turns now and looks into the forest. There's a strange

longing in his gaze, as though even now he would like to plunge in after his daughter, to fight alongside her, to force into being the future he always intended for her. But he, like me, is helpless now. Everything depends on Rosie alone.

"Wait beside me then, dracori," Alderin says. "We are kin of a kind after all, are we not? Let us wait together to learn our doom."

Iliyani snorts explosively somewhere behind me. "You gentle-folk stand around and gawp all you like," she declares. "I've a pot of porridge calling my name, and *you*, pretty boy"—she points a gnarled finger straight at Taigan—"are welcome to come share it with me." So saying, she stumps off in the direction of the cottage. Norlan hastily urges his horse out of her way and makes a swift sign of holy protection, avoiding her eye. Taigan flushes to the roots of his tawny hair, while Warrick chuckles quietly to himself.

I, however, remain standing at Alderin's side. Waiting. In the end, what else can we do?

24

Rosie

It's been two days since I began my ascent of Bald Mountain. I'm starting to wonder if I'll ever reach the summit.

The air is devastatingly cold and thin up here in the higher reaches, where the trail leads steeply through jagged rocks and up slippery inclines. Master Gormon, my tutor back in Stromin, taught that the monks who watch over the Shrine of Lorayarus are human, but I can't imagine how that's possible. Humans don't often dwell in Utherlynd to begin with, unless they wander in by mistake. It's so foreign to humanity's way of existing, with its fluid timelessness and the magic which pulses so intensely through the air. Not to mention, most humans would simply freeze in this high, thin atmosphere. Were it not for the phoenix flame surrounding my own flesh, I'm not sure how I would survive.

I struggle on, gasping for breath with every pace, lungs struggling valiantly. How in the heavens did Durona make this climb all those years ago with my egg in a satchel on her back? But she must have managed it, and without the comfort of phoenix flame. I set my jaw. Somehow I've got to live up to my mother's heroic legacy.

A wall of rock looms before me. The path is still just visible, but it leads at a nearly vertical line up that sheer face of icy stone. My heart shivers in my breast. I'm not afraid of heights, and it's a good thing; even with my steady nerves, I find that prospect absolutely terrifying.

I bite my cold-chapped lips. An impulse comes over me suddenly, stronger than I've felt since I began this climb. Until now I've resisted, but thin air is making me lightheaded and more susceptible. I take a step toward that horrible cliff, stop. Then, even as I tell myself it's only going to make things worse, I turn and look out at the view behind me.

My heart lurches. Seems to stop entirely.

From up here, in the thin atmosphere and the biting cold, it's as though I can see the whole green wildness of Utherlynd. My vision expands, well beyond the range of both my human and dragon sight. This must be the perspective of angels—seeing vast distances and tiny details all at the same time. From this vantage, I can gaze all the way to the distant court of the elf king, the magnificent crystal palace which rises to the heavens in shining towers, many thousands of miles from here. Simultaneously, I can peer down into the valley below, between the petals of a violet, and spy the sleeping fairy child curled up within. I see sprites dancing in the river, shimmering creatures of fractured light and laughter. I see centaurs bounding in herds across distant steppes, their booming voices upraised in bellowing song.

This place, this world, is so beautiful. So far from dragon poison and dragon flame. What would it be like if I simply . . . stayed? The thought shocks my heart back into a tumultuous tumble in my breast. That I should consider such a thing, even as a passing whim! No, no, this isn't my home. This isn't where I belong.

Only . . . I look again at that wildness, that endlessness. The scope for adventure upon adventure, each more beautiful and terrible than the last. The chance to lie under open sky and sing with the stars, training my own voice into sweeter harmonies. This is a world where I could truly, for the first time, come wholly alive. Wholly myself, healed from the unseen wounds I've carried since I first became aware of selfhood. No pain, no hellfire. No dark destiny. No . . .

"Valtar," I whisper.

I breathe out slowly, the air frosting on my lips through the sheen of phoenix flame. *Valtar.* He's back in that other world. That world of hellfire and eternal struggle. And he cannot join me here; the very blood in his veins prevents him. But if he is not here, how can here ever be home to me?

I shake my head and turn away, facing the wall once more. I feel strangely as though I've passed a sort of test. I won't abandon my world to Mhoryga. I won't let my dragon brothers be reclaimed to the Dragon Queen's thrall, won't leave Enya to surrender Cyran back into enemy hands. I won't let Arun be burned alive, nor will I let Nyxia kill herself trying to please a mother who will always and forever hate her existence. They need me. All of them.

But most of all, Valtar. Valtar, *Valtar.*

No paradise, however enticing, will ever be complete without him.

So, thrusting frozen fingers and frozen toes into crevices, I begin my climb. Phoenix flame licks around me, a feeble protection but better than nothing. I climb the narrow trail, feeling that one stiff gust of wind will send me hurtling to my doom. I won't back down; I won't give in. I climb for all of them: for Rhangyl and Rathal, for Enya and Iliyani. For Philippa and Warrick and even damned Alderin and thrice-damned Taigan. For Rhyo and all my dragon brothers.

But when all their faces fade from my mind's eye, and I'm too numb to remember even my own name, Valtar remains clear in my head. I climb for him. My very heart beats for him. He gave me up so that I could make this climb, and I must, I will, honor his sacrifice.

My arm stretches over the upper edge of the cliff, elbow hooking for leverage. With a last gasp and a feeble cry of both pain and triumph, I pull myself onto that brink, crawl a little way from the edge, and collapse. Here I lie, panting in the too-thin air, and wonder if my lungs will ever feel full again.

Slowly, my dull brain becomes aware of several interesting things. First, that before my foggy vision lies, not another expanse of rock, but a carved and shaped doorway, massive, made by expert hands. Second, that I'm being watched. Numerous eyes peer out, both from that doorway and from various ledges and crevices all around me.

Third . . . those eyes are human.

I push up onto my knees, blinking against the icy wind, which seeks to knife right through my flame protection and split my cheeks and lips. Figures appear, seemingly out of the rocks before me. Clad in thick hide-and-fur garments made from some large, black-and-white-striped creature I do not recognize, they look strange, otherworldly. But they are human. Of that I'm certain. The monks of the phoenix's shrine.

"Hullo," I manage, my voice as thin as my strained breath. "I, um. I've come seeking the flame of Lorayarus."

A single figure steps out from the deep doorway, separating from his brethren. A little taller than the others but still of human height and build, he leaves the shadows for the cold, clear glow of the stars, which forever gaze upon the barren heights of Bald Mountain. He approaches me with an unhurried, somewhat hesitant stride. Not disinterested, I realize, but disbelieving. His eyes, peering through the white-fur trimming of his hood, are wide, brimming with mingled wonder and uncertainty and—oddly enough, though I have no explanation for it—joy.

Suddenly he kneels before me. He's so large, I'm obliged to peer up into his face even now. It's an old face, though there's no sign of lines or wrinkles anywhere. In fact, he might pass for a man of twenty-five or so, were it not for the extreme age nestled deep within his eyes. The age of epochs.

"*Valindra*," he breathes, his voice quavering with some emotion I cannot name. Then his mouth breaks in a wide smile. "You've come home!"

Before I can utter more than a squeak of protest, he leans forward and wraps me in his arms.

"I ALWAYS KNEW you'd come again one day," Brother Naeryndam says as he pours tea from a delicate jade pot into an exquisite mother-of-pearl cup. A bright spice, like cinnamon but not quite, fills the atmosphere, warming straight to the bones even before a sip is taken.

He hands me the cup, and I cradle it in my hands for comfort. I've still got my white flame surrounding my body, but it's lower, not as necessary now that I'm within the shrine house. The monks of Lorayarus have made quite a cozy nest for themselves here at the peak of Bald Mountain. A busy hive of interconnected tunnels in which I would be hopelessly lost after three turns, but they navigate in the near dark quite easily.

Here, in Brother Naeryndam's private room, a small starfire is lit, burning pale lavender on the hearth and casting the room in an ethereal glow. His furnishings are sparse but tasteful, and the walls are adorned in intricate finger patterns which simultaneously feel primeval and far more complex than my mind cares to comprehend.

"I don't understand," I say, turning the cup around in my hands as steam wafts over my chilled face. "You're saying I was here before?"

"Twice, actually," he replies with an irrepressible grin. "But the first time was your birth, so I wouldn't expect you to remember." He sighs, overcome with sudden nostalgia. "I gave you your first bottle. Moon-yak's milk—nasty stuff, but you drank it, bless your fiery heart. You wet on me, as I recall, but I bear you no grudge for that!"

"So, it's true then." I set my cup down on the low stone table, for my hands are suddenly trembling too hard to hold it steady. "The story was true: I really was hatched in phoenix flame."

"Oh, indeed, indeed." Brother Naeryndam smiles again, shaking his head in pure wonderment. "When Durona Harpwood scaled that wall with that rucksack over her shoulder, the brothers and I all thought perhaps the thin air up here had finally cracked our senses. She looked like some sort of avenging angel, her face so harsh and filled with purpose, her body scarred from a hundred battles fought and won just to bring you here. Such a formidable creature!" He leans forward, his broad smile slipping into a shy grin. "We take certain vows here, you understand, including a solemn vow of chastity, but . . . I don't mind telling you,

I may have fallen in love a little bit in that moment. She was so fine and brave!"

I laugh. I can't help it, any more than I can help the sudden tears springing to my eyes. Oh, gods above! What would Durona think if she were to hear her praises being sung in such glowing terms by this ancient monk? She'd probably take it with the same stoicism she took everything in life . . . including her own death.

"What of Alderin?" I ask curiously.

"Who?" The monk tilts his head, blinking.

And that single word tells me everything I need to know. The floodgates of realization open wide, and I think: *Of course! Alderin could not have been here. He is dracori.*

I'd seen the evidence for myself, the green flame he'd wielded on the night of my escape from Stromin. How had I not thought it before? Alderin was no more capable of entering Utherlynd than Valtar or my dragon brothers. So that story he told me, when he claimed credit alongside Durona for this perilous journey . . . it was just that. A story. A lie. My father—the legendary warrior, who braved Mhoryga's realm to bring back a dragon egg. The greatest hero Belanor has ever known, with the blood of demigods flowing in his veins. A fraud.

Without Durona, he would even now languish as Mhoryga's slave. Without Durona, I would never have come to be—not this version of myself. Not *Valindra*.

Belanor may never know it, but its greatest hero wasn't the man they made High King after all. It was a stern-faced woman with a will of iron, who cared more for her honor than for glory. But I swear, if I come through this whole messy world-saving business in one piece, I'll do whatever I can to set the record straight.

"Never mind," I say to Brother Naeryndam. "You said I came here another time as well. When was that?"

"Oh, yesterday, I think," the monk says. Then he blinks, his smooth brow puckering. "Or was it last year? I'm not certain—I don't really live in *time* so much anymore, haven't in months. Or eons." He shrugs. "You were a small child then, I do remember that. Just a tiny slip of a thing. You'd somehow gotten back into Utherlynd on your own, and Lorayarus fetched you here. You stayed with us for a season. Or a day. I don't remember exactly. But I do remember quite enjoying that time! You were such a dear little chick."

"I'm sorry," I say, frowning. "I . . . I don't remember any of that."

"No." The monk sighs sadly. "No, you wouldn't. Just as you won't remember this either when you leave. It's the air up here—it doesn't let memories hold once you leave the mountain. Memories are such a time-based phenomenon, you see."

I don't see at all. But I nod as though I do, uncertain I dare pursue this line of thought further.

"Lorayarus was loath to let you go," Naeryndam continues. "He's never had a chick before, you see, and he was quite keen on you, insofar as a being of pure flame and creative universal force can be keen on any living thing. And the brothers and I, oh! How we wept to see you go. But, you see, in the timebound realm, you had a destiny yet to fulfill. You weren't old enough yet to manifest, so . . . back you went to grow a little. You wouldn't grow here, of course. Again, time!" He laughs like it's some great joke.

I take a sip of tea, savoring the sensation of warmth and spice sliding down my throat. Strange to think that I won't remember this moment, this chamber, this odd man in his fur robes. "I . . ." I hesitate, turning the mother-of-pearl cup in my fingers. "I am not a chick, you know. Not a phoenix, I mean." I swallow another mouthful, then chew the inside of my cheek before lifting my eyes to meet the monk's solemn gaze. "You do know I'm a dragon, right?"

"Oh, of course, of course." The monk nods his assurance. "Durona told us as much when she was here last week. I haven't forgotten! But you are the first and only egg to rest in Lorayarus's pyre since the creation of the worlds! I think it brought out something rather . . . paternal in him. He's eagerly awaited your return. Indeed, I can't wait for him to see you!"

My stomach pitches, the spiced tea no longer settling properly. "Is he here? On Bald Mountain?"

"Heavens!" Brother Naeryndam shakes his head, laughing. "He is off in worlds afar, of course. Everywhere that death has taken a stranglehold, and creation itself cries out for renewal, that's where you will find Lorayarus."

"Then when can I see him?"

"In about two minutes, I should think."

"Two minutes?" I echo. Perhaps the monk means two years. Gods, he might mean two centuries, for all I know!

But to my relief, Naeryndam reaches across the table to pluck the teacup from my hands. "Yes, indeed, which means we must get going," he says. "Oh, I wish I could see his face when he gets a look at you! I can't, of course—for mortal eyes to look directly upon the spirit-force of creation would mean instant death. But I'm sure I'll hear all about it after the fact!"

Still confused, I find my hand taken in the firm grasp of the monk. He helps me to my feet and leads me from his chamber back into the bewildering passages beyond. Even my dragon sight cannot make anything of this pitch blackness. Other monks move all around me, calling out cheerfully to one another from the various passages, their fur-booted feet slapping against cold stones. It's unnerving, like moving through a world of cheerful spirits.

Sudden light appears in my line of vision—a mere pinpoint, so small I would miss it were it not for the absolute darkness of this place. After several blinks, I realize it's nothing more than a single candle, burning in the center of what feels like a vast, empty cavern.

"We're here," Brother Naeryndam says, his voice strangely subdued in this space. "The Shrine of Lorayarus. Here we keep his light burning until he returns to the mountaintop for his great immolation. We are directly beneath the pyre here. When he burns, this whole place heats up like an oven, and it's best not to be anywhere near it! But it's safe enough now."

I turn to the monk. I can just about see an impression of his outline by the glow of that candle, but I *feel* rather than see the shooing motion he makes with both hands. "Go, go!" he says. "Go visit with Lorayarus. Oh! He will be so pleased."

"What about you?" I ask nervously.

"The brothers and I will hide our heads under our pillows and squeeze our eyes shut until it's all over. Safest that way, you know. Blessings upon you, Daughter! Do visit again next week if you can get away! Or next millennium. I'll brew the tea and make some of my famous moon-yak-milk biscuits."

I almost reach out to catch the monk's sleeve, but he shuffles off far too quickly, disappearing back into the tunnels. I'm alone in this great empty cavern with nothing but a small white candle for company. Well, I've come all this way. That fire doesn't look anywhere near enough to manifest a great transformation, but . . . I might as well get a little closer and see what's what.

I step forward into the emptiness. My breath sounds very

loud, echoing in my ears. There's no other sound as I cross the ice-cold floor. It's like my physical senses have been all but stripped away save for sight, which focuses with desperation on that little candle. As I draw nearer, I see it's a simple white wax taper. The flame burning from its wick might be ordinary candlelight, save that it's pure white. Like my own flame.

I kneel before that light. The ground is very hard under my knees. I press my shaking hands into my lap and draw a long breath. "Lorayarus," I whisper. "Lorayarus, I'm here. I'm here for my . . . my transformation."

Nothing. Just the sound of my voice, drifting away softly into darkness. I bite my lip. I've been so focused on simply *getting* here, I never thought through what it might mean to *be* here. What am I supposed to do? If I'd pictured anything over these last weeks, it was images of a vast pyre of burning white flame, and me walking into it . . . a terrifying image, but at least it was clear.

But there is no pyre. Of course not—Lorayarus only burns once a century, right? At least, that's what I was taught. But what does a century mean in this place where time is more an oddity than a fact of existence?

I stare at the candle. The flame dances delicately, moved by my shallow breaths. "Lorayarus," I whisper again. "Please, come to me. I need your help. You said I had a destiny to fulfill, didn't you? That's what Brother Naeryndam tells me anyway. Well, I'm here. Ready to fulfill it. I'm ready to become . . . whatever it is I am. I'm ready to be . . . to be . . ." My voice trails off. I drop my head, reluctant suddenly to say the word. But it's there on the tip of my tongue, and I know it must be spoken.

I breathe it out into the darkness: "*Valindra*."

Something stirs in the air. A wind? No, more like a . . . pressure.

A presence. The candle flares a little brighter, growing bigger and greater, despite its small wick. I stare at it, skin prickling. Then, in a moment of pure impulse, I reach out and grasp it, my fingers blocking out the light.

Fire explodes in my head.

At first there is nothing but rushing, roaring, wild heat. It's like being dropped into the center of a molten star. My soul jolts with pure terror, and I try to fling out my arms, but I don't have arms anymore. I am nothing but spirit, writhing within this far greater, far vaster burning.

"Lorayarus!" I cry, not with lips or tongue, but with everything that remains of my personhood. "Lorayarus, where are you?"

Here.

The voice is so great, I fear for a moment that it will crush me. But after the initial hugeness washes over my soul, I find myself caught and buoyed up and up, through the fire, through the roaring, the roiling, the wildness. I burst out through the surface, blinking at a world of starlight and spinning constellations. I seem to be standing on the surface of a burning sphere—a star? And the heavens themselves are displayed above me, over my head, all around. Rather than the blackness of night, this sky is filled with innumerable colors, including many for which I have no name. This, I realize, is what exists in the dark between stars—a world of energy and beauty and pulsing life, only my mortal eyes could never see it before.

Valindra.

I turn slowly. There, rising from the horizon of this burning sphere, like a living sun—the phoenix. A tremendous being, like a bird and yet utterly unlike. Huge and glorious, with pinions of flame and eyes like volcanic infernos. He is beautiful beyond all bearing, and I love him immediately with all my heart.

Valindra, the phoenix says. Do I imagine delight in that fiery voice? *My child, my chick. Come home to me at last.*

"Lorayarus!" I cry, and try to throw myself to my knees before him. Only I don't have knees, just my own little ball of spirit fire, so frail and small by comparison. "Lorayarus, I . . . I have come to manifest."

The phoenix seems to consider me through those firestorm eyes of his. "*You are not here to stay this time, then?*"

And I find myself filled suddenly, brimming with longing, much stronger than what I felt when overlooking the Utherlynd landscape. No, this is far more than that—a certainty, a truth, that this is where I am meant to be. This place of stars and fire and beauty and song. This is my home. I want to stay. I want to live here, singing with the stars, dancing with nebulas. I want to burn with this mighty being across the endless eternity of sky.

But even as I start to form the words, my heart clings to one final truth: *Valtar.*

I love him. I love him beyond all other loves. Beyond my own desires, comforts, or needs. I love him enough to give up everything for his sake. I cannot leave him behind, cannot leave him to Mhoryga and hellflame.

"I must go back," I say to the phoenix earnestly. "I must face my mother and defeat her. And for that I need fire. I need to fully manifest."

Though I would not have believed it possible a moment ago, Lorayarus begins to shrink. He pulses his wings, angling toward me, and as he approaches, his enormity compresses until he is about the size of a dragon—still huge and terrible, but no longer verging on incomprehensible. He lands on the roiling sphere before me, white flames writhing in the space's energetic wind.

I can help you, he says, *but I must warn you, my child—I do not know what you will be. You will become greater than you are, and you will burn brighter than any flame of your own world. Far brighter than the flames of Dracora! Other than that, I cannot say. You will not be a phoenix.*

"I understand," I reply. "I am a dragon. I've known that all along."

Yes, he replies. *But a dragon born in phoenix flame. And phoenix flame, you must understand, will inevitably consume you. It is part of the sacred cycle—life, death, rebirth. You cannot escape it, any more than I can.*

"Will I . . ." I hesitate, uncertain if I want to know the answer. "Will I be reborn? Like you?"

Lorayarus bows his proud head. *Am I reborn? Or am I made new each time? It is a question I asked myself at the instant of my awakening and will ask myself at the moment of my death. A question my new self will ask as well, each time the cycle repeats.* He looks up at me again, his blistering-hot eyes strangely filled with compassion. *All I can tell you for certain, Valindra, is that, should you return, you will no longer be what you are now. You will no longer be a dragon—for the fire of creation must and will purge your being. Whatever is left of you, whether it will return in a form you recognize, I do not know.*

"How can you not know?" I demand. "Aren't you supposed to be some ageless and eternal entity? Shouldn't you have some sort of omniscience to go along with it?"

The phoenix makes a sound so strange and wild, it takes me a moment to realize it's laughter. *What do I look like to you? A god?*

"Sort of."

Another laugh. *You flatter me, child. But no, I am but an instrument of the gods, the same as you. I know only that which I have discerned or experienced. But I have never experienced something like you before. You are new! Such a thing as you has never existed in all the worlds and realms beyond.*

"Lucky me," I mutter.

Blessed, perhaps. Fated, certainly. Lucky? I think not.

"How long will I have? Before . . . before my own flame consumes me?"

That I cannot say. But you will fulfill your fate. Of that I am certain.

"And does my fate include destroying Mhoryga?"

Your fate is to honor the purpose the gods intend for you, whatever that may be.

"You know, I've always hated enigmas."

The phoenix laughs yet again, tongues of fire bursting from his beak. *You are a delight, child of my flame! I wish I might keep you with me. But no, I see your heart longs for the world you know and for the love you've left behind in it. I will send you back there now, and you will do what you were intended to do from before the foundations of reality itself. Are you ready?*

My soul shudders. "No."

An honest answer. Prepare yourself then, Valindra. All heaven has sung of this moment since time immemorial, and the song will echo on into the beyond of forevermore. Now . . . go!

I GASP, MY lungs constricting on ice-cold air. Blinking up into pitch darkness, I struggle to pull my awareness together. I seem to be in a mortal body once more, lying on the stone floor of a cavernous chamber. My heart races, and my mind is full of images of fire and dancing constellations that simply won't *fit* inside my head. If I try to hold them, I will go mad. I can already feel my sanity reduced to crumbling pieces.

Turning onto my side, I curl up tight, clutching my head with both hands. Squeezing those ideas back down into small enough shapes that they can fit within a mortal consciousness. Finally, after what feels like hours of struggle, I let out a long, slow breath.

So. I'm still here. Still alive.

Still human.

Gods damn me, that was some vision! What was in Brother Naeryndam's tea? More than cinnamon, I suspect. I should have a word with the monk, teach him to go slipping dream-chasers into a girl's cuppa without asking! Sitting up slowly, I groan at the ache in my bones. The candle continues to burn, straight and true from its wick. No more flickering. No more dancing.

Funny, but I'd really thought something was about to happen. I wasn't exactly prepared for it, but . . . but now that it's *not* happened, I'm strangely disappointed. And relieved. Hard to say which feeling will dominate in the end. Oh, what a waste this whole long journey has been! And I still have to get back to Valtar somehow.

This thought brings a smile to my lips. *Valtar* . . . He will be so glad. When I step out from the forest, unchanged and rather humbled, he will wrap me in his arms, and for a few moments, nothing else will matter. We'll start putting together pieces of a plan after that, return to Cyran perhaps. Maybe an invasion force is the only answer after all, and—

The candle erupts, igniting the air, filling the chamber with a raging conflagration of white flame.

25

VALTAR

A glow shines deep in the shadows of Inamaer. As though some great light has suddenly ignited, miles from this place. It chases shadows before it like squealing, frightened things, a light too pure and brilliant for darkness to dare look upon.

At first it's so faint, I scarcely notice, even though I stand on the edge of the tree line, watching, watching.

Then it begins to grow brighter. Stronger. More intense.

My mouth drops open. Words of warning freeze on my tongue. I can only stare as that wall of light burns through the trees, bearing down upon me in a great, overwhelming wave.

Alderin's voice bursts through throb of blood in my ears: "*Take cover!*"

Some men turn their horses about and apply their spurs. Others throw themselves to the ground as their horses rear and bolt, screaming, fleeing the forest, away from that light, that wave of heat. I stand where I am, eyes wide, unable to move or think or even breathe.

A powerful grasp takes hold of my arm. The next moment I'm yanked from my feet, dragged to the ground. I have just enough wherewithal to throw my arms over my head, even as a distant, quiet, thinking part of my brain realizes such an action can't possibly do any good.

Then the wall of light consumes us.

In the first instant, I feel only heat and believe it scorches the flesh from my bones. The second instant, however, I realize no—this fire isn't devouring. It washes over me, hot and wild and strong, but not destructive. In fact, I feel a certain freshness rippling through my soul, and it occurs to me that, were I to bathe in such a fire for long enough, it might finally purge the hell from my veins.

By the third instant, it's over. The heat, the frenzy, the fear. The wonder.

I blink hard, my dazzled vision slowly clearing enough to discern that the world around me is not on fire. Instead there's a freshness to the air, a scent like exotic flowers. It reminds me overwhelmingly of the perfume which had filled the eldrin's wagon when Rosie's flame first manifested, only ten thousand times stronger.

"Look!" Warrick's voice, full of terror and awe, bursts through my stunned senses. I lift my head to see the prince of Anfalen point upward, his eyes so round the whites ring the irises. I roll over and gaze up into the sky.

"Gods save us," I breathe.

She rises into the sky above Inamaer. Vast—far greater and more terrible than I ever imagined. As big as Mhoryga in her true form, bigger even. A dragon, but also not, for this being, though as terrible as others of its kind, is also beautiful. A creature of grace and perfection, trailing white fire in her wake. Her wings pulse the air, sending clouds scurrying in her wake, and those wings are fledged like eagles', like angels'. Golden horns arch from the back of her head, creating a halo effect that catches her own light and radiates glory. She could burn this whole kingdom in a day if she chose, the fire of her being utterly devastating.

She climbs into the sky, higher and higher, and somehow the distance and perspective only make her seem greater than before. Her wings spread, blocking out the sun, but she herself is so shining, so beautiful, she could light up the very world.

"Valindra," I whisper. Even as my heart cries out in despair: *Rosie! My Rosie!*

The next moment, I'm on my feet. "Rhangyl!" I shout. "Rathal!"

The two dragon spawn, trembling with awe, pick themselves up and turn staring eyes my way. I stagger over to them, gripping Rhangyl by the arm. "Quick!" I growl. "We've got to get away from this place, get to where you can transform. We must follow her. She's going to Mhoryga, and we can't let her go alone."

The dragon spawn don't argue. They follow me, dodging between the prostrate king's men lying scattered here and there across the ground, stunned by that blast and that vision, which struck some of them with more horror than wonder. I don't wait to see whether they are hurt. They don't matter. All that matters is Rosie, getting to Rosie, not letting her fly to this battle unaided.

"Dracori!"

I stop. I don't want to, but something in that tone makes my feet disobey my will. Even as Rhangyl and Rathal hasten ahead, I turn back, watch Alderin rise, his golden armor somewhat worse for wear but still shining. "Take me with you," he says in a voice of command.

I shake my head, sneering. "Your horse will never keep up, High King."

"Damn you, man, have you forgotten?" Alderin strides toward me, his eyes bright, his face fixed with purpose. "I am dracori too. I can ride the dragon spawn." He waves a hand, indicating the two dragons even now crashing through ferns as they make for the cart trail. "You have a second mount. Give it to me. Let me ride with you to this battle. I too would see Mhoryga's end."

I want to resist. Hatred for this man burns deep in my gut. After everything he's put Rosie through . . .

But then I look into his eyes and see the fire burning there. Green fire—hellflame. I know too well what Alderin has suffered in his struggle to bring some measure of good into this evil world. Can I truly blame him for the harm he's done along the way, when my own ledger is splashed with far more red than his?

"Very well," I growl. "You fly with us."

Alderin nods and takes three steps after me, but another voice cries out desperately, "Uncle!" The High King turns back to see Prince Taigan just picking himself up off the ground. "Uncle, let me come too!" he cries. For all his faults, the prince of Gorduin is not lacking in courage. "Let me fight this battle alongside you!"

Alderin shakes his head. "You cannot, my boy. Your blood is pure, your heart true; no hellfire burns in your veins. You must stay here. Stay and fortify Belanor, for you are my heir."

With those words, he takes the crowned helmet from his head. Stepping swiftly to his nephew, who is still down on his knees, he lifts the helmet high, as though they are even now beneath the sacred dome of a temple. "I hereby crown you, Taigan

Aumanus, High King of the Unified Kingdoms of Belanor." While Taigan gapes up at him, astonished, Alderin places the helmet on his head. "Rule wisely and well, sister's son. And remember—it falls to you to defend your people, even to your very life."

Taigan shakes his head, eyes staring out from the helmet. "But, Uncle . . . you . . . you aren't . . . you can't—"

"There is no time," Alderin cuts him off. "Gods be with you, Nephew. I pray we'll meet again." Then, deaf to the prince's protests or questions, he turns and strides back to me. "I'm ready, dracori."

"Very good, dracori."

We set out at a run, soon catching up with the dragon spawn at the cart trail beyond Iliyani's cottage. They both struggle to take dragon form but manage it in the end with great gouts of hellfire. Though I will probably regret it, I don't waste time fetching our supplies. I simply mount Rathal, while Alderin climbs into Rosie's place on Rhangyl's spined back. The king looks to me, silent but intent.

"After her now, Rathal," I command. The dragon spawn spreads his wings and leaps into the air. We climb up above the trees and perform a wide circle, waiting for Rhangyl to join us. Then, the two dragons flying in formation, we set out in pursuit of the bright white flame which burns in the sky, speeding northeast toward Cyran. Valindra, the Angel of Fire. The dragon princess, now a queen. Mhoryga's daughter and Mhoryga's doom.

But not Rosie.

My Rosie is no more.

26

Nyxia

Not once does Nyxia allow herself to doubt what she will do.

Blood throbbing in her veins, she grips the horns in front of her, fixing her gaze on the horizon, as Zoar flies back across the Rothomir Wastes to Heleris. When she reaches her destination, she will do as Mhoryga bade her. She will drag Arun up from the dungeons, carry his broken, crippled body to Drathoridan. Merely alighting in that shrine will cause him terrible pain, as he hasn't the hellfire in his blood to protect him.

But that is nothing to the pain Mhoryga will inflict upon him.

And she will be right to inflict it! Nyxia reminds herself firmly. Valtar must be punished, after all. Yes, and Nyxia too. She failed worse than Valtar in the end, failed to live up to Mother's expectations. She might hate Valtar with all her being, but the truth is, if she had kept him under control, if she hadn't allowed him to slip from her grasp, then Arun would be permitted to live.

It's her fault. Her fault.

And Arun must die. Of course he must.

The hours pass in a blur. After the seemingly endless flight across the ocean, this return trek over Rothomir should seem like nothing. Yet somehow it is the longest stretch of the entire journey. Every beat of Zoar's wings is pure torture, every thud of Nyxia's heart a condemnation. And at the end of this journey . . . Arun. *Arun.*

For the last time, he will lift his head at her approach and say, *Is that you, little fierceness?*

For the last time, she will look upon his ruined face, so dear, so beautiful.

Then he will burn.

He will burn.

He will burn.

She startles, choking on her own gasping breath as Zoar begins a sudden descent. Several desperate blinks, and the world around her comes back into focus. They've arrived at Heleris. Zoar descends to the courtyard, while other dragon spawn circle the skies above, utterly uninterested in these newcomers. The stronghold feels abandoned—no sign of dracori patrolling the walls, no sign of slaves going about their inconsequential tasks. The once-graceful towers and arches, now long since blasted by dragon fire and blackened with dragon smoke, might well be a great, elaborate tomb. A mausoleum housing the remains of the last prince of Inithana.

Zoar lands hard, his horned head bowed low, his chest expanding and contracting in great heaves of exhaustion. Nyxia dismounts and hesitates, one hand poised in the air above his shoulder. She wishes she could speak to him. She wishes she could get into his mind and know his thoughts. But she hasn't dared attempt it again for fear he might read something in her mind as well. Something she can't bear for him to know.

Turning, she begins to cross the courtyard, intending to leave him behind. But his voice calls after her: "Sister?"

A little thrill runs down her spine. She looks back over her shoulder. To her surprise, she finds that Zoar has fallen to his knees in human form. It must have taken him tremendous effort to reassume that shape, and why? What purpose does it serve?

"Zoar," she says, and pauses. Then, in a rush, "You did well, Brother. You've been faithful through the worst trial we've yet faced. I'll . . . I'll be sure Mother knows—"

"Sister, you don't have to do this."

He lifts his heavy head, looking up at her, and both that look and those words freeze the hell in her heart. Nyxia stares at him—at that human face of his. At those gold eyes which they share, and those features which are more akin to his father and his father's people, very different from hers. She sees the great torture tearing his soul apart, but there's strength as well. And determination. "We . . ." he says, forcing the words out as though they hurt him to speak, "we were not born to be . . . slaves."

Nyxia grits her teeth. Until this moment, she'd not even considered the possibility that Mhoryga hadn't reasserted her connection to Zoar. Most likely, the Dragon Queen hadn't even noticed. He is nothing but a lowly dragon spawn, after all, of no interest to her. Any one of her dragon sons could easily take his place. Nyxia peers into his eyes, sees that his mind is still free as it was when Naevya first cut his connection, both to her and to Mhoryga. And yet he has not abandoned her; he has remained faithful, and he will continue to remain so. Whatever happens next.

"We are her children," Nyxia says, clenching her fists. Her voice sounds hard and venomous in her own ears. "Blood of her blood. Flame of her flame."

To her dismay, Zoar shakes his head. "She stole us. From our families, from our people. Stole the seed of our fathers and forced us into being against their wills and ours. We owe her nothing."

His words are treason. If any dragon flying over their heads even now suspected what he had just said, they would not hesitate to swoop down on him from on high and rip him apart, one vicious mouthful at a time. But there is no fear in his gaze. Exhaustion and entreaty, but no fear.

"Wait here," Nyxia says abruptly. Unable to bear one more word of this conversation, she turns on her heel and flees the courtyard.

The first door she tries opens to her, and she steps into the shadowed passages of Heleris. It's hot inside, the air filled with the latent heat which infects all Khylmira. Compared to Drathoridan, however, it's cool and fresh. She presses her back against a wall, breathing hard, panic thrilling through her limbs. What is she going to do? She must lose Arun—his fate is already sealed. But must she lose Zoar as well? Because she will, inevitably, if he does not fall back in line. Why did she not realize until now how dear he had become to her? Why had she not realized she was capable of such feeling, even for a dragon spawn?

If Arun and Zoar are both taken from her, she will be alone. Truly alone.

"I will have Mother," she whispers.

For once there is no comfort in the thought.

Pushing away from the wall, she forces herself to keep going. The halls of Heleris are familiar to her; she did spend her entire childhood here. She recognizes the way that leads to the throne room where, years ago, she watched Mhoryga pluck the eye out of Arun's head as punishment for Valtar's disobedience. And that passage on her right leads eventually to the prison wing and the tower where she and Arun languished for many years, until she was old enough to be of use to Mhoryga, and he was sent below.

She takes that passage, her footsteps quickening. Beneath the prison towers lie the cavernous dungeons of Heleris, and she needs to get there, to get this over with. Every turn she makes, she expects to bump into dracori guards, but still meets no one. Have all Mhoryga's forces been mustered? Does Mhoryga know something? Is an attack being mounted? Naevya may have dragons at her command now, but so few, and she herself is not powerful. Nyxia can't imagine she would be any real threat to the Dragon Queen.

But what if . . . what if . . . ?

No. She shakes that thought off. What's the point of dwelling on it? She has a job to do. Around another bend, and she comes to the door leading down into the bowels of Heleris. She lifts the heavy bolt and hauls the door wide, taking care to push a large stone block in place to make certain no stray wind blows it shut.

Then she plunges down the winding stairs, into the dark.

After several turns, even her dragon sight struggles to perceive anything, and she wishes she'd thought to bring a lantern. Too late now. She picks along carefully, deeper and deeper. She doesn't fear becoming lost in the labyrinth; she knows the way to Arun by heart.

Finally she stops before a low, bolted door. Her heart thuds in her throat, and she wonders briefly if she has the courage to go through with this. But what other choice does she have? No choice. There's never been any choice. There never will be.

She lifts the bolt and pulls the cell door open. Inside, a hellfire lantern burns from the ceiling, though the occupant of the cell cannot benefit from its light. But Nyxia can. By that glow, she sees him. Not bound to the wall like the last time she came, but crouched in a corner, hunched over himself, his skeletal arms wrapped around his withered legs. Shaggy hair falls across the ruins of his face.

When he lifts his head, however, the hair falls back, and green firelight illuminates his features, revealing the empty eye sockets and gouges of flesh, all the poorly healed scars. But when he smiles, his teeth are still good and strong; Mhoryga never did get around to ripping those out. "Is that you, little fierceness?" he says in a voice like dust and ashes. "I did not think I'd be graced with your presence again. What brings about this happy occasion?"

Nyxia stands for a moment, drinking in the sight of him. A sight she's longed for far more deeply than she ever let herself admit. But she cannot let herself be distracted from the task at hand.

She shakes her head sharply. "This is the end, Arun. Valtar has failed Mhoryga for the last time. He betrayed her and joined the cause of my damnable sister, Naevya."

"Did he now?" Arun tilts his head, and his smile grows. Not quite a sane smile—not after all he's been through. But still strangely beautiful. "Well, thank the gods he's finally stopped protecting me."

"This means you'll die," Nyxia snarls. She steps into the cell, strides toward him, while the hellfire lantern casts her shadow in demonic contortions across the floor and up the stone wall. "You will burn. Don't you understand that?"

He shrugs. "I've been dying by inches for years now. It'll be good to get it over with." He rises to his feet, unsteady on bones which have been broken and poorly mended. Somehow he pulls himself upright, and Nyxia is shocked to discover all over again how tall he is. His frame once promised to flesh out into a figure as broad and powerful as Valtar's, had the circumstances of his imprisonment not reduced him to this husk. Nonetheless, his spirit shines so bright, Nyxia can almost see the radiating aura.

"Shall we then, my fierceness?" he says with a lopsided grin. "I have an appointment to keep with destiny."

In this moment, when he smiles like this, Nyxia knows one thing for certain: There is no chance this side of hell she's taking him to Drathoridan.

Shocked, she reaches inside herself, searching for her connection to Mhoryga, for the compulsion that will force her to obey. It's there still, a powerful link, holding her in bondage. But not quite as strong as it once was. And there is that secret door, that center of her soul which she kept shut, hidden from her mother's perception.

"I'm sorry, Arun," she says, snarling the words through clenched teeth, "but destiny is going to have to wait for another day." Then she wrenches that mental door open.

White fire explodes in her mind.

27

Valtar

We fly without rest. Why should we rest? The dragon spawn have their inner fire to sustain them for days at a time, and they are eager for the battle to come. Their eyes fixed on the shining glory of the white Dragon Queen flying before them, they pursue her with everything their fire-scorched souls have to offer.

I reach out sometimes, trying to find some connection to that great, burning mind. Every time I do so, I touch only fire—fire so hot, so beautiful, but far beyond my ability to comprehend—and I'm forced to retreat. I can only hope that, with time, when she adjusts to her new form, then perhaps Rosie—the dragon, Valindra—will reach back for me. It would be a comfort to feel her in my mind, whatever she may have become.

As it is, this glorious being in whose wake I follow feels like a creature apart, something belonging to another world, another realm of existence. Nothing about it feels or looks akin to Rosie, save for the white fire which lashes from her wings in long, feathery tongues. That and the aroma of sweet flowers are all that remain.

I bow over Rathal's neck, focused on the flight, on the journey ahead. If I let myself start to think on what I've given up, I'll lose the strength I need for what is coming. I owe it to Rosie, to my wife, to give everything I've got to this final great struggle. I won't let her down.

Valindra flies on. I hope she doesn't mean to fly straight to Drathoridan without stopping. Even a newly transformed dragon queen could not sustain such a flight; she'll arrive at the Dracor Flame weakened. While Mhoryga may not be the power she once was, she is at her strongest there in the center of her kingdom. And there will be thousands of dragon spawn to fight our way through.

Impossible. The word burns in my mind.

But when I look at the shining being before me, I think, *But what if it isn't impossible? What if Rosie was right all along, and this is the way? The only way . . .*

Cyran appears on the horizon, the stronghold of Eirbalar standing tall on its promontory above the River Cy. Perhaps Enya set watchmen on alert, though they are hardly needed. No one could help seeing the mighty creature bearing down upon the city, larger than a thundercloud, with a wingspan that could encompass all of Eirbalar in its shadow. The dragon spawn are ready, eager. Even as I watch, I see them rise up from the city, like a flock of birds startled from their nests. Wings fill the air, soaring in funnels of bursting flame up and up into the sky. We fly in among them, and I see the Cyranian dracori clinging to the backs of their mounts. Lady Enya guides her own dragon close beside Rathal. I salute her, and she inclines her head in response.

As of one accord, we fly on after our queen, making for the

ocean and the long crossing to Khylmira. I have now been in flight four days and three nights without pause. But Valindra does not appear inclined to stop.

I take a look around at the sky armada we have gathered. Enya has been hard at work reclaiming the dragons who fled. There are many more present now than when Rosie departed for Inamaer. Our force numbers a hundred strong, maybe more—not bad, all things considered. But compared to the numbers we fly even now to meet, we may as well have no force at all.

I focus my gaze on the white dragon. She may be able to turn Mhoryga's children to our side. So far I've not felt her in my mind at all, but could she be made to remember this aspect of her power? Perhaps . . . if I could find a way to reach inside, to make her remember, then the battle for the soul of this world might yet be won. But how to connect to a mind so vast?

Rhangyl overtakes me. I look up at the one-eyed dragon, but it's Alderin's gaze I catch. The High King looks back at me, his golden hair whipping across his stern face. Something in his expression makes my blood run cold. I urge Rathal to break away and put some distance between us.

We fly into the night and on until dawn. As the sun rises, I think our numbers may have grown. Other dragons are drawn to Valindra, whether she connects to their minds or not. They fall in with our great flock, like a massive migration over sea.

By sundown we approach Rassumen, a cluster of islands known as the Pirate Kingdom. We pass over the larger, populated islands, but as we come to the remote isles on the far side of the cluster, Valindra finally begins to descend. She chooses a slab of uninhabited rock with a beach long and broad enough to hold her great bulk. There she lands and stretches out, filling the entirety of the space. The dragon spawn find places to land as well, little perches across the rocky terrain. Some disperse to other islands, and I can only hope Mad Melarue, the Pirate Queen, won't panic and muster her forces for a dragon hunt before the night is through.

Rathal lands not far from where the great white dragon lies. He's breathing hard; those days and nights of flight have finally caught up to him. Lucky Valindra landed when she did, or her loyal brothers may have started dropping from the sky like flies. Rhangyl settles not far away. His big, coiled body simply collapses in a heap of scales and wings. He puts his head down and utters a loud snore, complete with a billow of sulfurous smoke from his nostrils. Alderin, unflappable as ever, slips from his back and strides directly to me. "I don't suppose you thought to pack provisions for this journey."

I grimace.

"So it's hellfire for supper, brimstone for breakfast," Alderin says dryly. "It could be worse, I suppose. But what's say you and I make our way down to those tidal pools and see what we may find?"

We aren't the only ones to settle on this idea. All along the shores of the rocky island, dracori men and women pick through the pools, searching for crabs and mussels, anemones and seaweed. Alderin proves an effective scavenger. Between the two of us, we've soon gathered a small feast. I light a hellfire blaze and roast large crabs in their shells over the coals. While we wait, we use our knives to pry open mussels, slurping the innards greedily. All this while, the great white mound of the dragon lies still upon the beach, inert and apparently unaware of the world around her.

Alderin catches me looking her way. When I turn and find the king's gaze upon me, I hold it, long and level. His eyebrow tips. "Hard to see anything of Roselle in her now, isn't it?"

"She's still in there," I say firmly.

"Maybe. Maybe not. It doesn't make any difference, I fear." Alderin stretches out his legs and laughs at the furious look on my face. "Don't mistake me, dracori! I loved her too in my way. I brought her into this world, did I not? Sacrificed both body and soul to bring about her existence. How could I not love her? She is truly flesh of my flesh, the only child I have ever fathered. My legacy. But," he adds, sticking his knife between mussel shells and wriggling it vigorously, "I always knew she was meant for a purpose. A purpose which must be fulfilled, no matter the cost."

He looks at me again, his brow dark in the flickering light of the hellfire blaze. "You are not the champion I had in mind for her. That man . . . he was to love her, yes. But not as you love her. He was to love the ideal she represented, to honor her as a great and terrible weapon of destruction. He was to guide and enable, to give everything he had to bring about her eventual success. And when her great purpose was accomplished, then—"

"Enough," I growl. "I will not hear more of this."

"Ah, but Valtar, you know this task now falls to you. Look at her!"

I do. I look at the mountainous being, the scales and wings, the lashing flame, the cresting horns. A truly terrible creature. Terrible and beautiful and beloved.

"You know as well as I," Alderin persists, "a monster like that can and will overthrow Mhoryga. But what then? What will it accomplish for this world if one dragon queen is replaced by another, greater queen? Who will we find then to overthrow this one, to give the world of humans back to humankind?"

My breath is short, tight in my throat. The violent urge to throw myself across the fire and stick one of my knives into Alderin's skull is strong.

Alderin smiles, however, as though he knows exactly what I'm thinking. "You must consider it," he says, leaning back on one elbow comfortably. He stripped out of his armor long ago and looks much smaller, more approachable, despite his extraordinary beauty, lounging there in a simple white shirt and trousers, his feet bare. "The woman you knew is gone. She will not return. You must mourn her now and prepare yourself for the ultimate act of courage and sacrifice which the gods demand of you. For somehow, in a twist of fate not even my truthseer could have foreseen, *you*, Valtar Skylock, have become the last bastion. The final hope of this world."

I get to my feet, fists clenched. I stare down at Alderin, and for a few breaths, we strive against each other silently, while fire leaps and dances in the space between us. Finally, I say, "You have always underestimated Rosie. You've never understood her, never seen her true strength."

"Perhaps." Alderin inclines his head in acknowledgment. "Or perhaps I have simply not loved her too well. Not let myself become blind to the truth."

I draw a long breath through clenched teeth. Then I turn and walk away before I commit murder right here on this shore, beneath the watching eye of the moon.

28

Valindra

Little souls surround her, like stars, but so much smaller, so temporary and inconsequential. Sometimes she wonders, if she inclined her attention toward them, would she find them worth knowing, worth understanding? Ultimately, she can't be bothered.

What matters instead is that greater, hotter fire burning on the horizon of her mind. Great and green and full of poison. She sees it, not with her eyes, but with her very soul. It repulses her, yet she is driven to it. Driven to hunt it down, that source of so much pollution and destruction in this world. It must be brought to an end, and then . . . renewal. The fires of creation course through her veins, and this whole world cries out to be made new. But it cannot happen until that devasting green flame is put out. Forever.

Mhoryga. Yes, that name means something to her. But what?

Mother. She's uncertain what that word is. But it's important.

It has something to do with birth and death and this inferno inside her. She must ponder it awhile.

But for now, she is tired. Since the moment she came into being, she's been flying with driven purpose, surrounded by all these little flickering star souls. She'd thought she wouldn't stop until her goal was reached, but abruptly came to the end of that initial burst of strength. Now she must lie still for a time, let the fire in her soul replenish. Then she will fly on, and this time . . . this time . . .

One of those bright souls seems to peel away from the others. It approaches through the bigness of space all around her, growing larger as it comes, but still so very small. Strange . . . it seems to be singing. Soft and low, a simple song for a simple soul, nothing like the complex music of the heavens which pulses through her being. But, simple though it may be, she likes it.

"Rosie?"

Her heart stirs. Like a ripple on the surface of a great, still ocean. Memory—long forgotten. But that's impossible. She was born only days ago, wasn't she? She has no memory, save of fire and of sky and of that green flame on the horizon toward which she strives. Nothing else. And yet that voice moves her.

"Rosie, can you hear me?"

She watches his approach with some trepidation. He wears a physical frame, as all these star souls do, but her slitted eye struggles to make sense of it. Far easier to observe the light inside him. Up close, his spirit is bright and warm, but she sees now that it's surrounded by wreathing bands of green flame which constrict the burning light at his core. It reminds her of the flame she pursues. An evil, a sickness, a force of destruction which must be purged.

She begins to rise, flaring with inner fire, ready to destroy this thing here and now, but . . . no. That glowing heart at the center is beautiful. And she has no desire for senseless destruction. When she destroys, it will be with absolute purpose. She settles her heavy head back down on the sand and allows the small star soul to draw nearer. The impression of his physical form clarifies. A face—human, hard planed. Sad. Dark hair and darker eyes. So small and puny, she could swallow him whole and not realize she'd done so.

He stands for some while, his face upturned. Then he takes a seat, leans against her side. He stays there so long, she almost ceases to be aware of him and drifts back into a space of gentle darkness and distant stars and the far-off dance of celestial night.

When he begins to sing again, she doesn't notice it at first. It's such a small sound, made with his frail human throat. But the song blends with the pulsing light of his spirit, gives it greater strength and, at last, draws her attention. It reminds her of the song of the spheres, of the great expanses in which she longs to fly and dance. But it's also grounding. Full of unutterable longing.

As the stars pour down from heaven,
I sit alone with you in my mind.
Day to night, night to day, my love,
Even to the dying of the moon.
Alas, we are not side by side.

She stirs uncomfortably. Something about that song calls to a part of her buried deep, deep down. Down under flame, down where a still, small spirit curls tight in her core. That piece of spirit uncurls slightly. Awareness radiates through the great caverns of her soul, a whisper from the depths.

"Valtar?"

His voice chokes, stops. For a long while he is silent, but she senses how the glowing orb of his spirit brightens, almost dousing out the ugly green flames. Just for a moment . . . but in that moment, she thinks: *He is beautiful. Truly beautiful. A soul worth preserving.*

After a time, he begins to sing again. She closes her eyes and lets the melody wash over her, resting in its sonorous vibrations.

"Turn your eyes to me, my love.
I'll be there. I'll be there.
In the still of the night, I will dream of the time,
When my land and my love are mine."

29

Valtar

We fly on. Another four days without rest.

I begin to fear the dragon spawn will drop from the sky in pure exhaustion. But they hold a V formation, with Valindra at the peak, each branch like an extension of her own vast wings. I maintain position as close to her as I dare get, painfully conscious of her utter unawareness of me and all those who fly with her. We are simply too small, too insignificant to be of any concern to her vast mind.

Though I search for it again and again, I never hear that faint echo of a voice deep inside her, calling my name. I must have imagined it that night on the rocky shore of the lonely Rassumen island. My own desperation simply echoed back to me what I longed most to hear. I concentrate on the flight before me. My fears, my struggles, my heartache—none of them matter now. Not with the miles of ocean passing beneath us and the destiny which awaits in Khylmira so fast approaching.

At dawn of the fifth day, we reach the shores of Khylmira at last. The forbidding Umenoran Cliffs rise sheer before our eyes above the pounding waves but are no barrier to dragons. Valindra soars to the very topmost edge and lands there at last, her huge white wings arched over her horn-crowned head. She utters a roar that echoes from the cliffs and, carried by the ocean wind, rolls across the land. A trumpet blast announcing the conqueror's arrival. Though there's no sign of a living soul anywhere to be seen—either human or Draconan—the very foundations of the continent seem to tremble in acknowledgment.

To my great relief, Valindra does not immediately set forth into the mainland. Once again, she stretches out her great bulk, right here on the edge of the cliffs, and settles her huge head down for rest. The dragon spawn alight all around her, and the mounted dracori fall from their backs and lie spread-eagle beneath the sky, exhausted to the very limits of their endurance. We can only hope our mighty queen will give us time to catch our breath before the next great push. Rhangyl lands close to where Rathal and I settle, Alderin on his back. I don't meet the High King's eye.

Instead I dismount and, with a wordless pat on Rathal's heaving side, make my way across the clifftop toward Valindra's mountainous form. It takes time to walk the length of her tail, her haunch, her long, sinuous body, and finally come to her head. The great disk of her eye opens slightly to observe me. Am I mistaken in thinking I feel a faint vibration of pleasure from her soul? Does she remember me from the other night?

I press both hands against her broad, scaly cheek and lean heavily. Closing my eyes, I search for any trace of connection. "*Rosie?*" I whisper inside my head. "*Rosie, Rosie.*"

Suddenly a voice of fire burns in my mind: "*Why do you say that name?*"

For a moment I'm too shocked to reply. That voice is simply so great, so fiery, and so . . . *other*. Not even Mhoryga's voice was ever like this, for Mhoryga has learned over time to adapt herself to human modes and human forms, while this being struggles with the very concept.

I swallow hard. Then: "*What do you wish to be called?*"

She is silent for a time. Then, another burning wind wafts through my awareness: "*I believe I was called Valindra by . . . someone . . .*"

"*Valindra,*" I repeat. "*Yes, you are Valindra.*"

This seems to please her. She nestles down a little more comfortably, the huge coils of her body relaxing. But I haven't come here simply to chat. There's something on my mind, something I want to know for certain before we venture any deeper into Mhoryga's realm. "*Have you connected to the dragon-spawn minds, Valindra?*"

"*The what?*" If I didn't know any better, I'd say there was a yawn in her mind-voice, so complete is her disinterest.

"*Your brothers,*" I persist. "*The dragons all around us, right now.*"

Her slitted eye opens again, and the enormous iris moves, slowly scanning the cliffs. "*Is that what all those little soul sparks are? My brothers?*"

"*Yes! Don't you remember? Rhangyl and Rathal and the rest?*"

Her eyelid shuts again heavily, and her mind drifts away from me. A growl in my throat, I lean harder. "*There are more dragon spawn coming, Valindra. Mhoryga will send them.*"

"*Mhoryga?*" This time, when the big eye opens, the enormous pupil dilates with interest. "*The fire burning at the heart of this world. The hellflame.*"

"*Yes!*" I answer eagerly. "*Yes, that is Mhoryga. She has ruled this world for two centuries now, spawning thousands of dragons in that time. They are all under her thrall. And they are coming for us.*"

"I will kill Mhoryga."

It's more a feeling than words, a threatening storm of fire in my mind. It's so hot, I'm forced to step back and away from her for fear she will burn me. *"Yes,"* I answer, no longer daring to touch her. *"Yes, kill Mhoryga, free the world. But you'll never reach her. Not through the dragon spawn."*

She opens her mouth in something like a grimace, flashing teeth longer than swords or lances. *"I will devour the soul sparks. They will not touch me."*

I grit my teeth. *"Rosie wouldn't want you to hurt them."*

The great white dragon makes a wordless, questioning sound in my head.

"Rosie loved them," I persist, her name like a dagger to my heart. *"Her brothers. She had compassion for them and for the dracori, even . . . even for me. Even after all I've done."* I look up at the dragon, at Valindra, struggling to see some sign of the woman I love in that vast eye. But she is gone—and the more I search and fail to find her in this new incarnation, the more my heart threatens to shatter in my breast. Not even the faintest echo of memory remains.

But I know what Rosie would want from me in this moment. I cannot let her down.

"Don't destroy the dragon spawn. For her sake. The dracori perhaps . . . well, perhaps we deserve it. But your brothers cannot help what Mhoryga made them do. They were born into slavery, never given any choice. Not even the choice to die." Can she hear me? Can she understand? She's just so enormous, so far away. So not part of this world. *"You don't have to overtake their minds,"* I persist. *"Not like Mhoryga."*

The white dragon snarls, smoke billowing through her teeth. *"Not like Mhoryga!"*

"No, not like that. But you can break her hold on them. That should be enough. If they are not enthralled to her, they won't attack. Most of them, at least. They have no love for her but every reason to hate her." I reach out, touch her again. Her scales sear my palm, despite the hellfire in my blood. But I don't back away. *"Please, Valindra. Set them free."*

She looks down at me, that same faraway look in her eye. Not quite interested, but faintly curious. Almost as though she's forgotten who I am and what I'm doing here, as though the conversation we just shared was too meaningless in the scheme of the universe for her to bother recalling even a second later. Despair swells in my breast.

Suddenly all around us, the dragon spawn begin to stir, to rise, wings fluttering. A shout goes up from somewhere in the ranks, then numerous voices join in a raucous chorus just as they take to the air. Rathal appears behind me, wearing his human form. "They're coming," he growls.

I step away from Valindra, craning my neck. A cloud rushes in from the mainland, black as the fall of sin itself—a churning mass of dragon spawn, bursting with bolts of green-like lightning. There must be a thousand of them, two thousand. Maybe more. Far too many for our small force.

I turn to Valindra. She's lifted her massive head and tilts it curiously. A small gleam of sunlight breaks through the atmosphere of fumes and glints from her gold horns, causing them to shine like an angelic halo. Her expression is far from angelic, however; it's positively bloodthirsty.

She lumbers to her feet. I stagger back to keep from being crushed under her great forefoot. In a burst of hellfire, Rathal transforms back to dragon form, and I leap onto his back. We take to the air, along with the rest of the Cyranian host, rejuvenated at the sight of that oncoming attack. Captain Tanyl peels off down the left side of the cliffs, bellowing orders to a contingent of dragon spawn, desperate to get them into order. Lady Enya, spying me, urges her own dragon close to Rathal. "What can you tell us, dracori?" she demands. "How do we fight them?"

It is now that I realize: None of the Cyranians have fought an air battle before. They were only enslaved and transformed a year ago and have had no opportunity to learn dracori ways of combat. I see many of them summoning hellfire in roiling, green balls of energy around their fists, but what use is hellfire against other dragon spawn and dracori? No, that power which burns through their veins is all but useless. This is going to be the work of blade, claw, and teeth.

"Their underbellies are not well armored," I shout back to Enya. "Don't let them get beneath you. A thrust through the upper palate will pierce the brain, but try not to get a blast of hellfire in the face while you're at it!"

Enya nods in acknowledgment. "See you on the other side," she says, then turns her dragon to face the oncoming swarm.

I veer away to the right, shouting a formation command to the nearest dragon spawn. Their riders, all newly created in Cyran, do not understand, but their mounts are all from Khylmira. They know our formations and battle tactics. We gather in an arrowhead: a three-wing form in front, and two three-wing forms to the left and right. Rather than wing tip to wing tip, the dragon spawn know to stagger, protecting the soft underbelly of the dragon above them. The lowest in formation are most vulnerable, but the larger, more seasoned dragons with tough outer hides know to take those places. I see Rhangyl joining me at the tip of the arrowhead, taking the lowest position in the front three-wing form. Alderin sends me a sharp salute, as though he too understands the strategy. He did spend years as a dracori in Khylmira, after all. Who knows how many formations he has flown.

I position Rathal at the uppermost tip of the arrowhead, the foremost offensive position. Gripping his scaled back with my legs, I flick my wrists, knives appearing in each hand, ready for whatever may come. So, moving as one entity, we fly to meet that wall of dragon flesh and dragon flame. We fly to meet our doom.

The space in the air between us shrinks rapidly. Already I see the most aggressive of our own forces diving into the cloud, suicidal in their eagerness to strike back against Mhoryga. They will be swarmed almost immediately, disemboweled, their crumpled bodies falling in a spiral of broken wings. But I won't think of that. My only thought now is to take down as many foes as I can in the name of my queen. In the name of Valindra.

As though my thought has summoned her, the white dragon below spreads her wings at last and leaps into the air. She is so huge, it does not seem possible that such a being could get airborne, but her coiling body is so graceful, so natural in this element, she might be made of wind. Her powerful wings pulse hard, knocking her own dragon spawn tumbling on either side of her, breaking formations. She does not acknowledge them but fixes her gaze on the mass of Mhoryga's approaching children.

Her heavenly face breaks in a dragon's smile. With a roar of flame and force, she surges forward.

"*Go!*" I cry, and my own arrowhead speeds forward in perfect synchronization, as though we've practiced a hundred times. We cannot keep up with Valindra, but we speed through the air like the arrow we are, straight for our foe.

The white dragon breaks the front ranks of our enemy, plunging into the writhing host. She all but disappears, swallowed up in their fumes. Then a huge burst of white fire flashes across the sky, and I glimpse her again. Brilliant and shining, glorious and devastating.

There's no more time for thought, for fear, for hope. My arrowhead pierces the outermost ranks of the dragon spawn, and suddenly I'm in the thick of claws and teeth and lashing tails. Poisonous fumes fill my lungs, and though I ought to be completely overwhelmed, I am not. A sense of distant calm comes over me. As though none of this is truly happening to me, and I can, from a safe distance, control my actions and make decisions.

I bellow commands to my eight, and we tear through the ranks of dragon spawn. I would have expected our enemy to hold formations of their own; we've all had the same rigorous training, after all. But there's only chaos all around, as though their minds are disordered. Or rather, as though the single mind which directs them is disordered, unfocused. Frightened.

I balance on Rathal's back. We come up underneath a large green dragon. Without a second thought, I drive one of my knives up between scales, piercing vital organs. A spew of burning hell-inflamed blood bursts in my face, but we speed on to the next dragon, the next vicious thrust, twist, cut. I don't dare ask myself what Rosie would say if she could see me killing her brothers. Rosie is not here. Rosie is gone.

And that which is left of her even now tears into the dragon spawn with terrible relish, great jaws gnashing them out of the sky three, four, five at a time.

My formation banks again, but the larger arrowhead splits into smaller trios. It's simply impossible to keep the nine of us together in this chaos. I slice again, slitting the throat of a dragon as it passes over me. A burst of hellfire erupts on my right, strikes me in the side. I catch hold of Rathal's spines and let the flames wash over me. Some excitable young dragon has forgotten his fire doesn't work on his own kind.

Through the mayhem, I see a dragon spawn scrape Tanyl off the back of his mount. The dracori falls through the swarm, and though I urge Rathal to go after him, it's impossible. There are simply too many beating wings and lashing tails. Something strikes us from the left, and we're driven off course, leaving Tanyl to disappear into the churning smoke below.

Rhangyl, who has kept close formation with us until now, breaks away suddenly and attacks the exposed belly of a large dragon spawn. Alderin clings to his back as Rhangyl rips into the softer scales of the beast, all thought of brotherhood utterly forgotten.

Rathal carries me on. My view seems strangely to expand. I stare ahead, through the storm, to where Valindra even now gracefully dances, her long, sinuous body a mass of flashing coils. Strange how she can be so divinely beautiful, even as she wreaks such carnage.

A shriek somehow draws my attention. I turn, looking overhead in time to see a dragon spawn ripping at the underbelly of Enya's golden-scaled dragon above me. Her mount's wings fold up around her, and they both begin to fall from the sky. Enya manages to spring free of her dead dragon, and free-falls through the air.

Rathal doesn't need urging. He darts swiftly to one side, and I reach out, just managing to grasp Enya's arm and pull her hard against me. She clutches Rathal's spines, clinging desperately, her eyes white ringed with terror. "Hold on!" I bark, even as Rathal darts up underneath the dragon who just gutted her beast. I spring upright and thrust with my blade. Unfortunately, Rathal is obliged to pull away to one side, and I lose my grip, leaving the knife behind me, jammed into the dragon's belly.

I crouch against Rathal's neck, reclaiming my balance. All around me, I can see our people becoming separated, swarmed, torn apart by dragon spawn. One after another, they fall. Dragon spawn and Cyranian dracori, dropping like stones from the sky. Our force is in tatters; soon it will be nothing at all. Rathal is quick and nimble, but more and more dragon spawn close in around us. With no one to protect his underbelly, he can rely only on his speed and agility. There are just too many of them, pressing in closer.

And suddenly I realize—Valindra has gone. Though I crane my neck, I can see no sign of her anywhere. Has she abandoned us to our fate, fixated as she is on her own goals?

A dragon drives in close. Snarling furiously, I swing down, hang one-armed from Rathal's long neck and hurl a knife into the approaching beast's eye. It shrieks and falls away, but Rathal banks. I lose my grip, begin to slip. Rathal manages to snatch me from the air with his claws. I hang suspended underneath my mount, vulnerable and exposed, legs dangling in empty air. A dragon spawn spies me, surges toward us. Its mouth opens greedily, hellflame rising, and I stare into the jaws of approaching death.

30

Valindra

Green soul sparks surround her. Thousands of them.

When first she saw them approaching on the horizon, she'd momentarily believed she saw Mhoryga herself coming to her, so great was the mass and the pulse of evil light. But no—these are not the one she seeks. These are but small souls, inconsequential. Little gnats to be snapped from the air, all between her and her ultimate goal.

Stop!

That voice, deep inside her head—it makes the white dragon pause even in the midst of ripping the wing off one small dragon. She spits it from her teeth, sends it careening to the ground far below while its ugly soul flickers out of this existence.

You're killing them!

She roars, shaking her mighty head. This voice—it feels like her own, but she doesn't recognize it. It's a part of her from long ago, from back before she became who she was always meant to be. A part that should be forgotten, stilled forever.

She dives into another, denser cloud of spirit orbs, her mouth opened wide. A blast of white fire bursts from her center, burning through them, making their little green lights wink out in droves. That feels better, satisfying. She banks and arches back up and up, her body spinning as she propels herself higher.

But the voice in her head is furious now: *They are our brothers! Stop it! Stop at once!*

The white dragon climbs all the way out of the cloud of poisonous fumes, out into open sky, high above this world. Out above the storm of green soul sparks. Here she hovers, her vast wings outspread to keep her steady in the thin atmosphere, far removed from the chaos below.

They must be destroyed, she tells herself, her inner voice full of conviction. *The green fire must be eliminated from this world before renewal can take place.*

Yes, that second, smaller voice replies. *The flame inside them, but not they themselves! They are enslaved to it.*

Valindra considers this. She finds herself reminded of that one soul spark, the one with the essence of green flame surrounding its central orb. That one had claimed something similar, had it not?

You've got to reach into their minds, the voice persists. *Break Mhoryga's hold over them. It's the only way! The only way to save them and our own people.*

I must fly on, the white dragon says, turning her gaze in the direction of the green pulse of flame, which still calls to her from the horizon. *I must fly on and face Mhoryga.*

Not until you free them!

They don't matter.

They do! The voice erupts in a burst of white fire. For an instant, Valindra sees an image in her head—a human silhouette, dark against the ferocious burning of phoenix flame. It spreads out its hands, either in entreaty or fury. *They matter! All of them!* Eyes flash in that dark face, momentarily illuminated. *You cannot abandon them!*

I am to purify this world, Valindra says.

And what good will that do if you destroy everyone in it? You are meant to save them! Liberate the captives, set them free.

The white dragon shakes her heavy head. *I don't know . . . how . . .*

I'll help you. The voice speaks in a gentler tone, as though to a frightened dog. *I have . . . I have a bit of experience with it now.*

Valindra heaves a great sigh, emitting a cloud of smoke. But what can this intrusive voice be other than a part of her own self? And it is so adamant, she can't very well ignore it. *So be it*, she says with reluctant submission. *Show me.*

The image in her head vanishes. She senses that flaming presence joining with her, becoming one with her own consciousness. How easy it would be to suppress it entirely, to return to her own purpose! But for some reason, she doesn't. She allows that subtle thread of willfulness to have its way, moving in and through her.

Pivoting in the air, she dives back through the clouds, back into that storm of chaos and spinning green souls. She opens her mouth to devour, but the voice merged in her head snarls, *Don't you dare!* Valindra shuts her jaw again. This time, the spirit moves inside her, pushing at her mind, at her fire. It sends out spirals of light toward the nearest of those green souls. It connects, and to Valindra's surprise, she experiences a sudden influx of feeling. Dread, despair, rage. It's all there, but underneath is something else. Something which reminds her of that spirit orb who sang to her a few nights ago.

They're trapped, the voice in her head, merged with her own self, persists. *You've got to save them.*

More fingers of flame stretch out from Valindra's heart, touching other spirits. Each time, she feels that same combination of senses, that same pulse of a living soul underneath the green hellflame. A beautiful soul, a soul worth saving. More and more of them she reaches, the vastness of her spirit no longer struggling to connect. Fifteen, fifty, a hundred souls are in her grasp.

But then she feels something else within those souls. A presence. Massive, invasive. A parasite of the conscious mind. "*Ah*," says a voice of poison, rippling in multitudinous complexity from all those minds into Valindra's head. "*You have come at last, my daughter. What a fire you carry in your heart!*"

Mhoryga. Valindra can't guess if it's her own thoughts or that secondary presence who speaks the name. It doesn't matter. This, she knows, is the reason she's here. The reason she's flown across oceans. The reason she came into being.

Mhoryga.

Mother.

"*Yes*," the Dragon Queen hisses. "*You came to me right away, didn't you? Because you know what you are. You know what you are meant for.*"

"*I am meant to destroy you*," the white dragon replies. A ripple of terror bursts from all the dragon souls to whom she is connected. But the terror isn't Mhoryga's—it belongs to her children. Her presence within their minds simply laughs, and a jolt of pain passes through the dragon spawn. They crumple up, begin to drop from the sky.

Save them! The second voice rings desperately in her head. *Break their connection to her!*

Mhoryga, still stretching out through the minds of her children, sharpens her attention. "*Who is that with you?*"

Valindra doesn't answer. Her mind extends, many ropes of white fire reaching out to all the falling dragons simultaneously. It's easy now that she knows how to do it. They're so small beside her greatness, little motes of dust held in the palm of her clawed hand. She touches the spaces inside them where Mhoryga sits, knotted tight, wreathed in hellflame. Mhoryga looks out at her, a spirit of such ancient malice, the white dragon feels a flash of momentary dread.

"*You cannot stop me*," the Dragon Queen declares. "*I spawned them and you alike. All of you belong to me!*"

But Valindra gazes into those multitudinous minds held by that singular mind. And she says: "*Not anymore.*" A storm of flame streaks out from her, coursing into each and every dragon. It overwhelms the knotted presence within their heads, and she hears many voices screaming: the dragon spawn and, deeper down, another voice. Mhoryga.

The secondary presence in Valindra's head whoops joyfully. *The old bag wasn't expecting* that, *now was she?*

Valindra pours forth more fire, hotter and hotter, scorching those minds. She feels how easily she might destroy them, engulf their souls in her flame and snuff them from this plane of existence. But she doesn't. With elegant finesse, she focuses the blast directly on that knot in each of their heads, that snarl of green and sin-black coils.

Mhoryga fights back, throws a surge of hellish intensity against the white fire. Valindra feels it like a blow. Her great body rocks in the air, losing altitude. With a pulse of her wings, she catches her balance, then redoubles her efforts, even as the dragon spawn to whom she has not linked hurl themselves at her, tiny jaws biting, tearing, trying to make an impression on her scaled hide. She ignores them, her concentration fixed on the hundred souls already in her grasp.

A burst erupts from each mind. A simultaneous shock of pure white, so hot, so intense, but invisible to mortal eyes. It explodes in the atmosphere, vaporizing the poisonous clouds and exposing blue sky once more. Mhoryga screams as she is ripped out of those newly sundered minds. The liberated dragon spawn blink like newborn babes, unsure what to make of the world around them. The rest, still connected to their queen, screech with Mhoryga's own pain, her voice reverberating from their throats in hideous chorus.

Of one accord, the enthralled dragon spawn turn about-face and fly, a great exodus of snarling terror. Their brothers watch them go before slowly gliding down, down, down to the ground below. There, one after another, they collapse, losing Draconan form to lie sprawled on the earth, like a field of corpses. But they aren't dead. Valindra, hovering above them, looks down and sees their pulsing souls. Still alight with hellflame, not as purged as they need to be. But no longer bound to that central mind. No longer enslaved.

You did it! the voice in her head—her own voice—cheers. *Oh, I knew you could, you great, big, gorgeous hulk of a dragon, you!*

Valindra's teeth flash in a snarling grin. She looks around at the handful of dragon spawn still in the air around her. Her own Cyranian force, their numbers greatly reduced, but not utterly devastated. She even spies the little spirit orb she's come to think of as the Singer. Apparently he survived the altercation and . . . oddly enough, she's glad of it.

With a roar of triumph, she beats the air with her wings, soaring up into the blue sky. Sunlight glints on her beautiful wings, even as she fixes her gaze once more on that pulsing glow on the horizon. Her goal. Her purpose. Her reason for being.

All right then, Angel of Fire, the voice in her head says grimly. *We've got her on the run. Let's put an end to this now, shall we?*

Another sky-shattering roar, and Valindra pulses her great wings, tearing through the sky above Khylmira, her sights set on Drathoridan and the Dracor Flame.

31

Nyxia

Nyxia stands on the brink of a great chasm, gazing out across the sweeping plains of Yllajor. Once fertile farmland, peopled and cultivated, now shrouded in dragon smoke, lost to despair.

It's been many days now since she stole Arun from Heleris Stronghold, wrapped him in a dracori cloak, and fled with him across Khylmira. Much to her surprise, no one has come after them. She and Zoar keep a constant watch between them, expecting at any moment for a squadron of dragon spawn to appear suddenly through the clouds and set upon them with fire and fury. But all remains painfully quiet.

When not on watch, Nyxia has hunted snakes, scorpions, and local rodents known as dust-rats, which she's cooked over hellflames to keep her captive alive. He hasn't complained at this repulsive diet. "Better than what they served in Heleris," he said with a shrug, "when they remembered to feed me at all." He devoured roast snake with relish.

Nyxia shivers. Not from cold, for the air is sultry, but the stillness unnerves her. Mhoryga must be distracted elsewhere, too busy to search for her lost, half-formed daughter. And that can only mean one thing.

Naevya.

Her sister is coming. With her white fire. And Khylmira will never be the same.

She bites her lip. Sometime in her early childhood, someone—possibly her nursemaid Aeshlin, before she was fed to the dragon spawn—had whispered to her of another sister, from a few cycles previous. Heliar the Dreadful, who had the temerity to make a stand against Mhoryga. According to Aeshlin, Heliar was cast down in utter disgrace at the last, an embarrassment in the eyes of all the worlds and the gods themselves. Mhoryga ripped her still-beating heart from her chest and devoured it before her eyes even as she died. A gruesome tale—more than effective enough to douse any fires of rebellion which might have sparked in Nyxia's young breast long ago.

But now she has to wonder: Was it as easy as all that? Or did Heliar perhaps give her mother reason to fear? Is it in memory of that fear that Mhoryga now prepares to meet yet another daughter in battle?

"Well," Nyxia mutters to herself, "it won't be much of a battle. Naevya may have manifested fire, but unless she can get to the Dracor Flame, she will still be trapped in that pretty, human form of hers. What can she possibly do against Mother's might? Nothing. Nothing at all."

She can only hope Naevya and whatever force she brings with her across the ocean will create a distraction, keep Mhoryga occupied long enough that Nyxia, Arun, and Zoar can make their getaway, fleeing as far from Khylmira as they can get. They will spend the rest of their lives on the run, of course. But it'll be worth it if it means she can stop Arun from being burned alive.

"What is that?"

Startled, Nyxia turns to find Arun stepping out of the little cave she found for him to use as shelter against the worst heat of the day. He's unsteady on his feet, and meals of snake meat haven't replenished much of his depleted strength. It doesn't help that he's lacking a foot and struggles to balance on the stump. But he is determined. His face angles beyond Nyxia, west toward the ocean. Though he wears a bandage to protect his empty eye sockets, he seems to strain his senses in that direction.

Nyxia shudders. It hasn't been long since she watched the aerial force of dragon spawn pass in the distance, a great cloud of dragon wings, billowing smoke, and spurting flame on the horizon. She can only guess they were on their way to meet invaders. "There's nothing now," she tells Arun. "Nothing to see anyway."

Arun tilts his ravaged face to one side, long strands of colorless hair blowing across his cheeks. Suddenly, his lips crack open in a smile. "She's coming!"

In the same instant, Zoar rears his head from where he'd been napping behind a boulder a few yards away. In dragon form, he clambers up onto a ledge of rock, craning his neck and flaring his scales eagerly.

"Who is coming?" Nyxia demands, though she suspects the answer.

Arun turns his smile upon her. "Just watch. You'll see."

In another few moments, his words prove true. First the great host of dragon spawn she'd glimpsed hours earlier speeds back from whence it came, like a thundercloud propelled by hurricane winds. It's such a great mass, Nyxia would be frightened were they not too far off and so obviously intent on flight. It's a magnificent sight in its way—she's never seen so many dragon spawn in one place before.

But then all thoughts of them is driven entirely from her mind.

The great dragon appears. Like a vision of fate come to life. Enormous, beyond any dream of beauty she's ever dared imagine in all her sad, broken, half-formed life. A true dragon queen, but trailing lashing tongues of white flame rather than green. Even from this distance, Nyxia's nostrils fill with the scent of exotic flowers, leaving her lightheaded.

"Naevya," she breathes.

So . . . her sister manifested after all. And such a manifestation! So huge, so glorious, she seems to ignite the heavens, setting the clouds ablaze in her wake. Hers is the glory of angels, bursting from on high into this world of hell. Nyxia staggers then falls to her knees, both horrified and sanctified by that sight.

The vision passes, vanishing over the horizon toward Drathoridan. A last gust of sweet perfume billows over the stricken plains and breathes into Nyxia's face, as though to convince her that what she'd seen was indeed real.

Arun inhales deeply. "The day of judgment has arrived."

"She . . . she's beautiful," Nyxia whispers, her voice thick.

Arun turns to her. She feels his eyeless contemplation, as though he sees through her in a way a sighted man never could. "She has discovered her purpose," he says. "It is a remarkable thing."

Despair bubbles up from a well in Nyxia's soul, threatening to drown her. "I have no purpose. Not anymore. I've never been what I was meant to be." A sob catches in her throat. She forces it back with a furious effort. "But it was all right! For a while there at least. Because I knew Naevya was like me. Broken.

Lesser than her destiny." She adds in a voice too akin to her mother's for comfort: "A half-formed thing."

Arun is silent for some while. The only sound which disturbs the hushed atmosphere is the perfumed wind whistling among the stones. Then he steps closer to where Nyxia kneels and drops to his knees beside her. His hand reaches out blindly, nubs of bitten-off fingers searching. She doesn't move, doesn't reach back for him, but he finds her hand at last and clasps it. "I think," he says softly, "perhaps you are exactly what you are supposed to be."

She lifts her head, peering sideways at him through a sheen of hot tears. He shrugs, as though aware of her scrutiny. "Even a demon like Mhoryga cannot alter the plans of the gods. Not much in any case, and not for long. I do not think you will fail to fulfill the purpose they have for you."

A breath huffs from Nyxia's tight throat, something close to a laugh but too disparaging. How could he still believe in his gods after everything they've allowed him to endure? "You really are a lunatic, aren't you," she says.

Arun laughs, a bright, golden sound, utterly at odds with his broken body and wasted frame. "Well spotted, my fierceness!" He lifts her hand now and, to her surprise, presses it to his lips. "So," he says, his mouth hovering above her knuckles, "are you and that strapping brother of yours ready to fly into battle?"

"Into battle?" Nyxia blinks uncertainly. "Against Naevya?"

"Perhaps." Arun shrugs. "Or perhaps your heart will tell you otherwise."

She turns from him, looking toward the horizon where the white dragon disappeared. For a moment, she feels a tug in her very soul, as though she might finally spread wings of her own and take flight. Then she frowns. "I can't leave you out here all alone."

"Oh, I'll be fine. I can await your return quite comfortably in my little cave. No doubt Zoar has stocked me up on snake meat enough to last a few days."

"What if I don't return?"

"Then I can wait here just as comfortably for death." He grins. "We all do our part in the great conflicts of the world. Unfortunately, mine is not the part of daring rides into last stands. But if I can send you, my dear, I will consider it my one heroic deed."

With those words, a certainty fixes in Nyxia's heart. She *must* go. It's like the call of destiny itself, strong enough to almost make her believe in Arun's gods. It doesn't matter that she cannot make any difference in the end. The hour is upon her, and go she will.

She gets to her feet and helps Arun rise as well. When she is certain he is stable, she turns, her lips parting to call Zoar's name. But Arun's grip on her fingers tightens suddenly, and he gives a tug, shocking her with more strength than she would have expected, strong enough to pivot her back to him.

"Before you go," he says, "would you do one thing for me?"

"What?"

"Kiss me."

"What?"

He laughs again, even as his face breaks into another one of those incongruous smiles, which transforms his damaged features into something beautiful, almost holy. "I seem to remember back when I still had an eye with which to see, that you had quite a kissable-looking mouth. I've often wondered, in the long, lonely hours of my imprisonment, what it would be like to taste it."

Her heart seems to have forgotten how to beat. Not once in all the years she's treasured a secret love for Arun in the hiddenmost recesses of her soul has she dared imagine such a thing as . . . as *kissing* him. He's too good, too pure, too perfect in her eyes for someone like her to tarnish in such a way.

But there's such hope in his face, visible despite the bandage covering his empty sockets. The scented wind picks up again, flicking his long hair across his forehead, and Nyxia fights the sudden urge to reach out and smooth it back. Before she can lose whatever courage remains to her, she darts forward and plants a little peck on his lips.

Arun's mouth falls slightly. "I understand," he says, "that I must be quite ghoulish looking after all the bits and pieces Mhoryga has taken, but . . . don't you think you could do a little better than that? If this is to be our end—"

She catches his face in both hands, pulls him toward her, and plants her lips on his. To her shock and delight, his arms slip around her back, pulling her to him. His mouth claims hers firmly with a confidence she never could have predicted. As though this moment, this touch, has always belonged to him, to them. A moment that can never make up for all the years of suffering and hurt but, somehow, can transcend them. Become a bright star of beauty in a world of utter darkness.

A rush of feeling floods Nyxia's limbs. Her arms slip around his neck, and what started as something impulsive on her part becomes hungry, desperate. But if she lets herself go any further, she will lose the will to leave. So she pulls back at last, breathing hard, her lips hovering just under his. She closes her eyes, leans forward, allowing their brows to touch, and feels rather than sees Arun's smile.

"That's more like it," he whispers. "Now get you to the fight, little fierceness. Destiny awaits."

32

Valtar

Rathal holds me fast in his claws as he swoops low to the ground. He drops me, and though I try to get my feet under me, the momentum is simply too much. I collapse, tumble in the dirt, battered and bruised across every part of my body.

Yanking back my hood, I push upright and stare into the sky. The white dragon is still there, wreathed in glorious flame. All around her, dragon spawn fall from the sky, gouts of green hell-fire erupting from their throats. They hit the ground with heavy thuds, like hail from heaven.

What happened? My mind still cannot seem to grasp it. One moment I was looking into the eyes of death as a dragon spawn charged, eager to snap me in half with its powerful jaws. The next, the dragon's eyes seemed to burn bright with white fire, and it fell away. Rathal swerved and dived through the swarm of his brothers, but they seemed to have no interest in him. All the dragon spawn were focused in a single direction. On her. On Valindra.

Now, staring up into the sky, I watch the swarm of dragons, still dense despite those who have fallen. Suddenly, as though all receiving the same order at once, they turn and flee in a mass pounding of wings and screeching cries. The cacophony is deafening, and if I weren't already dracori made, I would surely die, choking on the great influx of poisonous fumes in the air.

"Rathal," I gasp. Then I get to my feet, stagger, catch my balance. "Rathal!"

Dragon spawn litter the ground all around me. Some of them remain in dragon form, crumpled like dead flies, their wings askew, their claws upraised to the sky in piteous supplication. Others shudder and, with a burst of green flame, shrink down into man-shaped forms. All different ages, from callow youths to old men. So many of them, hundreds, everywhere.

Overhead, Valindra utters a terrible roar. Though I try to stand my ground, the sound is too shattering. I throw my hands over my ears, falling back to my knees even as her wings pound the air, and she sets off across the sky, leaving the rest of us behind. Pursuing that seething mass of Mhoryga's children. But it's not them she's after—no, no. She wants their mother. She won't rest until she gets her. The clash of the dragon queens is even now upon us.

My heart stabs against my breastbone. I can't let her go alone! Perhaps there's nothing I can do, not in such a world-altering cataclysm. But I can't stay here. I can't let her face whatever is coming alone.

"Valtar!"

I leap to my feet, spinning in place, and crane my head to the sky. Alderin circles above me on Rhangyl. So, the High King somehow managed to survive that altercation. There are others as well. Slowly, I become aware of them in my peripheral vision.

Many of the Cyranian dracori fell to their deaths or were torn apart in that fray, but the force is not wholly decimated.

"Go after her!" I cry, motioning with both arms.

Alderin salutes. Rhangyl angles about and sets off, fairly low to the ground but making good speed in pursuit of the white dragon.

"Rathal!" I cry again, searching for my mount.

"Here!" a voice cries as though in answer. "Valtar Skylock!" I pivot and spy Lady Enya riding toward me on Rathal's back. The young dragon looks, miraculously, none the worse for wear, but the Lady of Cyran is bleeding profusely from a wound in her shoulder.

I spring to them. "Get down from there," I command.

"We need to fly," she answers weakly.

Reaching up, I grip her waist and pull her to the ground as gently as I can. She immediately loses her footing and sits down hard on the bare earth. I grimace. That wound looks deep, and there's far more blood than I initially thought. Her shoulder looks dislocated as well. Now would be a great time to have a woman of Rosie's skill on hand to tend our wounded.

I cast about and spy a Cyranian dracori standing nearby, dazed and confused but apparently whole of limb. "You there," I bark. "Come, assist your Lady."

Enya grabs my arm. I look down into her eyes, which simmer with pain, terror, and, despite everything, grim determination. "You will go with her," she says, not a question but a command. "You will see this through."

I nod. "I swear it, Lady Balxidon. Gather whatever of your people remain here and join us as soon as you can. Fly due west—you'll see Mount Dracor soon enough."

Her jaw sets hard. "Gods go with you, dracori." In that

moment, dirtied and frightened, but still so brave, she reminds me painfully of her brother.

With a short exhalation of breath, I hasten to Rathal, leap onto his back. "Fly," I command. "Fly like the damned."

The young dragon tosses back his head, bugling a battle cry before he springs into the air. His blood is hot, keen for more action, and he streaks across the fire-seared sky, leaving the valley of fallen dragons behind. I look back once. What will happen to them? Did Valindra set them free of Mhoryga's hold? Or are they only temporarily stunned? Will they turn on the Cyranians as soon as they recover?

Heart heavy with unanswered questions, I face forward again. I cannot let my attention be split. I must see this through, help Valindra in any way I can. For Rosie's sake. For the world's.

Days pass. Days and endless nights.

Now and then I believe I glimpse Alderin and Rhangyl up ahead. Sometimes, my eyes trick me into believing I see Valindra herself, like a guiding star on the horizon. But mostly we are alone, Rathal and I. Flying over the damned landscape of our home country. Hoping, fearing . . . wishing we knew how to pray.

I make him stop every so often. Find us a stream where the water doesn't taste too strongly of brimstone and we can refresh ourselves. I beg him to sleep, but he will have none of that. The young dragon longs to reunite with his sister, his queen, to be with her in the final battle. While I know I should insist, my own heart drives me with equal fervor. Soon enough, I remind myself, we will both be dead. We can rest easy then, I suppose, in whatever hell claims us.

At dawn on the third day, we come within sight of Mount

Helera, looming tall above the Rothomir Wastes. Here at last I see Valindra again, perched on the mountain peak, above the topmost towers of Heleris. She looks almost comically large compared to that stronghold, her massive claws gripping boulders, her huge wings casting shadows as deep as night. She is unaware of my approach, her gaze fixed on some point in the distance. I don't have to look to know what it is that absorbs her attention. Mount Dracor casts its evil green glow upon the horizon.

But my vision is more immediately consumed with a different sight, for between the white dragon and that mountain lie the wastes. The sky above them swarms with dragon spawn in incomprehensible numbers. Thousands, tens of thousands. An impassable, impossible force.

My heart plunges to the pit of my stomach. Yes, compared to Valindra, each individual dragon spawn is as nothing—little more than a mosquito, an annoyance. But in numbers like this? Here in the heart of Mhoryga's realm? I don't know how she can get through. Mhoryga's influence over those damned beasts is profound. She holds them in absolute sway—no need for avatars. Empowered by the fires of Dracora, she can be in every mind simultaneously, watching through many thousands of eyes.

Valindra may never get her chance to fight Mhoryga. Not if she can't get to her.

The white dragon seems to be considering this conundrum, perched there on the mountaintop, so still she might be carved from the very same stone. But there's nothing despairing in her stance, only calculation. After all, whatever else she might be, she is still, in essence, Rosie. Undeterred, indomitable. Once her mind is made up, no power in this or any world can stop her save death itself.

I swallow painfully. Gods, how I love her! It hurts so badly, loving with all my soul a being that can scarcely acknowledge my existence. But I love her nonetheless, and I long for nothing more than to die this day in her service. Should the gods grant me this one boon, I will go to my grave with a prayer of gratitude on my lips.

A flutter of wings, and Rhangyl draws abreast of us, Alderin on his back. The High King nods. Together, we urge our dragon spawn to circle the mountain and the vast creature perched upon it. She blinks her enormous eyes and seems to be vaguely aware of us. Then, shaking her huge head, she focuses on the teeming sky above the wastes once more.

Rhangyl and Rathal alight on boulders a little lower down the mountainside, but still above the topmost towers of Heleris. I take a moment to look down into the stronghold. Is Arun still there? Still chained in the dungeons? Not likely—Nyxia would have arrived long ago and told her tales to Mhoryga. I do not doubt the Dragon Queen was swift and merciless in retribution.

"Well, dracori," Alderin calls out, dragging my attention across to him on his dragon mount. "What is to be our part in this upcoming performance?"

I raise a skeptical brow and turn my gaze back to the wastes. Neither Alderin nor I have any hope of making a dent in that dreadful force. Valindra might be able to claw and tear her way through half of them, but even she must be overwhelmed in the end.

But what if—the thought whispers in the back of my mind, subtle but strangely irresistible—what if the white dragon needn't reach Mhoryga at all? What if she need never fight her? I press my lips into a hard line, studying that massive cloud of fiery hellbeasts between us and our goal. Mhoryga's attention must be strained to the breaking point, split between so many different souls.

"We can get through," I say, turning to Alderin, hellfire in my eyes. "If we fly low, close to the ground, we can escape their notice. Then if we reach Drathoridan, while the queen's mind is elsewhere . . ."

Alderin tosses back his head and laughs out loud. All these long days and nights of travel, and still, he acts like a youth on holiday, so great is his joy. "You think Mhoryga will let you get close enough to plant your assassin's blade in her wicked heart before she turns you back to her thrall?"

I shrug. "It's worth a try."

The High King shakes his head, still chuckling merrily, and gazes out across the dreadful stretches of tortured landscape that are Rothomir. "It's as good a way to die as any," he muses. "Possibly better than some." Then he nods firmly. "Very well, dracori. When our fair queen launches her assault, we will make our own daring sprint for fate and glory."

So saying, we both turn our eyes up to the mountain peak once more. Up to the mighty form of Valindra, who remains like a stone, her wings outspread but not yet taking flight. Gods above and below, grant me patience here at the end! What is she waiting for?

33

Valindra

The white dragon holds perfectly still—not just in body but in soul, in essence.

Her awareness is sent forth, out into that teeming mass of ten thousand dragon spawn. She searches—leaping from one mind to the next, seeking even the faintest point of entrance. She expects to find it. Of course, she must. Now that she's done it once, in that aerial battlefield above the costal cliffs, she knows what she must do. Her fire is tremendous, her passion undimmed by long days of flight. All she needs is access to one mind, then she's certain she'll be able to leap from that one to the next and the next, spreading through the entire host like a plague, snapping their connection to their queen.

But the atmosphere here . . . this is very different from the coast. That pulse of green flame, no longer a feeling in her mind but a reality seen with physical eyes here in this world of physical matter, seems to fill up her senses. It reacts to the white fire in her soul, repulsing it. Her flame is powerful, but somehow power makes the repulsion much worse. If she were less powerful, perhaps she would be less repulsed and, therefore, better able to launch her attack. As it is, every time she casts her mind out, the hellfire seems to throw it back again, preventing her from getting anywhere near those dragon-spawn souls.

Valindra breathes out slowly. She is a being far above petty human emotions like frustration or anger. She is too great, too terrible, and, in her own way—though she was born only days ago—too ageless. A creature not belonging within the bounds of time who, therefore, cannot be prey to time's capricious vices.

But deep down inside, the secondary presence in her mind is disturbed. Frightened even. Valindra shakes her head. She doesn't like that: *fear.* It doesn't belong to her, and she won't accept it. If that puny little human consciousness wants to rail and wring her hands, then she isn't welcome in this fight. Here there can be room only for one feeling: rage. Rage against this poisoned air, this decimated land, this ruin and devastation crying out to be remade.

Yes. She can use rage. She'll accept that.

Still, she cannot find the access she needs. Impatience stirs in her heart, urging her to leap out from the mountaintop and tear through those ranks of dragon spawn, ripping them to pieces and carving a path for herself straight to the mountain. Caution holds sway, however. While a thousand dragon spawn couldn't match her strength and size, tens of thousands are a different story. And here, so close to the center of Mhoryga's realm, Mhoryga's own mind is viciously present within her children's heads. Valindra can hear her, just on the edge of her awareness. The Dragon Queen laughs at her and her futility.

"*You see, child of my flame?*" she seems to say, not in words, but in the flutter of wings, the spurt of green fire, the churn of clouds and smoke and fumes. "*You are mighty, yes, but what good is that might?*

"Here in my world, the only fire that matters is mine. The hellfire which you failed to manifest.

"You will never reach me without it.

"You pathetic, half-formed thing."

The white dragon's scales prickle. Her lip curls back, revealing fangs, as her throat vibrates with a long, low growl. She has not flown so far for nothing. She has not given up everything she once knew, become this vast and mighty entity, only to give up now on the threshold of the final conflict.

One last time, she sends her mind flying forth, seeking entrance into the multitudinous dragon-spawn consciousness. One last time, she feels the repulsion, the rejection of her white flame.

Well, flame is not all she has. If this task before her must come down to teeth and claws, so be it. She will rip through those brothers of hers until not one remains between her and the mountain. Then she will tear out Mhoryga's throat.

A whisper like laughter erupts from the throats of the dragon spawn, filling the air with horrifying chatter. And once more, Valindra hears Mhoryga's voice in that dissonance: "*Come and get me then, sweet daughter, if you dare!*"

At last, Valindra spreads her wings and, ignoring the feeble protests of the second presence in her mind, launches from the peak of Mount Helera.

34

Valtar

When the white dragon takes flight at last, the propulsive power of her haunches sends avalanches of stone tumbling down the rocky slopes. Rathal hastily springs into the air to escape being crushed, and Rhangyl joins him. The two dragon spawn, their riders clinging to their backs, circle the mountain, gaining altitude.

I crane my neck, watching Valindra's progress. It's an awesome sight, her greatness, her majesty, so shining and beautiful here in this poisoned land. But I feel the repulsive force of the Dracor Flame, pushing back against her white fire. Though I don't pretend to understand it, I feel in my bones that it is somehow impossible for two such tremendous and yet opposite powers to exist in the same plane. One must simply force the other out of being, and I wonder if Valindra is strong enough to prove the victor in such a contest.

There is no time to question outcomes or rethink motives, however. With a surge of her massive wings, she tears through the air, straight into the dragon swarm in the sky above. A screeching, ripping, soul-tearing cacophony shreds my ears, so loud I'm sure it echoes across all Khylmira. In moments, the glory of Valindra all but disappears. The only sign of her ongoing presence is the black snarl of dragon spawn surrounding her, so dense they seem to have become a new dragon entirely, black and writhing across every part of her body.

But Mhoryga's attention is surely diverted, focused intently on this threat to her very existence. She won't notice any lesser beings creeping across the low places like skulking shadows. I catch Alderin's eye across the length of my dragon's wing. The High King nods once. Then, flying in close formation, we swoop out of the sky, keeping as close to the slopes of the mountain as we dare. We pass the abandoned battlements of Heleris and glide out into Rothomir. A hundred miles and more lie between us and Mount Dracor, which looms so huge and foreboding on the far side of this desolate landscape. I curse bitterly, wishing we could gain altitude, but dare not venture any nearer to the storm of dragon fury overhead. Bursts of green hellfire lick through black clouds like lightning, and fatal fumes thicken the atmosphere. We could never survive that fray.

So, flying no more than twenty feet or so above the ground, we cut our way through the poison-thick air. The land itself is grassless, and the only trees which remain are charred ruins, still somehow clinging to blasted soil with dead roots. Once the Kingdom of Alinar, this land used to lie rich and fertile, nestled between peaceful mountain ranges. Alinar was the first Khylmirian kingdom to fall under Mhoryga's thrall, and the shadow of Mount Dracor was cast long and dark over all. Later, when Heliar rose in defiance against her mother, the ensuing fire battle scorched whatever was left, leaving behind an unforgiving hellscape populated by long shadows and *ilemaara*, demons of the Third Realm.

The ground itself is cracked in long black fissures, which exhale vapors of poison. Those cracks run so deep, some say they plunge through layers of reality all the way to the Tenth Realm itself, even as the fire bellowing up from Mount Dracor is said to originate in Dracora. No natural life can exist in this place, but I feel the presence of demonic forces, lured here by the poisons which feed their essences.

Silently, I urge Rathal on, faster and faster. We are painfully vulnerable out here, beneath that thrashing mass of dragon spawn. I glance overhead, see the thickened place in the sky where they envelop Valindra even now. Bursts of white fire cut through their ranks, and dragon spawn fall from the sky in droves. But there never seems to be an end to them. Mhoryga has been breeding large batches for centuries now, and they never die, save when killed. They simply accumulate, and the oldest of them have long since forgotten that they ever once had human form, their minds utterly overtaken by hellfire.

I tear my gaze away, focusing on what lies ahead. Rathal dodges nimbly between strange, tortured rock formations, burnt-out husks of trees, and the ruins of once tall and fair buildings which, long ago, graced this land. Rathal knows instinctively that he needs to keep to whatever cover he can get, a difficult feat in this blasted place. Now and then I glimpse Rhangyl and Alderin, off to our right. The older dragon is not so agile as Rathal and is forced to choose a smoother course, which in turn makes him more vulnerable.

No sooner does this thought cross my mind than, to my

horror, I spy seven dragon spawn suddenly drop from the black snarl above, angling down toward us. At first I tell myself I'm imagining it, that we haven't been spotted. But I cannot keep up the deceit for long, for the dragon spawn fall into hot pursuit behind Rhangyl, spurts of hellfire trailing like foam from their hungry jaws. They don't seem to have noticed me as of yet.

Alderin looks back at them once before focusing ahead. He knows there is no fighting them, no escaping them. Whether they are under Mhoryga's influence or simply acting on impulse, giving chase like dogs, either way, there are too many of them. They're closing in fast, flanking the High King and his dragon.

"Rutting hells," I curse. Then I bellow against the wind so that Rathal will hear me: "Veer right!"

He understands. Light and quick, he darts out from among the rocks and ruins in which he's been hiding and sets a course to intercept Rhangyl's pursuers. I see one of the dragon spawn descending from above, claws extended to rip Alderin from his mount's back. "Faster, Rathal!" I cry.

The young dragon puts on a burst of speed. Realizing collision is imminent, I have a split second to make a decision. Setting my jaw, I release my hold on Rathal's spines and push free. For a breathless moment, I seem to hang suspended in midair, and I feel the impact in the atmosphere as the two dragon spawn crash into each other.

The next moment, I hit the ground hard, rolling in dirt and rocks, expecting any moment to feel bones break. My armor protects me, however, along with my unnatural dracori strength. I come to a stop at last, pull my head up, and watch Rathal and the dragon spawn spin away through the air, roaring and spurting flame. Alderin and Rhangyl speed on, but their pursuers are distracted. Changing course, they set their sights on Rathal instead.

"No," I whisper. Then I leap to my feet. "*No!*" I reach for my knife, knowing even as I do so that it's too late. The dragons have swarmed Rathal. I hear his shriek, abruptly cut short. They rip into him like wild beasts—tearing, snarling, utterly savage. Monsters without thought or conscience or mercy. Hellflame bursts and fiery blood flows, and I look away, sick to my gut.

But I can't stay here. Exposed as I am, the dragon spawn will turn on me next, remembering that their prey carried a rider. We're too far from any ruins or rocks, but one of those hideous crevices yawns not far from where I stand. I sprint to it, grimacing at the stench which rises from the endless blackness, and hastily slide over the edge, clinging to the wall. I feel as though I hang suspended over the very mouth of hell.

Sounds of carnage seem to go on forever, mingling with the ongoing roar reverberating from the sky overhead. I look up from my hiding place, watch the churning mass like living clouds. Is there any hope for Valindra to make it through now?

One by one, the seven dragons fly over my hiding place, gaining altitude to rejoin their brothers above, seeming to have forgotten their original prey, now that they've had a taste of blood. I can only hope Alderin will stay on course. Even if he makes it to Drathoridan, I don't have much hope the High King will be able to resist Mhoryga's thrall. I seem to hear Arun's voice, whispering close to my ear: *It's a fool's hope at best, and yet . . .*

Perhaps I am a fool. I feel like a perfect idiot as I climb out of the pit and stand in the midst of Rothomir, without a mount, without an idea of what I can or should do next, still fifty miles or more from Mount Dracor. My skin is blistered, despite the dragon blood in my veins, which ordinarily protects me from heat.

I shake myself out, still amazed that I've broken no bones, and turn at last, looking over to where Rathal met his fate. The young dragon's carcass lies in a pile of limbs and gore. My stomach turns over. I must do something, must honor him somehow. He is Rosie's brother, and he served her faithfully from the moment of his liberation. I take a few steps toward the body, uncertain what I should do. Say a prayer? What prayer is appropriate to be spoken over the corpse of a demon-born monster? Surely the gods must acknowledge that he died in struggle against his kin, against his very nature, for the sake of a hoped-for world. A better world, a dream which seems more impossible by the moment.

I take another three steps, staggering a little, winded and in pain. Before I can take a fourth step, a little windstorm kicks up between me and the dead dragon. It moves and stirs, dragging dirt and debris into itself, rising in a long column ten feet high, thickening, solidifying.

"Gods damn," I hiss, stumbling back. "Gods *rutting* damn."

Instinct tells me to run, but there's no fleeing this. Instead I sink into a defensive crouch, my blade at the ready, just as the demon manifests before me. It's an *ilemaara*—a monster of the Third Realm, one of five known to inhabit Rothomir. Vaguely humanoid, pale and rotten, with a jaw five times too large for its size and a long, sinuous tongue that tastes the air with rapacious curiosity. Its limbs are elongated, the joints all strange and backward, giving off a sense of absolute wrongness in the way it moves, the way it breathes and exists. It turns its awful head, looks down on me. That hideous mouth twists in a wide, toothy grin.

"All right then, pretty boy," I say grimly, teeth clenched in a grimace. "You want to wrestle? Let's wrestle."

The demon lunges. I hurl myself forward, churning up stones beneath my boots as the sky overhead writhes and bursts of white and green flame erupt like the end of worlds.

35

Nyxia

With an earsplitting scraping of claws on clay tiles, Zoar alights on the roof of the highest tower in Heleris Stronghold. He pants in great gusts of smoke and spurts of flame, having flown without rest all the way from Yllajor.

Nyxia, clinging to his back, now wonders if she should have made him slow, take the journey more easily. Conserve his strength for what lies before them. She stares aghast at the nightmarish sight playing out in front of her eyes, the churning sky above Rothomir. The air is so thick with wings and fire and smoke, she can no longer see the Dracor Flame burning on the horizon.

And where is Naevya? She searches the turmoil with desperate eyes. Is the battle already over and her sister cast down, defeated? But no—a burst of white flame, like a bolt of lightning, burns brilliantly through the clouds. Dragon spawn fall in a shower of dark, burnt bodies, but there are more and more, far too many. And though Nyxia's own connection to the Dragon Queen is severed, she can feel the pulse of her mother's mind, moving through that swarm. The bodies may belong to her brothers, but the purpose, the intent, the malice is all Mhoryga.

Nyxia grips the dragon spines in front of her, fingers tightening. In her mind, the white fire she unleashed still burns bright, and she feels how the green flame of Dracora repels it—a stronger repulsion than before. She frowns. Even when the fire was low in her mind, it was nearly enough to drive her back from Drathoridan. She watches another bolt of white light explode in the sky. As powerful as the white dragon is, how much more powerfully does the hellflame of Mount Dracor drive her back again? Two opposing forces, incapable of existing in the same space. With her tremendous size and strength, Naevya should brush the dragon spawn off her like flies, breaking their bonds to the Dragon Queen the way she did back in Cyran.

But not here. Not so close to the mountain. Not in the heart of Mhoryga's domain.

A curse burns on Nyxia's lips, blending with the salt of tears which streak down her ash-filmed face. She had believed . . . oh, just for a moment! When she saw the enormity of the white dragon soaring across the horizon of Yllajor, she had believed she beheld at last Mhoryga's undoing, the counterflame to her great power that would cast her down in ultimate ruin. Now she knows—it's not possible. The white dragon cannot even reach Mhoryga. She will simply burn herself out trying and trying and trying again, until that seemingly unstoppable fire in her soul is snuffed and she falls, crashes, lies in a heap of scorched bones on the very landscape where Mhoryga and Heliar once contested for the fate of this world.

No, Naevya cannot defeat Mhoryga. Not with this strange

white flame. She needs . . . Nyxia blinks, the beginnings of an idea prickling the back of her numb brain. She needs hellfire. It is the only way to get through—hellfire of a strength comparable to Mhoryga's, strong enough to break her bond to the dragon spawn. But what good is this knowledge? Naevya never manifested the hellfire in her blood. She too was born defective, like Nyxia.

"A half-formed thing," Nyxia whispers, despair threatening to drag her down in its clutches. But then she says it again. "Half formed. Half . . . of a whole."

Two eggs in a clutch.

Two sparks, twin flames.

Meant to be together, meant to be one.

A ragged exhale gusts from Nyxia's tight lungs. Suddenly she knows what she must do. She doesn't know how she'll do it or even if there is a way for it to be done. But she will try. Gods help her, she will try.

Maybe she has a destiny to fulfill after all.

"Are you ready, Zoar?" she asks, her voice thick with mingled dread and certainty. Her blue-scaled brother cranes his long neck, eyeing her with a reptilian gaze. He blinks once in acknowledgment. "Then fly like you've never flown before," she says, sitting low against his neck and bracing herself. "Fly to Naevya. Fly to our sister. *Go.*"

Spreading wide his wings, Zoar leaps from the turret, glides smoothly out into the cracked and broken landscape of Rothomir. With a burst of speed and power, he propels himself upward, aiming for that churning mass in the sky.

36

Valindra

A sideways thrust of the head. A gnashing of teeth. The crunch of wings and spine. Blood spurts across her tongue before she spits out another dragon spawn and turns to catch another, and another.

There are too many. They keep coming, biting, scratching, clawing at every point of vulnerability. She must keep her eyes shut, or her attackers will burst them, blinding her. Hellflame scorches her scales, and while, at first, she merely felt a little heat, now it begins to wear her down, to hurt. To burn. She summons her own healing white flame, but every time she does so, another pulse of repulsion from the hideous mountain drives it back down inside her, leaving her once again exposed. Valindra roars, sending a pent-up gout of fire from her gut, which blasts through the swarm. Her huge head shakes, no thought or direction to that blast, just pure fury and destruction. But this violence is not what her flame was intended for!

Mhoryga laughs. Her voice ripples from a hundred different

minds, a thousand. From every side, every angle, every corner of awareness, there is Mhoryga.

"*You were a fool to come to me so soon, my sweetling,*" she says, not with words so much as feeling, communicated through eruptions of hellflame and tearing talons and savage teeth. "*You should have let your fire grow before you attempted to face me. But then, it was always a hopeless rebellion! The more your fire grows, the more mine rises to repel it. I feel stronger now than I have since the day that human worm plucked you from my nest.*"

Valindra roars again, snapping at another dragon spawn that got too close, breaking its spine. Deep inside, she still feels the presence of that second self in her head, begging her: *Please, stop! Don't kill my brothers!*

But what else is she supposed to do? She must get to Mhoryga. She must get to that fire and extinguish it. This is her whole reason for being, and she will fulfill her purpose. Nothing will get in her way, certainly not her own second self.

But she is weakening. This struggle is far greater than she anticipated, and she fights mounting despair. When she summons her white flame, it simply refuses to answer now, burning inside her but inaccessible. The dragon spawn rip into her flesh, finding soft places under her legs, around her ears, her nostrils. Blood streams over her white scales, burning and bright, falling like molten rain to the devastated land below.

"*Naevya!*"

Through the cacophony, the din of dragon-spawn roars, the pounding pulse of fire in her own head, and Mhoryga's ever-present laughter, Valindra hears it—a voice she does not recognize, but which the second self inside her does. Calling out a name which is not hers and yet, in some strange way, is.

"*Naevya! It's me!*"

Though she knows she shouldn't risk it, Valindra opens her eyes. Shaking away attacking dragon spawn, she peers through the chaos. She should not be able to focus on any one dragon in this tumult, but somehow, her gaze fixes intently on a single blue-scaled beast which dodges and darts, making its way through the fray toward her. A small figure clings to its back—a bright, shining soul, filled with both white fire and green.

Valindra roars again, pulsing her great wings. One of her clawed hands swipes ten dragon spawn from the air in a single blow. And still she watches through slitted eyes as that blue dragon and the soul spark on its back draw closer, closer. Should she snap them from the air as well? But the thought no sooner occurs than her second self deep inside utters a desperate cry of restraint. Against her better judgment, she lets them draw near.

Something in the green flame of that soul calls to her, to some part of her beneath the white fire. Down where another fire still burns in her core—fire bred into her blood, diminished but not defeated, despite the manifestation of her phoenix-born form. For, despite the white fire, despite the flames of renewal that burn through her, she is still, at heart, a dragon.

There is something about this hellflame that feels different from all the burning green souls of the dragon spawn surrounding her, different even from the mountain of flame she pursues. Something about it calls to her, begs her to reach out for it. To take it. To claim it.

The blue dragon flies alongside her great eye. The little creature, the soul spark, looks at her—so small, so insignificant. Some distant part of Valindra's awareness hears Mhoryga's voice rippling through the dragon spawn: "*Nyxia! What are you doing? Nyxia, no!*" A bolt of compulsion goes out from that voice, but when it tries to overwhelm that soul spark, the white flame in her core drives it off. The little creature gazes into Valindra's eye and speaks aloud in the tongue of mortals, which the great white dragon can scarcely be bothered to comprehend.

"Naevya," she says, "take it. Take whatever I have. We were meant to be together, meant to be whole. So take my flame and become what we were meant to be."

Valindra doesn't understand. She can't understand. And now the dragon spawn are swarming worse than before, attacking the blue-scaled dragon, driving it off course. Valindra is forced to shut her eyes once more. But the second self inside her reaches out. Through the madness, through the storm of furious bodies and flapping wings, she latches hold of that soul spark, so bright, so different from all others around.

"*Take it!*" the soul spark cries.

"*Are you sure?*" the second self answers. "*What will happen to you—*"

"*Just take it, Naevya! Take it now!*"

So Valindra—Naevya, dragon, woman, whatever she is—catches hold of that soul spark and, very neatly, yanks the green flame out from it. She feels the little body in which it was housed shudder, collapse into itself. Fall. But she can't be bothered with that. She pulls that green flame to her. And suddenly it seems as though she sees a vision: a large nest, in which two smoke-blackened eggs lie nestled together, pressed against each other, surrounded in a green flame. One flame, whole and profound and deadly.

The white dragon drags that flame into her soul, pushes it down, down, down into her depths where it meets at last with the other twin flame burning at her core.

"*No!*" Mhoryga roars through the throats of her dragon spawn.

In the same moment, Valindra's eyes open wide, erupting with furnaces of hell. She opens her mouth and utters an earth-shattering roar, which ripples through the dragon spawn and, just like that, severs Mhoryga's connection to their minds. The dragons fold up on themselves, fall from the sky in a great shower of crumpled wings, even as Mhoryga's voice echoes across the barren plains of Rothomir, wordless in her rage and despair.

The white dragon—no longer white but suffused in green flame, eyes blazing like twin windows into Dracora itself—twists the coils of her body around in the sky, reveling in the freedom of movement, the liberation from all those slashing, tearing, tiny claws and teeth. She shakes her horned head, utters another bellow of triumph.

Then she turns her head to the burning mountain, the path to her goal clear at last.

37

Valtar

Claws shred the air mere inches from my flesh as I hurl myself to one side and spring to the top of a boulder. Using this added height to my advantage, I propel myself upward and slash my blade across the demon's face, aiming for its bulging red eye. The blow strikes wide, gashing across its wrinkled brow instead, but it's enough to make the *ilemaara* roar and double over, shocked by the sudden burst of pain.

I land lightly on my feet, whirl, and narrowly avoid a backhand swipe. My feet are perilously close to one of those black crevices in the ground. A cloud of steam belches from below, heating my heels. I dance nimbly to one side, thinking perhaps to distract the demon and drive it back into that gorge.

The *ilemaara* turns its heavy head, leering at me with its grotesquely wide mouth. It lunges on all four elongated limbs, its bent back bulging with hideous spinal bones. Opening its jaw, it shoots out a long tongue, which lashes like a snake. I'm not quite quick enough, and it wraps around my ankle and whirls me off my feet, up into the air, dangling above the demon's head. Slowly, it lowers me toward that mouth, a cavern of razor-sharp teeth that ring all the way down its gaping throat.

I stab viciously at the tongue, again and again, my blade piercing the soft tissues. The demon shakes its head, flings me through the air. I land hard, roll, nearly go over the edge into yet another crevice. My knife hits the ground several yards away. Scrambling to get my feet under me, I lunge after it, my only remaining weapon.

An enormous, long-toed foot comes down hard on top of the knife, covering it beneath big, arched claws. The demon grins toothily down at me, even as its bleeding tongue sags from its jaw. Grimacing, I reach for a rock, intending to hurl missiles if I must.

Overhead, a burst of green flame cracks the sky.

This is not like the small but constant eruptions of hellfire which have lit up the dragon-spawn swarm. No—it's as though the whole atmosphere momentarily *becomes* green fire as a wave of flame pulses out from the center of the churning mass above. I throw up my hands to protect my face, knowing as I do so that it will do no good. In a last impulse of self-preservation, I call up my own hellfire, wrap it around my limbs. Either the hell in my blood will protect me or I will be incinerated.

Heat rolls over me. The demon's shriek shreds my ears, and I think for a moment that I will share its fate, that my feeble shield will not save me. But the wave of green passes over me in a roar, and I fall to my knees, half blind but still alive, still whole. Fire dances before my vision, but when I look down at my own hands, they do not seem to be ablaze.

I yank my head up in time to see the demon standing before me, no longer alive, but a statue of ash. Even as I watch, it disintegrates on the wind. I catch a single breath, then lunge forward, grab my knife by the hilt. Only now do I dare look up. My heart sinks with dread.

The white dragon is no more.

A monster of epic proportions supported on vast pinions hovers in the air above Rothomir, while dragon spawn fall from the sky, striking the earth in a series of thuds. Above them all is Valindra—but this is no Angel of Fire anymore. She is demonic. A true queen, born of the Tenth Realm, birthed in fire. A monster so akin in appearance to Mhoryga, I almost believe it is Mhoryga herself come out from Drathoridan to slay her foes. But no—the shape of those horns crowning the once-beautiful head is familiar. It is the same dragon, only hideously altered. A hellish rebirth.

What happened? What has become of Valindra, of the phoenix flame? I don't understand. Despair crushes my heart. I fall to my knees, unable in this moment to think, to move, to do anything beyond merely exist.

A small figure catches my eye, tumbling with the dragon spawn through the air. There are so many falling bodies all around me, I shouldn't even notice, but somehow, I do. Possibly because it isn't a dragon; it's a human shape. Dracori? Strange, for I've seen no sign of dracori anywhere over Rothomir. No doubt they are amassed around the base of Mount Dracor, a last guard to protect their mighty queen.

But there is that one figure, tumbling like a straw doll through smoke and flame. A dragon spawn swoops toward it. For some reason, this beast was spared the fate of its brothers, untouched by that burst of flame. Its blue scales shine in the green hellfire glow, and it darts through its falling brethren to catch that little human shape out of the air with its front claws.

I look around. Dragon spawn hit the ground, some quite close by. I throw myself to one side, narrowly avoid being crushed underneath one, then scramble beneath the ledge of a nearby rock formation. Soon the landscape around me is littered with fallen dragons, just as the plateau above the Umenoran Cliffs was days ago. Only this number is far greater. My mind can scarcely take them in. Are these all the dragon spawn in Khylmira? I cannot tell if they are dead or merely stunned. Some of them, even as I watch, twitch, burst into flame, and reduce to human form. Bonfires blaze around me, and part of me wonders if I am dead. If this is hell.

As though in answer, Mount Dracor utters a terrible roar. The ground beneath my feet trembles, and the crevice erupts with great clouds of putrid steam. I turn. Look. See the dread mountain, still some fifty miles distant, emitting a gout of green magma and black ash thousands of feet into the air. Out from that magma, out from that ash cloud, bursts a being which has haunted my dreams since childhood. Vast, tattered wings churn storms of lightning into being. Black and pulsing with power, with evil, her cruelly horned head and blade-scaled body a nightmare made flesh.

Mhoryga, manifest, has come at last to fight for her throne.

38

The Dragon Queen

She watches her mother rise like a green sun over a dead world. As she gazes through her own hellish flame, she thinks: *She is beautiful.*

And following that thought: *I will destroy her.*

With a roar of joyful bloodlust, she pulses her wings, speeding across the newly emptied sky, sending spirals of black clouds and fumes in her wake. Mhoryga makes a lazy turn around the mountain before setting her sights on her approaching daughter. Then, with a surge of power and flame, she propels herself headlong into the inevitable clash.

The whole world waits in breathtaking stillness—the silent suspense when the heart stops and the blood freezes, just before the final blow falls. Pressure builds in the atmosphere, heat and electricity only just contained.

When the two demonic forces collide, that pressure bursts. Another wave of green flame ripples through the air, across the tortured ground, destroying and disintegrating all not born to its blaze. Any eyes that can bear it stare in abject horror and wonder and loathing and love at those tremendous beings, beyond all mortal comprehension, which claw and bite and flame each other across the fire-wreathed sky.

Deep in the younger dragon's mind, she hears that pathetic second-self voice crying out, *What have I done? This is not what we were to become! We were supposed to be different from her! We were supposed to save the world!*

But the younger queen cannot pause to heed that voice, that weakness. This is a time for utter strength and brutality, for wrath and unleashed hell. She rips at the older queen's tattered wings, kicks with her hind claws at her underbelly, long talons scraping uselessly against hide so thick, so dense, nothing can penetrate it. In a frenzy of fury, she opens her mouth and spews hellfire into the face of the monster who is her mother.

Mhoryga smiles. "*So,*" she says, speaking directly into her daughter's mind, "*you have become a true dragon at last with a heart worth eating.*"

"*Not if I eat your heart first!*" the younger queen replies. They tumble through the air, locked in combat, and hit the ground at the base of the mountain so hard, the earth quakes all the way across the Rothomir Wastes. The highest tower of Heleris Stronghold cracks, topples, and the fortified walls shudder.

But Mhoryga shakes her daughter free and stands tall, taller than castles, great as a mountain, while green flame leaps from her eyes, her mouth, between her black scales. She smiles again, roaring and shaking her horns in triumph. "*Have you not yet understood, my sweetness?*" she cries, her voice echoing against stones and down into the deepest depths of her daughter's soul. "*No matter what happens, I will live on. Should you kill this weakened frame of mine, I will live on in you.*"

Suddenly, within the young queen's head, a vision appears, vivid as life. She sees another young dragon, as great as she or greater still. Proud and beautiful and terrible, seething with hellflames. She sees the old queen rise up from the mountain, sees the great clash, and the terrible fire that scorched this land.

One dragon queen died in that battle. The other survived, lived on, ruled this realm. Became the Dragon Queen, the enslaver of nations.

"*Heliar was killed!*" the second self deep in the young dragon's mind protests. "*They told me Heliar died!*"

"*She did,*" the Dragon Queen replies, her forked tongue flicking out from the cage of her teeth, tasting the sulfur in the air. "*For when she killed my former self, she became me, and I her. I am Heliar. And I am Mhoryga. For Mhoryga cannot die! She is ageless, she is endless, she is undying.*"

She spreads her ragged wings, muscles coiling. The next moment, she shoots up into the sky, pulsing higher and higher, until she hovers in the poison-laced clouds above the mountain, gazing down at her daughter below. "*Come, sweetest darling!*" she roars. "*Come, make an end of this body. You have manifested your hellflame now, you have made yourself into a worthy vessel. The time is ripe for you to take the next step in your ascension. Become me, become Mhoryga, and reign over this world.*"

The second self deep in her mind moans. *No, no, no, it wasn't supposed to be this way! We were supposed to be different! We were supposed to heal this land—*

But the young queen doesn't wait to hear more. She launches into the sky, claws outstretched, jaw gaping, hellfire billowing from her gut in wave upon wave of heat and fumes and black, choking clouds. Her gaze narrows to a single fixed point, to that place just behind the wall of Mhoryga's breastplate scales, where her seething heart beats a harrowing pulse. The end is nigh, and she will not hesitate, she will not doubt. She will be what she was born to be.

The end—and the beginning—of dragons.

The two queens crash, a snarl of titanic limbs and wings and lashing tails. Down they plummet from the sky, a streaking comet of destruction, plunging through smoke and ash and poison into the yawning maw of Mount Dracor.

39

Valtar

The dragons fall entwined together, plummeting through the smoke-laced atmosphere, and vanish into the mountain. I watch in horror as a fountain of green, molten lava erupts two thousand feet high. The world trembles, and the ground beneath me cracks. The fissures already scarring the landscape suddenly widening, breaking into new jagged lines. I'm only just quick enough to fling myself backward before tumbling headlong into a chasm cutting from this realm into the very heart of hell. Sweat pours down my face, even as the fire in my blood struggles to protect me from the blast of heat rolling across the wastes. All around me, fallen dragon spawn lie as though paralyzed. Many of them topple into opening fissures, lost in clouds of flesh-searing steam.

I turn my face back to the mountain. *Valindra!* my heart cries desperately. But I know the truth—that monster I saw, whatever it was, wasn't Valindra anymore. The Angel of Fire is gone. The being which grappled with Mhoryga may have been Mhoryga's own reflected self.

Rosie! Another part of me, deep down in my soul, weeps. *Oh, Rosie, my Rosie, this is what you feared. This is what you never wanted to become. How could I have let this happen? How could I love you and not spare you this fate?* Better to have driven my blade into her heart at the moment of our first meeting, even as her lips pressed against mine. That end would have been kinder than this.

"Valtar!"

A voice is shouting my name. Over and over again. Too lost in horror, too lost in regret, I kneel in this hellscape, staring up at the mountain, unable to respond. But when a dragon spawn alights on the ground beside me, I shake my head and dully turn, looking up. Nyxia, her black hair singed, her face streaked with ash and blistered with burns, looks down at me over the shoulder of her blue-scaled mount. "Valtar," she says, holding out one hand. "Get on. Before this whole place collapses."

"*Rutt you!*" I snarl. Gripping my knife, I launch to my feet and stagger three steps toward her. But her dragon deftly swipes a wing and knocks me flat on my back. He plants a heavy forefoot on my chest, pinning me in place.

Nyxia's eyes appear above me once more. "There's no time for this, Valtar," she snaps. Something in her voice sounds strange. Not like Nyxia. There's a freshness breathing out from inside her that I don't understand—a lack of venom and heat. And, though I never would have expected it here of all places, my nostrils suddenly fill with the scent of exotic flowers. "I'm free of her hold," she says. "Naevya . . . Rosie . . . she broke me free. And I gave whatever was left of my own hellflame to her, to help her in the battle. I am not . . ." She chokes, shakes her head, her face wondering and terrified and glad all at once. “I am not a dragon anymore.”

I bare my teeth. “You have destroyed her then.”

Her eyes flash. “I gave her what she needed to defeat Mhoryga.”

“You’ve made her what she never wanted to be!” I shake my head, despairing, ready to weep for Rosie, for Valindra, for the beautiful Angel of Fire and her indomitable spirit, lost forever. Staring up at Nyxia, I’m not certain I could hate her more. Foam spits through my clenched teeth. “Give me one good reason not to spill your guts on this cursed ground!”

“Well.” She shrugs, tilting her head to one side. “I know where Arun is.”

Despite the chaos, the heat, the heaving hell on all sides, and the cracking world, my heart goes suddenly still. “What?”

“I broke him out of Heleris and took him into hiding.”

“You’re lying.”

“He’s safe. A few days’ flight from here, waiting for me to come back to him.” She swallows then slides from her dragon’s back and approaches me. When she pushes against his leg, her dragon reluctantly lifts it, giving me a chance to scramble to my feet and tower furiously over Nyxia. I adjust my grip on my blade, ready to thrust, to stab, but Nyxia holds my gaze. “Kill me if you must,” she says, “but don’t hurt Zoar. He’s the only other person who knows where Arun is.”

“Zoar?”

“My brother.” She nods to the dragon.

I hesitate. Though I’ve noted the similarity in color and shape before, it now strikes me profoundly how similar Nyxia’s eyes are to Rosie’s. No longer brimming with poison and hatred and malice, but shining with the light of newly claimed freedom. Here, in the face of her twin, I can almost make myself believe I see my wife again.

Mount Dracor utters another shattering roar. The world quakes. Nyxia, her dragon, and I all stagger hard, and Zoar's wings outspread to help him keep his balance. I turn from them, my limbs suddenly weak, my face slack, as I stare across Rothomir to the burning mountain.

A dragon emerges from its depths. Shooting out from the magma and fumes, soaring into the tortured sky. One dragon, triumphant. The reigning queen of this world. But from here I cannot tell if it is Mhoryga or Valindra or . . .

My lips form the name, breathe it into the swirling ash: "Rosie."

40

Alderin

The black stone walls of Drathoridan drip with lava, which oozes green from open crevices, running in shimmering rivulets. The walls shiver with impossible heat, as though Dracora itself has finally passed through layers of reality and come into being here in the world of men. No mortal could survive such temperatures or walk this floor or pass through these molten halls.

But a man with dragon fire in his blood may do so. A man who is no man anymore, but a monster.

Alderin knew from the beginning that he would not survive the mission set before him. That noble young prince of so many years ago, with his heart full of ideals of sacrifice and virtue—even he did not deceive himself. He could not endure what was coming and remain the same man. But he entered into his destiny with his eyes wide open, and when he felt the very essence of his soul chipped away, his virtue warped, his ideals crumbled to ash, he told himself it was all worth it if he could bring about that one great purpose.

Pandracor.

The end of dragons.

Now the end is near. One dragon queen destroyed, the other uplifted. It hardly matters which is which, so long as he is able to get close while she is momentarily destabilized following her altercation.

He arrives at the door of the shrine, which stands partially ajar. He knows this place quite well, for it was here that Mhoryga welcomed the handsome young prince, gave him her blood to make him like her, loved him, took from him, begat his only children. Five years he dwelt in this damned temple, worshipping his dark goddess, all other purpose and meaning forgotten. So he would have remained until the end of his days, were it not for Durona.

But Durona is not here to save him this time. Nor is there a brave champion, seasoned in prayer and prepared for the final thrust and twist. It doesn't matter. Somehow he always knew it would come down to this. The High King and the Dragon Queen. The figurehead of mankind and the embodiment of all that is Draconan. A final struggle for the soul of this world.

He will prove himself before the eyes of the gods, here at the very end.

He stands at the door, looks inside to the shrine—the great platform, which overhangs the seething mouth of Mount Dracor, that yawning doorway to the Tenth Realm. His heart leaps to his throat. She is there. Huge, but not so vast as she was in the first moments of her triumph. Following her rise from the volcano's depths, she circled high in the sky seven times before alighting here, her frame reducing slowly from its magnificent proportions into something no less terrifying but less tremendous. She's mostly dragon, but there is a vaguely humanoid shape to her now—the tail is shorter, the wings no longer great enough to block out the sky. She pants heavily from the exertion of battle, black streams of smoke issuing from her flared nostrils.

Alderin watches for some while, patient, awaiting the right moment. To move too soon, to draw attention to his presence while she is still mostly in draconic form, would prove disastrous. He knows the *meorise* blade hidden on his person could never pierce the armor-plate scales of her dragon hide. But if he can catch her in a moment of vulnerability, if he can get close enough . . .

She continues to shrink. From the size of a small mountain to an elephant and at last to a giantess—nine feet tall, long of limb, powerfully built, wrapped in a golden snakelike skin. A warrior angel of fire and death, lying naked on the platform above the volcano's mouth.

He steps into the chamber, soft footed, his breathing light. Even his heartbeat is slow, almost undetectable. If she becomes aware of him, if she gets into his mind, it will all be over. Like a shadow, he glides across the superheated stones, his feet bare, for the soles of his shoes have long since burned away. He is more dracori now than he has ever been, trusting only the hell in his blood to keep him alive just a little longer, just long enough.

She lifts her head. Shoulders bowed, hair tumbled, she turns, fixes him with her gaze. He freezes in place, heart jammed in his throat. Then he whispers, "Roselle?"

It is she. And it isn't she. A golden goddess, with the face of death and carnage. Slit-pupiled eyes and teeth like blades, a forked tongue flicking between her lips. Beautiful beyond all description. But where the Dragon Queen he once knew boasted a head of black hair, now he sees golden curls, shining through a coating of ash.

"Roselle," he says again. "I've come to find you."

"No," she whispers. In his mind, he feels her presence closing in upon him like a fist. "*No, no, no. No Roselle. No Valindra.*" Echoes ring inside his head, like the tolling bells of fate itself. "*I am the Dragon Queen. Goddess of this world, daughter and doom of Dracoris.*"

He knows he has but moments before she takes hold of him, before he belongs to her, as all dragon spawn and dracori belong to her. The time is now.

With a roar, he breaks into a run, covering the distance between them, sprinting across the platform. She is weak from her altercation, weak from her transformation. She will never be weak again, but in this moment, this blade of his, this bright *meorise* tooth, may bite through her breast, plunge into her fiery heart, and—

She rises. Her limbs unfold, first into the long, sensuous arms and legs of a humanoid creature, then longer, greater, huger, as the dragon bursts into being. Her elongated neck extends, her enormous jaw widens, opens. Alderin stares up into a cage of teeth, limned with green flame. "Roselle!" he cries again.

Then in a whisper of terrible understanding: "Mhoryga."

Blackness closes around him. Heat. Pain. Teeth piercing flesh.

Alderin Aumanus, High King of Belanor, knows no more.

41

Valtar

The nearer the blue dragon spawn flies toward Drathoridan, the weaker Nyxia grows. No longer protected by hellfire inside, she begins to go limp, sagging over her dragon brother's neck until I fear she will fall. If I needed further evidence of her humanity, this is it.

"Set me down here," I command the dragon spawn. We are still many miles from the mountain, but I simply cannot risk Nyxia's life. Not if she is truly the only person besides this dragon who knows where Arun is. They both need to get out of here; both need to survive, return to my brother, and flee.

Though we share no mental link, Zoar seems to read my mind. He swoops lower to the ground, but the heat rising from the fissures is so great, he dares not land. "That's far enough!" I bark, when we are still a good fifteen feet from the ground. He pulls up into a hovering position, and I spring from his back.

My landing is hard, but I roll into it, tumbling across sizzling rock. I come to a stop a mere foot away from another plunging fissure, roll over, and watch Zoar gain altitude once more. The young dragon makes a slow turn, careful not to unbalance his half-fainting rider. Then he sets off with all speed for clearer skies and unburnt air, leaving me behind.

Rising, I face the journey before me. A good twenty miles of broken landscape lie between me and the base of Mount Dracor. It may take me days to navigate these fissures, days more to climb the mountain. And what do I hope to find there? A dragon queen, a new goddess? My wife?

I set my teeth and begin walking, taking care to numb my mind against all thought save progress. Here and there, I spy more fallen carcasses of dragon spawn. Not as many this close to the mountain, away from the center of battle. I still can't discern if they are dead and don't bother to inspect more closely. There's no time for distractions now. I fix my gaze on the green and burning flame of Mount Dracor and march doggedly onward.

As though from a distance, a voice whispers in the back of my mind: *You must mourn her, Valtar.*

I shake my head, wipe sweat from my eyes, and stagger on.

Mourn her and prepare yourself for the ultimate act of courage.

A fissure lies before me, some five feet across. I give myself a running start and spring over it, just as a gust of hot steam billows forth. My skin reddens, and my nostrils fill with sulfurous stench. I land hard on the far side, stagger, go down on one knee.

Somehow, in a twist of fate, you, *Valtar Skylock, have become the last bastion. The final hope of this world.*

"Damn it," I growl, one fist pressed hard into the dirt as I struggle to reclaim my breath. Ash dances across my tongue, coats the inside of my throat. But the hellfire burning in my gut keeps me alive. I am a creature of hell, remade by the ungentle hand of my dark goddess. I can survive this place.

But I'm not sure I can survive what lies before me. Or that I even want to.

There's hope yet, Valtar.

The new voice whispers in my ear, soft and gentle as a spring breeze, refreshing even to the most tormented soul. I squeeze my eyes tightly shut. I can't bear to hear that voice, not here, not now. Not my Rosie.

And yet, with that same invincible spirit I've come to both dread and admire so profoundly, she continues: *It may truly come out all right in the end. The world saved. Your people and mine spared. And then we'll have the rest of our lives to—*

"Gods!" I cry, whether in prayer or blasphemy, I cannot say. "Gods damn me, but let her not be gone from this world!" In my mind's eye, I see that monstrous creature grappling with Mhoryga above the burning mountain. Could there be anything of Rosie left inside such a fiend?

I forge on, hour upon scorched hour. The day neither waxes nor wanes. There is no difference between dawn and dusk, noon and night. All is shrouded in black smoke, illuminated in Dracor's hellish flame. Time loses all meaning, and I begin to think I really am in hell, and this is the torment the gods have appointed for me, payment for my many sins. To trek this stricken land for all eternity, pursuing Rosie, pursuing my heart's desire, knowing all the while she will not be at the end of this journey, but striving for her hopelessly, nonetheless. I cannot imagine a perdition more vicious.

A flash of movement catches my eye. Another demon? But no, all the *ilemaara* who made Rothomir their home must have been incinerated in that first great blast of fire. I look again, straining my eyes through the swirling ash. Wings—dragon wings. One of the dragon spawn? I'd not thought there were any survivors other than Nyxia's brother, whose mind was not connected to Mhoryga and, therefore, not susceptible to that shattering bolt which broke her connection to the others and brought them crashing to the ground.

I continue marching, keeping half an eye on the approaching winged figure. As it draws nearer, however, a jolt of recognition races through me. "Rhangyl," I say, lifting my head. Then I wave my arms wildly and bellow for all I'm worth. "Rhangyl! Rhangyl!"

There's no sign of Alderin on the one-eyed dragon's back, but I won't try to guess what has become of him. All that matters is that I have an ally here in this burning world. An ally and a pair of wings.

I scream, shout, climb up onto a boulder, and all but dance a jig to get Rhangyl's attention. It works in the end. The battle-blackened dragon circles and lands before me, his powerful wings stirring up clouds of ash. I leap from the boulder, run to him, and scramble up between his wings. "Take me to Drathoridan," I command.

Though Rhangyl cannot speak in this form, and we share no mental link, I feel the momentary resistance in his soul. He does not want to draw any nearer to the seat of the Dragon Queen than he must, not while his mind remains free.

"Please, Rhangyl," I urge. "I must find her. I must know."

The dragon spawn heaves a huge sigh, little sparks of green dancing between his teeth. Then, resigned, he takes to the air once more. I cling to his spiny back, my eyes narrowed against the drifting ash which chokes the atmosphere. Now and then, Rhangyl opens his mouth and emits a bolt of flame just to clear the air in front of him. The heat rolls back over me, but I scarcely notice. My gaze is fixed on the mountain. On the black temple towers built of volcanic stone. And still, though I know I shouldn't, I dare to hope . . .

Rhangyl doesn't carry me all the way to the temple but sets me down partway up the mountainside, on the narrow road the dracori use to march to the temple gates. I slide from his saddle onto the oven-like rocks. "Thank you, my friend," I say, meeting his solemn eye. "Go on now. Get away from this place."

Rhangyl growls and shakes his horned head.

"No," I answer. "Don't wait for me. Be free if you can."

He holds my gaze, resistance and relief warring for dominance in his heart. Then he bows once, his single eye closing for a moment, offering me a simple salute. The next moment, his wings spread, pulse, and he springs aloft once more. Circling higher and higher, he vanishes into the ash-filled atmosphere.

I turn, gazing up to the twisted towers of Drathoridan. Now that the last leg of my journey lies before me, my courage flags. But what have I to fear? Certainly not death. It's been many years since the promise of a gruesome end had any hold over me. But I do fear what I will find up there, in the shrine above the Dracor Flame.

I begin my climb. Step after step, sometimes hand over hand, scrambling up loose stones, pulling my way against the pressure of the pulsing air. Strange, but as I climb, I seem to hear my own voice speaking out of memory: *I have even walked the path to Drathoridan and even seen the Dracor Flame which burns without ending in the heart of the shrine. Can any man here claim as much?* An image appears in my head: I see myself, standing bare chested in the receiving hall of Stromin Palace. King Alderin stands before me on the dais, with his stolen princess a few steps behind him. I'd made a daring gamble that night, opening my shirt to reveal my brand as proof of the false story I told. The gamble had paid off in the end, but only thanks to Rosie.

Even here, in the depths of hell, a smile pulls at my lips at that memory—the way she sprang forward just when the tension in that hall had reached a fever pitch and declared: *While I wouldn't want to speak for the company at large, personally I am quite ready for the dancing to begin.* How we'd all stared at her. That bright little figure, with her hair shining in the *scintil* light, thrusting herself into the fray with such ease and defusing what should have been an explosive situation. Though her voice was airy, it had commanded every soul in that room, my own included.

And when Alderin asked her to choose her partner for the first dance . . . she had chosen me. She always chose me. From the moment she dragged me out of that curtained alcove and planted her mouth on mine, she claimed me, made me her own. And though I fought with all my strength, resisting, telling myself I felt nothing for her . . . the truth is, I was a lost cause from the instant our lips met. Something inside me fundamentally changed under her influence. I became a different man, a better man—a man akin to the one I once dreamed I would be. Someone who could make my noble father proud, who could stand tall against the great evils of this world. That version of myself, whom I believed was crushed from existence years ago, Rosie brought back to life. Because that is the ultimate truth of who Rosie is. She never needed phoenix flame; she was herself a being of restoration and healing, a miracle worker in her own right. The white fire she manifested was only an extension of her true soul.

Grinding agonized breaths through my teeth, I struggle on up the mountainside. The heat eats away even my dracori garments until they hang in tatters from my limbs. I don't stop. I won't. If there's even a chance she's there, waiting for me at the top of this mountain, I need to know.

There's hope yet, Valtar, her voice whispers in my head.

"Yes, Rosie," I snarl, fighting against my own weakness and dread, fighting to reach that summit. "Hold on to that hope of yours. Just a little longer."

No guards stand at the temple doors, neither dracori nor dragon spawn. The whole place is abandoned. I feel the emptiness the moment I step inside. But I cannot help feeling that I walk in someone else's footsteps, someone who was here not long ago. Perhaps Alderin made it this far before parting ways with Rhangyl. Not a comforting thought; I know too well what Alderin has planned for his daughter. Gods, if that man lays a finger on her, I'll gut him where he stands!

I break into a run. I don't think I'm quite sane anymore. Some distant part of me, standing on the outside of my body, observes dispassionately the burnt, blistered, perspiring, lunatic creature staggering through these hellish halls, sweat or tears pouring down his cheeks. A madman, focused on a singular, mad obsession. Nothing to be done about it, however. There's no reasoning with such a man.

So I make my way silently through the labyrinthine passages. Green lava pours through cracks in the wall, oozes in rivulets, and pools on the floor, slowly hardening in ugly formations. And yet Drathoridan never falls, held in place by some ancient magic stemming from another world entirely. The air is painfully thick; I should have suffocated long ere now, but my body keeps on functioning, propelled by the fire within.

At last the door to the central shrine stands before me. I stagger to it, lean heavily against the doorway, breathing hard, my head bent. Now that I'm here, courage fails me. It would be easier to die right here in this moment than to look inside. But I cannot do that to Rosie. Not when she gave so much. Not when we've come so far.

I lift my head.

She's there. Standing on the circular platform above the volcano pit, she seems to admire the view. Not a dragon, but certainly not human either. More like an angel—nine feet tall, golden skinned, golden haired. Shining and shimmering with a gleam of green fire.

"Rosie?" I rasp in my burnt throat.

She turns, looks at me. Her brilliant eyes light up from the inside, leaping with flames. "Valtar, my sweet," she greets me in a voice of pure gold and thick smoke. "I hoped you would come." She spreads her arms as though to welcome me into her embrace. "You did not think to find me like so, did you?"

She is naked. Naked and glorious, a perfectly sculpted ideal of womanhood, wrapped in snakeskin. Her limbs are muscled, powerful; her breasts large, plentiful, succulent. Her neck is a long, graceful column to support that magnificent head, that bountiful mane of shining curls which falls nearly to her ankles.

My heart seems to have forgotten how to beat.

She comes toward me, moving with slow, seductive grace, one foot planted precisely before the next, toe to heel, toe to heel, like a dancer. Every curve of her body undulates gently, giving an impression of a snake's fluid grace but without the slither or the coils. "You see?" she says in low, simmering tones. "You feared I should not take mortal form again in your lifetime. But once I cast down Mhoryga, I received everything from her—her fire, her knowledge, her memories. Including the memory of how to become like this." She smiles, flashing pointed white teeth. "Your fears were all unfounded, sweet prince. You should have put more faith in me."

I watch her approach, and the blood, which had ceased to flow in my veins, surges suddenly like shards of ice, freezing me from the inside out. The contrast between this inner cold and the heat in the air around me is almost too much, more than I can survive.

She stands but a few paces in front of me now, towering and glorious, a dream made true. When she smiles, she is more beautiful than anything I could ever imagine. "We have done it, my love," she says. "Every dream we ever cherished is now within our grasp." One hand stretches out, trails a talon along the line of my jaw, tilting my head back so that I must stare up into that shining face of hers. A face in which I can almost recognize Rosie's features, but deified, exalted. A being of worshipful majesty. She tips her head a little to one side. "You always did belong to me. From the very first, you were destined to be mine."

I hear Rosie's voice . . . but another as well. A voice which caresses even as it kills, slipping in at the edges of my mind. In another moment she will be inside me, and I will be consumed by her. Part of me wants to let it happen. Part of me wants to give in, to turn myself over. If this hell is the closest facsimile to heaven I may ever know, is it not better than nothing at all? But in this moment, while my will is still mine, I know the bitter truth.

"Valindra." My breath stirs the ash before my lips. Her hand moves, taloned fingers wrapping around the back of my neck. She draws me toward her, lowers her mouth to hover just over mine. "Rosie." The name is like a razor blade on my tongue, cutting painfully as it's spoken.

"No," she answers softly. "I don't think those names suit me anymore, do you? What was that other name they called me? Pandracor?" She smiles. "The end of dragons."

My eyelids grow heavy. My gaze lowers, focusing hard on her mouth, on her lips, so full and sensuous, so near to my own. Her fingers tangle in my hair, and her naked breasts press against my body, eager and offering and demanding all at once.

"You are not the end of dragons," I whisper.

Her breath is hot on my face, blistering and seductive. "Am I not?"

"No." I lift my gaze, stare up into her eyes. Gold eyes, like twin suns, which seem to fill my entire world with light, with life, with heat. "I am."

As my lips meet hers, as she crushes me to her in a devouring kiss, I slip the hidden blade from my sleeve into the palm of my hand and drive it under her breastbone, straight into her heart.

A spasm rips through her, body and spirit. Her eyes flare wide, staring down into mine, as she wrenches her lips free. Mouth curling in a hideous snarl, she grabs me by the front of my burnt cuirass, lifts me from my feet, and hurtles me through the air like a doll. I fly, hit the far wall, crash to the floor. Dazed, I wrench my head up to see her striding toward me, even as she clutches her breast where the knife protrudes and blood pours green and hot as Dracora magma down her naked body. My death is written in her eyes. She begins to change, to warp, the dragon emerging from the woman in strange contortions, all beauty lost in monstrous fury.

But then I see it—a flash. Another face. Young, sweet. Determined to the point of muleheadedness. Even as the dragon seeks to yank the knife from her body with one hand, the other hand wraps around it, holds it in place. Mhoryga's golden eyes blaze at me with infernal hatred, but for a blink, an instant, they aren't Mhoryga's eyes anymore. They're Rosie's.

She wrenches away from me, staggering back, turning. Even as a roar of wrathful protest bursts from her throat, she lurches awkwardly a few steps, stops, and lurches again. Pain and loss of blood make her footsteps unsteady, but somehow, she carries herself to the edge of the platform.

"Rosie!" I cry.

She doesn't look back at me. Nor does she pause. Not even when her body, resisting, struggles to change shape, to fight against that valiant spirit which, just for a moment—a moment of searing, indescribable pain—has wrestled back control. Still clutching my knife to her breast, she steps right to the brink of the platform, her contorting body illuminated in green light.

Then she casts herself over the edge. Falls from my line of sight.

I FEEL IT. The moment she plunges into the magma.

The foundations of Drathoridan shake, every stone cracking as old magic disintegrates in bursts of green embers. A roar bellows from the throbbing core of Mount Dracor, rattling the poison-choked sky. The shrine platform crumbles, breaks, falls.

I pull myself to my feet, bracing myself with effort. The floor beneath my feet is crumbling, and the heat from below builds with each passing second. I have mere heartbeats remaining before I too will fall, will join her. Then we will burn together in the Dracor Flame, fulfilling at last the dark destiny neither of us foresaw. I close my eyes, hold out both arms, ready for the death which must claim me.

Only death does not come. A rush of wings fills my ears, followed by a sudden impact. Claws wrap around my arms, and I leave my breath behind me as I'm jerked from my feet, up into the air.

"*No!*" I scream to no avail. Rhangyl carries me. Up and up, out of the temple, even as it falls. Soaring with me clutched in his powerful claws, resistant to all my thrashing struggles. I plead. I curse. I threaten and weep. And, when none of these prove any use, I despair. The dragon spawn bears me away through smoke and ash. I look back over my shoulder, and through tears and an encroaching darkness on the edges of my vision, I see the last of Drathoridan's towers break and fall as the flames of Mount Dracor erupt in a pillar of dancing green fire.

Thus the Last Dragon Queen vanishes from the world of mortals.

42

Rosie

I flee through tunnels of fire, seeking escape, though I know there can be none. A desperate survival instinct refuses to give in, even as I feel life's blood pouring from my body and flame eating at my flesh.

The outermost layer is destroyed first. I feel her at a distance—the Dragon Queen, writhing and screaming, fighting to keep hold of this life, this world, this existence. Part of my heart is sorry for her. She is part of me, after all . . . that part of me which is born of Mhoryga, shaped by hellfire into something I utterly reject. She would have swallowed me up in the end. I already felt it happening, the suppression of all that made up the *me* of my soul, and the rising force of dragonness. What Mhoryga told Valindra in that last great brawl in the sky above Mount Dracor was the truth—when I killed her, I would become her. For she was far more than a dragon; she was a force, an eternal entity.

And now she writhes in her death throes as the green lava of Dracor drags her into its depths.

The agony of dying stabs down deep through layers of self and soul. Down to that place where Valindra—my dragon self—roars with fury. Here the true pain begins. Fire eats at my spirit. I have to plunge deeper still into my innermost self to find a place where it does not lash me. My mind presents me with pictures, trying to make sense of both the fear and the flight. I see myself in the stone halls of Stromin Palace, green flames shooting up the walls on either side of me, melting rock with its heat. I throw up my arms and run and run, desperate for relief. Ahead of me I see a familiar door. I plunge into a small, dark box and slam the door shut behind me. There's a lever; I pull it. Feel the box begin to rise. Here, in this dark place, the air is cool at last, and the fire cannot burn me. I exhale a ragged breath and smell the stink of sulfur. Dragon breath. Even here I cannot escape it.

The lift box comes to an abrupt stop. Can I escape? Flee out into the cold night air of the mountaintop? I don't mind that I am dying; it's the pain I wish to avoid. Perhaps the angels will meet me here, carry me away to heaven before I must experience that final sensation of burning flesh and burning soul.

The box door slides open, and I stagger out. A despairing cry rips from my chest. This is not the tunnel leading to the open mountainside. Instead I find myself once more trapped within the four flame-devoured walls of Durona's cottage. I've never fully escaped it, not really, not in all these years. Somehow I always knew I'd end up back here.

But no. No, I will not be beaten! If this is to be my end, I will make it the end of my choosing. I rush to the chimney, and though I'm no longer a child, I plunge inside, climbing, scrambling, pulling myself up and up, while flames lick at my flesh and fumes sear my lungs. As I climb, the chimney becomes the air shafts of Stromin once more, black with blinding smoke. I want to give in, to stop fighting. To let the fire claim me, even as I know it inevitably must.

Something drives me on, however. Some stubborn part of my soul that does not belong to Mhoryga and does not belong to Valindra but is entirely mine. I don't want to die. Not like this. Not burned in the flames of Mount Dracor with Valtar's knife protruding from my chest. There is another death I would choose instead, if only I can reach it, if only I can—

I burst through the top of the air shaft, out into ice-cold air beneath a star-spangled sky. Pyre wood surrounds me—great logs of whole trees, flown here from distant places and arranged in an intricate construction. I gasp in a short breath, struggling to inhale in the painfully thin atmosphere. So this is where my dying mind has brought me at last: Bald Mountain, and the great pyre of Lorayarus.

As though summoned at the mere thought of his name, one of the shining stars overhead suddenly sprouts wings and descends from heaven at tremendous speed, growing larger and more brilliant with each passing second. Even as he comes, green flames burst through the mountain rocks and lick at the wood of the pyre, surrounding me on all sides. But Lorayarus pays them no heed. The great phoenix lands on the edge of his pyre nest, and where his wings beat, hellfire instantly snuffs out, and the stink of sulfur is overwhelmed by the perfume of exotic flowers.

"Lorayarus!" I weep, scrambling across the pyre toward him. "Lorayarus, I failed! I tried to carry your flame to the heart of Khylmira, but I couldn't do it. I couldn't reach it. I couldn't get anywhere near the mountain." I crumple to my hands and knees, sobs racking my body, my soul.

And yet, Lorayarus says, gazing down at me from his vast, inferno eyes, *I find you here, at the center of yourself. True to your purpose to the last. True to the phoenix flame in your heart.* He tilts his crested head to one side. *I would not be able to be here with you were it not so.*

I shake my head, despairing as fire closes in upon me. "But it was hellflame I brought to Drathoridan." The shameful words fall like stones from my lips. "I became like Mhoryga in the end."

The phoenix takes a step closer, one great wing brushing off a tongue of flame. *You are a phoenix, my child. Born on my pyre, true to the pure fire of your creation. You have done what even I could not, what none believed possible: When you fell into its maw, you carried that fire to the very center of Mount Dracor. Renewal will come to this world at last, and all traces of dragon poison purged from this world.*

I look up at him, comforted by his words even as the hell-flames leap higher and the pain intensifies. "Thank you," I whisper, shuddering as my skin begins to blister. "I can endure it now . . . now that I know it was not for nothing."

Lorayarus takes another step toward me. *I can take you away from here,* he says. *You can fly with me back to the celestial fields. As my child, that is where you truly belong. Even the gods would not gainsay me.*

I want to. Oh gods! As the dragon fire eats away at the pyre, I want more than anything to escape it! But one thought, one hope, one desperate desire holds me back.

"What will happen if I stay?" I ask.

I do not know, the phoenix admits. *Your dragon self will be burned away. What will be left when it is gone, I cannot guess. Maybe nothing at all.*

"But . . . maybe something?"

He nods.

"There might be something of *me* left? Something for Valtar to find?"

It is possible, my child.

I grimace against the heat, against the searing agony in my soul. "In that case I will stay. If there's even a chance I might see him again, I will take it."

Lorayarus is silent for some while, his shining self almost obscured to my vision as the flames leap higher. Then he says, *That hope of yours is the brightest flame I have seen in this or any world.*

I wrap my arms around my burning body, desperate to shield myself, unable to find relief. "Will you leave me now, Lorayarus?" I cry, tears boiling on my cheeks.

But the great phoenix draws nearer. *I will remain with you a little longer*, he says, and covers me with his shining wings as the pyre goes up in a great conflagration of green flame. Here, in its center, I am surrounded by white light and sweet fragrance and the beating heart of creation itself.

43

Valtar

Dragon spawn emerge in waves from the ash-strewn wastes. Staggering like the undead, eyes staring out from masks of black soot, flesh burnt in patches, they have lost all trace of their dragon forms and almost all trace of manhood. Some support one another; others walk alone. No dragging wings or spined tails. No bursts of green flame.

I stand behind the battlements of Heleris, watching them come. The stronghold suffered great damage in the multiple quakes which rocked it to its foundation, but the primary structure remains firm. It proves as good a place as any to regroup and regather, and the dragon spawn make for its gates in silent hope of help.

There is little help to be had, however. Lady Enya and the surviving Cyranian force arrived two days ago, battered but determined. Rhangyl met them for me, assuming human shape and relating what he could of all that took place here in the last sky battle above Rothomir. Enya found me some while later. She stood a few paces behind me. Though I did not turn to greet her but remained standing with one hand resting on a stone balustrade, I felt her gaze on the back of my head. We stayed like so for some while, saying nothing. I don't know if she meant to offer comfort or if she hoped to receive comfort from me. In the end, she left.

And I continued to watch the burning mountain a hundred miles away.

Sometimes the smoke and ash are far too dense, obscuring my view. Sometimes gusts of wind blown in from the sea will partially clear the punishing skies, and I will see again that great column of green flame, burning straight and high, seemingly without end. Regardless, I refuse to my leave my post. Once in a while, voices speak on the edge of my awareness, entreating me to come away, to rest. I ignore them. They are part of another world, not this space of existence where I hang suspended between terrible hope and crushing despair.

After four days, a strange feeling comes over me. A sudden and inexplicable weakness, as though some essential force is being drawn out from my body through the invisible spaces between me and that mountain. I can almost see it: a thread of burning green light, spooling from my heart and out across Rothomir, drawn to the distant flame of Dracor. How long the feeling lasts I cannot say. Hours. Days perhaps.

Then, abruptly, a burst of greater light erupts from the mountain. I see the explosion, like the sudden birthing of a star. Sound follows after, a wave of energy, rippling out from that epicenter. The foundations of Heleris groan, and I grip the stones in front of me, expecting that this, then, is the end. The stronghold will crumble, crushing me beneath its broken towers.

But the final fall doesn't come. And when the swirling ash clears, when the ground settles, I look out once more to the mountain and see a strange sight. The green glow of the Dracor Flame is no more. The mountain continues to burn, but with a clear, white light.

A scent of exotic flowers wafts over the land and fills my nostrils.

I feel hollow. Hollow and clean, somehow, as though something has been scoured from my very soul. Curious, I look down at my own two hands, turning them over, unable to discern any difference. It isn't until I try to summon hellfire that I learn the truth: The dragon blood inside me is purged. Where once hell itself burned hot in my center, now it is empty. I am dracori no longer.

I gasp, lifting my gaze to the mountain once more. Is it possible? Did Rosie carry phoenix flame into the heart of Mhoryga's realm after all? Is the fire even now burning there not the fire of destruction but . . . renewal?

Sudden weakness overwhelms me. So long as hellfire sustained me, I could live without food or rest. Now my own humanity crashes down on me like a vengeful fist. I fall to my knees, still gripping the balustrade, still straining to keep my eye on that distant peak. Still watching, hoping, praying for a miracle I already know can never be. Darkness closes in, a welcome oblivion. I close my eyes, sink into it, and hope this is the end.

I AWAKEN TO find myself lying on a narrow bed in a small, cell-like chamber, with no idea how I came to be here. I blink many times, struggling to clear my vision. Every time my eyelids fall, I see again that searing image of the mountain, burning bright with white fire. When my eyes open, I stare up at a stone ceiling. My body feels heavy and, simultaneously, gutted. An odd combination.

Slowly I breathe out a tightly held breath. Then, summoning what strength I can, I lift my hand. Turn it slowly. Flexing my fingers, I strain after that power which has dwelt inside me all these many long years. No flame responds. Not even a spark.

So it's true. The power of Dracora has gone from me. My stomach knots. Does this mean what I think it means? Is Mhoryga's influence purging from this world in the wake of the Last Dragon Queen's death? Is that pale fire burning at the top of Mount Dracor cleansing the poisons which have so long saturated the atmosphere of this realm? I don't understand it. My mind and body are both too weak to make sense of anything right now.

"You know, this was my room for a number of years."

My heart jolts. I turn my head to see a tall, emaciated figure standing at a window, leaning heavily against the sill. I would know that frame, that voice, that stance anywhere, in any world.

"Arun!" I gasp.

He turns to me. A band of torn fabric wraps his temples, covering the gruesome eye sockets, but it cannot hide the chunks of flesh torn from his face, the mangled hands, the twisted limbs. In the overcast light of day pouring through the window, he is a ghastly thing to behold. And yet I have rarely seen a sight more beautiful.

"Hullo, Brother," Arun says, smiling gently. "They tell me you fainted when the hellfire purged from your system. Don't worry. All the dracori reacted similarly, and the dragon spawn worse still! Nyxia and I were lucky that Zoar had just alighted in the courtyard when it happened, or we would have found ourselves plummeting from a great height, riding on the back of her lanky young brother. Not the end I ever envisioned for myself."

I push upright in bed, swing my legs over the edge. The room pitches, but I grip the hard mattress with both hands, knuckles whitening. "Arun," I say again, "you're . . . you're . . ."

"Alive, yes." He comes toward me slowly, leaning heavily on a makeshift crutch tucked under one arm. I don't know how to react. I don't know how to think, how to feel, how even to exist. I stare at my brother, this phantasm I can scarcely believe in, drinking in the sight of him.

Then suddenly I slump forward, fall to my knees, my hands, pressing my forehead to the stone floor. "Forgive me!" I cry, even as a surge of shame and pain and sorrow overwhelms me. "Forgive me for what I did to you. Forgive me for not being willing to let you go. Forgive me for . . . for what I became . . ."

Arun crosses the little chamber to my side. His crutch clatters to the floor as he drops down beside me, wraps his arms around my shoulders, and pulls me into an embrace. "I forgive you," he says, his voice thick with emotion. "I forgive you, Valtar." He touches my face with his mangled hand, rocking me like a small child. "I forgive you for everything you ever did or were forced to do. But you must do something for me. Promise me. Promise me!"

"What?" I ask desperately. "What can I do?"

Arun lets out a long breath, his arms tightening around my quaking body. "Forgive yourself."

I begin to weep. For Arun and the torment he suffered all those long years. For our father's death and the death of King

Hagra and the genocide of the Magjor. For Durona Harpwood and the people of her village. For the deaths I dealt in secret and in shadows at the behest of my dark goddess.

Most of all I weep for the child, Valtar. Who gave his blood, gave his soul, gave everything on the mere chance that he could save the brother he loved.

44

VALTAR

Two Years Later

Years of dragon flame and dragon smoke have corroded the wooden elements of my father's palace in the heart of Inithana. But the stone foundations remain strong, testimony to the fortitude of our forefathers and the indomitable courage of our people. Fresh wind blows through gaps in the ceiling and broken windows, purging the halls of sulfurous scent, and carrying with it a delicate trace of exotic flowers. The throne of our ancestors stands at the end of the great hall, alight with a beam of sunshine, which pierces through the windows and the broken roof, illuminating the new king of Inithana—Arun III of the House of Skylock.

The floor below the dais is crowded with dignitaries from across the continent and over the sea, all gathered for this momentous occasion. I chose not to stand among them. And when my brother asked me to stand at his side, I begged leave to remain in the shadows, unseen by all those watching eyes. So I lurk in a hidden gallery above the throng, observing from a safe distance as my brother receives his crown.

Arun looks unexpectedly comfortable, seated on that throne. He wears a gold-threaded bandage around his eyes, hiding the ugly scars. He refused to wear gloves to cover his mangled hands, however, determined that his people should see him for exactly what he is: a survivor. Proof to the world that if he can endure all Mhoryga inflicted on him, then our land can endure as well and come back stronger than ever. In many ways, he's unrecognizable from the skeletal man I embraced in Heleris Stronghold two years ago. His frame has filled out, strength and muscle returning as he's learned how to move through the world in a crippled frame.

But one thing has not changed, and, I've come to realize, never will—the greatness of his spirit. That heroic tenacity. Not to mention his ability to inspire tremendous loyalty in the hearts of all who know him.

I lean out from behind my sheltering tapestry, peering down at those gathered on the smoke-stained and broken tile floor below. Many of the lords and ladies of Inithana were slain during Mhoryga's conquest, and the rest were either enslaved or transformed or fled into exile. But Arun has pardoned all those who became dracori, even as he pardoned me. I spy Lord Dusklore and Lord Rivenscar, both of whom were dracori alongside me. Their faces are solemn, marked with the remembrance of their enthrallment, filled with gratitude for this man who has extended such grace to them.

Other familiar faces appear in the crowd as well. The High King of Belanor sailed across the sea to be at this coronation. I covertly take in the sight of Taigan Aumanus, looking much older and grimmer than he did two years ago. The weight of rule has settled heavily upon him. I never thought much of the young prince, hot-blooded, impulsive, and far too concerned with his own legend as he was. The queen on his arm, however, I hold in high esteem. My gaze shifts from Taigan to Queen Enya, once the Lady of Cyran. When I heard that she'd accepted the High King's proposal of marriage, I thought perhaps Belanor might do all right after all. With such a woman at his side, Taigan may indeed become a great ruler someday. Something in the way he stands leads me to suspect he defers to his wife's guidance more often than not.

She, in turn, still bears some resemblance to young Lord Elis, though all the bright laughing lines are nearly obscured in her face. Her time as a dracori essentially changed her. I suspect it was no easy thing for Enya to return to Khylmirian shores, but I do appreciate that she made the effort to honor the new king of Inithana.

Prince Warrick of Anfalen is present below as well, along with his wife, the beautiful Princess Philippa. I recognize Rosie's onetime lady-in-waiting from back in Stromin Palace. A wry smile pulls at the corner of my mouth. Of all the champions, Warrick was the only one I ever saw as potential competition, but the man was simply unmotivated. Now I can better guess the reason for his distraction.

Shaking my head, I return my attention to the front of the throne room. The high priest of Eidolo even now performs the final benediction, standing behind Arun's throne and holding the silver-wrought crown above his head. A guard of honor stands at the back of the dais, one-eyed Rhangyl chief among them. Rhangyl was offered a lordship in Inithana following the fall of Mhoryga, but he turned it down. He prefers instead to serve as captain of Arun's guard. It's difficult these days to see the dragon that was once so prominent in Rhangyl's features. The same is true for all the surviving dragon spawn. Now that the Dracor Flame has gone out of this world, they have lost their ability to transform, even as the dracori lost their power to summon and wield hellfire. We are all of us mere men now.

Many of the dragon spawn never made it out of Rothomir. Their mortal flesh, without the dragon nature to protect them, simply could not survive in that blighted realm. I mourn their loss, knowing how it would have pained Rosie. All those brothers, thousands of them . . . and her great heart would have held love for each and every one. So I mourn them and rejoice for those who survived. Sometimes I wonder about the boy Rhyo, whom I have not yet succeeded in finding. Maybe one day. Rosie would like that.

The priest comes to the end of his prayer and lowers the crown to my brother's head. For just a moment, I glimpse a flicker of emotion on Arun's face. It can be hard to read his expressions through all the scarring, but I know him well enough to guess at his thoughts. He's remembering our father and the sacrifices he made for the sake of his kingdom. I set my jaw, lifting my head a little higher, even as a strange tightness fills my chest. How proud Father would be of the man Arun has become. Of his courage, his fortitude in the face of impossible odds. Of the king he will be, walking in Travarn Skylock's footsteps.

What of his second son? Would our father be proud of the role I ultimately played, of the sacrifices I made? I'm not sure. I don't know that it matters anymore. Truth is, if I could have done otherwise, I never would have made that final sacrifice. I never would have given up Rosie. Only the knowledge that Rosie herself could not bear to become another Mhoryga gave me the strength to drive that blade into her heart.

No, I do not see myself as any sort of a hero, worthy of my father's legacy. But as the priest leads the gathering in solemn prayer, as the words echo to the rafters and out through the broken rooftop to the open sky above, my heart lifts with sudden gladness. For better or for worse, I kept Arun alive all those years. Perhaps my reasons were selfish, but in the end, the gods have used my selfishness for the good of the world.

As the echoes of prayer die away, Arun rises from the throne, his crown flashing from his brow. A young acolyte steps forward to take his scepter, and a second priest advances, offering a velvet pillow on which a second, smaller crown rests. Arun lifts the crown in his mangled hands and turns to the throne placed alongside his. The throne on which his queen waits, her face solemn, her eyes downcast.

My stomach knots. Even now, two years later, I cannot stand the sight of her. *Nyxia* . . . No, not Nyxia. For she took a new name when she stepped into her new life as a human woman. *Valinala* she is called now: *Angel of Mercy*. The name is incongruous to my ear; I never knew mercy under her thrall. But I appreciate that she took the elfin name in honor of her sister, Valindra.

I watch as Arun places the crown on her head. She no longer possesses any dragonish traits, no gleam of scales, no fire in her eyes. Even the long, talon-like nails are no more. In this thoroughly human form, she looks more like Rosie than she once did. Something in the set of her chin, the shape of her nose. And, of course, those striking gold eyes. There's something there which haunts my heart and makes it even more difficult to bear the presence of my brother's wife.

His *wife*! Great gods on high, I'll never get over that particular madness of Arun's. I tried to talk him out of it, tried to tell him how foolish it would be for him to take a dragon as his bride.

But Arun was adamant, and there is nothing that can change him once his mind is made up. So Nyxia—Valinala—and I have learned to navigate a simmering, mutual dislike for the sake of the man we both love.

The silver crown settles in Valinala's bounteous black hair and across her brow. Arun takes her hand, and she rises. The two of them turn to face the assembly together as a great cheer goes up: "*Long live the king of Inithana! Long live King Arun! Long live the queen of Inithana! Long live Queen Valinala!*" Voices echo to the rafters, while music begins to play, horns and drums and the voices of priests blending in triumph.

Through it all, my gaze does not leave my brother's face. Just as the music swells, Arun turns suddenly and seems to look without eyes up to my hiding place behind the tapestry. I promised him I would be here for the ceremony. Arun knows I kept my word, and the knowledge lightens my heart.

I draw back a step, let the tapestry fall between me and that sight of celebration. Someday I will return to Inithana. Maybe when Arun's first child is born. That would be a worthy occasion indeed, one I must be present to celebrate. In the meanwhile, he knows where to find me if he needs me.

I slip from my hidden gallery and down the back stairs. I will not take time to speak to the King of Belanor and his queen, nor to greet Prince Warrick and Princess Philippa. The lords and ladies of Inithana and Khylmira, come to witness this triumphant moment, need not be bothered with my presence. I don't feel part of any of these doings or even part of this world anymore.

It's high time I got back to my wife.

45

Valtar

Eight Years Later

A drop of sweat rolls down my nose as I plunge my spade into the dark earth, turning it over in search of grubs. They have been working a destructive streak right through the roots of my roses, and I've been obliged to wage all-out war. A grim smile tips the corner of my mouth as I overturn a fat, juicy one. A quick slice of the spade, and I toss the two halves over my shoulder for a waiting starling, which hops along in my wake, eagerly coveting more such treats.

Sitting up on my heels, I swipe the back of my hand across my brow and take a moment to admire my handiwork. Half a mile distant, a sturdy little house with mud-and-wattle walls stands on a hilltop, surrounded by young trees, all past flower and beginning to put forth tender fruit. Neat rows of vegetables and herbs line the fields on every side—practical things, necessary for the ongoing survival of one man, alone out here in the wilds of Rothomir. But I don't spend all my days growing my next meal. I indulge in roses as well—bountiful splashes of color such as one never would have believed could grow in these once-wasted grounds.

But Rothomir is not what it was. Lying in the shadow of the burning mountain, it breathes in the perfume of sweetness which permeates the air. Over the years, the raw, cracked, broken land has begun to heal. Now, as I cast my gaze across the lonely miles, I see green and growth, the beginnings of new forests, rivers, and lakes. Even the deep crevices which once belched poisonous fumes have closed up, leaving nothing but narrow cracks to betray their former presence.

I breathe in deep. The air is scented with both rose perfume and that strange, unnameable scent of exotic flowers which has grown familiar to me over the years. The Kingdom of Alinar will never be reestablished—not like Inithana. It was utterly decimated by Mhoryga over the centuries of her rule in this world. But someday, I believe, when this land has fully healed, people will return here. Fields will be tilled, towns will be established. Great cities of men will rise and flourish. For now? I share this wild place with the deer, foxes, and birds of a hundred varieties. Not to mention the grubs.

I turn my attention back to my spade. Practice has taught me to locate my fat, white nemeses with expert precision, my spade an effective instrument of death. With the eager starling fluttering at my back and whistling tuneful encouragement, I set to with a will, making my way down the line of rosebushes.

I'm near the end of the row when awareness prickles down the back of my neck. Someone is behind me. My assassin's senses have never lessened, despite the singular lack of need for such skills out here in the lonely wilds. I listen to the sounds of footsteps in the middle distance. Two sets—one short and quick, the other longer, staggered, more layered. I would know those footsteps anywhere.

"So, you've come to visit your hermit brother again," I call over my shoulder. Sitting upright, I turn and look up the hill to where two figures stand on the edge of my rose plot. The taller of the two leans heavily on an elegantly carved crutch, his face half hidden behind a fine silken eye band. Despite these accessories, he carries himself with a quiet strength and dignity. Even a fool would recognize in him the right of kingship. At his side is a child of some seven years. A boy child with a mop of black hair. Arun named him Travarn after our father. Sometimes I wonder what our father would think if he knew his grandchild had the gold eyes of his dragon mother.

"Uncle Valtar!" the boy cries, and darts in among the roses to throw himself into my arms. I rise and spin him about, flinging his legs over the heads of bobbing rose blooms.

"How now, little troublemaker!" I say, setting him back on his feet. "Are you ready to wage war?"

The boy's eyes brighten with a ferocity that reminds me rather more of his mother than his noble father. Upon being handed my spade and urged to hunt and slaughter grubs to his heart's content, he falls to his hands and knees, digging into the black soil with relish. The starling abandons me in favor of this new provider, hopping along at the boy's heels in the long shadows of the roses.

Trusting the strong roots will survive my nephew's enthusiasm, I turn to Arun. My brother stands respectfully at the edge of the plot. He tilts his head in my direction. "Are you well, Valtar?"

"Well enough," I reply, striding to his side.

"Have you gone and grown a wildling beard? Anytime I picture you, I tend to see the boy you were when we lived with the Magjor Tribe. Only I like to add a beard these days, in keeping with your hermetical status."

I take hold of my brother's hand and slap it against my bare cheek. Arun shakes his head. "Still bothering to shave then," he says with a sigh. "I confess, I'm disappointed. I was hoping to find you'd turned full-blooded lunatic in the three years since last I saw you."

"Lunatic or otherwise, I've always known how to wield a razor's edge," I answer dryly.

Arun smirks. His son lets out a whoop, drawing his attention to where young Travarn triumphantly waves a fat, wriggling grub in the air while the starling flutters around him. "Is my boy wreaking havoc on your solitary paradise?"

"No more havoc than a boy his age ought to wreak."

We stand together in silence for some moments, enjoying the sight and sounds of childish glee, each remembering our own abbreviated childhood. Neither of us bothers to speak of it; the memories are strong enough.

"How is the baby?" I ask after a little.

Arun smiles at mention of his new daughter. "Loud, fractious. Perfection." He breathes deep now, turning his head in the direction of the distant mountain. "I forget sometimes how good the air here smells."

I too lift my gaze to that place on the horizon where white fire burns, my eyes ever hungry for that sight. "Another few years and I believe this land will be fully healed." We are silent again for a little while. Then I ask, "And how fares Inithana these days?"

My brother's face is grave. "The poison runs deep, but I see signs of healing everywhere. Now and then, when the wind blows down from Rothomir, I think I smell this same scent, and I know renewal is at hand, whether or not I can perceive it."

"A man more faithful than I would remind you that the gods work their miracles in their own good time," I say.

"True enough." Arun turns to me now. His searching hand reaches out, and I grasp it, feeling the strength in his mangled fingers. "When will you return to Inithana, Valtar?" he asks.

Sighing, I let my gaze run across my garden, my nephew, my house on its hill. Then slowly, inevitably, it is drawn back to the mountain. "You know I cannot leave her," I answer softly.

"Valtar?"

I won't look at him.

"Valtar, it's been ten years."

"To the day," I acknowledge. I don't bother to add how I've experienced the passing of each and every hour like a blade slicing across my heart. Even now I feel the heat of dragon's blood pouring over my hand as I drove my knife into her naked breast. And, despite the sweet scent on the air, sometimes I still wake with the stink of brimstone in my nostrils.

Arun's hand comes down heavily on my shoulder. "You are still a young man. You have a whole life ahead of you, not to mention people who care about you. Why not return with me to court? I could use someone with your talents by my side."

"An assassin?" I raise an eyebrow. "Are your courtiers getting uppity, good king?"

My brother snorts. "I mean your intelligence. Your courage, your insight. Not to mention this new skill you seem to have developed for growing things."

A chuckle rumbles in my throat. Once more, I cast my gaze across my garden, my home. This place I've carved out of nothing, all in pursuit of a dream I've long since ceased to hope will manifest. But it's a dream I cannot let go. Not yet at least. "No, Arun," I say at last. "I feel close to her here. So long as I can see her fire burning, it's as though part of her is still with me, in this world. The true her, not the monster, not the demon. Not even Valindra. But Rosie herself."

Arun nods. He does not try to argue; he's done so in the past to no avail. He's learned to respect my choice, even if he cannot fully understand it. Instead he lifts his head once more, his blind face turned toward the mountain. "Does the fire ever show signs of going out?"

"It has burned steadily since that dreadful day," I answer. "I believe it will go on burning until all the poisons of Dracora are purged from this world." After a little silence, I shake my head and speak in a lighter tone. "And was this the sole reason you traveled two hundred miles from home? Or have you decided to make Rothomir your new summer destination? Perhaps the ruins of Heleris could be converted into a holiday palace."

He chuckles. "Well, I certainly didn't come to discuss such matters on an empty stomach. Tell me, is there anything in this eclectic garden of yours which might mix up in a hearty stew? Perhaps you could be prevailed upon to assassinate a rabbit for the pot?"

"Come up to the house," I say, slapping his shoulder and turning him in the right direction. "I may have a little coffee squirreled away somewhere. And if that boy of yours works up an appetite, then . . ."

My voice trails off, for Arun stops abruptly, and the color drains from his face. It's difficult to read his expression behind the eye band, but there's something there, something that sends a shiver through my heart. "Arun?" I say, my brow lowering. "Arun, what is it?"

He turns to me. His mouth tries several times to form words. "It's happening," he manages at last in a strained whisper. "Now."

"What?" I grip him by the shoulders. "What are you talking about? Arun, are you all right?"

Much to my surprise, his face breaks into a sudden smile. "Look to the mountain, Valtar," he says. "Look to the flame!"

Ice floods my veins. Turning slowly, almost unwillingly, I obey my brother's command, gazing across the sweeping plains of Rothomir, verdant with summer and new life. My heart turns over in my chest. The massive slopes of the mountain loom over all, fifty miles distant and more. But there, above the clouds, at the peak . . .

The white phoenix flame abruptly vanishes.

I stare. Stare at that empty place in the sky where there should be dancing flame. Clouds part, revealing the blue vault of sky. A huge gust of wind blows across the plains, rippling the grass and causing my garden plants to toss and writhe. It catches my nephew's hat from his head, sends it tumbling past my feet while he shouts and chases after it. But I scarcely hear him, scarcely notice anything in the immediate vicinity.

Inhaling deeply, I breathe in the perfume of a hundred thousand fragrant flowers.

"I must go to her, Arun," I whisper, my voice a rough scrape in my throat. "At once."

46

Valtar

Arun gives me a horse from among his entourage, and I pack supplies for a twelve-day trek and set off before sundown. I ride as far as I can before darkness forces me to stop, no longer possessing the advantage of dracori eyesight to help me navigate at night. I sleep very little and rise with the sun, urging my poor mount faster and faster across the green countryside.

We meet with no trouble on our journey. Only the occasional narrow fissure which must be navigated. No demons, no dragons—just wide-open sky and new green growth as far as the eye can see. Occasionally an eagle or hawk will pass overhead, and my heart will jump with remembrance of greater wingspans and deadlier talons. But those days are now gone, and even the memory of dragons will soon pass from history to legend, and from legend to myth. In time, no one will be left to remember the Last Dragon Queen.

I grit my teeth and ride on. Day follows endless night in a cycle that feels as though it will last forever. But by noon on the sixth day, I find myself on the lower slopes of the mountain. The ground grows steeper, and I dismount rather than urge my poor horse into uncertain terrain. As I have no way of guessing what I will find at the summit of this climb, I remove the beast's bridle and set it free. Gods willing, it will find its way back to Arun. I don't expect to return myself. I'm far too afraid to allow expectation or hope any room in my heart. I dare not think anything other than *Go to her. Go to her. Go to her.*

I begin my climb. The old Drathoridan path is still there, the same treacherous route I once marched as a dracori in Mhoryga's service. I use it now, my mind crowding with far too many evil memories for any one of them to settle and take root. I simply sweep them aside and breathe the perfumed air, which clings to the mountainside like a gracious mantle. There's growth on the lower slopes. Green stems push through even the harshest, blackest stones, unfurling leaves and delicate blossoms of white, flame-shaped petals which I do not recognize. I never would have believed it possible for anything to grow on Mount Dracor. Even now, a decade later, Rosie continues to bring about small miracles.

Evening falls, forcing me to stop once more. I build a fire, eat from my sparse supplies. And I gaze out across the landscape of Rothomir from my tucked-away place between two great stones, watching the last of the setting sun illuminate the land. In the distance, I can almost imagine I glimpse the towers of Heleris; in between is a lush and beautiful paradise. All thanks to Rosie. Rosie and her stubborn refusal to give up. Her willingness to sacrifice personal happiness for the sake of a world that never really knew her.

If she were here beside me now, how pleased she would be.

I don't let myself think about what awaits me at the top of the mountain. I don't let myself question why I'm making this pilgrimage, driven back to the place of her death. All I know is that I must see it—the site of her final burning. And I must know for myself that she is truly gone.

At dawn, following a night of fitful dreams and perfumed air, I continue my climb. It's cold up in the higher regions, and the air is much thinner. My footsteps slow, my limbs trembling with fatigue, but I push on regardless. Strange how the higher I climb, the more densely those white, flame-shaped blossoms grow around me. Almost as though they are spilling up from the mouth of the volcano itself.

The day is lengthening by the time I reach the ruins of Drathoridan. Much of the temple has crumpled and fallen at last into the mountain, but here and there walls and bits of towers or winding staircases are still to be seen, the last remnants of Draconan presence here in the human world. The white-flame flowers bloom with particular profusion here, as though eager to cover up and swallow these last ugly memories. I walk through the ruins, pursuing the same route I took on that fateful day, ten years ago, and come at last to that place where the central shrine once stood. There isn't much left—only the base of the broad platform which once extended over the mouth of the volcano.

Here at last I gaze down inside.

The inner walls are blackened, but it's difficult to see them, so profusely do those white flowers bloom. There are more flowers inside the volcano, filling it up entirely, transforming it into the most fertile of valleys where once was all molten green lava. My vision is so stunned by the sight, I cannot make sense of it, cannot believe my eyes. Surely I must be driven beyond sanity, as my air-starved mind plays tricks on me.

It is beautiful though. Even if it is only an illusion. Like a piece of heaven. A wind blows, chilling the tears on my cheeks.

Strange . . . I lift up one hand, touching my face. I have not wept in ten years. Not since that moment when my brother held me in his arms and asked me to do the impossible. Asked me to forgive myself. But it would be impossible not to weep at such a sight as now lies before me.

I fall to my knees. This beauty in a place where once was only terror and death and loss is more than I can bear. Something inside me breaks, unleashing the last thing I would have expected: a prayer. A simple prayer of gratitude, welling up from the depths of my soul. "Thank you," I whisper, my voice soft as a song on that cold breeze. "Thank you for her life. Thank you that she once moved and breathed in this world. And that I knew her. Oh yes, thank you for that most of all."

A cloud of white petals wafts around me, carried up from the volcano valley. I close my eyes, breathing in their scent, a scent I have become familiar with since the first time I encountered it in the eldrin's wagon so many years ago, the night my Rosie's flame manifested. I breathe it in, along with every memory of her I can summon. There are so many, though my time with her was painfully brief. She herself brimmed with enough spirit to fill an entire lifetime all in a matter of a few short weeks.

When I open my eyes at last, my gaze catches on something I'd not noticed before. From this distance it's difficult to see clearly, but . . . in the center of that huge valley is an oddly shaped lump of gray stone. Flowers grow densely all around it, but not over it. Now that I've seen it, I find it difficult to look anywhere else. From this distance it looks remarkably like . . . like . . .

Like a woman curled up with her knees to her chest, her face tucked in tight.

I scramble to my feet, heart throbbing. Frantically I search along the edge of the volcano for some path, some place of descent, but there is nothing. So I kick off my boots and simply begin to climb down the wall. Fingers and toes find crevices, and I force myself to go slowly, carefully, to make no foolish mistake that will send me hurtling to my doom in a bed of flowers. Time loses all meaning—the descent may take hours, but it feels like mere moments before I'm leaping from the wall into that lush growth and running barefoot through blossoms, heedless of how many I leave crushed in my wake. They spring back upright behind me unharmed in any case.

The stone is not large. It's a miracle that I spied it from such a distance. I throw myself to the ground beside it, a gray lump, featureless and yet . . . and yet I could swear I see an impression of a face. The line of a jaw, the curve of a cheek, the shape of an ear under locks of hair. Obscured details, and yet I would know them anywhere.

"Rosie," I whisper, my voice on the edge of breaking. Before I can talk myself out of it, I reach out and touch the stone. Only it isn't stone at all. It's ash. A thick layer of ash. A strangled cry in my throat, I begin to brush it away, harder and harder, choking clouds filling the air, coating the blossoms all around us. There, beneath the ash, I find naked limbs, pale olive skin, and a bounty of glorious golden hair. There are no scars to be found on her shoulder and neck, no blemishes of any kind. Everything is healed, renewed, restored.

"Rosie," I cry, desperate joy mingled with terror. She lies so still, like a wax doll. And she does not breathe. Gods above, why does she draw no breath? I pull her into my arms, weeping, shaking. What is this? Is it real? Is she alive or dead or some bizarre in-between? I press her to my heart, tears trailing down my ash-streaked face, and bury my nose in her soft, flower-scented hair. For some while I can do nothing but sit like so, quaking in every limb, scarcely believing that she is even now in my arms. The hope and the pain are too much, beyond any mortal capacity to endure.

Finally I relax my hold, let her head fall back over my arm. Her face, uptilted to the sun, is a perfect replica of that face I have cherished all these years in my heart. I stare down at her, studying those features which I have not seen for a decade. It feels like so much longer, as though centuries have passed in the world outside, while she and I have gone on existing in a little timeless space of our own.

Hardly knowing what I do, I lower my mouth, gently press my lips to hers. I taste ash and tears, bitter and sweet. In that taste, in that touch, I breathe one last heartfelt prayer: "Return to me, Rosie. Return to me, my love."

Her lips move under mine.

My heart leaps, and I start to draw back, but her arms reach up, wrap around my neck. I utter a strangled cry—half joy, half terror that this is all nothing but a dream. Dream or not, I kiss her—kiss her hard, unwilling to let this moment pass, unwilling to let this connection break, convinced that when it ends, I will awaken alone.

At last her arms around me shift. A hand rests against my cheek, gently pushes me back. I part from her reluctantly by mere inches and stare down into a pair of golden eyes. They shine with the light of distant stars and dancing galaxies. For a moment, she does not seem to see me, to know me. It's as though we are still part of two separate worlds.

But then she blinks. Her vision clarifies. And those are Rosie's eyes I see, looking right at me.

"Valtar!" she exclaims.

Her voice is the song of heaven itself in my ears. And so it will be, forevermore.

Keep reading for a preview of Sylvia Mercedes's

BRIDE OF THE SHADOW KING

Available now!

Faraine

"If you'd managed to snare the crown prince of Cornaith for a husband, we wouldn't be in this situation, now would we?"

I close my eyes, trying to still the shiver running down my spine. My brother's words hit me like slaps. They fall from his lips so casually, one would think he remarked on the weather or the cut of his tunic. But the bitter and unspoken emotion behind the words makes me wince and wish I could somehow sink into the cushions of my carriage seat and vanish.

I draw a long breath before raising my lashes and peering at Theodre seated across from me. He's resplendent in a fur-trimmed travel cloak and a plumed hat that takes up far too much room in this small space. A purely decorative sword is propped by his knees, the jeweled hilt wrought to correspond with his belt. Six fat rings, large enough to fit over his velvet-gloved fingers, flash at every move of his hands. He polishes one of them now, blowing on the faceted stone and rubbing it against his sleeve.

"War is such a fright, you know," he says, as though the

thought would never have occurred to me. "Hard for the average man to go about his business, what with having to drop everything and turn out to fight. Crops are left to spoil with only the women to do what needs to be done. And such ugly scarecrows they are! All hollow eyed and bony hipped. It quite turns the stomach to look at them. Out there with their plows and their scythes, and a gaggle of ragged brats trailing behind. It's like they have no pride in king or country."

He looks up at me, his dark eyes flashing in the dimness of the carriage. "Nothing an alliance with Cornaith wouldn't have fixed. Their cavalry would have made our enemies take to their heels! Instead, we've got those gods-damned fae crawling all over the countryside, running raids, burning crops, stealing livestock, all like it's good sport. So the people come crying to Father's gates, wailing and holding up their starving children like there's anything he can do about it. Other than send more of them out to fight."

And it's your fault.

He doesn't say it. He doesn't have to. I feel the accusation underscoring every word, every gesture, every glance. I feel it so profoundly, I begin to believe it.

My fault.

Burnt crops. Displaced people. Starving children.

My fault.

I should have done better. I should have *been* better. When Prince Orsan of Cornaith came courting, I should have smiled and flirted and danced and teased. I should not have sat quietly off to one side, keeping to the shadowed edges of the room, striving to find places where the light and the noise and the laughter and the tremendous press of people wouldn't break through all my defenses and leave me gasping with pain. I should have pushed that pain into the farthest recesses of my awareness—it's mostly in my head anyway, isn't it?—and pretended not to feel it. Pretended to be what I ought to be; what I was born to be as the eldest daughter of the King of Gavaria.

But I couldn't.

Even so, Prince Orsan might have taken me. Negotiations were well advanced, all the offers and promises between his kingdom and mine nearing culmination. Perhaps I wasn't the bride he'd always dreamed of. Perhaps every time he looked at me, I felt nothing but disappointment and resignation emanating from his sharp hazel eyes. But he knew the value of a good alliance as well as the next man. He knew the wisdom of uniting Cornaith and Gavaria against the threat of fae invasion. Plus, there was my substantial dowry to consider. Yes, in light of these temptations, he would have gone through with it.

Until he tried to kiss me in the garden.

Oh gods! I close my eyes again, trying not to remember that terrible moment. We'd been strolling in the moonlight, to all appearances the perfect picture of a courting couple if one were to ignore the careful way I kept a good three feet of distance between us. He was quite handsome in a silver-embroidered tunic, his fair hair swept back from his forehead, a jeweled circlet ringing his brow. I wore a romantic, off-shoulder gown of delicate pink, my hair adorned with pearls. Music trailed after us, played by musicians hidden behind a screen of blooming flowers. I'd turned to the prince, intending to make some remark on their playing.

To my utmost surprise, Orsan had taken two swift steps, caught me by my shoulders, his fingers digging hard into my bare flesh, and pulled me against him. His lips crashed into mine. The abruptness of that contact was too much. Everything he was feeling washed over me in a wave—frustration, determination, fear, anger, embarrassment, inadequacy. All of it. All hitting me in one painful collision of lips and teeth and tongue.

My body surged in reaction. And I vomited. Right down the front of his pretty embroidered tunic.

The party from Cornaith left my father's house the next morning, all negotiations abruptly ended. The day after, Father sent me to the Convent of Nornala. He didn't speak to me, not even to tell me how deeply I'd disappointed him. It was as though he wanted to forget I existed entirely.

That was nearly two years ago. I'd heard nothing from home since then, not even a letter from my sisters. Theodre's arrival shocked me three days ago, when he strode unannounced into my private room, filling the doorway with his big, plumed hat.

"I've come to fetch you home, Faraine," he declared without preamble. "The Shadow King is looking for a bride, and you're needed at once."

I'm still not entirely certain why Father sent for me. Whoever this ominously titled *Shadow King* might be, I'm quite certain I am not the bride he's looking for. But apparently, my younger sister, Ilsevel, declared she would not be bartered off in marriage. She'd thrown an enormous fit and locked herself in the east tower, dropping bits of crockery on the heads of anyone who tried to approach.

"Father seems to think you can talk some sense into the foolish girl," Theodre had said as he looked sneeringly around my small, sparse room at the convent. "No one else can, gods help us. But you've always had a way with Ilsie. Get her to recognize her duty to the crown and all that. Make yourself useful."

Suppressing a sigh, I turn to the carriage window and lift the curtain, peering out at the countryside. We are on a decline, descending the mountain pass. My view extends over miles of lowland beneath a twilit sky. I spy what looks like the remains of a village not far from here: a caved-in hall, smoke still rising from its collapsed roof. Burnt-out cottages, blackened walls. Ruin. Devastation. And what became of those who had once called that village home? Are they dead now, run down and slaughtered? Or do they wander the countryside, homeless, helpless, even as early spring storms batter the land?

The whole world seems to exhale despair.

I sit back, letting the curtain fall. Though it's bitterly cold, I pull the glove off my right hand and slip it under my cloak, feeling for the crystal pendant hanging from a chain around my neck. My fingers close around it, squeezing so that its sharp edges dig into the flesh of my palm. At first, it feels cold and lifeless. Slowly, however, it warms in my grip. I detect the faintest vibrating *thrum* deep inside. Closing my eyes again, I try to synchronize my breathing to that pulse. Pain recedes; the roiling in my gut diminishes. I let out a sigh.

Feeling Theodre's gaze upon me, I open my eyes and look back at him. He raises an eyebrow. "Not a pretty view, eh?"

I shake my head. "I'd not realized just how bad things have gotten." My tongue feels thick and heavy when I speak.

My brother snorts. "You've been hidden away in that convent too long."

Hidden away. Not married and producing babies. Not ensuring the military support of our nearest neighbors. Useless. Disappointment. It's all there. Hanging in the air between us. Unspoken but real.

I drop my chin. Perhaps I'm not being fair to Theodre. After all, I don't know him very well. He's several years my senior and spent most of his childhood away from Beldroth Castle, where my sisters and I were raised. I saw him for state occasions and a precious few family gatherings, nothing more. This journey from the convent is the most time we've spent in each other's company. I doubt we'll seek each other out in the future.

"Ah well," Theodre sighs, twisting yet another of his rings as though it's pinching him. "If Ilsie can snag this Shadow King for her groom, it'll all be made right. From what I understand, he's got quite the impressive army at his beck and call, and no love for our enemies. Never thought I'd see the day when Father bargained with trolls, but hey! Desperate times and all that. Ilsevel's not at all keen on the idea, but Father says you can use your godsgift and make her see reason. I hope you can, for all our sakes! Though I can't say I blame poor Ilsie when I think about it. I mean . . . *trolls*."

He makes a face at the last word, a wave of disgust flowing out from him. I grip my crystal a little harder, breathing in time to its faint pulse. I've heard tell of trolls, of course: stories from the caravan merchants who stop at the convent for shelter on their way over the Ettrian Mountains. They tell of hideous stonehide monsters towering seven feet tall and more, with fists like boulders and teeth of shining gemstones. Man-eaters. Bonecrushers. Brutes without brains or conscience.

I struggle to imagine such creatures having a king. I struggle still more to imagine my father bargaining with such a king for Ilsevel's hand. Whatever he may think of me, Father has always loved my sister, with her ready laugh and sharp temper, her recklessness and courage. Of all his children, Ilsevel is the most like him—and many's the time I've heard him sigh that she should have been born a boy.

How bad have things become that he would wed her to a monster?

The carriage lurches to a stop. It's so abrupt, I nearly fall from my seat. My brother curses and flings out both hands to brace against the walls. "What in the seven secret names is going on?" he growls, grabbing his sword and using the hilt to hit the ceiling with three sharp taps. "Oi! Fantar! What's the holdup?"

A muffled shout. Followed by a *thunk* on the roof of the carriage.

My heart begins to race. "Theodre?"

My brother, heedless of me, mutters another curse and flings back the curtain over the window, sticking his head outside. "Fantar! It's gods-spitting cold, man. Don't leave us sitting around all—*argh!*"

A burst of shock ripples out from Theodre. I just have wherewithal enough to reach out with both hands, grab hold of his jeweled belt, and haul him back into the carriage. There's a flash of fire on the other side of the window, the gleam of a sword edge slicing down where his neck had been a moment before.

Theodre falls back in his seat. "Spitting heavens!" he gasps, blood draining from his cheeks. "It's those gods-damned unicorns!"

I don't have the words to question him. All hell has broken loose just outside the carriage door. Men are shouting, horses screaming in terror. Through a crack in the curtain, I see flashes of red heat, flickering flame. And in my head—explosions of terror. Terror not my own. Hitting me with the force of a battering ram.

I sink from my seat onto the floor of the carriage, gripping my crystal pendant. My brother stares down at me. His fear is the worst of the assault. It pounds me with brutal intensity. He blinks once. Then, grabbing hold of his decorative sword with one hand, he fumbles with the door on the other side of the carriage, pushes it open, and falls out. For a moment, I'm overwhelmed with relief as he takes his terror with him.

Another scream bursts in my ears. Theodre? One of our men? I cannot tell, cannot guess. What should I do? Crouch in here like a mouse in a trap, waiting to be found and dragged out by my hair? Surely that must be worse than facing whatever waits outside.

Setting my jaw, I work my way to the half-open carriage door and ease the gap wider. A mistake. Utter mayhem meets my eyes. Riders streak past on creatures shaped like horses with monstrous, flaming horns protruding from their skulls. They're beautiful, terrible, glorious creatures ridden by beings equally beautiful, terrible, and glorious. Long hair streaming, shining faces alight with bloodthirsty joy, they wield swords that flame as bright as their mounts' horns. They wear no armor—in fact, they seem to wear next to nothing at all—their muscled, godlike bodies fully displayed as they circle their prey and cut them down.

I spy the silver helmets of my brother's guards. They fight valiantly from horseback, struggling to defend the carriage. One by one, they're pulled from their steeds. Blood, terror, and death assault my senses. I am frozen in place, paralyzed.

Once again, my gods-gift proves to be a curse.

A rider turns suddenly, violet eyes alight in a face of such heartbreaking beauty, it takes my breath away. He sees me and smiles, flashing sharp canines. Digging his heels into his unicorn's flanks, he urges the beast straight toward me. My vision is full of flames and laughter and the edge of an upraised sword.

Acting on survival impulse, I fall out of the carriage, hit the ground hard, and roll underneath. My skirts drag and catch, but I manage to get myself fully concealed just before cloven hooves skid to a stop at my eye level.

The next moment, a pair of bare feet land on the road. My pursuer drops to his hands and knees, turning his head to smile at me where I'm hiding. "Hullo, pretty thing," he says in a language I do not know, but which somehow communicates perfect meaning as it reaches my ears. "Come out and play?"

He reaches his hand under the carriage, long nails snatching at my face. His savage lust hits me like a knife in the head. I scramble backward. The horses squeal with fright, and the carriage lurches. I narrowly miss being crushed under a rolling wheel that catches my skirt and cloak, trapping me in place. Choking on a scream, I release the catch of my cloak, then grip my skirt with both hands and wrench free. The fabric rips in a long slash all the way up to my thigh. I stagger back from the carriage, struggling to find my balance.

Movement draws my eye. I look up to see my attacker, who has sprung to the top of the carriage, looming over me. He holds his sword out to one side for balance, but when he spies me, he raises it high. Tossing back his head, he utters a deep-throated, ululating cry of triumph.

As though by magic, a knife appears in his throat.

His eyes widen. A wave of surprise rolls over me. He drops his sword, and his hand comes up to touch the hilt of that knife. Wondering. As though he cannot fathom how it got there.

The next moment, he falls in a lifeless pile at my feet.

I stare down at the being, so beautiful even in death. The stillness of him is stark, the sudden silence of those powerful emotions that battered me only heartbeats ago. I'm numb, frozen.

Before I can pull a single coherent thought into my head, thundering hooves pound in my ear. I whirl just in time to glimpse a huge dark shape bearing down on me. A figure leans far to the side in a saddle; an arm reaches out. I let out a little bleat of surprise just before the breath is ripped from my lungs and I'm swung up into the air. For a terrible moment, I believe I've been struck.

Then, suddenly—*calm*.

I hardly know how to describe it. Where an instant before, the whole world stormed with horror, my every sense exploding with pain, now there's stillness. Peace. I'm so shocked by it at first, I can't even try to make sense of my surroundings. I can do nothing but close my eyes and lean into that calm, that quiet.

Slowly, my awareness returns. I realize I'm not standing on my own two feet anymore. I'm seated. Seated on the back of a large lurching beast and encircled by a pair of powerful arms. I choke on a gasp and twist in place, trying to get some sense of my captor. A pair of startlingly silver eyes look down at me. It takes me several breaths before I realize the face in which those eyes are set is an unnatural blue. For the moment, his eyes dominate everything.

Staring into them, I recognize immediately the source of that calm.

His lips are moving. He's saying something, but I have no idea what. "I . . . I'm sorry?"

"Are you all right?" he repeats. He speaks my language, but his words are strongly accented with a husky, growling burr unfamiliar to me.

"I hardly know!" I blink, shake my head, and look down at my quivering body. "I think so?"

"Good," he says. Then, "Keep low."

A hand on my back forces me to bend over the neck of the beast on which we ride. A thick, muscular neck with a shock of black mane, which I take at first to belong to a horse. But no, those are scales I see between patches of fur. This is definitely no horse.

I don't have time to question further before a flash of fire draws my gaze to one side. A unicorn rider pounds into our vicinity, his mouth open in wild, murderous laughter. He swings his weapon, but the man at my back pulls on his reins, and his beast sidesteps. Steel and flames whistle past my ear. There's a thick sound of a blade hitting skin. The unicorn lets out a bloodcurdling scream. Both steed and rider go tumbling.

I stare in open-mouthed horror. And yet that quiet, that calm, continues to surround me. The strangest, most unexpected sensation.

An arm wraps around my waist, pulling me back against a solid chest. "Best hold on," the accented voice murmurs close to my ear. I just have time to grab a handful of thick mane before he spurs his beast into motion. It lurches forward, but it doesn't feel like galloping. It's as though the monster has become a streaking shadow. I can still feel the warm solidity of its body beneath me, but I can see no more than an impression of rushing darkness.

We bear down on another flaming unicorn and rider. I turn my face away, closing my eyes even as my rescuer's sword arm moves. Distant screams of rage and death burst in the air but seem to belong in another world while I, here in my own small sphere of existence, am surrounded by peace.

The stranger pulls on his reins. His beast skids to a stop, suddenly solidifying. Its huge hooves clop on the stones beneath us. We're no longer on the road but have ridden straight up the mountainside. No horse could scale such a steep incline. When I look back, the view makes my stomach pitch.

The arm around my waist tightens slightly. "Have no fear, my lady. Knar is as sure-footed as they come. Shall we rejoin the others?"

I seem to have forgotten how to talk. I can do nothing but nod and tighten my grip on the mane. Am I imagining the pulse of a heartbeat at my back? A beat so strong and steady, it works its way into my bones. Like the pulse of my crystal, only much greater, much stronger.

I shake my head and peer down to the road below. The unicorn riders have fled; I can still see a few of them vanishing into the deepening twilight, flaming horns and wicked swords flaring. But far too many broken and crumpled bodies lie around the carriage. "My brother!" I manage to gasp, finding my voice at last. "Where is my—"

I don't have time to finish before I hear a familiar voice shouting, "Get your hands off me, you filthy rock biters!"

Turning toward that sound, I spy Theodre a short way up the road, surrounded by three tall figures. They are startlingly pale, their skin faintly blue, their hair pure white. Two male, one female, each with their hands up, exchanging uneasy glances. Theodre stands in the midst of them, swinging his decorative sword in erratic arcs. He's lost his hat, and his long, oiled locks gleam in the firelight. He looks rather like a lapdog snarling at a pack of wolves.

"I take it that's the brother in question?" says the voice at my back.

"Yes, indeed." I flush as Theodre spews another stream of invective at our rescuers. Or are they our rescuers? Looking around, I spy more of the strange scaly monsters like the beast I'm currently astride. They're just as frightening as the unicorns, if not more so. And these people, they must be fae. Have I been saved from one set of foes only to be taken captive by another?

"Please," I say, turning to look up at the rider behind me. "My brother is frightened. He doesn't mean what he says."

"Gods blight your nethers with pustule sores!" Theodre shrieks.

The stranger raises an eyebrow. "He sounds fairly impassioned." His mouth quirks in a half smile. "But here, he's had a fright. Not all men are built for battle. Shall we see if we can ease his fears?"

So saying, he rides his monster up to the little circle. Theodre spies him coming, his face paling at the sight of the awful steed. His knees knock, and I fear he will faint then and there.

"It's all right, Theodre," I call out. "You're safe now."

My brother's gaze snaps to my face, his fear momentarily displaced by surprise. "Faraine! What in the seven gods' names are you doing up there?" His voice is accusing, as though I've betrayed him somehow.

I press my lips into a line, then start to slip from the saddle. The stranger immediately moves to assist me, setting me lightly on my feet. I wobble, a little unsteady, but manage to make my way between the tall figures to my brother's side. His churning fear lashes at me like a whip. I wince but extend a hand to him even so. "You're safe, brother," I say again. "These are our rescuers. I don't sense any threat from them."

"They're fae," Theodre spits, his lip twisting with disgust. "They're always a threat."

"Perhaps." I glance around at the crumpled bodies surrounding us, both human and otherwise. "But not to us. At least, not this time."

Theodre struggles to master himself. After a moment's hesitation, he takes my offered hand. I bite back a cry as that contact of our skin sends his emotions jolting up my arm. Bracing myself, I try to send something back through that connection, some small measure of the calm I just experienced so unexpectedly.

Theodre shivers and starts to pull back, but when I squeeze his fingers a little tighter, he stops trying to resist. After a moment, he seems to gather strength. Lifting his chin, he turns and addresses the stranger still mounted on the beast's back. "This road belongs to King Larongar of Gavaria. I demand to know who you are that you would dare ride it."

Cringing with embarrassment, I glance up. The stranger tilts his head to one side, looking contemplatively down at my brother. That half smile is still present at the corner of his mouth. "I am the man who has just saved you from becoming unicorn fodder."

Theodre draws himself up, chest swelling, nostrils flaring. "I will have an answer from you! In the name of the King!"

One of the pale figures standing close at hand takes a step forward, touching a hand to the sheathed sword at her belt. "I'll warn you, sir, to show proper respect," she growls ominously.

"Peace, Hael," the stranger on the monster says. He swings down from his mount and approaches us. A flaming sword lies close at hand, its red gleam shining against his blue-tinted skin and making the planes of his face stand out at sharp angles. "I'm sure the little human means no harm."

"*Little human?*" My brother sounds as though he's about to burst. I try to squeeze his hand again, but he shakes me off. "Do you know who I am? I am Theodre, Prince of the House of Cyhorn, heir to the throne of Gavaria!"

"Indeed?" The stranger looks down at Theodre, his brows rising ever so slightly. "And I am Vor, King of Mythanar, Lord Protector of the Under Realm."

I stare up into those shining silver eyes. My heart seems to catch in my throat. I realize suddenly who our rescuer is: the Shadow King.

Photo by Chelsea Ann Photography

Sylvia Mercedes makes her home in the idyllic North Carolina countryside with her handsome husband, numerous small children, and a menagerie of rescue cats and dogs. When she's not writing, she's . . . Okay, let's be honest. When she's not writing, she's running around after her littles, cleaning up glitter, trying to plan healthy-ish meals, and wondering where she left her phone. In between, she reads a steady diet of fantasy novels. But mostly she's writing.

VISIT THE AUTHOR ONLINE AND LEARN ABOUT
HER TWENTY-PLUS BESTSELLING ROMANTASY NOVELS

SylviaMercedesBooks.com
AuthorSylviaMercedes